Eli is in the process of completing a BA with a major in English and a minor in French. He lives with his family in Morinville, Alberta. *The Opportunity* is Eli's first published work. He hopes that it will become the first of many.

To Franny, wherever you are, I hope you are reading this and smiling.

Eli Trenchard

THE OPPORTUNITY

AUSTIN MACAULEY PUBLISHERS™

LONDON • CAMBRIDGE • NEW YORK • SHARJAH

Ordering Information
Quantity sales: Special discounts are available on quantity purchases by corporations, associations, and others. For details, contact the publisher at the address below.

Publisher's Cataloging-in-Publication data
Trenchard, Eli
The Opportunity

ISBN 9798886933420 (Paperback)
ISBN 9798886933444 (ePub e-book)
ISBN 9798886933437 (Audiobook)

Library of Congress Control Number: 2023908541

www.austinmacauley.com/us

First Published 2023
Austin Macauley Publishers LLC
40 Wall Street, 33rd Floor, Suite 3302
New York, NY 10005
USA

mail-usa@austinmacauley.com
+1 (646) 5125767

Chapter 1

The story I heard for the first time in the stale awkwardness that is a train car from New York city to Quebec, Canada, starts in the small town of Medora, Montana.

The night was the coldest the little town had been dealt in years. The small, beaten oak door swung open allowing a fresh batch of snowflakes into the bar. "Close the door, kid," the barkeep yelled. The young man stepped inside hurriedly, letting the door slam shut behind him, making his way to his usual seat in the far-right corner.

The bar was old, rundown and smelled of cigarettes, but the young man felt safe there. He shed his satchel, unzipped his hoodie and placed it on the back of the chair. He pulled a book from the leather satchel and began to read. As he read, the waitress Maria wandered over and asked, "The usual?" To which the young man murmured, "Yeah." Lost in the pages of the book that had been assigned by his English professor earlier that same day, he barely acknowledged the triple shot of cheap whiskey that Maria set down beside him. His classes had been okay that day, nothing special. It hadn't strayed from normality, not even an inch. He didn't mind however, out of the five classes filling his final semester, his favorite was English. The books he was obligated to read were fascinating and gave him a break from the mundanity his life had become. So did the alcohol, but he didn't like to ponder on that for too long. It was a crutch, always present but became no less shameful as the days passed him by.

As he sat sipping the cheap alcohol and reading, his mind began to wander. It was the last semester of his 3 year graduate degree in English literature. He would finish his degree, go on to a prominent job at a publishing house or literary agency and finally be an 'adult'—even though he had been one for five years at that point. He still hadn't found his one true calling and had resigned to the fact that he may never find it.

Jack Hanson was, by all accounts, an outsider. He made good grades, wasn't unathletic but wasn't 'athletic', although he tried to work out at least once a day. Jack was just another piece in the little town's cog. Not inconspicuous but by no means someone who you would notice as you walked down the street. His ability to blend into his surroundings wasn't on account of his outward visage but was more accredited to the fact that a cloud surrounded Jack wherever he went. The cloud wasn't filled with depression or failure, but instead was brimming with loss and uncertainty. It made people look the other way when they walked by him or suppress their innate instinct to go and talk to him. That was the way it had always been until Charlotte arrived.

Engrossed in the book, Jack didn't notice the woman that had just walked into the small, rundown bar. She had dark brown hair that somehow moved by the touch of an invisible wind, one eye blue like the sea, the other chestnut brown like a violins polished surface. Her skin, flowing brown, like a milk chocolate bar that has been left out on a hot day. Not to mention the physique comparable to that of the goddess Aphrodite. In every way, she was perfect. As she strode purposely through the humble, time worn oak door, her presence stole breath from every person that laid eyes on her. When she finally took a seat the bar, she asked John the bartender, "Do you know a Jack Hanson? I was told he usually hangs out here."

"Yeah, sitting at the table in the corner," John answered, pointing over in Jack's direction.

"Why haven't I seen you in here before? This is the only bar in town and your face isn't one so easily forgotten."

"Not from around here I'm afraid," Charlotte said, with a thin film of superiority covering each syllable and then glided over to Jack who still hadn't noticed anyone or anything new about the bar where he so often spent his free time. She pulled a chair from an unoccupied table and sat down. The movement was enough to startle and awaken Jack from the stupor he had found himself in. He looked up only for a moment, but a moment was all that was needed to realize he was in the company of someone who was very special or just as equally dangerous. "Jack?" Charlotte asked.

A moment passed and then another. Jack, a person who never had trouble finding the right words, had lost the art of speech. So, she asked again, "Jack Hanson?"

This time he cleared his throat, paused, then spoke, "Yes, and your name is?"

"Charlotte," she answered, "Charlotte Jones. I am a graduate student at New York University. Your Professor Laurent told me you were the brightest literary mind that he had ever had the pleasure to teach."

Jack's cheeks reddened at the compliment. "Ah well, that's very nice of him but I'm afraid he overestimates my talents," Jack responded respectfully but no less dismissive. Charlotte stared unblinkingly into Jack's bright blue eyes and completely disregarded his statement.

"I was sent by a group of three very influential men who sponsor one student from the United States of America to go to New York University for the last semester of their university careers so that they may graduate from one the best English programs in the country and go on to either work for them or go out into the world one rung higher on the social ladder. My employers are very generous, and they would love for you to be their next sponsored student."

Jack heard the information and knew that he should be responding but he just couldn't make his lips formulate the words. He was dumbfounded that a woman his age could be that beautiful. He had seen very attractive women before, but Charlotte was different. It was as if he was looking at an eclipse. Jack knew he shouldn't stare too long but he couldn't help it.

After many moments had passed, Charlotte spoke again, "If you need the night to make your decision that is totally understandable. I am leaving at 12:00pm tomorrow afternoon and I hope to get a call from you by then. This is the opportunity of a lifetime, I promise you. My number is (212)-460-8093."

Jack jammed his hand into his satchel, pulled a pen out and begun tattooing the number on his arm. Still not able to speak, he watched her leave just as she entered. Charlotte's exit seemed to have the same effect on the occupants of the small bar as it did when she walked in. Only this time people seemed sad to see the woman they had never laid eyes on before that day, leave. Jack sat at his table not quite believing what had just happened. It had been his dream since high school to go to NYU and get his degree from a school as prestigious as theirs was, but something didn't feel right about the proposal. Who were these important men and why did a girl like Charlotte work for them?

Jack tried to go back to his book, but questions kept swimming around in his head. He tried drowning them in whiskey—which was his usual method of dealing with problems—but after the fourth glass he decided he had better

9

retire to his bed for the evening. After settling his bill with John and giving Maria a modest tip, he stumbled and swayed his way to the humble oak door and pushed it open. As he did, the cold hit him like a semi-truck. Thankful the walk wasn't far; he began his journey home. His affordable but rundown bachelor suite was just four buildings from the bar, so the walk never took him more than five minutes.

But that night, walking through the snow, wind and stabbing cold that seemed determined to pierce through his skin and freeze his heart, the walk seemed to take an eternity. He was thankful to open the door to number 7, remove his bag, lay his jacket over a chair and sit on the couch to begin warming up. His little hole in the wall of the Iners Plaza wasn't much. It reeked of TV dinners, ramen noodles and whiskey but it was home. It wasn't quite his true home but close enough.

Charlotte's offer swam through his head. 12 hours from that exact moment he could change the entire course of his life, or he could stay where he was and regret giving up the perfect offer forever. Although, the offer had to be too good to be true. What type of wealthy men gave away their money to strange kids? Wasn't the reason they were rich because they didn't foolishly spend their money? The same string of thoughts circled around his head so many times that he was eventually spun asleep sitting on the couch, dreaming of the massive halls, atmosphere, and prestige of NYU.

Screeching tires woke Jack from his light, unrestful sleep. Groggy and freezing, he made his way to the kitchen to make a cup of coffee. As the coffee was brewing a light turned on in his brain as if awakening him from a coma. The thoughts, memories and emotions from the previous night came rushing back in hoards. Frantically spinning and grabbing his phone from the kitchen counter, he flipped it open and checked the time: 9:30am. 2 hours and 30 minutes on the clock, it was decision time. New York held his dream school, the most stunning girl he had ever seen and a great set up for his future. Not to mention it was an entirely free option.

Medora on the other hand, held his favorite bar, one more semester, and a safe life inside the hole that was number 7 Iners Plaza. He would probably move to New York anyway after his graduation and his adult life would start. In that moment, the doubts and questions he had the previous night seemed to be erased from his memory. Still, change made him uneasy. It stretched his mind and weighed his heart. The prospect of leaving the haven he had created for himself was terrifying. It almost pushed him back to bed, leaving the whole experience in the past. Almost. As he sipped his coffee, he realized the decision had already been made; the leap was scary but the pot of gold on the other side could erase every problem that he had ever faced.

Packing didn't take long. Four pairs of pants, a couple shirts, a few sweaters, a jacket, underwear, socks, quite a few books, a picture of his mom, a throw blanket, some toiletries, and his MacBook pro. The rest of the contents of his apartment came with the place when he was handed the keys. Every belonging he owned fit in the duffle bag he had brought when he moved there from the orphanage in Sidewinder, Maine. After all his belongings were safely tucked into the trunk, the picture of his mom wrapped in the soft blanket, he flipped his phone open and called (212)-460-8093. It rang for three painstaking chimes but finally he heard Charlotte on the other side. Even her voice was perfect. The tone and tempo of the slow, melodic notes matched her body like a glove, it was beautifully poetic. "Hello? This Charlotte Jones," she said.

"Hey, this is Jack, Jack Hanson. From yesterday...If you don't remember..."

"Good to hear your voice Jack, I was getting worried. So, what have you decided? Will you let me, and my employers change your life?"

"Yeah. I mean thank you very much for your offer, I would be honored to accept it." His mother was always very stern with Jack about using his manners, *The manners of a man show the world what kind of a person he is on the inside,* she used to say.

"Very good to hear! Have you packed?"

"Yes, I have. I am all ready to go, just waiting on you to let me know what the next step is."

"Great, what is your address?"

"25 Bonté St."

"I will have my car pick you up and take you to the airport. I will be waiting for you there. Shouldn't be longer than 10 minutes."

"Thank you, I will watch for it," Jack said as the line went dead. While Jack sat by the corner window overlooking the street below, he thought of his mother and how she would have been so proud of him going to college there in Medora, imagine if she knew he was heading to New York on a full scholarship. She would have had a stroke.

Lost in thought, Jack almost didn't hear the honk of a horn coming from the street. Looking down, he saw the car—more like a limo wealthy people arrive to fancy events in—jumped to his feet, grabbed his satchel and trunk, and ran to the door. When he took one last look at the apartment, a twinge of remorse reverberated throughout his entire body as if he was leaving an old friend.

For 5 years, those walls had seen him in his darkest hour and on the days of his greatest triumphs. Touching the wall gently, he whispered, "Thank you." Then without another look, he shut the door and ran down the flight of stairs and through the front door.

The cold was manageable that day and the snow had stopped but, in its wake, left snow drifts up to his mid-calf. At the car, the driver took his duffle bag and satchel, opened the back door and motioned for him to get in. The inside of the car was entirely covered in black leather, with a U-shaped couch in the back and a TV screen in front. It was wealth like Jack had never seen before. He looked intently out the back windows for the entirety of the ride. Taking mental pictures of the small town as he drove past all the places he had come to know in his tenure there. The small town would always have a soft spot in his heart because it was the first place he could call home since his mother had passed.

All too soon the town passed by and all he could see for miles were the Rockies. They fascinated him but didn't touch his soul like the town had. As the car pulled into the airport parking lot and passed through the chain link fence. Jack wondered where they were going. After all, he had only ever been through the front doors of the airport. Then he saw it, a small white private jet like the ones he had seen so many times in the movies. As the car came to a stop, he realized it was what he would be flying on.

Charlotte was standing on the stairs into the plane, wearing a dark blue dress, so tight it left little to imagination and a small black fur lined coat thrown over her shoulders. He looked down to his own clothing and realized he was still wearing the exact same clothes as the night before. Which was not a good look. He knew he must smell like a bag of dead chickens. He didn't know how he was ever going to get on a plane with the most breathtaking woman he had ever seen smelling like he did. Opening the door to the car, the driver discreetly handed him something. It was a stick of deodorant. The driver must have smelled him when he got in. Feeling completely humiliated, Jack thanked the driver, used the deodorant, and stuffed it in his pocket for later, just in case.

When Jack stepped on the plane, he couldn't believe what he saw. The plush black leather recliners, champagne in buckets of ice and a fully stocked bar at the back end of the plane. The same feeling that he had felt earlier in the car came rushing back. The endless amounts of money the people who were sponsoring him must have been in possession of baffled his narrow-minded, poor brain. Having never lived with people who weren't at least struggling to make ends meet, he couldn't fathom the money that was on display in the plane alone. Suddenly, the trance he had been stuck in was snapped by Charlotte's voice. "Was the car ride up to your standards?" She asked.

"Yes," he said, "I've never even been in a car like that before. It was like I stepped into a movie."

"You have never taken a ride in a limo?"

"No, never."

"Well, you live in New York now and you have been placed into a very wealthy circle. You will have to get used to living lavishly."

"It's going to take some getting used to. I have never not worried about money before," Jack said, almost laughing.

"Money isn't an issue anymore, I promise you that much," Charlotte said as her phone went off and she answered, disappearing into a room behind the bar. Jack wondered what it was about. The look on Charlotte's face was one Jack could only compare to the look his mother wore when the bills for their house came in and she wasn't sure how she was going to be able to pay them. He wondered why she wouldn't just answer the call in the main room. The call must have come from her boss or boyfriend. Jack pleaded with the universe to let it be her boss. When he looked back down after pleading with the almighty God, he once again spotted the bar at the end of the plane. It was late enough for Jack to reconcile a drink, so he walked up to the bar and ordered. "Triple shot of whiskey, please," Jack asked.

"What kind, we have Four Roses, Jack Daniels or a Canadian whiskey called Crown Royal," the bartender said.

Jack hadn't tried any sort of Canadian whiskey in his life so he thought he might give it a try. When in Rome and all that. "I'll give Crown Royal a try."

"Great choice," the bartender said, handing Jack a glass filled to half with the amber liquid. "Thanks!" Jack said as he returned to his seat, drink in hand.

When he looked out the window, he realized they hadn't even left the ground and remembered the massive snowstorm they'd had the night before and wondered if air traffic control would let them take off at all. As if she could hear his thoughts, Charlotte appeared out of the mysterious door behind the bar and said, "That was the air traffic control. We have been cleared for take-off. We are going to head out momentarily." Something in the beautiful tapestry of her face told Jack that the call had most definitely not come from the air traffic control. Although he did not know her well, Jack thought about asking if she was alright but then thought better of it.

"Sounds good," he said as his mind drifted back to the last plane he took from Maine to Montana. The flight that was supposed to be his ticket to the promise land. The ticket that should have allowed him to finally leave his messed up high school years in the past and start anew. Of course, that wasn't true, his past had just followed him like a salivating dog looking for treats and incessantly wagging its tail. The evidence of that was the glass brimming with hard liquor beside him. The plane took off without any issues and they were finally air born. The next chapter of his life had begun.

As soon as the captain had notified the passengers it was safe to roam around the cabin once again Charlotte slid into the seat beside Jack. "When we get to JFK, there will be a car waiting for us and it will take us to the boss' office. They have everything prepared for you. You will pick an apartment and they have a few forms to you need to sign so that you can accept your offer to the English department at NYU and a couple others saying that you accept their sponsorship"

"Sounds good," Jack said as the excitement began to bubble up in his stomach.

"You will love New York. I will take you out, help you get situated in the apartment, take you to purchase furniture and anything else you may need for the semester."

"Thank you for everything. This is a dream come true," Jack said.

"No problem I know what you're feeling. I felt the same way when I was in your seat on this very plane," Charlotte said and then without any warning, disappeared into the secret room behind the bar once again.

Jack knew she was beautiful; he knew she was one of the most physically attractive women he had ever seen in person but there was something about her that he couldn't quite put a finger on. He could tell there was something she wasn't telling him; something more. But as he sat on the plush private planes chair that felt like was sitting on a cloud, he made his first mistake. He threw his intuition to the wind and made himself believe that's she was just tired.

Awoken by the sound of the captain's voice on the loudspeaker letting him know they had arrived he sat up groggily wondering how long he slept. His hair must be a mess and he realized that he hadn't been to the bathroom since last night before he got to the bar. *Of course, there was no time to go right now,* Jack thought, but he couldn't wait so he asked the bartender, "Where is the bathroom?"

"Front and to the right," the bartender said. Half jogging, half walking, Jack got into the bathroom, relieved himself and then looked in the mirror. He knew he looked like a homeless bum but there was nothing he could do about it, so he settled for reapplying the deodorant the driver had given him and messing up his hair so that it resembled something of what a sane person might look like. When he got out of the washroom, the foldable stairs were down, and he could see Charlotte getting in a car that was an exact replica of the one that carried him to the airport in Medora.

Quickly grabbing his satchel, he ran down the steps and into the car. When they arrived at the 'office', Charlotte got out of the car and waited for Jack to get out and then whispered in his ear.

"Make sure you show Paul respect. He doesn't take kindly to being disrespected."

"I will do my best," Jack said.

The lobby was huge. Cascading marble floors that had been polished like ice sparkled underneath his feet, a gawdy chandelier loomed above his head, and a massive mahogany reception desk sat in the center with two elevators standing guard on either side. Without even a curt nod directed at the receptionist Charlotte led him to the right elevator. The doors opened like they were waiting on his arrival, and she pressed the button for the 8th floor. The 8th floor was the second highest floor, only one more floor laid above them, but it was marked with a numberless button. *Funny thing to have,* Jack thought, *why wouldn't it have a number?* Must have been scratched off or faded over the years, he reassured himself.

When they reached the 8th floor, the doors opened again to a room with only a heavy wooden desk in the center. The resemblance to the desk that sits in the oval office was uncanny. Behind it sat a man in his 50s with a grey hair showing streaks of white with a beard to match. He was muscular and wore a

15

crisp three-piece suit. The man stood up immediately and walked out from behind the desk giving Charlotte a hug and then turned to Jack. "You must be the famous Jack Hanson I hear so much about," he said as he stuck his hairy, scarred hand out for Jack to shake.

Jack stuck his hand out to meet Paul's and shook it firmly but respectfully. "Jack Hanson, very pleased to meet you sir. Charlotte has told me wonderful things about you and your associates."

"Pleased to meet you as well, Jack, the ride here was pleasant, I hope?"

"More than pleasant sir, it was fabulous!" Jack said immediately regretting his choice of words. He was surrounded by the largest accumulation of wealth he had ever been in the presence of and he used the word fabulous as if he was a dewy-eyed schoolgirl.

"Good to hear son. I've got some papers for you to sign here, and I would love you to choose an apartment to live in while you're in New York."

"Sounds good sir. I really don't need anything fancy, I'm not fussy."

"That's perfect we have an apartment that overlooks Central Park. Two bedrooms, one bath, gym and laundry in the budling and a bar just down the street." The mention of a bar just down the street sounded nice but why did Paul feel the need to let him know that it was there? Had Charlotte somehow found out about his drinking? Maybe it was just because he and Charlotte met in the Medora bar, but it was just as equally possible that the comment meant something. The comment could have been harmless, or it could have revealed how Charlotte really came to be in the bar that night, Jack just wasn't sure which it was yet.

"That sounds lovely, thank you sir," Jack said taking the contracts and giving them a glance over, he never was one to look too hard at the fine print, so the whole process took less than 5 minutes. A couple John Hancock's and his birthday in a few other spots. Jack thanked Paul again, got back into the elevator with Charlotte, and they were off.

Chapter 2

The next few days of the break Jack had been given flew by in a blur. They were filled with dinners, shopping, tours, and orientations. The money still left Jack mystified. He could not comprehend the amount of money that was being thrown around without so much as the blink of an eye. When the second last night before the first day of his next academic chapter rolled around, he realized hadn't eaten at a home cooked meal or even a bowlful of ramen noodles in his new apartment. The apartment he had been given was great, but it still didn't feel like home.

All the furniture was new, the chandelier didn't have any dust on it and the massive oak desk in the center of the second bedroom had yet to be christened with the first letters typed onto his trusty MacBook. As he sat on the Italian leather that covered the couch Charlotte had picked out earlier that same day and watched *Yellowstone* on the massive 50 inch TV, he couldn't help but feel homesick. Not for the home he had made for himself in Medora, but the double wide in Cielo, Maine. It wasn't much but it kept Jack and his mother warm, and he always felt safe there as if the paper-thin walls were instead made from titanium.

As he thought of a time before the cancer, orphanages, and whiskey his mind wandered to Jessica. She was the type of girl that would keep a 16-year-old boy up at night, wondering what her lips might taste like. The girl next door that was so close yet so far. He remembered her face in the church the day of his mother's funeral, tears streaking down her cheeks like pity and sadness falling from her big brown eyes that used to be filled with so much warmth. The way she looked at him that day made him feel like damaged goods, he didn't even have the stomach to say goodbye the day the social worker came to take him to the orphanage in Sidewinder, Maine. Her face danced in his mind until he slipped into back void of sleep that night.

His own internal clock woke him at 7:30am the next morning. It was Saturday, January 7th. He turned on the fancy Keurig—Charlotte had said would 'revolutionize' his mornings—drank his coffee, got dressed, grabbed his gym bag, and made his way down to the gym. That day was a chest and arms day so Jack was very much looking forward to the bang and clanking sound of the plates and not dreading the same noises as he usually did on leg days. The gym had become almost as much of an escape as the whiskey was. The burn and exertion helped his mind stop thinking and created a space where he felt peace.

Peace had become a scarce commodity for Jack. When the workout was over, he headed back up to the apartment to take a shower and then go meet Charlotte at Four Roses for breakfast. The shower was monstrous. The faucet was affixed directly above and rained freezing water down on him like he had stepped into one of London's winter rainstorms. It gave him the exact opposite feeling that the gym provided. It felt like the world was falling down on him from above. Once the shower stopped, he threw on some of the new clothes Charlotte had picked out for him and headed back out into the tornado that his life had become.

The Four Roses was a great breakfast joint. It had a warm 60s diner feel, and the waitresses were always kind. It was almost like the bar back in Medora Jack had grown to love so much. He took his place at one of the main counter seats and just as he sat down the door opened. Charlotte walked in wearing jeans, an oversized sweater, hair in a messy bun with glasses that completed the look. She hadn't dressed up the way she had in Medora for a while, but she was still breathtakingly beautiful.

"Sleep well last night Jack?" She asked.

"Yeah, that king bed is a whole lot bigger than the old twin mattress I was sleeping on when you changed my life. But I guess I will get used to the extra room," Jack said with a chuckle, he found his own joke quite amusing.

"Yeah, it took me a few weeks to get the swing of things here when I arrived, but this becomes your new normal soon enough."

Jack wasn't convinced that he would ever get used to living up on the high horse he found himself on, but he didn't want her to know that. He often found himself wondering what Charlotte's life consisted of before Paul came and flipped it like one of the Four Roses famous pancakes.

"I'm sure I will," he assured her.

"I know you will. Today we don't have much to do. So, I thought I would take you to the University and show you where your classes are, then we can get some lunch and then we are going out for supper with Paul. He wants to take you out for a fancy meal to celebrate the new beginning you are starting on Monday."

"Sounds like a plan," Jack said. Then proceeded to order four eggs, sausages, and a few pieces of toast. The Four roses always put some fruit on the side but he never ate it because according to Charlotte, restaurants always reused the fruit from other people's plates. Charlotte talked about textbooks and teachers for the rest of breakfast. Jack ate quietly, nodding and agreeing at all the right times. After they both had their plates cleared and Charlotte settled the bill they headed off to the university. The campus at NYU was incredible, it was like New York had been built around the university. It truly was the beating heart of the city, feeding it with bright new minds to sustain its youth. Jack had 4 classes in 3 different budlings. French, Creative writing, Old English, and Forensic Sciences.

The classes were easy enough to find and he felt at home there inside the revitalized brick buildings. They gave him a sense of new beginnings. Each warm face, professor lost in deep thought and janitors smile placed the feeling of safety on him like a warm blanket. Once Charlotte had finished showing him the buildings he would be in and the quickest ways to get to them in relation to each other, they grabbed a hot dog at one of New York's many hot dog vendors. Charlotte turned to leave and then remembering Jack had no idea what the plan was, turned back to tell him what to do for the quintillionth time that week.

"I will meet you at 7:00pm on the sidewalk outside of your building to take you to dinner. We will be meeting Paul at Gorggios for dinner. It's a very fancy restaurant so wear the new grey pinstripe suit we bought the other day."

"Sidewalk, 7:00pm, Grey pinstripe," Jack verified, as a boyish grin cut across his face.

"That's right. Don't be late," she said and then spun on her heels and walked away, fading into the constant bustle that was New York City.

The university was about a 20min walk from Jack's apartment and he still didn't have any money to spend on taxis, so he decided to walk. Contrary to Charlotte's belief that a fancy car service was the only mode of transportation, New York was well suited for walking. By the time he got back into his apartment, the time read 3:37pm. That meant he had about three and a half hours to himself. Once he started setting out his outfit for the night, he realized he had a few choices to make. He needed to pick the perfect belt, tie, shoes, and shirt. He decided to go with a plain white shirt that night, paired with a black belt and black oxfords. He knew he should keep it simple; Paul did not like to be disrespected. Being better dressed than him could be taken as disrespect.

Given his money bought all the clothes and just about every other possession Jack had acquired that week Jack knew he should try to stay as thankful and respectful as possible. The tie was the more challenging part. He had narrowed it down to three choices: Forest green, the red of a worn barn door and one that was as black as the ace of spades. After 5 minutes of weighing the options and much deliberating, he chose forest green. Not too plain but not flashy. He also decided he would wear the watch Charlotte had picked out for him. It sported a black leather strap and a plain black and white analog watch face with silver casing. Everything looked crisp and as far as his fashion expertise went it was the best he could come up with.

Everything was ready and he would leave himself an hour to get ready, so he had an hour to do whatever he wanted. Jack had bought a bottle of Crown Royal from the liquor store down the road earlier that week and he figured now was as good as any time to crack it open. He filled half a fancy drinking glass— a glass he usually saw powerful, wealthy people drinking from in the movies— and sat down with one of the books he had brought.

It was called *I Am Number Four* by Jobie Hughes and James Frey. It was great book written about a boy that is on the run from aliens from a different planet and he himself turns out to be an alien. The improbability of the book gave him a break from the whirlwind that had become his life. It helped him suppress the feeling that there was something Charlotte and Paul hadn't told him yet, he guessed that night would be the night they told him the whole story, which made him very uneasy.

The hour of peace flew by in a whirlwind of letters, words and sentences. Their fluidity and poetic rhythm had lulled Jack into a near hypnotic trance. Once he reached the third chapter he looked up and realized he only had an hour left until he needed to be in the lobby ready to meet Charlotte. He decided he would shave first and then hop in the shower. After he had shaved, showered, and brushed his teeth, he coaxed his hair into place with the help of a little bit of paste and went to his room to put on the suit. Pants, belt, socks, and shirt were easy enough but by the time he got to the tie he realized he had no clue how tie one.

Jack had never met his father and wasn't mad or bothered by that unfortunate fact in any way, but it had left a gaping hole in his manhood training; after all, a mother can only teach you so much about being a man. Jack decided that anything a runaway dad could have taught him, YouTube would be able to do just as well. After he had tried 3 times and fiddled with the tie so much that he had almost creased it. It was finally on his neck. Just in time too, it was 6:55pm. Go time. He slid the suit jacket over his broad shoulders and made sure everything was tucked in and he looked presentable. Leaving the room with one more glace in the mirror he went into the kitchen. He didn't think one last drink could hurt. The amber liquid flowed down his throat, and he left the apartment with an almost imperceivable, yet nerve settling buzz.

Once the elevator doors opened, he saw Charlotte standing in the middle of lobby looking down at her watch as if she had been waiting for him awhile. She was wearing a stunning, forest green, flowing dress with a beautiful silver necklace that held a large red jewel. The dress perfectly accented her feminine features but in an almost coy way; like she didn't know they were there. The pendant however stood out like a sore thumb. It didn't match the dress or the shoes and didn't look like an accessory she would have chosen to wear. The dress most certainly was a true reflection of the woman beneath, but the pendant was not. He reassured himself that it must have some special meaning from her past as he pushed the thought out of his mind.

"Cutting it close there, aren't we Jack?" She said, politely scolding him as she turned and headed out the door, silently instructing Jack to follow her.

"Yeah, but I have a minute to spare," Jack said jokingly, trying to diffuse the thick tension he knew was growing between the two of them.

"Little too close for my comfort but I'll let it slide this time given you do look quite handsome tonight."

"Thanks," Jack said, completely stunned. He couldn't believe a woman like Charlotte would have ever taken notice to his appearance. He couldn't really believe the compliment was genuine, but he said thanks just in case. "You look stunning tonight as well, but that's not really a surprise. I like the green. It's as if you told me what you would be wearing tonight."

"Yeah, it's funny the way the universe works sometimes, isn't it," Charlotte said, as a smile snuck quietly across her face. "Here," she said as she handed him a mint. "I can smell the whiskey. I have no problem with it, but Paul might."

"Thanks," Jack said, embarrassed but thankful she told him before he got to dinner. 'I don't have a problem with it' is what she had said but Jack didn't believe what she was saying, or why she felt the need to let him know she didn't have a problem with it. The assurance struck Jack as slightly odd and even bordering on being completely out of character. Maybe there was more to this goddess than met the eye.

The black car that had picked him up from his old apartment—his old home—pulled around the corner and he opened the door for Charlotte before stepping in himself. The drive took about 15 minutes and as if appearing from a cloud of smoke he saw it. The huge gold letters, Gorggios, like something out of a movie. The glass doors opened as he and Charlotte walked toward them. The tables were covered in white linens and a remarkable gold elephant sat in the middle of each table with a massive gold chandelier looming above the entire seating area.

Compared to the bar he used to frequent in Medora with the scratched wooden tables and wobbly chairs, it looked like a dining hall straight from heaven. The waiter immediately took them to a table in the back despite the overwhelming line of patrons at the door. If these people were 'well off', then Jack assumed he was now 'rich'. Paul was already seated in the corner with a view of the doors and the rest of the restaurant in front of him. He stood up from his seat as they approached. He was wearing a jet-black suit with a white shirt, black belt, black bit loafers completed with a blood red tie. He pulled Charlotte's chair out, she sat, and he pushed it back in. Jack took his place and once they were all seated, he spoke.

"How has your first week in the big city been Jack?"

"Great Sir, Charlotte has been a great help. She helped me furnish my apartment, showed me around the city and the university. I couldn't have asked for a better guide."

"It was nothing, I—"

"Good. We are very pleased to have you here Jack. Your writing speaks for itself, and I respect a man who takes care of his body."

"Thank you sir, I hope I can keep your respect for as long as I am here."

"Me as well Jack, me as well," As the final word left his mouth the waiter appeared as if from thin air and asked if the 'guests of honor', as he put it, were ready to order or if he could start them off with some drinks.

To which Paul responded, "We will all have the seafood dinner, and I will have a dark rum straight."

"Gin on the rocks for me please," Charlotte said, meekly. It was a tone Jack had not yet heard from Charlotte's lips. It made him wonder what type of relationship she and Paul really had.

"Crown Royal neat for me if you have it, please," Jack said.

"Excellent choices, I will bring the drinks out right away," The waiter said hurrying away in the direction of the bar that was situated at the back of the dining hall.

After the drinks had been served and the waiter had left Paul began to speak again.

"I too was a writer, but I took business at the university once I arrived in New York. I still have quite a few friends in the writing department at NYU so if you have any issues with teachers or classmates let me know. I will see what I can do to remedy the situation. Same goes for any issues with the apartment. I am always here to fix any situation that you need fixed."

"Thank you very much sir," Jack said but he wasn't sure he would tell Paul even if he did have any grievances. There was a certain dangerously sharp edge to his words that didn't sit well with Jack. They talked about sports teams and Broadway shows that Paul could get Jack tickets to if he so desired until the food came. When the food arrived three waiters came to the table, one pushing a cart loaded with gold plates overflowing with food, one with salt and pepper and the other with a shredder for parmesan cheese.

After the food had been served, salted, and the shredded cheese sprinkled on top, they dove in. The plates were filled with every sea creature you could possibly imagine. Crab, lobster, clams, mussels, calamari, and some that Jack didn't even know the names of. It all tasted like heaven, he had never tasted food so fresh and filled with flavors. His palate was overwhelmed with a wonderful firework show of stimulus. After the plates had been cleared, drinks replenished, and dessert offered—to which all three declined—Paul scooted his chair forward and leaned in as if to say it was time to get down to business.

"Jack, me and my associates are very pleased with the person we have selected to sponsor this semester. But our sponsorship has some conditions.

We expect you to come when I call no matter what time it is. This is non-negotiable. It may not be once a week or even once a month and you may not get a call the entire time you are here. I will never call during school hours but after school hours if your phone rings we expect you to pick up. Is that something you think you can handle?"

"Yes, sir I think I will be able to handle that," Jack said but underneath his polite visage he wondered what type of jobs he would be carrying out. He also wondered why there was such emphasis placed on the phone calls. What could be so important that a single missed phone call could revoke his sponsorship? Charlotte sure hadn't motioned any sort of late-night clandestine phone calls he was subject to receive.

"Good, because our tutelage comes with many perks as you already know," he said as he pulled a silver card from his inner jacket pocket and handed it to Jack. Jack recognized it. It was the same one Charlotte had used all week except his had the number 6 on it instead of Charlotte's 5. "This is a credit card; it has no limit, and I will not tell you how to use it. You are free to use it however you see fit as long as you answer when my call comes in. You understand?"

"Yes, sir I do, thank you very much," Jack said graciously. The man had literally just handed him all the money he could ever hope to earn in 10 lifetimes.

"Good, as long as we understand each other our partnership will be symbiotic. I have some business to attend to but I didn't want to leave without getting that formality out of the way. Goodnight, Jack, I wish you all the best this semester." Paul stood up, placed 7 hundred dollar bills on the table and walked across the hall and out into the night. With all that was said that night, Jack's head was spinning, but one curiosity was still gnawing at him. Why had Paul completely ignored Charlotte the entire meal? Maybe she was just there as his escort but still, to not even show a sliver of gratitude for showing Jack around all week? He hoped he would not be treated that way once Paul and his mysterious colleagues found another young writer to sponsor.

Once Paul left Charlotte spoke, "Ready to go? I can take you back home if you would like."

"Yeah, that sounds great, I just wanted to thank you for all that you have done for me this week I wouldn't know up from down here if it weren't for you"

"Don't mention it, my predecessor did the same for me," Charlotte said getting up, beginning to walk away.

Jack followed her to the car, and they drove away from GORGGIOS and back to his apartment. When they reached their destination, Charlotte said goodnight and Jack opened the back door and got out of the car but just as his soft impressionable cheeks hit the chilly New York air he decided to take a leap of faith. He stuck is head back in the car and asked, "Want to come upstairs?" He didn't know if it was the booze, fancy food or the fact that she had complimented him on his appearance earlier. Maybe it was a combination of all of that added to the fact that she was stunningly beautiful, and conversation seemed to come easy between the two of them. Whatever the reason was, it happened. In that moment, he was charged with whatever consequences his words elicited.

"Umm...Sure, as long as you have some clothes I can use because as gentle on the eyes as this dress is, it is so very uncomfortable."

"Yeah, for sure. I can lend you some sweats and a shirt, although I don't have any bras or women's clothes."

"That's alright," she said as she exited the car and headed into the building with Jack.

As the pair entered the elevator anyone around them could tell that there was a nervous energy in the air. At least in the air around Jack that was. Once they were in the apartment Jack hurried to his bedroom to grab Charlotte some clean sweatpants and a shirt. He knew both would be too big but that was the best he could offer. He came back out into the living room and handed the clothes to Charlotte.

"Sorry I know they're not your size but it's all I have. The bathroom is just down the hall, first door on your right."

"These are great, a little bigger is actually better. This dress is tighter than the crevasse the guy in *127 Hours* gets his arm stuck in," she said as she walked toward the bathroom. As soon as Jack heard the click of the locking mechanism on the bathroom door he rushed to his bedroom, quickly undressed, re-applied some deodorant—the stick the driver had given him before boarding the plane in Medora had come in handy on more than one occasion—then peeled his suit off and pulled on some loose-fitting sweats and a t-shirt. Just as he left the bedroom, he caught a glimpse of Charlotte. Even in his clothes that were draping over her body as if she was wearing elephant skin, she was beautiful.

She had folded her clothes in a pile—undergarments included—with the red pendant necklace on top and set it on the bar style island in the kitchen.

He walked up to her and was about to speak when he realized she was fumbling through her purse looking for something. Finally, she found it. A plastic bag with three little white paper sticks. At first, Jack thought they were cigarettes. He wondered why she would she have individual cigarettes but then he realized what they were. They were joints filled with marijuana. In his first year of university he went to a few parties and weed was always a party guest. Sometimes he would even partake in the activity so many enjoyed. Just as he thought back to his days in Medora a light switched on in his brain, this is what she meant when she said she didn't mind the smell of his boozy breath. She herself had a vice. He was proud of himself that every day he was learning more and more about the woman.

Charlotte turned around and gasped, "Jesus Jack, you scared the fuck out of me."

"Oh, sorry I didn't mean to…You smoke?" He asked.

"I do…is that okay? I can put it away if you like."

"No, it's all good, we can go on the balcony if you want. I just don't want it smelling up the entire apartment."

"Ok good idea, Thanks."

"Give me one second before we go, though," Jack said as he went to the counter where he had left his fancy glass and the bottle of Crown Royal. He quickly poured himself a stiff drink and led Charlotte though the glass door to the balcony. The chilled night air was cutting though his shirt and his muscles tensed slightly under the loose fabric. Charlotte lit one of the joints, the tip glowed red and she blew out a stream of smoke. Before either spoke, she took a few more drags and Jack took a few sips of his drink.

"Would you like a hit?" Charlotte offered.

Jack thought for a second. He had one of the most beautiful girls he had ever seen in his apartment and his week had been such a tornado so in the heat of the moment he decided that spacing out a little bit couldn't hurt anyone.

"Yeah, if you don't mind."

"Not at all," she said, handing the glowing white stick to him.

"Thanks," Jack said taking a long hit and immediately beginning to cough, which Charlotte found to be very amusing. Once the coughing settled, he took two more—smaller—drags and handed the nub back to Charlotte who smoked the last little bit, then snubbed out the glowing tip and threw the butt down onto the street below and headed inside. Jack's stayed looking out into central park nursing his drink for a little while longer. When he felt his hands start to numb, he headed back inside, locked the sliding door and sat down on the couch where Charlotte was sitting curled up in a blanket. The weed had started to grasp his conscious thought and released all the built-up nervousness he had been feeling.

Grabbing the blanket that had protected his mother's picture on his journey to the city that now sat on his bedside table he asked Charlotte, "Where did you live before Paul waltzed into your life?"

"Beatrice, Ohio. It's a small farm town 35 miles from the nearest skyscraper," she said with something close to nostalgia growing in her eyes. The truth surprised Jack to the point that even if a gun had been pressed to his head, he would not have been able to come up with a response. Charlotte dressed, spoke, and acted like she had lived in the big city her entire life. *Paul must have rubbed off on her,* he thought.

So much time had elapsed since anyone had spoken so Charlotte continued, "Me and my Father lived in this big brick house at the center of town. He was the chief of the local police department. I was 17 when he died trying to arrest a man who was holding the local convince store up at gunpoint. It was the same day that I won a national writing competition. I received a letter that morning saying I had won. So, after the funeral, I came here given the fact I had no reason to stay in Beatrice."

"Wow I don't even know what to say, congratulations on the award! But I am so sorry that your dad died. Were you guys close?"

"Yeah, we were. He was my whole world…" She said wiping tear that had begun to run down her cheek. "But enough of me, where did you come from, you know before Medora?" Jack wondered how she knew he had come from somewhere else before Medora, but the marijuana dulled his inquisitive mind and the thought slipped off into the black void he visited every time he slipped from consciousness.

"A few different places but my first home was in Cielo, Maine. It was a small town just as far from a skyscraper as your hometown sounds like it was. It was only happy memories, until I turned 16 and my mother got sick. It was a few months of hospital visits and one long week stay but eventually the cancer took her to the promise land. After that, I was shipped off to an orphanage. We

27

never had much money in Cielo, but they were the best times of my life. It always felt like home there. Well, it did to me, I'm not completely sure how my mom felt."

"Sounds like we had the same childhoods except for the orphanage part. I'm sorry to hear about your mothers passing."

"It's alright," Jack said even though in his heart he still ached for a mother to hug and talk to after a long day. He would give up every possession and dollar he had to have an hour more with her. "So, you have lived by yourself in New York Since you were 17?" Jack said trying to steer the conversation away from the jagged, painful cliff it was threatening to drive off.

"Yeah, well 18. I Turned 18 the day I got on the big white plane. New York has in some ways become my second home although I would love to go back to the endless fields of corn and wheat one day."

"Wow that's incredible, I don't know how you made it. I could have never done what you did when I was 18," Jack said, even though he knew that he would have been fine. The orphanage had changed him. Turned his body into one big callous that wasn't easily damaged but one that he was thoroughly ashamed of. It morphed his body into an endless pit filled with sorrow and regret.

"I'm sure you would have found a way. God this is getting depressing, do you have a speaker or a way to play music?" Thinking about it, Jack had no idea but then he remembered that the TV they had bought earlier that week was called a 'smart TV'. Maybe that meant it had Bluetooth.

"My phone doesn't have Bluetooth but I am pretty sure the TV has Bluetooth so you might be able to pair with it."

"Oh yeah, it does. I can play some music if that's okay with you," Charlotte said standing up and beginning to dance slowly to the pace of the song. Obviously, Jack had no say in whether they played music or not, but he didn't mind, he was too focused on the way Charlotte's hips moved. Jack sat on the couch just watching her sway. Her hair flowing through her hands, eyes closed letting the warm embrace of the mary jane and melody guide her. After a while, Charlotte stuck out her hand out, beckoning him to stand up and dance with her.

"Did you ever learn the Jive?" Charlotte asked.

"Yeah, in middle school and it was pretty popular at the bigger parties in Medora."

"Good, it's my favorite. Que up *Mambo No.5* on my phone."

"You bet!" Jack said smiling from ear to ear.

Charlotte took his hands in hers and said, "You better keep up," as the song started but as soon as it did, they were off. They moved in perfect lock step. Every movement executed perfectly. It was as if they had been dancing together their entire lives, as if their entire existences had been a warmup for that exact moment. As they danced Jack thought back to what his mother used to say to him, *in life you get 10 or 20 pure moments. When stumble upon one, don't over think it. Just let it happen.* Up until that point he didn't think he had ever had a 'pure moment' but that night, in that crazy situation, there was no doubt in his mind that he had stumbled upon a pure moment.

As the song ended and Jack swung Charlotte though his legs and let the momentum carry her up into the air, at her peak their eyes met and locked. Time was at a standstill the two dancers were bonded. Charlotte hung in midair suspended by Jack's arms. Even Rutherford wouldn't have been able to split the bond that was created. As Charlotte hit the hardwood floor, Jack leaned in and their lips grazed slightly, just hard enough to be called a kiss but it became harder, as if two wolves were fighting for survival. Jack and Charlotte were locked in a fight between love and lust. When the kiss finally ended and they became two separate entities once again, Jack and Charlotte both realized that something exponential had just happened.

They both knew it was a night neither of them would ever forget, hell or high water wouldn't be able to erase the moment from either of their memories. Every event, trial and turbulation that they had been through separately was one step closer to that point. Neither had meant for it to happen, neither thought a simple late-night dance would have held that type of gravitational event. But it had and neither of them knew what to say, do or how to act. So they both reverted to their usual escapes.

Jack to the kitchen to fill his glass of whiskey and Charlotte to the balcony. After the third or fourth sip, Jack's soul finally seemed to return to his body. He had finally found the catch of the too good to be true offer—even though he didn't know the extent of it quite yet. He had finally asked a girl up to his apartment, something he had only dreamt of since the first day he had lived on his own and quite possibly found his soulmate. Whoever was taking care of his mom since she had left sure had an odd way of releasing previews of the 'grand plan' they had for Jack. His deep thought was interrupted by a quiet voice.

"Would you like to watch a movie?" Charlotte asked.

"Yeah sure, I'm exhausted though. Want to watch in my room?" Jack said, and then realized that this sounded like he was asking her to sleep with him. "Or we could just watch in here, I don't mind sleeping on the couch." He didn't want her thinking he wanted to sleep with her. Jack did want to sleep with her, just not quite yet. He needed to know what picking up Paul's phone call meant and how deep she was in the business Paul was running.

"Bedroom's fine with me, I'm exhausted too," Charlotte said, reassuring Jack.

"Great, just have to finish this and I'll be right there," He said. Quickly emptying the overflowing glass of the smooth amber liquid down his throat, he made his way to the bedroom. Jack hoped Charlotte didn't think he wanted to sleep with her. *It would ruin the entire evening,* he thought, as ludicrous as that sounded. But when he walked around corner and through the corner of the room he saw Charlotte under the covers, sleeping like a small child. She looked so peaceful; leagues different than the goddess that walked into the bar in Medora. Jack hopped into bed and was fast asleep before his head even touched the pillow.

Chapter 3

The sound of a police siren awoke Jack. He slowly opened his eyes; he had kept drinking well past his limit the night before although he hadn't realized because had been drunk on Charlotte just as much as the whiskey. His head was pounding but an entire barrel of 100-year-old whiskey wouldn't have been able to wipe his memory. He looked down, Charlotte's soft cheeks were resting on his chest, her hair flowing down over his ribs, one arm draped over him, and one leg stuck between both of his. Jack was glad that the pure moment they had shared wasn't ruined by sex. He gently lifted her arm, set her leg free and lifted her head slightly so he could slip out of the bed and then replaced it just as gently on the pillow.

Once he was finally free, he walked into the kitchen, made himself a coffee and left Charlotte a note. *Went to the gym, be back in an hour.* Jack always found that no matter how hungover he felt a good workout released the toxins and shook off the cobwebs. As the weights worked their magic, he thought about all that had happened the previous night. It was a very eventful night but what scared him the most wasn't the fact that a sinking feeling had started to grow in his chest telling him that he was giving up more than he was getting out of his 'symbiotic' relationship with Paul. It was the fact that he had kissed Charlotte.

He couldn't stop thinking that now he had two choices; The first was to go down Charlotte's path and see what it was like not to be completely alone. To see what it would be like to have someone in his corner for the first time in many years. He hadn't had someone close to him since his mom died and it almost felt like he was betraying her by even considering the thought of letting another woman into his life. The second option was to tell Charlotte that the kiss and sleepover meant nothing. To let her believe that he was just an acholic who was a decent writer. Just an average guy, no different than the rest. No matter what decision he made he would still have to live with the fact that he and Charlotte shared a bond and a pretty strong one by his standards. No matter how good he was at fading into the crowd Charlotte would now be able to pick him out of the masses with ease. Their hearts had been connected by something much more powerful than sex and it terrified him.

Jack finished his workout and got back onto the elevator that would take him back to his apartment. When the steel doors opened, and he walked into his apartment nothing had been moved and Charlotte's clothes were still on the island. Jack walked to the bedroom and saw that she was still sleeping. Jack decided to let her sleep because he knew she must be exhausted. Then took a shower, cleaned up the apartment and then looked at the clock. 10:30am. He knew he should wake her up, she undoubtedly had something important to do. He felt bad waking her, but he shook her gently.

She opened her beautiful eyes and fluttered her eyelashes like a computer booting up. Then sitting up she asked, "What time is it?"

"10:30am, well probably 10:32am now," Jack told her.

"Perfect, have you been up long?"

"Hour, hour and a half. I had a cup of coffee, worked out and showered."

"Ah shit, you should have woken me up."

"You looked so peaceful; I couldn't bring myself to do it but then I thought you might have something important to do today so I thought I had better wake you up."

"I have to go see Paul later but that's it. Thanks for letting me sleep."

"No problem, would you like a cup of coffee?"

"Sure, then I had better get going. Can I wear your clothes home? I just can't bring myself to put the dress back on."

"Yeah, no problem," Jack said and then they headed to the kitchen. Even though her hair looked like an abandoned bird's nest, her face was creased like the folds of an origami crane and the elephant skin like clothes hung off her body she looked stunning. They drank coffee and talked about the upcoming week, she made sure Jack could recite his schedule, knew how to get to each class and then she bid him goodbye. She grabbed her dress, her high heels, blood red pendant and headed out the door so gracefully she almost looked like she was floating.

The fact Charlotte hadn't even alluded to anything that had happened the previous night made Jack uneasy. As did the fact that she was meeting Paul after he had been so dismissive of her at dinner last night. He realized he had come to genuinely cared about her. He didn't just see her as the stunning woman that was sent to pick him up from Medora. He honestly cared about her well-being, and the worst part of it was that he knew Paul didn't. Knowing he cared for Charlotte, the only thing left to decipher was if he could trust her. He knew it was possible to care for a person and still not be able to trust them but he hoped he would be able to have both.

Jack had already worked out, so he didn't know what else to do with himself. It was odd to have that much time to himself. All week he had been rushed around to just about every shop, café, and sandwich bar in the city. That day he was in charge, whatever his heart desired he would be able to do at the drop of a hat. However, having that level freedom left his mind blank. After a few minutes of nothing, he decided he would read for a while and then go from there. It was too early, even for Jack, to have a drink, so he just sat down on the couch with his book and read for hours. Before he knew it, the clock read 2:00pm. "Shit" he said out loud, realizing he had missed breakfast and lunch at that point.

Starving, Jack decided to put his book down and grab a burger from The Four Roses. Their lunch and dinner options were subpar, but Jack didn't feel like making something and with the limitless monthly stipend Paul had given him he didn't have to worry about running out of money. It was a foreign feeling to not care about money. He had lived his life with ramen noodles, budgets and ego crushing charity. On the way to the diner, his mind drifted back to the night before. The dinner, Charlotte, and the kiss raced through his mind like a forgotten song on replay. Being an outsider, Jack hadn't exactly had hordes of girls lining up to make out with him or sleep over at his home. But through his journey up to that point he had had kissed his fair share of women and based on that limited sample he knew that the kiss he and Charlotte shared had been 'real'.

There was no faking that type of passion. So then why hadn't she said anything that morning, was it because she was ashamed? Did Paul call and instruct her not to get close to him? Or was she just so void of feelings that she didn't feel anything toward him, didn't feel the passion he had felt? He knew it was going to be a long semester because whatever the reason she had for kissing him, he knew it was bound to happen again, and again until something finally broke inside him. The sheer amount of time he knew they were going to spend together was like a contract signed by the two of them allowing it to happen.

Once Jack reached the Four Roses he paused, peered into the window to make sure that the small diner wasn't the place Charlotte was meeting Paul. He didn't want to run into either of them today, he just wanted to enjoy his freedom if only for a few fleeting hours. After a quick check, he was sure neither one was in the diner, so he swung the door open and walked to what seemed to have become his usual seat. He ordered a double bacon burger and fries. Then turned on his phone—It was an old flip phone that only was able to take calls—to check and see if Charlotte had called while he was reading, she hadn't; Jack knew that he should probably buy a newer phone, but he didn't care. He didn't want a new one. As he looked at the phone, he wondered what it would be like the first time Paul called. Jack knew it wouldn't be an overly pleasant conversation. Even though Paul had given him no real reason not to like him. By all accounts, Paul was an incredible man who gifted him an opportunity of a lifetime. Although underneath all the compliments and charity Paul had given him, there was fear. An uncomfortable feeling of unease that told Jack, Paul was not who he wanted Jack to believe he was. Jack pushed the thought out of his mind when his lunch finally arrived and thanked the waitress. As he ate his mind was cleared, hunger was more important than any other thing that was happening in his life in that moment. After he had finished eating, tipped the waitress and settled the bill he opened the door to the diner and stepped back out into the cold New York air.

He had always dreamed of living in the city and studying at NYU, but he had never made a list of the things he would like to do once he got there. And even as he stood 20ft from central park he still didn't have any idea what activity he would like to do. He couldn't go back to his apartment because he knew that his mother would be irate if she knew he was whittling his life away drinking and reading in his apartment. *"Books and words are important, but they can't show you the world like your eyes can. God gave you them for a reason Jack,"* she used to say, and she was right.

All the books in the world couldn't bring his mother back, they couldn't answer why she had been taken and couldn't let him speak to her once again. He knew alcohol couldn't either, but he wasn't quite ready to fight the world all by himself just yet. Despite the thought of the depressing addiction Jack knew he had developed; he decided to take a walk and see where that went.

The cold bit at his skin through the thread bare 'trendy' shirt Charlotte had picked out for him, he hadn't bought a jacket quite yet. As he tried not to focus on the cold, he decided that's what he would do. Unlimited money meant he could buy any coat he could possibly imagine. All he had to do was find a store to purchase a jacket from. With time to think, he decided he would buy two jackets. One for day-to-day use and one to wear with one of the suits he had procured during the tornado of a week he had been caught up in. Out of the corner of his eye he spotted a Levi's outlet. They sold warm coats, one of the older kids at the orphanage had one when he had fist got there and Jack had always wanted to try it on.

Now he had the money and freedom to buy one of his own. Jack crossed street dodging taxis and cars and pushed open the barn style doors of the outlet. As he stepped inside, he was smacked in the face by the smell of denim and what he thought was the smell of a horse stable. It was worn wood, the sound of hooves pawing and pacing, moldy straw, the strong jaw of a horse crushing oats between it's teeth, the smell of well slept on hay and fresh manure. He didn't mind the smell but instead wondered how it got there, the city of New York was an eternity from the nearest barn. Jack wandered aimlessly around the shop until he found the coats.

There were jean jackets with wool lining and wool collars, jean jackets with no wool and corduroy jackets with and without wool. He tried on a jacket with blue jean and white wool, black jean with black wool and black jean with white wool. After careful consideration, striking many different ludicrous poses in the mirror he landed on the black jean with white wool. After paying for it, he ripped of the tags and stickers, stuck his arms through the sleeves and threw the jacket over his shoulders. It was the first purchase his writing skills had bought him, and he was quite proud that for once his ability had provided him with something more than student loans. The next order of business was to find a nice dress coat to wear with his suits. As he walked through the city— warmer on account of the heavy wool jacket—he felt happier, more content with his current situation.

He spotted a leather store directly ahead of him and thought that a nice leather jacket would keep him warm and make him look sophisticated. He pushed the door open and the smell of leather tickled his nose just as the stable smell had in the Levi's outlet. As soon as he looked up a sales associate stood blocking his path and brazenly asked him what he was looking for.

"A fancy jacket to wear with a suit," Jack told him.

"Are you sure this is the right store for you?" The associate said with the same air of superiority Charlotte had spoken with in the Meodrian bar. "There is a gap just down the street."

Jack looked at him and knew the man had just made a judgment based only on his outward visage. Little did the man know that he was one of if not the richest 25-year-old man in the city. Jack however was not a rich asshole, so he said, "Yes sir. This is the right store. Just a jacket that will look good with a suit please."

"Very well sir," the associate replied and led Jack to the back corner of the store. The jacket he had in mind was thrown on a mannequin's shoulders, collar turned up in the back, flared to the sides in the front and had buttons all the way down the front.

"Looks great. Can I try it on?" Jack said.

"Of course, sir. We don't let a costumer purchase any item without trying it on first," and grabbed the jacket off the mannequins' shoulders leading Jack to a small alcove with mirror lined walls and a podium in the middle for costumers to stand on.

"I can hold your jacket for you, sir?"

"That would be great," Jack said, shedding the new jean jacket and grabbing the leather jacket from the salesman. When he put the jacket on, he was overcome with a feeling of power, a feeling he wasn't accustomed to but enjoyed all the same. After standing on the podium for a while, he felt the salesman's eyes on him waiting impatiently for a compliment or some criticism.

"It's perfect, I'll take it!" Jack said.

"Very good sir, I will meet you at the till," he said handing Jack his jean jacket. After sliding the jacket back over his shoulders, Jack walked up to the counter.

"This is one of our best jackets sir. You have a very refined taste."

"Thank you, I think it will work for what I plan use it for."

"The total is $650. Will that be cash or credit?"

Jack couldn't believe his ears. A week earlier, he wouldn't have been able to cover the cost of the jacket with all the money in his bank account. Of course, now $600 was just a number that held the same weight as $1,000,000. The surplus of money still hadn't sunk into reality for Jack, but he thoroughly enjoyed the freedom that accompanied it.

"Credit please," Jack said as he stuck his card into the reader. As he pressed the button for a tip, he remembered the salesman's earlier snide remark and inputted $10,000 dollars in the tip value. He inputted his pin, grabbed the bag containing his new coat and thanked the salesman again as he headed out the door. He was finished with shopping and adventuring for the day. It was time to head back to the apartment for the night. After all, he had a big day coming up.

Once he was back in the apartment, he removed the tags from the leather jacket and went to his closet. It was a huge walk-in closet almost as big as his room at the orphanage in Maine. There was an island style table in the middle with a small rack coming out of the back of it. Jack decided if Paul called, he probably wouldn't have much time to leave the house and he never knew what state he would be in, so he should be prepared. He grabbed a white shirt with small black dots all over it, black pants, black dress socks, black tie with a forest green stripe in the middle, a black blazer with a forest green pocket square and his new leather jacket and hung them all on separate wooden hooks—apparently these hooks were the best for delicate dresses and suits according to Charlotte—and then laid out some clothes that he could wear to his first day of school at NYU.

After he made sure his bag was packed, his laptop was charged, and everything was in order for the momentous day that was just peering over the horizon. He headed back into the kitchen to check the time. 8:00pm, the clock read. He dug through the freezer until he found one of the individual pizzas he remembered buying earlier in the week, stuck it in the toaster oven and poured himself a stiff drink from the last of the whiskey remaining in the bottle of Crown. He would have to make a trip to the liquor store after school he thought making a mental note. Jack finished his first drink of the night by the time the pizza was ready. So, he took the pizza out, cut it into slices, placed it on a plate, poured himself another drink, sat down on the couch and found a movie to watch until he was ready for bed.

Halfway through *A Simple Favor* Jack headed back to the kitchen to pour a final drink. As he poured, he realized that Emily Nelson, who was a character from the movie he was watching, reminded him of Charlotte. Curious he thought as he walked back to the couch to finish the movie, curious that a fictional character and a real live human could be so similar. By the end of the movie, Jack was so invested that he almost forgot about his drink—almost. The character that reminded him of Charlotte had completely duped her husband and her best friend. As he made his way to his room to go to bed for the night he thought that it sure would be unfortunate if the movie drew parallels in his own life.

Chapter 4

Jack was pulled to consciousness by the same internal clock that had awoken him the previous morning. He coaxed himself out of the half conscious, half subconscious state that he always found himself living in in the mornings and headed to the kitchen for a coffee. He was still half asleep by the time the coffee was ready, but the first sip of the scalding caffine took care of that. As his tongue continued to sting from its contact with the burning liquid, he decided to say 'fuck it' to the coffee, poured it down the drain and picked up his gym bag to get a quick workout in before he had to leave for school.

As he felt the weight rip his muscles and heard the clink of plates hitting each other he thought everything over. He was anxious for his first day but also extremely excited. He knew the two emotions were biologically the same, but he liked to call it anxiety instead of excitement. It kept him humble, being the humble but friendly person without really getting in too deep had become his specialty since his mother had died. In the nine years since his mother's death, the only person he had ever talked about his past with was Charlotte. He didn't know why he told her the truth. Somehow, he felt warm, safe, terrified, and completely insignificant all in the same 5 minutes when he was in Charlotte's presence. It was an odd feeling to be sure, but Jack felt like he may have found the one he could really get to know, the one he wouldn't have to lie to.

Once the workout was finished, he finally felt clear headed and fully awake. All the cobwebs were shaken off and it was time to shower and get to his first class of the day. The first class was French followed by Forensic studies on Mondays and Wednesdays. Then on Tuesdays and Thursdays he had Creative writing followed by Old English. He also had a two-hour break between classes. The break was very beneficial because he might be too busy to accomplish any homework during the nights. Once Jack was showered and dressed, he put his new casual jacket on, headed out the door backpack slung over one shoulder toward the Four Roses to grab a breakfast sandwich. He couldn't remember the last time he had a meal that hadn't been prepared by a large brand name food company or a local restaurant.

Jack arrived at the NYU campus overcome with excitement. He felt like a 6-year-old boy who was just told he could pick out any Lego set he wanted no matter the cost. His dream was being realized, even though the incessant, nagging feeling that he was trading quite a bit to see his dream realized hadn't gone away, the excitement didn't waver. It was just too amazing that he was an actual student at NYU. His mother was crying tears of joy wherever she was, Jack was sure of it. Charlotte's tours had left Jack with a very detailed memory of the campus and how to get to each class. Finding the class was almost a trivial task. He sat down at the back of the first classroom, that way he wasn't likely to be picked out of the crowd and put on the spot to answer a question no one knew the answer to.

The class started and the teacher introduced herself. "My name is Professor Blanchette, but you can call me Mrs. B if you would like," she said.

Jack noted the deep-rooted French name and made a mental note to ask her about where she had come from one day. As she spoke Jack realized that she 'knew her shit' but it was held back by the thick French accent she was burdened with, which he would have to get used to but for now he was just happy to be sitting in an NYU classroom. Jack knew the pedestal that he had placed the university on would eventually fade closer reality as he got used to the city and university. But on that first day the pedestal was as high as the statue of liberty, and he relished in the shadow it cast.

The class finished with little real material being covered, pretty much just a bunch of handouts, class introductions and a large number of rules and regulations the school had obviously told all the teachers to cover for the new semester. Jack decided that given the lack of homework that had been prescribed, he would call Charlotte and ask if she wanted to meet up for some lunch. The call connected on the second ring and Charlotte answered. "Hey Jack."

"Hey. Want to grab some lunch, or do you have a class soon?"

"No, lunch sounds good. I have an hour break right now anyway. I'll meet you at the white archway in the center of campus and we will go from there."

"Sounds like a plan," Jack said, hanging up the phone. As he walked, his mind fixated on the night they spent together. He hoped Charlotte would say something, if for no other reason but the appeasement of his subconscious turmoil.

Jack spotted Charlotte directly underneath the massive white archway with her back turned to him. He snuck up and playfully grabbed her by the shoulders. She spun around with her fists clenched as if she was ready for a fight but then realized it was Jack and unclenched.

"Damn, you scared me. Don't sneak up on me, you jackass," she exclaimed.

"Sorry I was just trying to have some fun."

"All good," she said but for some reason unknown to Jack her voice was still unnervingly quaky.

"My bad. Where do you recommend we go for lunch?"

"I have a place in mind, it's not too far. Follow me," she said grabbing his hand and whisking Jack through the bustling crowd of students. After they escaped the mob, she let go of his hand and pointed across the road to a small burger joint called Ben's.

"That's it. They make the best burgers I have ever tasted."

"Perfect, after yesterday's burger at the Four Roses I am due for a good one."

"You had a burger the Roses?" Charlotte asked between laughing fits.

"Yeah, I did. Shut up. It was my first outing alone in the city," Jack said smiling.

"I guess, I'll give you a break this time but for future reference the Roses only make good breakfast food. Just down the road there's a small bistro that has a good lunch menu. I forget the name of it but it's worth the extra couple dollars," She said as she entered the small burger joint. As Jack entered, he could smell the burgers cooking. The grease and sizzle of meat against white hot steel made his mouth water. The restaurant had a solid steel counter that wrapped all the way around the kitchen but other than that they had no other tables or seating. Jack assumed it was strictly a takeout restaurant. By the time Jack reached the counter, Charlotte had already ordered two number threes and paid for them. She asked him to wait for them while she went to the bathroom.

Even though Jack knew all of Charlotte's money came from the same place his did, he felt a pang of guilt that she had paid for the meal. His mother always said that no matter how independent a woman was, they always gravitated to a man that could provide. So he wrote a mental note to himself to ensure he paid for all purchases from then on, no matter the cost because what was limitless money good for if he couldn't pass it on to others. When the order was done, one of the cooks handed him a paper bag with a grease stain starting to blossom into a heart attack flower.

Charlotte was still in the bathroom, so as he waited for her, he looked around the restaurant at all the different accolades, trophies and certificates displayed on the walls. Once she emerged, he held the door open and waited for her to exit, then thanked the cashier and followed Charlotte out.

"Where are we going to eat?" Jack asked.

"There's a nice bench near your next class, we can eat there," Charlotte said and started walking across the street, this time without grabbing Jack's hand. When they finally arrived at the bench, Charlotte grabbed the bag and dug around inside until she grabbed one of the burgers and handed it to Jack. Then grabbed her own and started to eat. Neither spoke a word until the burgers had vanished. After they had both finished and wiped the grease out of the corners of their mouths, Jack admitted that the burger was in fact very good.

It was much better than The Four Roses pathetic excuse for a burger and then finally cracking under the constant barrage of thoughts he asked, "Are we ever going to talk about what happened the other night?"

Caught off guard Charlotte choked on her own saliva and then paused as if thinking about her response and then finally said, "It was a good night. Hanging out with you is a great break from being alone for so long, and the kiss was incredible. I don't think I have ever been so filled with whatever that kind of feeling that was after kissing someone or after anything for that matter, but you are such a good person. Jack you are the definition of an innately good person. Sure, you have a bit of a drinking problem, but I have my own problems too, ones that you know about and many more than you wouldn't be able to guess. But being such a good person…such a pure person I can't. No, I won't do anything more with you other than being friends. At least until you do your first job for Paul. If you still want to be with me like…that after you find out what it is we do, then we can talk. You must know that this is my life, Paul's world is my world. His business is my business. It wasn't always my life, but I am too deep now to get out, so it's my life."

Speechless, Jack couldn't respond. It was as if her words had sewn his mouth shut. Instead of appeasing his questions, she had sent in reinforcements. After a few moments, he finally managed to get a few words out.

"Ok. Thanks for lunch." Then he stood up, threw the greased stained paper bag in the garbage, and walked in a haze toward his next class. He was an hour and fifteen minutes early, but he didn't have the brain power to do anything else other than sit on one of the leather benches outside of the classroom. Jack felt like he had punched in the face by Mike Tyson, like his brain had been scrambled. The only problem was that no one had hit him, instead Charlotte's words had slithered through his ears in into his brain with the sole purpose of causing chaos. The nagging feeling that he had sold his soul was now not so nagging.

Instead, it had both of its greasy, unwanted hands firmly placed on his brain's steering wheel. Jack just sat perfectly still, immobilized in the very center of his dream life until he started hearing a few pairs of footsteps at the end of the hall. Class must be starting soon he thought standing up and opening the door to the forensics study's class and taking a seat at the back of the room. The class was filled with introductions, rules, and handouts, much like his French class. Except from the professor's gender and name, Dr. Print, it was identical. Once the class was over Jack caught a cab back to his apartment and just as he was entering the building, he remembered he was out of whiskey. Jack closed the door and walked to the liquor store down the street, purchased two of the biggest bottles of Crown Royal he could find and headed home.

Once he was inside his apartment he took a large swig straight out of the bottle, then poured the amber liquid to the brim of the fancy whiskey glass, sat on the couch and turned on the TV. It was amazing how quick the alcohol reached his neurotransmitters and settled him down. He flipped through Netflix until he found a movie he wanted to watch and then headed to the kitchen to throw another pizza into the toaster oven.

Jack's mind was numb as he headed back to the couch, pizza and whiskey bottle in hand. That night was going to be a heavy night, there was no reason to lie to himself. Without warning, his pocket buzzed. Must be Paul he thought frantically fishing in his pocket trying to pull out the phone. "Fuck me!" He yelled into the empty apartment as he fiddled with the phone in his pocket for three entire rings. He finally grasped the phone, flipped it open and said, "Hello."

"Hanson!" The voice responded.

Jack recognized the voice immediately. His suspicions were correct, it was Paul. He knew he was in no state to be doing any sort of work that night, so praying to every god he could think of Jack said, "Yes sir, I'm here."

"How was the first day? Meet any interesting people? Any familiar faces?"

"It was great! We pretty much just went over the standard first day stuff. Didn't really focus on the other students, just focused on getting to class and memorizing the syllabus." It was complete bullshit, but he couldn't very well tell Paul what sort of thoughts had been running through his head for the better part of the day.

"That's good to hear Jack, remember if you need anything all you have to do is ask."

"Yes sir. I remember."

"Good. I was just calling to check up on my young Hemmingway. No jobs for you tonight but I have some business to take care of next week so expect another call from me then. Have a good night, Hanson," Paul said and then hung up the phone.

Jack's stomach finally fell back into place and he took another healthy swig straight from the bottle. Then as he poured another drink he dug into his pizza. By the time the movie had concluded, he could barely see the screen, he definitely wouldn't remember the end of the movie and his conversation with Paul would inevitably be a blurry memory. He decided he would have one more drink and then try to get some sleep. He poured another drink, spilling quite a bit on the coffee table. After he mopped most of the mess and finished what was left of his drink in one large gulp, he cleaned up a bit more and stumbled to his room. Crashing into the walls on multiple occasions, Jack finally made it to his bed and flopped down on the mattress.

No clothes would be set out that night. As he lay on the bed the room swam in front of his eyes and after a few minutes of the stomach lurching spinning sensation the room morphed into the interior of a rundown but clean trailer. Jack recognized it as the one he had lived in with his mother. Jack heard screams of agony coming from the room at the end of the hall. Jack moaned; he knew all too well the memory that was about to be replayed in front of him. The alcohol only suppressed the pain as long as he didn't consume too much and that night, he had unequivocally drank too much. Walking toward the thick wooden door, he steadied himself and turned the knob.

There was blood spattered on the pillowcase that sat on top the mess of sheets that were strewn about the mattress. He stumbled further into the room staring at the open door to the on-suite bathroom. Kneeling at the toilet his mother was vomiting frightening amounts of blood mixed with yellow bile. A boy was on one knee beside her holding her matted, sweaty hair back in one hand, messaging her back with the other. He recognized the boy as the 16-year-old version of himself, the sober version.

"Ambulance…Now," his mother grunted out between fits. The boy ran right through right through his chest to the phone in the kitchen. Jack could hear himself telling the operator his address through muffled sobs. He felt so bad for his former self, he knew the damage that had been inflicted on his own psyche that night but then suddenly, the memory disappeared. He was back in his new apartment, and that was the last thing he saw before his consciousness went completely black and he was pitched into a void. Blackouts had become commonplace since the first time he remembered drinking with the sole purpose of getting drunk and they were almost always preceded or succeeded by a painful flashback.

There must have been a terrible accident not far from Jack's house because the black void was rudely interrupted by many loud sirens. Jack rolled over trying to ignore the ear-piercing noises, but they were insistent. It was as if the city knew he had better things to do other than nurse his hangover. Reluctantly he sat up—eyes closed, he still couldn't face the light just quite yet—grudgingly removing the covers and feeling his feet hit the floor, Jack opened his eyes a few nanometers feeling his way to the kitchen on account of his limited vision.

Once he reached the kitchen, he opened his eyes fully or a wide as they would dare to go, loaded the Keurig, placed a cup underneath the nozzle and waited. Just as he thought the night was a fuzzy memory but contrary to his assumption, he recalled the entire conversation he had with Paul via telephone. No heavy drinking next week. Definitely a moderate amount of whiskey, enough to subdue his moral compass and his pain but not heavy by any means. His wits had to be intact if he was going to a 'job' for Paul. After the coffee had been deposited into his mug, he drank it slowly, then grabbed his gym bag and headed out. He didn't have to worry about getting dressed. He had slept fully clothed that night.

The rest of the week flew by, he attended his classes and completed a few assignments. Jack was really starting to get the hang of French; Professor Blanchette had taken a real interest in him, and his English classes were going very well. There was really no surprise there though, that was the reason he was in New York in the first place, wasn't it? By the time Monday rolled around once again, Jack had only blacked out once more, but no other flashbacks had reared their ugly heads, which was a rarity. A rarity he wasn't complaining about.

Oddly enough Jack hadn't seen or heard from Charlotte since their conversation. So, as he walked to his first class of the day catching a glimpse of a girl that looked a lot like Charlotte out of the corner of his eye he was truly hopeful it was her. The girl was walking toward him quite quickly and when she got close enough Jack could tell that it was in fact Charlotte. She was wearing tight black leather pants and a flowing white shirt. Stunning as ever.

"Hey jackass!" She said with a smile that Jack could tell was masking her nervous energy.

"Hey Charlotte," he responded.

"How was the first week? I'm sorry I haven't seen you since our little chat last Monday, but I thought you might need a little space."

"Yeah, I kind of did but I could've used your cuisine expertise. I've stuck to a strict frozen pizza diet for the last week," Jack said with a grin.

"Yeah, that won't cut it. We will have to meet up for dinner more often, as long as you are okay with spending time with me after tonight."

"Tonight?"

"Yeah, Paul is going to give you a call tonight about a job. I told him he was starting you off too fast, but I guess it's better to know what you've signed on for sooner rather than later."

Jesus, tonight is the night he thought silently to himself. His palms started to sweat, and he knew his capacity to learn that day had just flown out the window with his stomach firmly in its grasp.

"Yeah, better get it out of the way," Jack said not really agreeing with the words that slipped through his lips. He honestly didn't mind being an innocent bystander, but his signature was on the papers, so he really didn't have a choice did he.

"Yeah, well give me a call after if you want, if you need a few days to process that's fine too but just remember I am here to chat if you need." Then pulled one of her patented spin outs and left Jack standing alone with nothing but his own thoughts to console him. Jack had no other good options, so he headed to his French class. It was fun and it might actually take his mind away from whatever awaited him that night. The day flew by in a haze of anxiety and by the time Jack entered the apartment his hands had developed a mild case of Parkinson's. He poured himself a small drink to steady the nerves and then headed to the shower.

The cold water showered over him dulling his senses and once he was sure the cold water had done its job, he got out to start getting ready. Suit on, teeth brushed, hair done nicely and jacket laying on the back of the barstool-like chairs, he poured himself another drink and waited in silence. As he stared at the oven clock, the phone finally rang, and Jack's heart skipped a beat. It was 9:45pm.

Chapter 5

Jack flipped the phone open and spoke, "Jack Hanson here."

"Hanson, tonight's a good night to earn some of the money I gave you son," Paul said. Son. Jack hated that word coming from anyone's mouth, but it made his skin crawl coming from Paul's. He didn't have a father and this 'businessman' sure as shit wasn't it.

"It would be an honor sir, what time do you need me?"

"Be in my office in 20 min." Jack knew he would have been screwed if Charlotte didn't tip him off that he would be getting a call that night. He would have to figure out a plan that ensured he would always be ready when called upon.

"Yes sir, I will head out right now," Jack said hanging up the phone. He knew it didn't take 20min to get to the office from his apartment, but he was never late. At least, not when his livelihood hung in the balance. As he rushed to get his jacket on, he realized that he didn't know the address of the office. Embarrassed and reluctant, he called Charlotte and asked her if she could tell him the address of the office. She told him it was 100 Mal St. and wished him good luck. Jack thanked her and ran out the door and caught the first taxi, told the driver where he needed to go and let him know he would pay triple if he got him there fast.

10 minutes later he sat in the back of the car staring up at the building. His hands were trembling, and he knew he wasn't quite ready yet. Jack took a few moments to settle himself, paid the driver—four times what he owed—and opened the taxi door. Standing on the sidewalk looking up at the 'office' he felt very small and insignificant. The lobby somehow seemed smaller and less impressive than it had the last time he had been there.

Remembering how Charlotte had acted the last time, he walked purposefully past the receptionist without so much as a courteous head nod and stepped into the elevator that had already opened itself as if it already knew Jack was heading up.

Once the doors opened Jack saw Paul sitting with his feet up on the president's desk; Smoking a cigar with his left hand, drink in his right, a smug look painted across his face. The expression told Jack that Paul was excited for the proceedings; He had been waiting for it. Words slipped out of his mouth between the tendrils of smoke that encased his head in a sickly haze.

"Hanson…You're early. I admire a punctual man."

"Yes sir, It's a big night. I am finally being welcomed into the folds of the business that has given me so much, in so little time."

"You seem to be worth it as far as I can see. We will see how much you really are worth tonight," Paul said standing up. "Follow me," Paul strode past Jack into the elevator and Jack followed swiftly behind him. Once they were both safely inside the elevator's confines Paul pressed the button with no number or marking and clasped his hands together in front of his belt buckle. Jack had previously been under the impression that it had been faded with time but he realized then that it had been installed that way and that there must be a room coupled with the button that could didn't fit any sort of number value.

The elevator lurched to the left and then after a few second it dropped downwards. Once the elevator stopped the doors opened slowly, on the other side of the steel doors was a room made of stone. Each wall was made of massive flat rocks with mortar keeping them from falling out of the earth effectively filling the room. It was a small room with only one round low hanging light providing all the light that it guarded so dearly. The floor was made of cobble stone except a for a large black mat that had obviously been placed into the stonework post construction. Smells and sounds of the sewer faintly ran through the walls and the mortar had begun to grow moss in certain places.

Jack got the feeling that the room had seen and heard many different things. Things that were certainly nothing close to a charity function or a humanitarian aid project. He thought it could have been an old bunker from the world wars. He remembered learning about bunkers that rich people had constructed during the first world war to run into on the good chance they were bombed by the enemy. At the far end of the room, a man stood barefoot on the cold damp stones. He was about Jack's height, but Jack assumed the man had at least 20lbs on him. He was wearing a black wife beater with black shorts.

"This room is where our sponsored employees prove themselves," Paul said, "this isn't the job for tonight but if you fail this task, you will be relived of your card, apartment and any possession that you have been so graciously given." Jack chuckled, in essence he would be naked, homeless and alone in New York City if the task wasn't completed to Paul's standards.

"What is the task, sir?" Jack said with a faint quiver in his voice. He knew exactly what awaited him but deep down he prayed that he was wrong.

"You will fight this man. You will fight him until he or you are knocked out. You can place your jacket, suit jacket, tie, shirt, belt, shoes, and the contents of your pockets on the floor. You can choose if you would like your socks or not it doesn't matter to me either way." *Fuck me,* Jack thought to himself. If the fight was just proving himself, what would the actual job be?

Putting that thought aside, he said, "Ha, sounds like fun." Nervous energy that was so close to amusement filled Jack's body starting at his head and making its way down to the tips of his toes, it almost drove him into a full fit of laughter, but he fought to control his emotions. As Jack stripped, he thought back to the years preceding his mother's death. She worked 17hr days splitting her time between two jobs, so she wasn't able to be around all the time. Yet she didn't want him falling in with the 'wrong crowd'. That's what she called the kids who hung around the municipal skate park – although many were kids not so very different from him.

At the time he had never been to the skatepark but was told they got up to some stuff that at the time seemed like the worst things, people could possibly do. He couldn't imagine what she would have thought of him, watching him standing in the stone room with those men. Her way of making sure he didn't fall in with the 'wrong crowd' was to send him off to the boxing gym, that's where he developed his working out habit and after she left, he continued working out to make sure he wouldn't get in with the 'wrong crowds' wherever he was. During the last 3 years of living in bliss with his mother, Jack became quite good at boxing and even won a state tournament.

So, the man that was supposed to be intimidating, wasn't carrying out his job as well as he thought. Jack was quite confident that he would be able to drop the man quite easily. His knuckles were sure to be sore when he woke up, but he wouldn't let himself be the one waking up homeless, broke, and naked.

Once he had removed all the items Paul had told him he needed to remove—plus the socks he had the option to remove—he stepped onto the mat. The man was already standing on the black mat cracking his knuckles and gearing up to ruin Jack's life. Once the two men were ready Paul whispered, "Begin."

Jack raised his hands and held them a few inches below his eyes, tight to his body. The two combatants circled each other, each waiting for the other to strike first. The unknown man swung first; a heavy right hook meant for Jack's temple. Jack dodged the attack easily still circling, "Don't get horny," his boxing trainer used to say. The man swung again this time it was a light upper cut that caught jack in the ribs. Jack didn't mind the pain much; the daily workouts had helped grow muscle around his ribs that now served as padding. Still feeling his attacker out, Jack let him swing a few more times and evaded the onslaught with ease.

The man was practically foaming at the mouth after Jack evaded his last attack. It was dangerous, the man could land a lucky punch and Jack was human; His head would fall if it was struck in the right place. He knew the time had come to end the fight. The man threw another heavy right hook which Jack ducked under, then slammed his left fist into the man's open ribs. He heard the crack of bone snapping, raised his head, and drove all his weight through the man's head with a right hook of his own. The man's lifeless body fell like a 1000-year-old oak deep in a forest and hit the mat with a merciful thud. A feeling of pride and accomplishment filled Jack's chest, warming him against the chill in the small stone room. Not unlike a healthy swig of whiskey on a cold winter night.

Jack turned around and saw a look of admiration and glee on Paul's face. The warm feeling left his breast as quickly as it had come. In its place, Paul's expression left him heavy with shame.

"There's the outcome I was hoping for," Paul said with a smile. "Get dressed, we are heading out; you have a job that needs tending to" and handed Jack his clothes. Jack got dressed again, pulling the jacket up his arms he turned up the collar and flared it out at the front. Although it was the same movement he performed at the store, he didn't feel the same sense of power. Paul made him feel small, like a caged bird. They walked back into the elevator, and it brought them back to the lobby.

The pair stepped out of the left elevator doors, through the lobby and out onto the sidewalk where the same car that had delivered Jack to the office the first time sat waiting for them. They got in the car. Jack first, followed closely by Paul. The driver must have known where they were headed because he immediately drove off.

Paul began to speak, "Now that you have proved yourself you need to know who you are now employed by. I manage the largest betting company in the world. It is called the GWA or the Global Wagering Association. We run every betting booth, online betting website and casino in the world. I run the American piece of the larger puzzle and I also sit on the council that runs every gambling network on earth."

Now Jack understood where the absurd amounts of money came from. It had been earned through the exploitation of ruined lives, failed marriages and the crippling debts of every gambling addict that inhabited the earth. "We have thousands of people trying to steal from us every second of every day but today is special. A man had stolen 14 million dollars from us. We need to make an example of him Hanson. Stealing is one thing but 14 million is a lot of money, even for me. You are going to be my weapon of choice in the resolution of this little problem. We are keeping him in a warehouse in the Bronx. When we get there, I will give you a choice of which tool you want to use to 'carry out the deed'. I don't think I have to tell you what will happen if you don't complete the task," Paul said.

He was calm as if he had just instructed Jack to grab him a coke from the gas station down the road. But he hadn't, he had instructed Jack to kill a man, or rather was going to force Jack to kill a man. Jack was sure the man was joking but the look of pure placidity told Jack he was deadly serious. Jack would have never signed any papers regarding the death of any human even if it was the death of criminals, no matter what sort of cash incentive was placed above the signature line. Jack thought about jumping out of the car but the doors would undoubtedly be locked and even if they weren't, he didn't think Paul would have reservations about shooting him in the street like a stray dog. Then, even if he got away, where would he go.

He had no one to run to. So, he shakily said, "Any whiskey in here?" It was the only thing he could think of that could even come close to numbing him enough to take a man's life.

"Yeah," Paul said cheerfully as he pulled a bottle of very old, very expensive scotch and two glasses out of the console that divided the two men.

Handing Jack the bottle he said, "Take as much as you want and pour me a little."

Jack poured a small amount in the first cup and handed it to Paul. Then poured as much whiskey as the small glass could hold in his own and drank until it had all been liberated. Looking down at the empty cup he poured another glass, just as full, and once again swallowed it in one gulp. Jack no longer cared what the man thought of him, he was angry and scared, and if a wolf's reaction to being cornered was to snarl and reveal his teeth, Jack's reaction was to drown the problem. If he was able to fight, he would have fought to the death, but he knew a fight would be in vain. Although his reaction to the problem should have worked, it didn't seem to matter how much alcohol he consumed, his brain wouldn't allow him to escape. He was going to have to complete the job all by himself.

Neither man spoke for the rest of the ride. Once they arrived at the steel building, Paul stepped out first, followed shortly after by Jack. They walked in the large warehouse through a small metal door on the left side of the building that showed signs of battering with two men standing like sentries on either side. Jack noted the state of the neighborhood. It was dreary, dark and smelled like crime. The cigarette, marijuana and cigar smell filled the air as if it was warning him against entering the warehouse. Jack knew the place reflected Paul's soul like a mirror. The large space was empty, save for a chair occupied by a man dressed in a suit with a black bag tied over his head. Next to him there was a table littered with weapons and a mountain of a man that resembled a silverback gorilla, holding an automatic, military issue rifle in his massive hands.

The man in the chair had a pin on his chest. It was a United States flag. The type usually worn by politicians. Jack pushed the thought from his mind and turned to the table. The table had a police issue Glock pistol, a heavy looking revolver, a large hunting knife, a bow with one arrow, a bat with nails hammered through its 'sweet spot' and some black gloves that were missing leather on the fingers and the knuckles.

"Choose your weapon, take care of the issue and then the car will take you wherever you would like to go," Paul said.

Jack had never fired a gun, shot a bow and arrow, played baseball or messed around with knives in his entire life so there was really no choice that would allow him to make sure the man died quickly and painlessly. But all in all, the revolver looked like the best option. He picked up the heavy gun in his right hand and felt the cold dangerous metal in is hands. He imagined lifting the revolver, shooting the behemoth behind the poor sod with the black bag over his head and then spinning and shooting Paul. Then running to the door waiting for the two men to come rushing in, killing both and then fleeing but that only happened in the movies. So, he instead walked toward the man in the chair, his hands were tied to the chairs arms and his head hung low.

Jack knew he was most likely sedated or knocked out. Jack held the gun in both hands, contemplating the choices and people that had brought him to that very moment. Obviously, he was taking too long because Paul yelled, "Do it!"

Terrified, Jack lifted the gun in his right hand and held it to the man's head. It was shaking so much that he had to bring his free hand up to level it to the point in which he could rest finality's iron on the man's forehead. He pulled the hammer spur back, listened to each individual click, closed his eyes, and silently asked his mother for forgiveness. Then turned his head away from the man, eyes still closed, he pulled the trigger. BANG. Brain tissue flew out of the back of the man's head hitting the behemoth standing guard behind him.

The gun immediately slipped out of Jack's clammy hands and bounced off the concrete floor, chipping a piece of concrete as it did. Jack felt his face draining its blood and his head started to spin, on the fifth revolution he vomited all over the concrete beside the dead man's chair. Jack looked up helplessly and the behemoth handed him a rag he had readily available in his pocket. Jack wiped his mouth clean and handed it back to the giant who threw it at his feet as a wildfire of violence spread across his face. Jack turned and looked at Paul, his face was calm, and he had a look in his eyes that almost made Jack throw up again. The man almost looked proud.

Paul walked silently toward Jack and put his arm around his shoulders to lead him out of the warehouse, stopping briefly to speak to the men behind him.

"No trace," he said as he removed his arm from Jack's shoulders and reached in his pocket. He slowly pulled out a silver necklace with a blood red pendant in the shape of an Aztec sun. "This is yours now; you've earned it," he said as he walked away and got into one of the two cars that now sat in front of the warehouse, but Jack couldn't move. He just stood there, welded to the ground for a long time. He had just killed a man. Ended the man's shuffle on this mortal coil as Shakespeare would have put it. Jack had stolen the unknown man's one and only soul. In that moment, he wished it was him in the poor man's place, but he only let himself feel helpless for one fleeting moment.

54

After collecting himself or as many of the shattered pieces of his former self as he could, he loaded himself into the remaining car and saw the bottle of scotch sitting in one of the cup holders where he had left it.

"Where to?" The driver asked.

Jack took a large swig straight from the bottle and said, "Charlotte Jones's apartment." He had never been there, but he assumed the driver had driven there enough times to know the way without an address.

Chapter 6

Charlotte's house was a long way from the warehouse and for the entire duration of the ride Jack sat shell shocked in the back seat starting at the Aztec sun in his hand, trying to drink the memory from his mind. He had finally poured himself glass full after the 5th or 6th swig straight from the bottle. The adrenaline finally ended its blockade and allowed the alcohol to rush in an overwhelming flood to the receptor sites, allowing a numbness to wash over Jack's consciousness. It swam freely around his brain like the guest of honor, and he welcomed the numbness that it brought as a party gift with open arms.

As he wallowed in his own self-pity, he stared at the medallion. It was cold and felt wrong in his palm not because it was large—it was only about the size of a quarter—but because somehow it felt like he had a 50lb weight in the palm of his hand. The silver chain was shiny and most definitely real. There was no real surprise there, Paul obviously had every red cent in America just sitting in his bank account waiting to be spent. Jack couldn't help but think back to what he imagined shitty days to be when he was 18. A shitty day back then consisted of a failed exam, a slap in the face given by the orphanage supervisor's—the Callust twins—or maybe being late for class and getting detention. The sheer contrast between the hellish situations almost made him laugh. Now shitty days held bullets, booze, and murder.

Only God knew what his mother would think of her little boy now. The worst part about the whole damn thing was that he could no longer escape his bad days, there was no avenue that seemed even remotely viable. He thought about how simple life was back then. Days filled with gym, biology, history, and English with the best teachers he had ever had. Mr. Deviant was the shining star standing above the rest. The man had helped Jack so much. He nurtured Jack into the writer he had become. Mr. Deviant was able to bring Jack out of his pit of tears and show him the best parts of the world once again and then once he was ready, the lowly teacher showed him how to write once again as if Jack was uncovering a lost artifact in some distant desert.

Jack had been working on a novel when he was taken to the orphanage but once he was finished, he vowed never to write again. It took almost a full year for Mr. Deviant to show him what he was really capable of. The man was even the one who had gotten Jack his spot in Professor Laurent's class at the University in Medora. It was the closest thing Jack ever had to a father, the image of Mr. Deviant dancing in his brain brought him all the way back to reality. Jack was literally sitting atop a chair made of wealth and was on the verge of tears.

Of course, back in those days, he didn't think he was in the 'good days', even then, in the back seat of a limo, he still didn't whole heartedly believe that those were the good old days. He had lost his mother in those years, became an alcoholic and witnessed things no kid should ever see. However, anything was better than picking up a cold, hard and powerful weapon in your hands, resting it on an unconscious man's head and pulling the trigger. The bang and the hole that had been careved through the black hood made Jack shudder.

As he reminisced on the past a story popped into his head. 'Gawain and The Green Knight' was a poem Mr. Deviant had read to them in the last week of high school. It was a tale about a knight in King Arthur's court who embarks on a journey to find a green chapel where a green knight resides. The knight was supposed to be the most moral and perfect man in Camelot. A true Camelot knight through and through, but by the end of the story he accepted a sash that is supposed to save him from any stroke that may harm him. Being a knight, a 'pure' soul, it was—in the knights' eyes—an appalling thing to do. So, when he gets back to Camelot, he always keeps the sash on him as a token to remind him of the sin he has committed against God and his own 'purity'.

As he thought about the fable Jack wondered how a human could be pure. Rationally thinking everyone makes mistakes, there is no person alive who hasn't even committed one sin, but he assumed that it may have been the purpose of the story. To show the fantasy or impossibility of the knight's condition. The sash the knight wore around his body reminded Jack of the red medallion that literally embodied his sin. It was a literal medal of appreciation for his sin. As he thought of the complete absurdness of the gift Jack held the chain in both hands. He noticed it was big enough for him to slip it over his ears without undoing the clasp. So, he slipped it over his ears and let it rest on the green tie. It looked out of place, just like Charlotte's jewel. He knew that he needed to wear the necklace, but he wasn't ready for the world to know about his sin quite yet.

Jack loosened his tie and unbuttoned the top button of his shirt, sliding the medallion into the hole he had created, letting it rest directly on his skin. Maybe if he bore the chain around his neck from then on, he wouldn't forget the feeling that filled him that night and it would motivate him to stay away from the 'wrong people' from that moment forward or at least remind him of the person he used to be. Even though he knew that to be impossible and that he was a member of the worst group of humans in New York.

At least, he did in that moment of weakness as he sat on the bedrock of his life. He knew the medallion was just symbolic, but in some crazy way it might even keep him alive while he conceived a plan to get himself out of the situation he had so hastily thrown himself into. He realized that haste was the foundation of the plan Charlotte had when she walked into a bar gave a drunk man 8hrs to choose his fate. She obviously couldn't afford to give him too much time to think the proposal over. Jack still didn't know what he was going to say to Charlotte once he arrived, but it was the only place that popped into his head.

"We have arrived sir," the driver said.

"Thank you," Jack said grabbing the bottle of scotch, opening the door, and stepping onto the pavement in front of Charlotte's building.

The building was less fancy than his own building but looked well-kept and existentially more comfortable than the one he called home. He assumed Charlotte hadn't moved apartments since her arrival to the city back when she was 18. He took his first step and soon realized he was drunk. Struggling to keep his balance he heard the driver yell out, "Number 405."

After what felt like hours, Jack finally made it to the fourth floor and looked around for some signage telling him which direction 405 was. He decided to take a right, the left sides of buildings hadn't been kind to him that evening. After a few second of walking and checking door numbers, he knew chose correctly, he could see the door to 405 at the end of the hall. He steadied himself on the door frame and tapped the bottle lightly on the door. A few moments passed with no answer, so he tapped the door again. He assumed she was most likely sleeping but he didn't care in the slightest, she had brought him into this world, and she would be the one who explained what exactly Paul brought him to New York to do. After a few more taps, he heard Charlotte say, "Be right there."

"Hurry the fuck up!" Jack drunkenly yelled at the door. He knew he shouldn't be there at that hour or in that condition, but he didn't care. Standing in the hall, combined with every other thing that had happened that night had left him impatient and angry. Charlotte swung the door open. She was wearing tiny shorts that barely contained her ass and a shirt that was doing a horrible job of wrangling her breasts into place. She looked tired but oddly calm. Her eyes were almost completely red, and she stunk of weed. *Stoned,* he thought. Jack almost chuckled they were like two plastic bags that Paul had snatched out of the wind. The broken were always the easiest for men like Paul to take advantage of and Paul was nothing if not a man void of morals.

"Hey…you don't look great, jackass," Charlotte said, obviously trying to make a joke so that the white-hot anger would leave Jack's eyes. The result was like throwing a glass of water on a fire fueled by gasoline, Jack didn't have an ounce of humor left in his bones. "Paul called me, he said you set a record among recruits. He said you knocked henry out in 45 seconds, and it only took that long because you were playing with him."

"Oh, you know, that's great! I'm fucking honored," Jack said with a bow. "Now I'm atop a mountain of killers," He said almost spiting as a result of the seething rage and guilt. "You know when you said I would have the opportunity to go to NYU you didn't mention I would be trading my life for it. Must have forgot about that part, hey?"

"Yeah, well misery loves company I guess," Charlotte said quietly. A little bit of rage left Jack's eyes when he heard the sad tone in her voice. Charlotte must have sensed the crack in door because she started speaking again, "You know I've watched fifteen other recruits just like you and me die since I've been here. I have been dealing with the devil long before you got here. While you were getting settled in Medora, going to parties, and making a name for yourself. I was here choosing my weapon off the god forsaken black table and murdering thief after thief. So far, I am the only one who didn't cave after the first night so the fact that there are two of us now makes me happy and I don't really fucking care how that makes you feel," She said as her breath started to become shallow gasps and her voice rose to an octave Jack had never heard a woman speak in.

"Every other recruit took the gun and put a bullet in their heads right after they killed their target, and one even did it before they 'Carried out the deed'." The thought of killing himself hadn't even crossed Jack's mind. Maybe because of the shock but the more likely explanation was the fact that from an early age his mother had drilled the fact that people who 'offed' themselves were the lowest of low, into his impressionable brain. They had taken the 'easy' way out, she used to say. His mother had no sympathy for people who didn't give everything they could summon until their final breath. She was no hypocrite either, she had fought the cancer every step of the way until it finally spoke the last word.

"Sorry, I didn't know," Jack said. The anger had all but vanished. He thought about how lonely she must have been. How sad and helpless she was against Paul's tyranny.

"It's okay, I didn't know how bad I needed to get that out. It felt really good to finally set all that free," Charlotte said wiping the spit from Jack's eyes and drying her own cheeks.

"Why haven't you runaway yet? You must have thought about it. You could go back to the endless skies of Ohio. Hide in a small town where Paul wouldn't even think to look."

"No, I can't. I can't find a way to get out. I've gone over a thousand scenarios, even tried once. They all end up with me hypothetically dying, getting captured and tortured or arrested. Paul's reach is too wide. There isn't a way, at least not alone."

"Well, it's a damn good thing you are not alone any longer," Jack said pulling her into his arms, holding her head to his chest, telling himself if he held her close no one would be able to touch her. Tears fell down her beautiful cheeks, staining her creamy cheeks red. Letting her go he looked around the apartment, it was clean and neatly organized. Not ODC organized but organized enough to make it feel cozy. Jack assumed she had worked very hard to make the apartment feel like home.

Even though the anger had left, he still needed to know what his place was in Paul's regime. He needed to know what the reason was that had implored Paul to choose him.

"I know it might he hard, but I really need to know why Paul chose me. Why not someone else? I know it's hard, I know but I need some explanation,"

He said as he ran his hand over Charlotte's tear-stained cheeks. Her eyes started watering again as she walked away.

"Come out to the balcony. We can smoke and I will explain why Paul decided to ruin your life."

Charlotte walked to the kitchen, opened a small brown box, gently removed two joints and a zippo lighter. Then headed to the sliding glass doors picking up a blanket on the way. Jack followed her and slid the door closed once he was outside. There were two comfy chairs outside so they each took a seat. Jack sitting on the right, Charlotte on the left. He was still weary of the left; it had been the birthplace of so much pain in just the last 5 hours alone. She lit both joints and handed one to Jack and they sat in darkness a while, the only light coming from the embers at the tips of the stark white paper.

"He chose you because he loves reading and writing. Before he was the leader of GWA, he was a writer. He would have become a bestselling author, but he had a gambling addiction. He got himself on the GWA's radar and found himself sitting in the chair with his head covered by a black bag. Somehow the anesthesia didn't work, and he woke up before the 'deed' was done so he pleaded with his would-be murderer and for some reason the man decided to give him a chance. That was when he was 22. He has worked his way up in the organization over the years and now, as you probably know he runs the operation. That experience changed him."

"The man that was placed in the chair that day was killed, and a new man emerged from the metal door. Lucifer accepted his soul with open arms that night. Every good quality he possessed was vanquished. Over the years the evil has warped him into the man he is today. He chooses writers because he wants to punish everyone that might have a future. Any writer that he deems good enough to become something is brought at his request to the office. When they arrive, he assesses them and from that assessment he either has them die in a tragic accident or tries to poison their souls. Like he is attempting and might have already succeeded in doing to you and me."

"A few have slipped through his fingers, and a few didn't accept when they were presented their 'opportunity'. But for the most part he has succeeded in his vendetta. Not one writer that has walked out of the left elevator has ever made it past their final semester of university. However, because he was given a chance by his executioner, he can't pull a trigger to kill the people that attempt to steal from the organization. He relies on us and the men you saw at the warehouse to do it for him." She paused for a second, to steady her breath and to steel her herself against the constant barrage of sadness threating to open the flood gate of tears. "That's why he chose you Jack. He chose you because your special, in his eyes your worthy. You have endless potential." Charlotte said.

Jack sat on his chair in disbelief. The man who was evil incarnate was once just like him. A writer with an addiction. Paul at one point, had a soul. Jack couldn't even begin to think of what to say, he didn't know how to respond to that type of revelation. Wow didn't cut it, there were no words to sum up what had just been said. So, he took another drag from the joint and sat still, looking off into the distance, watching the cars driving along the roads beneath him. He had been told New York never slept and he didn't think he would be able to anytime soon either.

Charlotte's words had lifted the drunken stupor and Jack felt his mother's hand on his shoulder, "I won't let him break my soul. My mother would be appalled by my actions tonight, but she would be even more ashamed of me if I let him win. In her lifetime, she fought so many battles, including but not limited to the cancer she fought to her dying breath. So, I will fight Paul until I prevail, or I will die trying. My soul will stay intact so long as there is air in my lungs," Jack said knowing, but not caring, that he sounded like a knight in an old renaissance movie.

"Sounds like something I can get on board with. You sure are something different Jack Hanson. The first time I saw you in that sad little bar someone could have given me 10 000 guesses, and not once would I have guessed you would have turned out to be this person. Before you came, I was pretty sure I was going to die in Paul's employ." As the comment hit his ears, Jack smiled for the first time that night. He knew it was about time he picked up his mother's pen and started writing the next chapter.

"You know we can't do anything for a while though right Jack? He will be on high alert for at least a month or most likely longer. Paul won't let his guard down until he trusts you fully."

"I know. I can wait."

"It probably means you will have to kill quite a few more people."

"So be it. If a few souls must be taken to end Paul's wrath, I think it might be worth it. It's not like their innocent women and children." The pair finished smoking, headed back inside and Jack slid the door closed on his way in.

"Heading home tonight?" Charlotte asked.

"Umm…"

"Never mind you can stay here. You opened your doors to me the other night, I owe you one."

Jack breathed a sigh of relief. He was in no state to be alone that night. "I can sleep on the couch, don't worry about me," Jack said.

"We will see how the night goes jackass. Don't think you're going to bed right now do you?" She said with a weak smile as she started walking toward the vinyl record player in the corner of the room. A silent tear fell down her cheek as she dropped the pin on the vinyl and turned up the dial. "You still dance, don't you? Haven't forgot the steps since last weekend?" Charlotte said grabbing Jack's hands starting to sway back and forth.

Jack spun her underneath his outstretched left arm and caught her with his right-hand landing on her waist. They circled each other holding each other close, parrying every step with a counter step of their own. It was the second time he had been locked in a dance that night the only thing still up for debate was the question of which dance was more dangerous. Was it the dance he was currently dancing? Or was it the more primal dance he had been an avid participant of earlier in the night? Despite the baggage she had unpacked at his bequest Jack was still wary of Charlotte. Paul had told him every recruit needed to prove themselves. That meant that Charlotte beat Henry into submission as well and despite the grace Jack had won the fight with, Henry was not someone to dismiss.

Henry wasn't an easy opponent to submit which wasn't evident in the ease Jack was able to win the fight with but was unequivocally true, nevertheless. That meant Charlotte was trained somehow, otherwise she would have been killed in the 'selection process'. Plus, there was the fact that she obviously had Paul's trust. 'Paul's business was her business'; the words had come straight out of her own mouth.

So, Jack still wasn't completely sure if he could trust the woman in his arms. Was she a snake that would eventually shed her skin and reveal the sly, more dangerous snake underneath? Or was she just wearing the skin to survive in the nest she found herself in? No matter what, Jack was going to have to slip into a snakeskin of his own to keep his head six feet above the ground instead of six feet under it as Paul had promised.

Sunlight burned Jack's eyelids and he cracked them open to find himself laying on a couch. Startled he jerked up into a seated position. Where was he? Whose couch was he on? After a few seconds the nights memories started to replay in his head. All the thoughts, feelings and sights came rushing back. No amount of alcohol or drugs would be able to erase those memories, they had been etched into eternity just like the night of his mother's death. Those memories would never leave him. At least, not until the gentle kiss of death finally granted him peace. Jack remembered the dancing, the look on Charlotte's face and the soft skin just above her waist.

Jack looked down and saw that his clothes were still on his body and in the same state they had been last night which was a good thing. Jack stood up and was immediately sat back down, his head pounded. Like the evil was trying to break down the walls and escape. Once the pounding subsided, he stood up and walked down the hall to check if Charlotte was still in the apartment. He needed to make sure she hadn't gone running to Paul as soon he passed out. He opened her bedroom door and found her lying on top of the covers sound asleep.

It didn't necessarily guarantee that she hadn't told Paul everything he had said the night before but that was an issue that could be dealt with later. He shut the door carefully and rummaged around in the kitchen drawers to find a piece of paper and a pen. Jack didn't want to have a conversation about the previous night just quite yet.

"Headed home. Thanks for letting me stay the night. Talk soon."

"Thanks, Jack." He wrote.

Chapter 7

Once Jack arrived at his apartment—it wasn't home yet, and he didn't think it ever would be—he took off his clothes that had been stained with sin. As he removed articles of clothing, his leather jacket, his suit jacket, his tie, his pants, socks, and finally his shirt he uncovered the forgotten Aztec sun. The token Paul had given him for his 'performance' had completely slipped his mind. He rubbed the silver and the thick gem between his fingers just to find that it was still cold even after all the hours it should have been warming against his skin.

As he rubbed the pads of his fingers over its uneven surface, he remembered what he had decided it stood for, the physical embodiment of his crime. It was proof that he was a sinner; proof that he was no better than his would-be oppressor. He knew he never would be. It didn't matter that he was coerced into killing, he was the one that had pulled the trigger. Even though he wanted nothing more than to throw the medallion through the massive sliding glass doors that led to the porch, Jack decided that he would stick to his earlier decision to bear it like Gawain had borne his own symbol of sin.

Jack walked out of his room toward the bathroom. He turned the shower dial on and left the temperature ice cold. He needed the freezing water to bring him back to reality. The numbness could only last so long, once the morning came reality always needed to be reinstated. The ice-cold water showered over him in sheets, he scrubbed the cobwebs off and got dressed. Despite the very unusual circumstances of his life, the usual problems still needed to be tended to. Jack had already missed his first class of the day and decided that he would take the day off school. Laundry needed to be done, his suits had to be dry cleaned, he needed to eat, and he had to buy a gun of his own.

It was not a usual chore but one that was absolutely necessary given his extenuating circumstance. It was something he had never had any occasion to do before that day but after his eye opening night it seemed wise to have at least

65

some chance to defend himself if Paul came knocking. Grabbing his wallet, laundry bag and dry-cleaning he threw his jean jacket on and headed out.

The laundry was in the apartment building but the lady that attended the front desk told Jack that residents had to drop off their laundry so that the staff could clean it. After what felt like hours of going back and forth, Jack handed the bag of laundry to Angela—the desk attendant—and told her that he would stop at the bank on his way back to the building and pull out some cash to give to her for a tip. She told him that it wasn't necessary but thanked him all the same.

Jack stopped at the drycleaners he had seen just down the street; the man told him the suits would be ready by 5:00pm that night. Jack thanked him and continued on his journey. The normality of the chores made Jack happy. They made him think of Medora, the routine he had there and how much he missed his old, boring and uneventful life. On his way to the gun shop, Jack saw an atm inside the window of a convince store and decided that an atm was just as good as a bank. He would have never thought so haphazardly in his old life but having all the blood money he now had access to allowed him not to be worried about the insane markup credit card companies put on cash withdraws.

After he stuck his card into the machine, Jack decided $500 would suffice and he took it all in $50 bills. Anything smaller and he wouldn't be able to fit the cash in his wallet but as he was leaving the convivence store he thought about the gun purchase he was about to make. He thought it would be smart if he bought it in cash, that way Paul might not find out about the purchase. He would most likely know that Jack had taken a considerable sum out in cash but might not find out what he had spent it on.

Jack pulled another $14,000 dollars in $100 bills out and stuffed it all in his jacket pocket. His next stop would be the gun store he saw when he went coat shopping the other day. It seemed like an eternity since he had stepped into the Levi's store that smelt like a barn and was gently embraced by the warm innocent smells. Jack wasn't even sure he would be able to recognize the smells of innocence anymore.

The steps of the gun shop were cracked and pieces of chipped off cement laid around them like fallen soldiers. As Jack looked at the lonely pieces of cement separated from their once strong whole he thought of his own soul. Before he pulled the trigger it was strong, it was whole. When he pulled the trigger and heard the bang of the gun, it shattered. The bullet may have struck the hooded man's skull, but his own soul was caught in the crossfire. Little pieces of the once greater whole would forever lie on the cement of the warehouse floor as the little pieces of the steps did now. He could feel his soul crumbling as he made his way up the steps to buy a weapon of mass destruction.

It was a purchase he had told his mother he would never make but as he fell further and further into Paul's mud pit, he found himself doing more and more things that seemed necessary, making them no less wrong. Jack reached the top of the steps and paused before he stepped into The Gun Emporium. As he paused Jack's mind flashed back to the warehouse, and the black table littered with the tools of an executioner, but he pushed on into the store and made his way to the front desk.

Every muscle fiber in his body wanted to turn away and run from the store, but his primal survival instincts pushed him further inside. The emporium had massive guns lining every wall. Knives, grenades, and other tools Jack didn't recognize sat on shelves in the middle of the store. Images of the hooded man and the warehouse swam in-front of his eyes replacing reality. The ear spitting bang the gun emitted when he pulled the trigger rang in his ears and all of a sudden Jack's legs felt weak. He knew they would give way soon if he didn't leave. So, through the haze he stumbled into the rack of shooting magazines and turned toward the door.

A few steps more and he would be home free he told himself as his vision started to go completely black. He slammed headfirst into the door, pushed it open and immediately felt the relief of the cold air. A fresh breath of air returned the strength to his legs. The memories vacated his vision, and he was able to see once again. He was going to have to find a way to defend himself some other way. As he moved down the street, aimlessly walking in any direction that wasn't in the general direction of The Gun Emporium, he thought of other ways he could defend himself.

The solution couldn't involve weapons because all he could see when he thought of them was the table and he 'tools' that lay on it. Self-defense would have to suffice, it may not have been the best decision and he may be killed due to his lack of resolve, but he didn't care. A gun was too final, it lacked humanity. These new, humane skills would also have to be kept from Paul and never used to carry out a job. Weapons would be used for that. Tools would be kept in that part of his life; separate from the world of peace he had lived in for the last 25 years.

They would symbolize the ugly, dark side of his life, never to slither into his pure life. It was the same principle that is used when common sense tells a person to leave their dirty boots at the front door to avoid tracking dirt into the house. It was the only way he could keep his sanity intact. Of course, his sanity laid in Paul's palm no matter how innately good he strived to be.

Jack opened his phone and looked at the time. The screen was blank, maybe it was the world telling him that his old life was over. The past was behind him and all he could do was move forward. Without an operating cell phone, he decided he had better find a phone shop, if Paul's calls got missed, he would die. As much as Jack hated Paul and everything he stood for, a degree from NYU was what he had traded his life for. He would get that piece of paper no matter the cost or at least that's what he thought in that moment of defiance. Jack hailed a taxi and asked the driver to take him to the nearest phone store.

Jack wondered if that was the correct term, he couldn't think of what else that type of store could possibly be called. The driver drove for about 5 minutes and then pulled to the side of the road. Jack paid the man, got out of the car and entered the store. Hours later, he left with the newest Apple phone, which according to the salesman was the best on the market. Jack had made sure he still had the same phone number which was vital because he didn't quite know how to get to the office yet or Charlotte's apartment so he wouldn't have any way to let Charlotte or Paul know his number had changed otherwise.

He also got an unlimited data plan with unlimited texting and calling. He had never texted before in his life, but he imagined that it would be a whole lot easier than calling someone every time he just had something quick to say. Jack didn't even ask how much the monthly cost would be. As he stuffed the new phone in his pocket, he was very aware that the sale of his soul had come with a noticeable number of perks.

After a few minutes of aimless walking, he looked at the digital clock on the new phone. 3:45, it read. He had wasted a lot of time in the store but still had an hour and fifteen minutes until he needed to pick up his dry cleaning. So, he decided to look up some martial arts gyms near him and sign up for a class or two. Even if Paul ever found out about his new hobby, he would just think Jack was honing his skills, becoming a better 'employee'. Jack finally found a gym called Justice. They taught boxing and MMA. It was perfect and was only a 5-minute walk from his apartment. He could go after school, but he would have to make sure he could have his own locker; A locker he would be able to put his own lock on so that he could store a suit there.

He never knew when Paul would call so it was always better to have a backup plan. The driver finally pulled over and Jack could see the old block letters that sat above the glass door. The gym was small, there was a large ring in the middle of the room and a large cage just to its right. The room smelled like B.O and blood. It filled his nose with the same smells that drifted through the air at the warehouse but somehow, in the small gym, they were different, softer, more familiar. The floors were covered by black rubber mats and in some places, there had been blue gymnastic mats laid out over top.

Jack recognized the mats as those designed to cushion the blow when you were thrown to the ground. The gym was rundown and in serious need of a makeover, but Jack got a warm feeling standing there watching the students train. It felt as close to home as any place had in the city. Jack was so lost in his own head that he didn't even hear an employee ask him if he needed help. When the man asked for the third time, Jack finally heard him.

"Sir?"

"Hey sorry, I was just thinking about something," Jack said feeling quite embarrassed. "That's fine sir, my name is Jason, I own this gym. Would you like to purchase a membership?"

Jack looked the man up and down. He looked a lot like Paul except for a few details. Jason had muscle that had seen many winters, his hands were scarred badly, and his hair was greasy showing signs of white—not unlike Paul in that sense—but his arms were covered in tattoos and his eyes didn't have the sharp dangerous quality that Paul's eyes always held. In its place, his eyes held a broken quality, a fire that had been doused with water many, many times while continuing to defiantly burn bright against the adversity. Jack got the feeling that he would be able to trust this man.

"Yeah, I would. But I need to make sure you would be able to provide me with a locker that I can leave clothes in for days or weeks and I like to shower after a workout. Do you have showers here?"

"That's understandable sir, every one of our clients gets his or her own locker and we do have showers for all clients to use whenever they want. They aren't private showers though, there is just a wall of shower heads in a long room. Does that work?"

"That's perfect, I would also appreciate it if you would be able to work with me one on one when I am here. Would I be able to purchase an hour or two of your time per day? I would pay whatever you want."

"Umm…That would cost about $1500 dollars a month sir," Jason said with the same prejudice the leather salesman had spoken with. Jack smiled, he liked that people still saw him in the same light that once shined upon him back in Medora and Cielo. It gave him hope that he may not have changed as much as he thought he had.

"That's fine, tell you what, I will pay you $3000 a month for you trouble," Jack said knowing it was the first time in his life he had offered more than the regular sales price. Does 4:30 to 6:30 or thereabouts work for you?" That way Jack knew would be done classes and would have ample time to get to the gym. Plus, it would still be early enough that Jack most likely wouldn't have to leave early to get to 'work'.

"Thank you, sir. That's very generous. 4:30 to 6:30 sounds good to me. When would you like to get started?"

"Tomorrow at 4:30. Does that work?"

"Yes sir, I look forward to working with you," Jason said. The title, sir, that Jason kept using sounded wrong in Jack's ears, like nails on an old-fashioned chalkboard. It was like Jason was referring to him in the same light as he referred to Paul in, it made him sick.

"My name is Jack by the way. Jack Hanson. I look forward to working with you as well." And as he turned to walk out of the gym Jack remembered the $14,000 dollars in his pocket. The money was taken out to purchase something to protect himself and it still was going to be used for that purpose just in a less blood-spattered manner. "I have money to pay for four months, can I pay now?" Jack asked.

"Yes sir…I mean Jack. Would you like to pay debit or credit?" Jack pulled the wad of cash out of his pocket and slapped it on the counter.

"Cash please."

The look on Jason's face was pure astonishment. He had probably never seen that much money in cash before that day. After all, Jack had only seen so much in one place for the first time that day as well. Back in Maine his mother would have passed out if she laid eyes on anything near that amount of money.

"Wow, that's a lot of cash sir. If you don't mind me asking, what do you do for a living because I may have to change my profession," Jason said, with a nervous laugh.

"I am sponsored by an anonymous donor to be a part of the NYU writing department." This was of course a lie. He was paid to kill; he was an assassin; or more correctly he was an executioner. Not a voluntary job but that was his job. There was no way of getting past that fact, no matter how badly Jack wanted to forget it.

"That's incredible, I wish I had a mind that could write," Jason said, to which Jack forced a smile. He used to be proud that he could write. Proud that he could create worlds, make up stories, and dissect even the most acclaimed authors works. Now his gift was tainted, Paul had tainted the thought of creation. Charlotte's story had made Jack see his gift as the thing that had landed him in the muddy life he found himself in. That of course wasn't true, it was his greed and stupidity that landed him there, not to mention his drinking but that was only a subsidiary to the larger issue. "No, you don't. It brings dangerous attention," Jack said as his spirits took a freefalling dive and his reserves of hope drained from its leaky bucket. He turned and left the gym without so much as a look behind him.

Jack walked through the steady stream of bodies that New York seemed to produce from within, stopped at the drycleaners tipping him one of the crisp $100 bills. Then stopped at the liquor store to grab another bottle of Crown Royal making an impulse decision to buy a flask at the till. He knew it would come in handy on the next drive to the office. As he headed into his apartment building, he stopped at the front desk to grab his laundry. It was neatly folded a carboard box with the bag he had dropped it off in sitting on top. He tipped Angela a $100 dollar bill and gave her another $100 to give to the person that had cleaned his laundry.

Jack knew she might not actually give it to the person that deserved it, but he didn't care, he was determined to spend as much of the unlimited money as he could in ways that would completely contradict Paul's belief system. Jack entered his apartment and removed his shoes, making his way to the closet to put his freshly cleaned clothes away. He neatly placed all the folded clothes in their respective spots making sure to put an outfit on the small table in the middle of the room and hung the pinstripe suit on a hanger in the back with the rest of the suits that had been purchased with the blood of addicts. Then hung his 'work suit' on the rack at the end of the table, went into the kitchen to pour himself a drink, grabbed his book and sat down on the couch. He was feeling much calmer than the night before. He was beginning to make peace with the fact that his new life wasn't perfect but there was nothing he could do about it.

He was also filled with a new sense of determination, a burning fire in his chest that craved revenge on Paul for the pain he had already caused and would continue to cause him. After three glasses full of whiskey, the words on the page of his book started to swim, telling Jack that it was time for bed. As he lay in bed his mind wandered back to Jessica. Her face was a warm light in the dark room. Her unincumbered visage made Jack believe that there were still good people in the world, made him believe he still had a chance to live a normal life again. He remembered walking to school with her when they were both young, her smile lit up the early morning dew like a swarm of fireflies emerging from the grass as the sun kisses the horizon goodnight.

Unlike Charlotte she emitted a warm energy, she always seemed like she cared about everyone she spoke to. Charlotte was much more conventionally beautiful, but Jessica was beautiful in a wife sort of way. Charlotte had a movie star beauty. The type of beauty that is stunning but cold and impossibly far away. Jack wondered what she was up to these days. She used to dream about becoming a nurse. She wanted to save the lives of the destitute and wounded. He wondered if she ever made that dream a reality. As her face danced through his mind, Jack slipped off the ledge into the void of sleep. If she had become a nurse, he knew she would be saving lives; meanwhile, he was taking them.

Jack woke the next day to the sound of an alarm. It was coming from his new phone, quickly he remembered setting it the night before. Waking up to an alarm was a new experience for Jack but he didn't feel the way he usually felt after a night of drinking. He had found the perfect balance between oblivion and sobriety. Throwing the covers off, Jack pulled an old t-shirt and sweats on, grabbed his gym bag, and headed to hit the weights before classes. After he was done classes for the day, he would head over to the new gym he had found.

Jack was excited for the first time since finding out his patronage hung in the balance between his murderous potential and his passive heart. Now he had a real outlet for his pain and would receive the added bonus of being able to kick Paul's ass if he ever came knocking. Jack knew he would probably be able to kick Paul's ass already but the hours every day practicing would cement that reality. When Jack got back to the apartment he showered, got dressed, cleaned his teeth, fixed his hair, and made some eggs. The eggs were the first food he had eaten since the 'job', at least he thought they were, he couldn't quite remember. Food hadn't seemed too important over the last 30 hours or so.

But that day, the eggs were just the thing he needed. The burst of energy required for a successful completion of the day. His first class of the day was creative writing, the teacher was Dr. Confucius, who was…interesting. The old man seemed strong and powerful but weak and frail at the exact same time. The old teacher had thick white hair that was slicked back by what Jack hoped was product because if not it was the most disgustingly greasy hair he had ever seen. The man's beard must have brought a sense of pride because it was the one thing on his body that looked perfectly trimmed and cleaned to perfection. The old man criticized every work that had been published after 1975 as pathetic excuses for writing.

Jack felt that his evaluations of the works were completely of line, he thought that people like Confucius were just stuck in the past. Stuck yearning for their youth. A class of individuals that didn't understand modern society. They had just began studying *Death of a Salesman* in the class. Jack didn't mind the book; he knew it revealed the disgusting lie that was shown to the American public through the 40s and 50s. One that still crumbled families to dust and drove people to madness in today's day and age; The American dream was what he sought all his life—probably because he never lived it.

The 'dream' was what made him accept Charlotte's proposal, and just like Biff the 'dream' had led him to the devil and quite possibly death. The essay that had been assigned was to be written about how the American dream can uplift or destroy every American. He and his classmates were given 1500 words in which to make their case. Jack decided he would write about how it destroyed people, to write how it laid waste to every aspect that held America together. Even the people who achieved the American dream always wanted more and more times than not the people who displayed what it meant to possess the American dream, usually led different lives behind closed doors.

The news was always interested in rich families and their problems; spoiled children who spent their daddy's money on drugs, cheating wives, and abusive husbands were just another Tuesday to the families living the 'American dream'. The essay was due the following Monday but if Jack wasn't called into work, he would be able to finish it with 4 hours and 3 glasses of whiskey. Once Dr. Confucius was finished giving his final lecture on the book he dismissed the class early, leaving Jack with 3 hours. until his next class which was Old English taught by Dr. Primeval, his name fit him like a well-worn pair of shoes. The man was losing his hair and all that remained were a few long strands of snow-white hair. The man barely weighed 90 pounds and his skin clung to his bones like it had been vacuum packed to his figure.

Before Jack left for lunch, he decided to try his new texting app out and ask Charlotte if she would like to grab some lunch.

J: Lunch?

C: Sure. Didn't know you could text on that prehistoric phone of yours.

J: Got a new one yesterday. Old reliable finally quit on me. Where do you want to meet?

C: Same place as last time. Got a new place for lunch to show you.

He quickly walked to the massive white arch. The morning classes hadn't quite wrapped up yet so there was only a small crowd in the courtyard. He spotted Charlotte easily and walked up to her, making sure he announced himself instead of startling her. He didn't want a redo of the last time. She turned around and offered a feeble 'Hey'. Charlotte looked like shit, which was very unusual for her. Jack hadn't yet seen her looking anything but perfect. Her hair was a mess and not in a cute, just woke up sort of way, but instead, a sleepless night dragged into a phantom morning sort of way. Her makeup must have been yesterday's because it had been smudged off in places. She was wearing a hoodie with stained sweatpants and was smoking a cigarette. A broken shell of her usual self.

"Are you okay?" Jack asked, completely at a loss for what to say.

"I'm fine, Paul called me into work last night and the job was harder than usual. So, I haven't slept for a good 24hrs or thereabouts."

"Jesus, are you sure you want to go to lunch? Maybe you should go home and get some sleep."

"Nah I'm fine. Just need a drink. There's a good place that has a pretty good lunch menu and serves drinks 24hrs of the day." Charlotte reassured Jack as she started walking in the direction of the 24hr bar. Once they had reached it Charlotte opened the door and let herself inside without holding the door for Jack. It was an odd show of blatant disrespect, but he cut Charlotte some slack. She looked like she had been runover by a bus.

"I have to go to bathroom, grab us a table in the back," Charlotte told Jack. The bar was pretty typical. The actual bar was the length of the building and had 20 bar stools lined up underneath it. There were booths lining the walls, a few tables scattered in the middle and posters and signs lined the wall behind the bar. Jack sat down at the booth farthest from the door and a cute waitress came over to take his order, but he turned her away saying that he would wait for his friend to sit down before he ordered. Once Charlotte returned from the bathroom, she had a lot more energy.

If her internal battery was at 5% when she left for the bathroom, it was now at 120% and she kept touching her nose as if it was itchy or was chalk full of dried snot. When the waitress came back to take their orders, Charlotte complimented her outfit, saying it was cute and asked where she had bought it. Since Jack had met Charlotte, he had only ever heard her utter one compliment and it was directed at him. He was completely perplexed by the entire situation. But having lived amongst drug dealers and users at the orphanage, he could guess what had happened in the bathroom.

Jack ordered fish'n chips and a Jack and Coke. Charlotte ordered a cobb salad and a 'heaping' glass of gin straight. Something was definitely wrong with Charlotte, but he didn't know what to do or say to make her feel better or at least stop her from acting like a maniac. Her personality had completely changed, twice, in the last hour alone. Once the drinks came Jack sipped his slow and set it down on a coaster meanwhile, Charlotte was in the process and inhaling hers. She didn't stop until all the liquid had entered her system and slammed the glass down on the table.

"Whoo-hoo, that hit the spot," she yelled. As the words left her mouth every eye in the bar turned to train directly on them. "The fuck are you looking at?" Charlotte asked all the patrons of the bar. They all looked away quicky, as if they were embarrassed but Jack assumed there were just as equally terrified.

"Seriously, are you okay?" Jack whispered.

Charlotte must have been thrown back into reality because she whispered so quietly Jack could barely hear her. In a voice that was barely audible, she told him what had happened, "The table didn't have the abundance of choices it usually does last night. The hooded body wasn't asleep either. He kept screaming and pleading for mercy, of course Paul wouldn't let me give in. Tears flew down my cheeks like my eyes were fucking Niagara Falls. I picked up the only weapon on the table, it was knife and a dull one to boot. I have never chosen the knife before; I always choose the gun, it's much quicker and less painful for the poor soul in the chair. So, I had no idea how to kill him quickly or painlessly with a knife. I won't make that mistake again, I am going to have to figure out how to kill with a knife and practice."

Practice? It sounded like she was talking about a sport or brushing up on how to drive stick for a manual labor job. It sounded like she thought killing wasn't anything that important.

"I stuck the knife into what I thought was his heart, but I must have missed because he just started to scream louder and louder until I couldn't bear it, so I removed the knife and tried to slit his throat, but the knife wasn't sharp enough it only scratched his throat. Paul made me stay until the man died. Blood pooled at his feet and ran out of his mouth and I could see it dripping down his neck from the, admittedly superficial, slash I had made. I don't think the screams will ever leave me Jack, I smoked enough weed and drank enough alcohol to kill a human last night, but the screams soaked up all the booze and trapped all the smoke. The joy that was written on Paul's face when he finally allowed me to go home won't allow me fall asleep, it's going to haunt me until I die Jack. I want to get my degree so bad but without sleep I don't know how I'm going to accomplish that. He is going to win, Jack."

Jack sat still, immobilized by shock. He wanted to believe Charlotte, wanted to feel empathy for her, but he still felt uneasy in her presence. Still felt like she was hiding things from him. After all, she was the one who had brought him to the city. Surely she and Paul had grown close over the years. It had been 6 years since she arrived on the plane. Why would he do something like that to her? Was she really telling the truth the other day? Was she today? And if she was being punished for what she said, what was in store for him? And most importantly how did Paul even find out? There of course was the possibility that she could be making all of it up, Jack knew her to be capable of lying. From the first moment she met him, she had lied.

Misery might like company, but that didn't mean she wasn't capable of lying to him for other reasons as well. No matter what he believed, he had to keep up the fake relationship he had with her; Just in case she was telling the truth. There also was that pesky bond they had created all those nights ago.

"Jesus Charlotte. That's really messed up, why would he ever do that? That's evil, even for Paul that's evil."

"He does things like this every once in a while. Just to make sure I know he is still the boss. To make sure I know he can still do anything he wants," she said. As she finished her story the waitress came back with the plates of food.

Jack ate quickly and waited in silence for Charlotte to finish eating. After they were both finished eating their meals, Jack went up to counter and paid the bill adding a $100 tip to make up for Charlotte's earlier outburst. The pair walked in silence all the way back to campus and Charlotte only broke the silence right before they split up and went their sperate ways.

"Be prepared the next time Paul calls, he may have a treat for you too."

"I will," Jack said walking away toward his next class. He told himself that no matter what the story turned out to be, lies or truth he wouldn't let Paul win; he would go along with whatever Paul threw at him—perhaps drunkenly—because he would be earning what he had been promised by Charlotte in Medora. His innocence had already been forfeited. Nothing would stop him from ensuring Paul's side of the deal was upheld.

Jack's Old English class held no surprises. Dr. Primeval talked slowly as if carefully choosing his words before he released them from his mouth. Primeval was in love with Shakespeare. In his eyes, Shakespeare was the only writer that had been prevalent in the history of literature. Shakespeare was one of, if not the best writer of his era but not the only one worth mentioning. Nevertheless, Jack had learned that in school it didn't matter what you thought, all that mattered was how well you could agree with the instructor.

How well you could read his thoughts, emotions and once you did that all you had to do was write something that was 'well written' in their eyes, but feigning your beliefs was the most important part. Smart successful people always had big egos and they rarely discredited your work as long as you played into their ego during its duration, not unlike Paul and his sadistic sponsorship. Jack was so grateful when the class was over that he ran all the way to is apartment to grab his gym clothes. He could barely contain his own excitement.

Chapter 8

When Jack finally arrived at the gym, he was almost giddy with excitement. He checked his phone and saw it was 4:15pm. He had given himself just enough time to get changed and stretch before training started. When he stepped through the front doors, he headed straight for the changerooms. As he pushed the male changeroom door open, he was taken aback by the massacre that time had laid upon it. The tile was yellowing, every shower head had calcium built up all over them like barnacles on the belly of a ship and the lockers bright blue paint was fading in the places they even had any paint left. Despite all of its outward issues, it was a place free from Paul, Charlotte and all the fucked-up, blurry parts of his new life.

By the time Jack finished changing, it was 4:25pm. It was close enough Jack thought heading back out in the main area phone in hand. He couldn't wait a moment longer. Even though the sanctuary he had found was free from Paul, there was still a chance he would call, and Jack would have to go running back to his apartment to change. So, he wanted to start as soon as possible. Jack spotted Jason across the room working with another one of his clients, so Jack sat down and started stretching. Engrossed in the stretch Jack didn't notice Jason walking up to him, so when Jason said, "Good to see you Jack," he just about jumped out of skin.

"Done stretching?" Jason asked.

"Yeah. I'm ready to go," Jack said as his heart continued to pulse at an alarming rate. "Do you have any experience? I mean I can see your in really good shape, but have you ever boxed or done any sort of hand-to-hand combat?"

"Umm, I have a little bit of boxing experience but maybe I should spar a little with someone just so you can see where I am at," Jack said even though he was pretty sure he could beat anyone in the gym 1 on 1 without breaking a sweat. He didn't fully understand why he said it, he wasn't sure if it was his own sense of inadequacy or if it was his inflated ego that had taken over, yearning for a compliment from a man it actually respected.

"Sounds good. That's probably the best way to figure out how much I have to teach you and how much I am going to have to tune up," Jason said, as he called over to another client and asked him if he would step in the ring with Jack just so he could see where he was at. The other client agreed, and Jason handed both men padded helmets, boxing gloves and grabbed a new mouth guard for Jack to wear.

"Don't go easy on him, Colin," Jason said. Jack couldn't help the smile tickling the corner of his lip. He had just been given a free pass to beat the other man senseless and show Jason what he was really made of.

"I want to see what the kid is made of," Jason said. The only thing Jack was worried about was the fact that he didn't know if he would be able to knock the man out with his helmet on. "Start whenever you're ready." Jack touched his gloves to the other man's before backing off and beginning to circle Colin. Jack immediately started to see Colin's weaknesses; His feet weren't placed purposely, and he tended to cross his legs over each other while circling. It was terrible habit. All Jack had to do was land one punch while his legs were crossed, and he would nosedive into the canvas.

As Colin started throwing jabs Jack saw that he also had a tendency to telegraph his punches with his right or left foot. After a few seconds of circling, Colin began to get impatient. He moved in closer and threw a few right hooks mixed with left-handed uppercuts. They all missed. Not because Jack was dodging them, they just missed due to nerves or lack of training. Jack wasn't sure which it was, but he was starting to feel bad for the man opposite him. After a minute of Colin throwing useless punches, he finally landed a pathetic blow to the ribs that had been hit by Henry when Jack was proving himself in the stone room.

The small amount of pain was all it took to release all the anger Jack had been suppressing. Colin's face morphed into Paul's and Jack's calm, excited, playful demeanor quickly changed. The seething anger that had been on display when he walked into Charlotte's apartment late Sunday night, returned. Jack swatted Colin's next strike to the side as easily as he would have if a fly had landed on his arm and threw a hard body shot. Colin wasn't expecting such a hard shot, so he leaned over to his right side. Which Jack exploited by throwing another huge body shot into his left ribs. Colin was completely taken by surprise and as a result his hands were nowhere near his head.

Jack tightened his fist even tighter, channeling all the anger, pain and rage he had into possibly the biggest right hook he had ever thrown and followed all the way through Colin's defenseless head. The punch carried twice the force that Henry had been hit with. Colin's eyes went blank, and it seemed to Jack that his soul had vacated his body. The soulless corps fell and laid limp on the ground. Which brought Jack back to reality quickly—a much better reality given the fact that he had released every emotion that had been eating away at his soul into the punch—because Colin still hadn't been brought back to consciousness. Jack knelt beside his unmoving body terrified that he had just killed the innocent man but a few seconds later Colin woke with a jolt.

"Jesus, you hit hard man," Colin whispered. Jack helped him to his feet and apologized for hitting him so hard. He honestly hadn't meant to do it. He just got caught up in his own head. Jack turned and saw Jason standing beside the ring with a look of shock on his face.

"Well Jack, I don't know what you are here for. I am pretty sure you could knock me out with a lesser punch than the one you just threw."

"I really don't think I could," Jack said sheepishly, cheeks warming with embarrassment. "I just need someone to show me how to protect myself, so that no matter what weapon someone tries to kill me with I will be able to come out the other side unscathed."

"Well, I would be honored to teach you that. You have the power and certainly a great right hook. But I can definitely show you how to defend or go on the offensive against a weapon and show you how to fight against a man much bigger than yourself."

"Perfect, that's what I was looking for," Jack said.

The rest of the 2-hour session was filled with holds, grappling, and evasive moves that would remove a weapon from the hands of any assailant. Jack was in bliss; he didn't like the reasons that had pushed him to the training but loved every minute of it anyway. The training challenged Jack to the point of complete exhaustion. A welcome exhaustion. Jason was teaching him the moves he would need to beat Paul if the occasion ever arose in which he had no other choice; Or at least had received his compensation and had nothing else to lose.

Jason was quick to say he would do all he could to teach Jack everything he knew about hand-to-hand combat but if the assailant decided to shoot him from a distance it would be out of his hands. Jack knew that was the risk he accepted when he chose his fists over a gun. The gun would have been easier, but his fists allowed him to disappoint his mother a little less. They also didn't make his hands shake and his legs feel like jelly. A gun would have been more powerful, but a gun didn't have to feel every bone, muscle and tendon it broke, tore or ripped to shreds. A gun couldn't feel remorse and once the trigger had been pulled there was no taking it back. His fists on the other hand could stop mid punch. Jack had full control over his fists and full control made his heart feel pounds lighter.

Once the session was complete, without a single buzz or ring from his phone Jack thanked Jason and headed to his locker to grab his bag. He didn't need to shower there, and he wanted to avoid the gym showers as much as he could. They were disgusting, even compared to some of the questionable showers Jack had been in. Once Jack made it back to his apartment he hopped right in his cleaner shower. The freezing water relived the sore achy feeling every one of his muscles seemed to be coated in. Despite working out every day, he hadn't felt that type of soreness in a very long time.

He couldn't remember the last time his muscles screamed out in pain the way they were in that moment. After the shower had finally silenced the screaming, Jack threw on some sweats and headed into the kitchen to slide an individual pizza in the toaster oven. Jack knew he couldn't keep eating garbage every night but that was tomorrow's problem. After Jack had eaten the entire pizza and inhaled a glass of water, he grabbed the fancy glass, the bottle of whiskey and headed to the study to start his English paper.

When he opened the door—for the first time since the first night he had slept in the apartment—he looked at the large desk and his MacBook perched atop it. The laptop was beckoning him toward it, willing him to open it and bring the talent that he had almost lost back from the grave. Jack opened the laptop to begin writing about the American dream and how corrupt the whole premise really was. He couldn't type fast enough to keep up with the ideas in his head.

The ideas, words, and the whole premise of writing had been so close to extinct, that once it was set free, he couldn't stop it. The essay called for 1500 words; Jack had that before he was even finished his first glass of whiskey.

After he had gotten the rough draft down on the page, he took a break and finished his glass. After circling the room a few times, he sat back down. Jack always checked every word meticulously. His high school English teacher said, 'a great writer is able to account for every word he writes' and Jack regarded the statement as if Christ himself had said it. He removed some, added in others in better spots and rewrote entire paragraphs altogether.

Once he was satisfied with his work, Jack saved the document, transferred it onto a memory stick and shut the laptop. He finished the second glass of whiskey and deposited the empty bottle in the sink along with the glass. *Tomorrow's problem,* he thought to himself heading to his room to sleep. He hoped no alcohol induced dreams ruined his perfect day, because aside from the absurd lunch he had shared with Charlotte that's what it was. The best day he had since he had come to New York City.

Chapter 9

It had been four days since the absurd lunch Jack had shared Charlotte and a full week since he had killed a man. Jack was still trying to rationalize the sin he had committed. In his own head, he wasn't calling it a crime because Paul would never let his sin come to light. So, it was just a sin there was no breaking of laws just the shattering of every rule and piece of advice his mother had taught him over the years. The experience was fading into a scar covered memory and it had started to become the author of less pain and suffering but he was still plagued with images of the man in the black hood and the way his head snapped back when the bullet exited his skull. Whiskey usually helped with forgetting and falling into the void of sleep had become a wonderful escape.

The void was exponentially easier to handle than its more sober counterpart—dreams—but Jack had been so tired once he got back to the apartment after his workouts at Jason's gym that he didn't want to waste his time trying to fall asleep without at least some help. The two workouts a day were becoming easier and easier as the days passed. The first day after his training session he couldn't move his arms or legs to get down to the gym and lift weights before school but after the second training session Jack was more than able to get back in the gym and lift before school. Although he still fit quite a few drinks in while doing homework, he hadn't been able to get blackout drunk in a few days which was as near to sobriety as Jack had come in a very long time.

Just as it had every day since he had set it, his phone alarm rang loudly. He had set the alarm to sound like an air raid siren, just like the ones that would have rung out over London's city scape in WW1 and 2. The sound always woke him up quickly making him sit up fast and then realizing it was just the phone he usually laid his head back down on the pillow. The new routine gave Jack's life stability, or at least as much stability as it could. Paul hadn't called in a few days and the radio silence left Jack feeling weary, always on his toes, never fully relaxed.

As Jack climbed sleepily out of bed and slipped into some workout shorts and an old tee shirt, he walked over to the Keurig, slipped a mug underneath the spout, and pressed the button that allowed the machine to release coffee. As he waited for the coffee to be ready Jack logged into his school account and checked his grades. Forensic studies had no grades yet; neither did Old English or French but there was a notification above the Creative Writing section. Dr. Confucius explained that it meant there was a new grade inputted. He realized his first essay had been graded, his cheeks warmed, and his palms started sweating. His finger hovered above the notification, not quite able to press it.

Summoning all the courage he could gather; he closed his eyes and pressed it. Jack knew he was a good writer, but doubt has started to creep into his mind poisoning his confidence. Was he NYU good? The University of Medora was a lot different than NYU. Sure, it had a pretty good writing program, but NYU was the big leagues. They produced some of the best writers in the United States. Jack slowly opened his right eye and saw in big black letters that his grade was 95%. He finally allowed the breath he had been holding in for so long to escape his lips. His body felt numb, not like it did when he drank but rather a euphoric numb. A tear escaped his right eye and rolled down his cheek, the grade was such a relief. He was, in fact, 'NYU good'. He deserved the opportunity he had been given, in terms of the school aspect anyway.

It wasn't just Paul affirming his prowess any longer, it was a real NYU writing professor. Dr. Confucius also thought he was talented. He could hold his own on one of the biggest stages in America. Jack wished he could call his mother and tell her the news, wished he could hear the pride in her voice. He knew she was always watching over him, but it would be that much sweeter if he could speak to her or just even look into her eyes. He would even settle for her warm touch against his cheek.

The mark left Jack feeling elated. He was able to lift more in the gym, take a warm shower and it even encouraged him to tip the waitress at the Four Roses $100 dollars after he had finished his breakfast. Every morning since the morning after his ridiculous lunch with Charlotte, he had been going to the diner for breakfast. Eating had become more important as of late. It had climbed up a few rungs on the ladder of prevalence, whiskey and the sweet numb of any alcohol still clung firmly to the top rung, but food was catching up.

After breakfast, he headed to the university, he had French and Forensics. Professor Blanchette had become more and more understandable, and Jack was starting to get a grasp on the language. The genders of words still baffled him, but words and phrases were starting to formulate in his head on their own. He even felt himself repeating sayings and questions in his head after class. Jack almost let himself believe he was a normal university student.

Following French, Jack had a long lunch break but he hadn't spent it with Charlotte since the scene she had made in the bar the Wednesday prior. That day he felt no different. As stunning as Charlotte was, she either had demons that Jack couldn't even try to deal with himself, or she had a promising acting career in front of her. So instead, Jack had been going to the cafeteria to each lunch by himself.

As he walked, he felt happy, he felt true contentment with his new life. That day's special was chilli and caesar salad for the obscene price of $20.49. Jack always heard lots of other students complain about the prices but yet again the murderous sponsorship had its perks. One of them being he didn't have to worry about the lunch specials price. Once Jack had paid for his lunch he sat down at his usual table in the back and took a book out of his backpack.

He sat quietly, reading, and eating, sporadically checking the time on his phone until it told him that there were 20 minutes until his next class started. He folded the corner of the page over and tucked it back into his bag, threw his garbage away and headed off to Dr. Prints, forensics class. Jack was fascinated with what Print taught. There was an art to catching criminals and the way in which criminals hid their crimes. That day's class had them learning about how criminals left DNA at the scene, and how to find and test suspects for the same DNA.

Science wasn't really Jack's forte, but he still found it very interesting. He usually found himself thinking back to the warehouse and how Paul had said 'No trace' to the guards at the front door. It made Jack wonder if Paul had taken the class and now used it to evade capture instead of catching criminals.

Once the class ended Jack walked all the way to his apartment and grabbed his training bag, which held new boxing gloves and hand wraps, as well as gym clothes. By 4:25, he was stretching and getting his head in the right space to absorb all the teachings that Jason had to offer. Jack was getting better every day and that day was set to be a big day. Jason had brought in a boxer from another gym to test Jack's skills against an actual opponent. They had been working a lot on the techniques that would help him prevail against a weapon or a bigger man but at the end of every session, they worked more on his boxing. He was a star boxer as Jason loved to repeatedly point out, but Jason always said that he could work more on his uppercut. That day he would get to test his newly tuned uppercut against a good fighter.

Once Jack and his opponent were properly warmed up and had got their protective gear on, they both stepped into the ring and tapped gloves. Jack could tell Jason was excited because he was basically jumping up and down beside the ring. Jack and the other man began circling each other, Jack was on the lookout for any chink in his armor but couldn't seem to find any. The man didn't have the bad habit of crossing his legs as his last opponent, Colin, had. The man swung first; the blow would have landed on Jack's temple, but Jack blocked it before it could find its target. The blow was hard and told Jack the man meant business.

They both traded jabs back and forth but neither man did any damage, after a few minutes Jack could tell the man was getting tired. His jabs were less frequent and were thrown with less purpose. Jack decided the next time the man threw a right cross he would duck and come up with a huge uppercut and maybe end the fight. Jack didn't have to wait too long. The man must have also wanted to end the fight because he threw a massive cross, meant to knock Jack out. But Jack stuck with the game plan and ducked and came up with as much speed and force as he could muster following through the man's chin. He didn't go down, but Jack could see he was rattled so he threw a huge right cross of his own. The life immediately left the big man's eyes, and his head was soon laying still on the canvas. Jack knew he didn't hit the man with even a fraction of the power he had hit Colin with.

So he didn't feel bad ducking under the ropes and fist bumping Jason, who said, "That was good. The uppercut needs more power but without the padded helmet and gloves he would have gone down on that punch."

"Thanks. I'll work on it some more tomorrow," Jack said. Then headed to the changeroom to get dressed. After he was fully clothed, he left the gym giving Jason a wave goodbye and shaking the big man's hand who was now sitting on the floor with his back leaning on one of the posts. The big man congratulated Jack on the knockout and told Jack he would come in again if he needed a 'worthy fighter' to test his skills against.

As Jack walked back to his apartment his pocket began to buzz. A call was coming in. Jack dug into his pocket and looked at the screen. It was Paul. "The devil always has to come and ruin a perfectly good day," Jack muttered under his breath. He answered the call and spoke, "Hey Paul."

"Hanson."

Jack hated that the man liked using his last name as if they were friends.

"I've got a challenge and a job for you tonight; I will have a car at your building in an hour."

Challenge? He didn't understand why the devil had to be so cryptic. "Sounds good," Jack said as the line went dead. He ran the rest of the way back to his apartment and hopped in the shower immediately. He focused on every drop of water running down his shoulders as he thought about how after that night, he would have two sins encased in the red sun that hung around his neck. It was a sobering thought. It effectively sucked all the warm fuzzy feelings down the drain along with the freezing water. He shut the water off dressed himself in a suit, tucked the blood-stained sun into his shirt and tied the green tie around his neck.

Checking his phone he saw a text saying that a car would be at is building in 10 minutes. He had just enough time to have a quick drink, fill the flask and tuck it into his jacket pocket. It was unnerving how quickly he turned to the bottle once Paul had once again poisoned his mind. After the flask was filled and secured in his breast pocket, two drinks poured down his throat and shoes tied, Jack headed out the door to face his demons head on. After all, there was no other option.

The driver didn't acknowledge that Jack had stepped into the car or acknowledge when he exited. Jack entered the big building that was referred to as the office, but he knew ten offices could have been stuffed into the monstrosity. He walked by the receptionist—that always seemed to be sitting at the desk, day or night—and into the elevators open arms. It rose and higher and higher until it squeaked to a stop and the doors opened again. Paul was sitting behind the desk letting the tendrils of cigar smoke encase his head as he flipped a large hunting knife from hand to hand.

As he exited the elevator Paul said, "Hanson! Good to see you son," and put down his knife. Jack swore to himself that one day he would summon the courage to tell Paul that he didn't have any right to call him son, but he did not possess the courage quite yet. He also didn't possess the piece of paper for which he traded his life. Instead of the string of curses he had lined up he responded in a happy tone. Trying to sound like he wasn't disgusted by the sight of Paul.

"Hey Paul! How's business?" The words tasted bitter coming out of his mouth.

"Good, good. Booming as always," Paul said standing up from behind the desk, sliding his suit jacket over his old but impressively muscled shoulders. "I have a quick challenge for you, downstairs, then we will head to the warehouse and then you are fee to go wherever you want. You can take the jet somewhere for all I care."

Wow, the jet, Jack thought. Tonight, must be a big night. Despite the generosity shown by Paul, Jack felt like the challenge would be just like proving himself on the very first night. He could feel that his fate hung in the balance yet again.

"Sound like fun," Jack said. He had decided that the best way to conduct himself around Paul would be to act like they were cut from the same cloth. It might just allow Paul to leave his soul intact. As they entered the elevator, Jack felt the familiar jerk to the left side of the building, and Paul began to speak again.

"Sure does son, I'm quite excited to see how you handle the challenge tonight. I don't know if Charlotte mentioned anything to you but last week when you knocked out Henry in 45 seconds, you set a record for the fastest knockout out of any sponsored employee. I think that you can do it even faster tonight."

Jack was correct, it was a fight. The second of the day but this time he wouldn't feel out his opponent, no circling mercifully. He held no sympathy for the men in Paul's employ. These men didn't deserve it. All he wanted to do was get out of Paul's presence as quick as possible. Being at the devil's side made Jack feel small and helpless, even though Jack knew he would be able to beat Paul in a 1v1 no weapon bout easily.

"I will do my best, Sir," Jack said, effectively ending the conversation. The pair didn't talk for the rest of the elevator ride. Once the elevator doors opened again and they stepped into the dimly lit, cobblestone lined room. The room was wet and cold. The wet chill cut all the way though Jack's clothing and made him shiver. The type of cold that made way for snow was one thing, but the wet, penetrating cold was different. It was more suited to Paul's personality, a cold that seeped into your bones and froze you from the inside out was more Paul's style.

A huge figure stood on the other side of the black mat; he was at least six foot three inches tall. His shoulders were huge. Every muscle in his body was on display given his lack of a shirt, but his face was hidden by the darkness. Jack was scared for the first time in a very long time. He hadn't been beat to submission in a very long time and he knew his shaky, newly acquired techniques would have to come in handy, no matter if they were ready or not. The only thing that was different this time around, other than the massive opponent, was the fact that there were three chairs in the room. They hadn't been present last time, but Jack quickly understood what they were here for, or at least he thought he did. As Paul Sat down in the one that was placed on the left side of the ring, in the perfect place to watch the fight and told Jack to get ready. Jack removed his jacket, blazer, shirt, belt, shoes and socks.

Once he was ready Jack looked down at his chest, the sun rested in the middle of his two pectoral muscles. Jack thought he better take it off. If it got broken in the inevitable violence, Paul might lose his mind and kill him. In the interest of self-preservation, he grabbed the cold steel in his hands and placed the necklace on top of his clothes that were neatly folded on one of the other chairs.

"Put your clothes in the corner, bring both chairs over here and place one on either side of me," Paul instructed. Jack's earlier assumption had been wrong; the chairs weren't for his clothing but rather for two more spectators. He collected both chairs and placed them on either side of Paul, and looked over at his opponent. The man still hadn't moved a single muscle, he just stood at attention still like Paul's personal statue. As Jack stared unblinkingly intimidated by his opponent, he noticed another door at the far end of the room. He wondered how he didn't see it last time he had been in the room. Maybe because he was so in shock, or maybe he was too focused on not becoming homeless. Whatever the reason was, it didn't really matter because as he ran plausible scenarios in his head the door opened, a small white-haired man wearing an entirely red suit, walked in accompanied by Charlotte who was dressed in all black, save for the red jewel that hung at the bottom of the necklace and showed no outward signs of being completely distraught less than a week ago.

Once there were both seated beside Paul, he motioned for both combatants to step onto the black mat and said, "Begin" in the same quiet, ominous voice that he used the last time.

Jack wanted the fight to end quickly but he didn't want to 'give away the farm' too quickly and leave himself exposed. He decided to let the mountain swing first no matter what. The man circled slowly sizing Jack up as if he was a lion and Jack, a terrified gazelle. He swung hard but Jack blocked the blow before it could snap his ribs. The strength didn't surprise Jack. He honestly expected more force. The mountain didn't know it yet, but Jack was a jaguar hidden in a gazelle's carcass. A terrified jaguar, but no less lethal. The man came back with the exact same punch and this time Jack was waiting for it; he grabbed the outstretched arm and pulled it over his right shoulder flipping the massive body over his shoulder and letting it slam to the ground. But being a gentleman Jack let the man stand back up. The mountain was shaken but otherwise, fine. Jack secretly hoped the fall would have knocked the man out because now the mountain was angry. He hadn't thought Jack would have lasted even that far into the fight. It had only been 15 seconds, but the man wasn't used to being thrown around.

The anger clouded his judgement, and he began to swing relentlessly. Jack parried, blocked, and evaded each blow with a considerable amount of effort but left the onslaught unscathed. The man swung one more time; a haymaker meant to knock out or even kill Jack on impact, but Jack saw it coming and the whole world seemed to slow. Jack flashed back to his earlier fight and thought about what Jason had said, and then thought that the mountain surely hadn't been hit very many times and if he utilized all his strength and channeled it all into an uppercut, he may be able to end the fight here and now.

His mind settled back into reality, but the world was still moving in slow motion. The punch aimed at his head was just about to connect with his temple, so Jack ducked underneath; Coming up with all the power he had in his legs almost jumping but instead transferring all the power into his arm at the last second and up to his fist that was locked in place then let it go like a rocket launching. The punch connected with the large man's chin and continued along its predetermined path until the mountain's head was pushed far enough back that his fist could move without restriction.

The man stood rooted in place and then Jack saw the all too familiar sight of consciousness leaving the man's eyes. The mountain's legs that were as thick as tree trunks swayed and eventually went limp, and the rest of his frame followed suit. His head smacked the black mat with a sickening thud. Lifeless, the body laid on the cold, damp floor chest rising and falling very faintly. Jack took no pride in his victory, but knew it had to be done to save his own sinful soul.

Jack quickly walked to the corner of the small room to get dressed once again and watched out of the corner of his eye as the man in red walked slowly over to where he was now getting dressed. He stuck out his hand and said, "That was impressive Mr. Hanson. Thank you for allowing me to witness such a work of art."

Jack shook his hand and almost laughed at the notion that he had a say in who watched him fight but he managed to hold it in. Jack didn't even know there would be anyone else at the fight, but Jack had a sinking feeling that this man was even more powerful than Paul.

"Thank you, sir. I wasn't all that confident at the start, but I was happy that the outcome turned in my favor." The man laughed a full belly laugh. One of the laughs that makes your abdomen ache if it persists too long.

"I too expected you to be squashed like a bug, but you surprised me. Paul speaks very highly of you. I thought he was full of shit as per usual, but I see that his praise is well placed. Congratulations," the old man said and then walked back through the mysterious door followed closely by Charlotte.

Jack didn't want Paul's praise or the old man's congratulations, but he knew the men liking him was better than them hating or being suspicious of him. Jack dressed as fast as he could making sure to place the necklace back around his neck. Once he was done, he and Paul stepped back into the elevator, through the lobby and left the building. Jack opened the back door of the black car letting Paul get in first and then entered himself. Once the car started driving Paul said, "That fight was 28 seconds long if you wanted to know and that man was the strongest man in my employ. You impressed me tonight, kid. You've proved without a doubt that no one should take you lightly."

Jack wanted to tell Paul that it was exactly what he was going for, but Paul wasn't finished.

"Anyone without a gun that is," he said chuckling lightly amused by his own joke. Jack didn't find the joke even slightly amusing but forced a fake chuckle out just to appease the horned beast beside him.

"Thank you, sir. That guy was huge I didn't really expect the uppercut to knock him out," Jack said as he pulled his flask out of its pocket, took a long swig and waited for Paul's response but it took five more swigs before Paul spoke again, "Amadi is not like you he has no gifts other than his obvious physical ones, but I have never seen him get knocked down, and definitely never knocked out before. Jack knew Paul was trying to make him quit. There was no question about it anymore, there really had never been any question to start off with but now it was crystal clear."

"You sure drink a lot don't you Hanson?"

"Just when I am in a situation I want to forget," the little voice in Jack's head screamed but he didn't let the thought leave his mouth. "Yeah, I'm trying to cut back," Jack said. It was an obvious lie, maybe when he was out of hell he might try but in that moment, there was no point. To his knowledge there was no better memory eraser.

"Good. Addictions grab hold of everything we hold dearest."

Jack knew he was right but hated him even more just for saying it. Once the warehouse came into view Jack tipped the last of the liquid left in the flask down his throat and exited the car, heading for the door on the left side of the building, Paul caught up to him, opened the door and walked in first letting the door slam in Jack's face.

The warehouse looked identical to how it had the last time except for the fact that the table only held one item this time around. At the sight of it, all the confidence that Jack had stored up deserted him at the door. His legs started to feel like jelly as he walked up to the table. At least, the man was still hooded and seemed to be sedated which was a small comfort but still better than the horror story Charlotte told which was sounding truer and truer with each step he took. As Jack reached the table, he realized the object was a knife.

A huge hunting knife that looked like it would cut you just by looking at it. Jack breathed a sigh of relief. It was a premature sigh but at least it wasn't dull or small. It would kill with little to no trouble at all. Paul stood beside the bound prisoner and waved his hand as to say 'whenever you're ready'. Jack looked down at the knife and the same fantasies of escaping came back to his mind, they were even less plausible than last time, but they calmed him. They made him feel like if he put all his effort in, he might be able to get out of this mud pit of a situation in the end; hopefully alive but that remained to be seen.

As Jack ran his fingers down the hilt of the knife, he realized he could feel every impurity. The alcohol had, once again, failed him. For the moment at least, he wouldn't have any help, let alone relief from the gut-wrenching guilt. The alcohol would inevitably numb every inch of his body after the deed had been completed but there was a mountain to climb before he arrived at the village of numbing peace. Jack clasped his sweaty shaking hand around the polished wood handle. He was consumed by the power held in his fingers; it terrified him.

He imagined that Paul would feel right at home with a murderous weapon in is grasp but it made Jack feel weak and evil. For the first time in his life, he pitied himself, but he couldn't let Paul see the weakness. So, he walked as slowly as he could, knife gripped so tight in his fist that his knuckles had turned white. Trying to feign as much confidence as he could muster, he kept putting one foot in front of the other. Instead of radiating confidence he was radiating BO. The smell filled his nostrils and made him feel weaker than he already felt. The Aztec sun felt warm against his skin it was somehow being heated by his shame or by the devilish act he was about to commit. When Jack reached the man, he looked him up and down. His clothes looked cheap, and his jeans were even torn in a few places, it was quite different than the suit Jack's last victim was wearing.

Jack prayed for forgiveness and pleaded to whatever power sat above him watching him commit these sins to cover his mother's eyes. He prayed she wouldn't watch the purely evil act he was about to commit. The hood that covered the man's face wasn't as long as the one the poor soul had been wearing the last time Jack tore his soul. Jack could see the man's throat; his jugular veins were exposed. As untrue as Charlotte's story seemed to be when he was listening to her tell it with the crazed look in her eyes, she was probably right.

Severing the jugular vein was probably the best way to go about killing a person with a knife. Jack wondered how the hell the revolting murderous thoughts seemed to materialize in his head. Before Charlotte walked into that little bar, he couldn't have even imagined what killing a person would be like, let alone the best way to do it. The man he was being forced to become made him deeply sad but there was no more time to be sad. He was wearing Paul's patience thin, Jack had to finish it. He had to end the life to save his own and more importantly, he needed to ensure the snakeskin he had slipped into stayed opaque. He needed to make them believe he was really one of them.

Jack pressed the cold, shiny steel against the victim's neck. Just the small amount of pressure caused by the weight of the knife had already started to draw blood; Jack could see it trickle down the man's neck. He pressed the knife harder into the man's neck. His hands shook so badly that he was sure it would shake right out of his grasp. He could feel all the blood leaving his face. If he didn't do it now, he wouldn't ever be able to, so he pushed all his weight behind the knife and slid the blade across the man's throat. It slit the skin perfectly opening every vein that ran through its path.

Jack stared in horror as the blood that had once warmed the man's body splattered all over his suit jacket and hands. Once the supply started to run low it flowed gently down the man's shirt like a babbling brook and pooled at his feet. Jack let the knife slip out of his shaking hand and hit the concrete floor with a loud clang. He waited until the blood had stopped flowing so strong and asked Paul if he was done. Paul said, "Yes, there's a car waiting outside to take you away. You did well tonight. Go out and spend as much money as you can, you deserve it."

It was a very odd thing to say but Jack didn't stop to think about it. He walked as fast as his jelly legs would take him away from the dead man and opened to the door wanting to get as far away from the god forsaken warehouse as he could. He practically jumped into the car, opening the same compartment he had last time and took out the bottle of scotch he knew would be there and began to drink. The driver asked, "Where to, sir?"

Jack was without a single clue in his mind as to where he wanted to go. All he knew was that by the end of the night he needed to be back in his apartment. He had school tomorrow and he wasn't going to let Paul ruin the things he held so dear. He could always go see Charlotte, but she had been in the damp room to watch him either fail or prevail. If it were him, Jack would have declined Paul's phone call, he would never watch Charlotte get beat to death, even if she had the chance to win. So, with no other options, Jack said, "My…apartment please."

Chapter 10

The driver delivered Jack back to his apartment and Jack entered the building feeling as though the images of the blood spilling out of the man's neck would never leave. They were burned into his psyche like Paul's personal brand. But as he walked into the apartment building a warm blanket seemed to wrap over his shoulders. He shut the knowledge that Paul had paid for and was somehow associated with the place out of his mind. The warmth and familiarity of the building made him feel safe. It wasn't home but instead, a safe house of sorts.

The words Paul left Jack with ran through his mind like a mantra, Paul probably expected him to buy some extravagant possession, or spend copious amounts of money in a place of sin but Jack had other ideas. His mother always preached that, *'If you ever are in a position to help, you must act. Someone created you and your hands, and they didn't create them to harm, they were created to help. Any chance to use them for their intended purpose must be taken.'*

Jack intended to give as much as he could, especially now that his hands were being used for the opposite of what his mother would have wanted. Maybe the act of giving would bury his sins deeper in the medallion but even if it didn't Jack knew he had to help in some way. Jack walked toward the front desk and saw that Angela was sitting in her chair fast asleep, she looked so peaceful, Jack almost felt bad for waking her by ringing the bell softly. She stirred and then woke with a start. Apologizing over and over again she asked Jack what she could do for him.

"It's alright, I am sorry for waking you. Can I ask you a personal question, Angela?"

"Anything sir. Anything."

"Do you have any debt?"

Angela sat very still; her sleepy, weathered face was covered in shock. She almost looked hurt by Jack's question but answered, "Yes sir. I do."

Jack looked up to the heavens and silently thanked his mother for giving him an opportunity to help someone, especially on a night in which he had hurt two men.

"Would you be able to write the dollar amount down on a piece of paper for me."

"Sure, please don't judge me for the amount, sir."

Jack didn't say anything. He still had his walls up, the ones put in place to shield himself from Paul. They were built with care, making them extremely difficult to break. Jack took the piece of paper from Angela's hands. $1,200,456 was the number scrawled on the paper. "I have had quite a bit of bad luck sir. I work two jobs to provide but sometimes my sons medical bills become too much." Angela reminded Jack of his mother, but in her case her own medical bills were her downfall.

"Give me 2 seconds," Jack said as he ran as fast as he could into the elevator and dug through his kitchen drawers until he found the check book Charlotte had given him during the first week he was in the city. Check book in hand, Jack got back into the elevator. Once the elevator hit the lobby, he ran back to the front desk and asked Angela for a pen. He made the cheque out to her in the amount of $2,000,000.

"Never speak of this to anyone. I could get in big trouble if anyone found out. Promise me Angela."

Angela's face had gone white, and her eyes started to become glossy. "Yes sir, I swear on my son's life I will not breathe a word to anyone. I don't know how I will ever repay you. Thank you, sir, Thank you."

Jack didn't know what he expected to feel after giving such a large of money to a complete stranger. A part of him hoped he would feel absolved of sin, but he didn't feel any different. Deep down he knew the act of kindness wouldn't change a thing, so he turned away without speaking and got back on the elevator. The doors reopened and he found himself standing in own apartment. All alone once again, with only his thoughts to keep him company. He checked his phone one last time, placed it on the charger to make sure the alarm would go off in the morning, grabbed a bottle of whiskey, the good glass and headed to the couch to begin drinking.

The familiar blare of the air raid woke Jack. He realized that he had passed out on the couch, covered in sweat and still wearing the suit from the previous night. He picked himself up, made his way to his room to change into some more appropriate clothes and headed off to the gym. It was arm day, so he was at least a little bit excited. Once he returned, he took a warm shower, threw on some clothes—not bothering with his hair, he was too tired—and headed down to the Four Roses.

When Jack reached the Roses, he ordered and paid for a cup of coffee and a breakfast sandwich. He checked his phone and saw that he had 30 more minutes until he needed to leave for school. He didn't usually have time to sit down and eat. He didn't time his workouts or have a plan, other than the relative area of muscles he wanted to work out that day. He just worked out until he didn't have any more time or until every muscle in the target area was screaming. It was an escape. He wasn't necessarily trying to get stronger or better at something, unlike his new training with Jason. When he was within the walls of Justice, he was most definitely trying to get stronger, faster, and more knowledgeable in the subtleties of war.

Jack sat down at a corner booth, unwrapped the tinfoil around the sandwich, and dug in. Charlotte was right, the Four Roses lunch and supper was terrible, but its breakfast menu was the best he had ever tasted, and the egg sandwich was the best on the menu. The bun was perfect; soft, and warm but slightly crunchy around the edges with sesame seeds topping it all off. Jack never really tasted the sesame seeds, but their crunch seemed to complete the experience. Then there was the sausage, egg, and cheese. The sausage was garnished with all sorts of spices, just spicy enough to interest his tastes buds but not to the point where his tongue burnt. The egg was juicy and full of flavor. Jack was so impressed by the egg that he even asked a waitress where they bought the eggs they used in the sandwiches sent from God on a day he had time to spare.

The waitress told him that the eggs came from a farm upstate. They were 'Free range' eggs. Jack had no idea what that meant but loved the sound of it. The cheese was nothing special, Kraft singles; But its artificial flavor complemented the rest of the sandwich nicely. Jack had been regularly observing breakfast because of the Four Roses' egg sandwiches. Something he had not done back in is old life. Maybe the new life wasn't all darkness and shadows after all.

As he sat in the booth eating and thinking about last night's events, a woman walked by. He barely looked up from his sandwich but once the small glance registered in his brain, he jerked his head up fast to catch another glimpse. The face was familiar. A face that had been buried under piles of old memories; a face locked so deep in his hippocampus that it almost didn't trigger a response. When he looked back up, she was gone. He wasn't even done his meal, but he grabbed his backpack and ran to the door.

Looking frantically side to side Jack scanned every face that passed, but she was nowhere to be found. Maybe he was mistaken, it could have been someone else. His overactive imagination playing tricks. No, he knew it was her. It must have been her. Jack wondered what she was doing in NYC if it was in fact her. If it was the woman he thought it was, she should have been all the way back in Cielo, Maine.

As he walked to class the thought of her set up camp in his brain. The smells, sights, and feelings connected to her overwhelmed his psyche. She had been 'the one', she had been the person Jack thought he would be with for the rest of his life; if they had ever gotten together that was. She was always so close, yet so far away. Jack was consumed by the thought of her and what she might be doing for the rest of the walk to class. Even as Dr. Confucius introduced the next book they would be studying, which was '1984 By George Orwell'.

Jack couldn't focus on anything; except the face he had caught a glimpse of. If he had been paying attention, he would have been able to draw similarities between the new text and his new life, but instead her face and his memories of her danced though his mind. The woman possessed a face he would never forget completely and would have to keep his eye out for in the coming weeks.

A voice cracked through the bliss, "Mr. Hanson?" It was Dr. Confucius; he had obviously called his name more than once, the tone in his voice and the annoyance in his eyes confirmed it.

"Yes sir? Sorry I didn't hear you; I was lost in thought."

Without an ounce of forgiveness in his voice, the Dr. said, "Since you have so many thoughts, surely some of them were about the new reading?"

Jack had thankfully read *1984* before so he did have some thoughts and insights on the book. Although none of his most recent thoughts had been on that topic. "Since it was mandatory for my students to have read all the material before they were enrolled in my class, you should know what the theme of the text is."

A few seconds went by, in which Jack was thinking of all the themes and broader issues the book had shed a light on, but the Dr. was very impatient that day, "Earth to Jack! What is the prominent theme of the text?"

"Yes sir, sorry sir. I do have a theme, but I am not sure if it is the prominent topic of the text," Jack said, even though he knew it was. Jack was extremely confident in his ability to dissect fictional books. He could always find the deeper meaning behind an innocent work of fiction.

"I believe George Orwell is trying to shed a light on the dangers of totalitarian government, he is trying to warn us that the future could potentially hold a reality in which the individual is not an aspect of our lives. He paints the picture of a future in which friend or lover can be someone who you never expected them to be. It shows the loss of individuals as a result of total emphasis being placed in the group as a whole." The look of shock plastered on Dr. Confucius old face made Jack grin. He had shown the man that he may not have been paying attention, but he still could share insights and correct insights at that. Jack knew he was exemplifying what it meant to be 'NYU good'.

"Yes, Mr. Hanson is right and despite the lack of confidence he has in his own observations, they are in fact the very basis that the book sits on." Jack slid down in his seat as a warm wave of confidence washed over him. The rest of class went by with compete normality, the Dr. reading aloud and the class jotting down notes and asking questions. As soon the class was over, Jack started packing up his items and out of the corner of his eye he saw Dr. Confucius walking up to him. "Jack, can I speak to you for a second?"

Jack had nowhere else to be, so he didn't have any issue with staying behind a while longer to talk. "Yes, of course sir. What would you like to talk about?"

"I just wanted to let you know that I believe that you are the most gifted student I have had the pleasure of teaching in a long time. Your essay and your comments in class today were both insightful and flawlessly presented." Jack kept his composure but inside his heart he was dancing around, it felt a mardi gras parade had just broken out in his chest. He so wished he had someone he could talk to about all the things that had been happening to him. Especially the good things.

"On account of your success, I would like to invite you to a meeting Saturday night. All the leaders from around the city will be there. It may be a good opportunity for you to put you name out there so that the most powerful people in the city can get to meet you." 'Powerful', the word powerful and an amazing opportunity had presented itself to Jack before. He was still caught up in that particular 'once in a lifetime' opportunity. Jack didn't know if he could handle another one. However, he couldn't say no to this man who had believed in him and reinstated a sense of pride and confidence in his own writing.

"I would love to sir, but I will have to make sure I don't have any other plans that night."

"No problem, Hanson," Confucius said handing Jack a black and gold invitation written on hard cardstock. The air of wealth reminded Jack of the dress and the power that had floated around Charlotte when she first waked into the small medorian bar.

"The gathering is at 12:00pm Friday night. A car will be at your house at 11:30pm Friday night and will drive you to the gathering if you decide you are up for a little bit of fun. It will leave by 11:45pm no matter the circumstance. So don't be late if you mean to attend," Confucius said and then walked away, out the door and disappeared.

Jack finished packing up his supplies and walked out of the empty classroom. As he walked to the cafeteria, he replayed the conversation in his head over and over, as he did the red sun that hung at his chest grew heavier and heavier. Reminding him that he was still shackled to Paul, and that his sins separated him from the elite in ways that Confucius couldn't even fathom. Or at least Jack hoped he couldn't.

If he accepted the offer and attended the gathering, he may have to leave midway through to add another soul to his ever-growing collection. The thought of it made him miserable, it wasn't enough for Paul to ruin his life, but his wrath was now seeping quietly past the line drawn clearly in the sand into the side of Jack's life that he was proud of. The side of his life that he had earned…twice.

Once Jack reached the cafeteria, he was unable to eat anything. He sat in the corner and relieved his spine of the load it had been carrying, then removed the invitation from his pocket. It was black with elegant gold trim and writing.

The Founders
New York's oldest society

The invitation reeked of the upper-class, Jack wouldn't have been surprised if the gold ink was actual gold. The lavishness made him feel uneasy, like its prestige wasn't meant to be grasped in his poor, orphaned fingers. Of course, there had been so many situations and possessions that made Jack feel inferior. So many that he didn't know what to make of it.

The rest of the day went by without any other unexpected conversations or gifts, until he had already started walking home that was. His phone buzzed and for a fleeting moment Jack thought that it was Paul calling to tell him he had was needed at the office, but it was too early for that. He slowed his breathing and pulled his phone out of his pocket. It was Charlotte texting to ask if he was free for dinner that night.

Jack didn't know what to respond, he didn't like the fear that arose when he thought of talking to Charlotte and he didn't want her making a scene like the last time he had broken bread with her. After some deliberation, he decided that he wanted to ask who the man in red was and wanted to ask why she had been in attendance for his fight the night before. None of it made sense and even if she lied to him at least he would have an answer to appease his fears.

J: Yeah sure, does 7:30pm work for you?

C: Sounds good I will come pick you up in a company car.

J: Just going to be me and you tonight?

Jack wasn't going to attend if Paul or the Man in Red would be in attendance. He did not want to see either of their faces unless his life laid in their crosshairs.

C: Just you and me Hanson.

Perfect. He honestly didn't mind Charlotte's company and he did miss having someone to talk to about things. He continued on his path, grabbed his training clothes from the apartment and rushed down to the gym. Training with Jason had become the highlight of his day. It had saved his life once already and he was sure it would need to save him again sooner or later. Jason had saved Jack's life without even knowing it and Jack was very thankful, but he would never be able to share the good news with Jason. Jack knew he wouldn't keep training him if he knew the manner in which his techniques were being utilized.

When Jack arrived at the gym and had finished stretching, he went over to where Jason was training another young apprentice to let him know he had arrived. Jason decided that day would be a great day to teach Jack a new set of moves. By the end of the workout, Jack could barely move his arms or legs and was drenched in sweat from head to toe. Jack's heart was about to beat straight out of his chest, and he felt as if all the blood was rushing from his head.

The world blurred and swayed around him for a few seconds and then came back into focus. He knew he was going to have to eat something before he left for dinner. He thanked Jason as he grabbed his bag, he ran all the way back to his apartment—which wasn't the greatest idea given the fact that he had almost passed out a few seconds earlier—and hopped into the elevator. Once the elevator stopped at his apartment, he quickly ate two granola bars and headed into the shower. The nutrients packed into the granola bars seemed to appease his depleted stores and as the cold water hit the top of his head the blood returned to his face, and he regained some strength. Once he was clean, Jack got out and with the towel wrapped around his waist, headed straight for the closet.

Charlotte had said 'company car' implying they would he heading somewhere fancy; thus, he needed to dress the part. It was a good thing Charlotte had picked out eight suits for him the first week he had been in the city, way back when his biggest complaint was that he had to spend large stretches of time purchasing items. As he thought back to that time he started to laugh, if that version of himself could see where he was now, the younger version would be completely horrified. The laugh started as an innocent chuckle but quickly turned into a laugh that twists joy into pain. One of the laughs that hurts more and more as it persists and just as he thought his core was going cramp up or explode the laughter died.

Jack couldn't quite tell why he had been laughing, maybe he was so broken that horrors were now amusing to him. Or maybe he was just so sad that his body didn't know how to process the emotion anymore—after all he had been suppressing it since his mother died. It was just easier that way. He had learned over the years that pain is always easier to fight into submission than to process healthily, especially emotional pain. As he flipped through the suits, trying to pick one, he thought about that last day with his mother, her face, her smile, and her unsettling wisdom filled words, until the pain became too great. Then doing what he did best, he repressed. He had gotten painfully good at repression over the years.

Jack finally picked out a suit. A midnight blue suit jacket, jet black turtleneck, black belt, and midnight blue pants with black shoes. He laid the clothes out on his bed and went back to the bathroom to make sure he smelled fresh, fixed his hair and looked at himself in the mirror. During the short time he had been living in the city he had gained quite a bit of muscle, he could see it rippling softly underneath his skin with each muscle contraction but while his physique had become more toned and stronger, his face had grown gaunt. His hair had become slightly unruly but there was an added pain etched into his eyes. His drinking problem always left his eyes looking sad and bloodshot but recently they had become worse.

People always said eyes were windows to the soul and if that was true, his soul was in serious trouble. Jack's eyes reminded him of what they had been exposed to in the recent weeks. The damp room, the office, the important man's brains sitting on the ground in front of him, the poor man's scarlet blood running down the front of his body pooling at his feet and his own trembling hands holding the murderous tools. Even though they had been forced to witness such ugly sights, they had also laid eyes upon her. Jack was sure of it. He hoped they would be forced to train their gaze upon less ugly things and spent more time trained on her from then on.

Once he finally finished getting ready, he made his way to the kitchen. Jack realized the sun was sitting outside of his turtleneck, shining bright red against the black back drop. Quickly stuffing it back under the black fabric like he was in possession of a stolen artifact, he checked his phone. The time was 7:15pm. He had a few minutes until he should head down to the lobby to meet Charlotte, so he headed to the liquor cabinet, poured himself a drink and put it down in one gulp.

Then he poured himself another, drank it in the same fashion, grabbed his 'work' jacket and stepped into the elevator. As much as Jack hated living in such luxury, having an elevator that opened to his apartment was very convenient. The convenience presented some security risks but under Paul's unwanted protection no one would dare try something anyway. All Jack had to fear was Paul himself. In the words of his high school biology teacher, they had a mutualistic relationship under the condition that Jack upheld his 'duties'. If not, their relationship would become extremely parasitic.

Once Jack reached the lobby, he realized Charlotte was already standing there, checking her phone. Her back was turned to the elevator, she was wearing a stunning black and red dress. The top half, the part that covered her breasts, leaving her back very much exposed, was blood red and then at the waist it completely changed its tune to a jet-black flowing material that danced

103

around in the breeze. A breeze that was somehow hitting it from some unknown angle. Jack decided he would surprise her, he wanted to see what her reaction would be. After all, she had seen him knock a man twice his size out cold. He creeped up behind her and whispered, "Boo" in her ear. She whipped around fast, her hands tensed ready to strike, but then unfurled them when she realized that it was him.

"Fuck you," she said, her face was twisted into a forced smile that attempted to tell Jack she wasn't legitimately angry, but Jack could see through her veiled expression quite easily.

"Good to see you too Charlotte," he said with a genuine smile. "Where are we going for supper?"

"You will just have to wait and see," she said walking away.

Jack hated when she did it, it was like she knew he had no choice but to follow her around as if he was a little puppy. Although he always did what she wanted anyway. Once they both got into the car, she lit up a joint and offered it to Jack once she had taken a few drags. Jack politely declined, making sure to say that he might say yes later. He wanted to ask some questions and he wanted to be as sober as possible while asking them.

Jack also didn't know how he would act if he was high in public, he had never tried it before and wasn't about to make that night the first time. They made small talk through the drive and kept taking about meaningless topics, avoiding the golden elephants in the room on the way into the restaurant. The venue was called Le Meilleur—a French restaurant. Jack had never taken a French class before and the word hadn't yet been covered in his class, so he had no idea what it meant. The name was written in red neon lights above the entrance and a quick glance through the glass windows confirmed Jack's assumption; The restaurant was ultra-fancy. No surprise there. They walked up the hostess who, with one look at Charlotte, showed them to a table upstairs, the only table upstairs as it seemed.

The table was set for two with all sorts of upper-class cutlery, glasses and plates which was all set to the backdrop of a scarlet tablecloth with gold trim encircling the hem. Jack pulled out Charlotte's chair and waited for her to sit before pushing it back in and then took his seat across the table. The waitress came back over and asked if they wanted any drinks. Jack couldn't help but think he had seen her before; he was having trouble placing her face but then as if from midair it popped into his head. It was Maria, from the bar in

Medora. "Maria!" Jack exclaimed. He couldn't express how comforting it was to see a familiar face in a place where he felt like a polar bear in the Sahara Desert.

"Jack Hanson, I'll be damned! You look so different I barely recognized you."

"Ha-ha, yeah I'll bet. What are you are doing in New York?" Jack asked trying to push focus away from his appearance.

"A week after you left, I decided I needed a change scenery, so I bought a ticket on the next plane out. And started looking for a job, these kind people offered me one and this is where I've been ever since."

"Wow, that's great to hear!" Jack said and he honestly meant it, it made him feel less out of place. Maria's presence made him believe that after the whole fucking situation was over, he could actually start anew somewhere else. "Well, it's good to see you, I will have a glass of whatever whiskey you have on the rocks and Charlotte will have…"

"A glass of your finest pinot noir. Thank you," Charlotte said completing Jack's sentence.

"Coming right up Ma'am. Good to see you Jack," Maria said and then walked away quickly. Jack turned back to Charlotte and his spirits fell into a freefall all the way back to reality's cold, stone floor. He decided to wait until he had a drink to sip in between questions and answers so he made some more small talk until Maria had come back with drinks and taken their orders. They had both ordered the French onion soup to start and then the Salmon en Papillote for their main courses. Jack sipped his drink and began to speak, "I wanted to ask you why you were at my fight the other night and I also wanted to know who the Man in Red was. Also…Why did you attend this fight and not the last one?" Charlotte choked on her wine, wiped her mouth, and then said, "We will get to that, but I must admit I have ulterior motives for inviting you to dinner tonight, other than just your delightful company. Paul has asked me to ask a favor of you. This favor is optional, but it would get you in his good graces, may even get you out of work for a few weeks."

Jack had come to hate favors, opportunities and things that were supposed to benefit him. They never seemed to actually move in his favor in the long run; There was always a catch that would inevitably ruin his life but if this favor would save him committing unwilling murder for a few weeks he knew he should at least hear Charlotte out. "He would like you to accompany

Alexander, he is the man that was with me at your fight the other night, to a function this Saturday."

Jack's mind thought back to the invitation Dr. Confucius had handed him earlier today, the gold writing and trim, and the heavy black cardstock. Was it the same event? Was his English professor associated with Paul? Was Dr. Confucius one of Paul's so-called 'friends?' If so, was he a good writer, or was it just all a ploy to make Paul happy?

"Is it a function for the Founders Society?" Jack asked wearily.

"Yeah!" Curiosity and suspicion started to form on Charlotte's brow creeping its way down to her lips. "How did you know that?" Jack slammed the rest of his drink back and answered.

"I got an invitation from one of my teachers today, Dr. Confucius." Jack felt doubt and detestation creeping into his heart. How could he have been so stupid, of course Paul was behind it. He always was. It seemed that every turn he took for the rest of his life would eventually end with him staring into the face of evil.

"Jesus, if you decide to go with Confucius's offer you better try not to run into Alexander. The Dr. hates Alexander and Paul. Confucius's ancestors created the Founders Society; Fergus Confucius is the latest in a long line of extremely influential men. He has never married or had a child, so he will be the last of the founder's pure blood line. Fergus only ever invites Paul and Alexander because they are part of the GWA and is slightly scared of them, I think. If he realizes you work for them, he will, without a doubt, drop you from his class or at the very least give you horrible marks the rest of the year."

Jack couldn't believe what he was hearing, the doubt and detestation were driven out almost as fast as they had come. Confucius was good, he was better than good. His teacher—that apparently wasn't just an old angry professor—felt that he was on the same plane as the man in red and Paul. Even, arguably, regarded him on a higher level than his two oppressors. "I can't believe he gave you an invitation, you must be a better writer than I thought," Charlotte said, with only a hint of jealousy coming through in her tone. Jack had no idea what to say, he fiddled with his knife for a while as he tried to summon the words. When he finally found them, he spoke, "I can't believe it; you better not be messing with me," Charlotte reassured him saying that she was being '100% serious' and that she would never mess around with something like this.

"Confucius seemed like a normal Professor. He actually seemed slightly stupid," Jack said in disbelief.

"Yeah, he just teaches because he wants to find his replacement. He believes that he will eventually find his replacement in one of his advanced classes. In the 20 years that he has taught at NYU, he has never invited a student to the only Founders meeting of the year. I am 90% sure you're the first student to ever to be invited by the leader. You must be a possible candidate for the leader position in his eyes."

Jack's mouth went dry, and his palms started to sweat. He was now not only caught up in one massive scary corporation but now the leader of a secret society might want him to be his successor. Jack so wished that Confucius' offer could have come well before Charlotte ever pulled out a chair at his favorite table. Even though he knew that her coming to retrieve him from the outer rim of the writing world was the only reason all of it was happening. Not one of the men that now led his life would have even known his name if she hadn't given him a chance, or at least that's what he believed then.

"Good god. This month has been the most exciting yet terrifying month of my life," Jack said as a huge grin spread like wildfire across his face. His comment had only been partly truthful, the actual 'most terrifying' month of his life was the month in which his mother had died. It was also the most life shattering month of his life. Charlotte had drastically changed his life there was no doubt about that, but his mother's desertion had obliterated it.

Jack could see the onion soup coming up the stairs, so he waited to say anything else. Once Maria had set the soup down and replenished their drinks he began to speak again, "How am I going to make this work? How am I going to keep my relationship with Confucius while staying in good graces with Alexander and Paul?" Charlotte sipped her glass of wine slowly, her face scrunched up as if in deep thought.

"I could offer to accompany Alexander instead, that way I could try to steer him away from you and Confucius while we are at the party. Of course, that would mean that you would probably be called into work at least two times in the next three weeks."

In essence, Charlotte was saying in order to have a chance at getting out of his current situation he would have to dive deeper into the mud. Forced to sell his soul to the devil so that he could enter heaven. It was an impossible decision. "But if I take the bullet for you, you have to promise that you will save me from hell from your seat in heaven."

It was the first time in a while that he believed what Charlotte was saying. It sounded like she was pleading, paired with a strong undertone of urgency. But the fact that he would have to kill in order to stop killing still poisoned the offer. It was just the latest application of fresh blood painted on the once purely white canvas of his innocence.

"I will make a decision by the end of the night, I promise. But I still want to know who Alexander is in relation to the GWA."

"I think he is the leader of the whole organization; he sits on the same council that Paul sits on. No decision gets made without Alexander's seal of approval and I am pretty sure he is also the man that spared Paul's life."

Jack realized that Charlotte had been telling what she thought the truth Paul's origins were. The most recent revelation confirmed it. Maybe he had been too quick in his judgement of her.

"Wow…Why was he at the fight then? Why were you? I am not that important, according to you I am just a kid that Paul means to break." Even though Jack didn't want to believe his own words, he knew it was the truth. He knew that if he let Paul break him all of his gifts would be effectively dismantled.

"Alexander was at your fight because you are becoming more important, you impressed them in your first fight. You impressed them so much that they feel threatened. The organization set up that second fight because they wanted to hurt you bad or even kill you to show their power. Yet again you surprised them. However, the surprise did not catch me off guard. I was there as a punishment for taking so…recruiting you. It was the second part of my punishment, the first was when I was forced to kill the hooded man with a dull knife."

A tear slipped from her right eye, but she brushed it away quickly and continued, "Now that they see that you are really the best of the best, in more ways than one but they only care about the physical side of things, they will respect you. You won't be given terrible jobs or left with only one weapon on the table any longer."

Jack thought back to the night of the second fight, the glinting steel, and polished walnut handle. The obscenely large hunting knife had terrified him, a knife was much slower and more intense method of killing. Even a razor-sharp knife like the one that had sat on the table that night was primal and inhumane. Paul had forced him to kill a man in one if the most savage ways possible. Where was the respect in that? Paul had watched as he slid the knife through the man's soft flesh and watched the scarlet blood flow out of the gaping canyon that was left in the cold steels wake. It was scarring, something he would never forget. Just another reason to drink himself to sleep every night.

"They made me kill a man with a knife, Paul made me stand there and watch him bleed to death. Where was the respect in that?" Jack whispered quietly.

"It was a demonstration, a horrible demonstration but he wanted to show you that no matter how powerful you may be, he still owns you. It won't happen again, they both agreed that it was better to have you fighting for them, instead of against them."

If they thought he was on their side, if they thought he was fighting for them, they had another thing coming. At least they did when he got his degree. As the hellish opportunities piled up Jack felt the degree and accompanying piece of paper start to seem less and less important.

The pair didn't speak for the rest of the meal. They ate in silence throughout the entrée and dessert. After the meal was done and they had both finished their third drinks of the night, Jack caught Maria's eyes and motioned to tell her that he was ready for the bill. The whole dinner, everything included, cost $500. Jack paid the bill and tipped Maria another $20,000. Maria's face lost all color when she read the bill and she stuttered, asking Jack if he had made a mistake. Jack reassured her that he made no such mistake, then wrote his phone number on his bill and handed it to her saying that if she ever needed anything all she had to do was call.

After saying thank you about 100 times, she said she would be in touch. Jack told her he looked forward to her call, slipped his jacket on and helped Charlotte put hers on; Then the pair walked down the stairs and out into the night.

"Where do you want to go?" Charlotte asked.

"My apartment. Is that okay? I have classes tomorrow, so I need to sleep at my place tonight. Would you like to come with me upstairs with me when we get there?" Charlotte's expression melted into a coy smile and said, "Sounds like a plan, I have to make a quick stop before we get there and then we are good to go. Is that okay?"

"Yeah, for sure, no problem." As he finished talking, the black car that had dropped them off pulled around the block. Jack opened the door, let Charlotte get in and then got in himself.

After a quick stop at a marijuana dispensary, they arrived at Jack's building. He exited the car and helped Charlotte out, then poked his head back in to let the driver they were staying put for the night. They walked through the front doors and Jack said goodnight to Angela, she wished him a goodnight as well and winked at him once Charlotte had passed. Jack eyes crinkled and he held in a chuckle. Even with the murderous ultimatum hanging above his head like his own personal storm cloud, he felt happy. The ultimatum was tomorrow's problem, he planned on having a good night.

Charlotte reached behind her back, grabbed Jack's hand and led him into the elevator, once the elevator doors closed, she pushed him softly into one of the cold steel walls. Even with heels on Jack was a few inches taller than her and he could smell the shampoo and hair spray wafting off the top of her head. They smelled like rosehips and bitter chemicals. An odd contrast to be sure but once Jack got past the chemical smell, he was overcome with infatuation. Charlotte looked up at him with her mismatched eyes and stood on her toes seductively pressing her lips against his and then pulling them away softly making Jack crave their soft touch.

The doors opened to his apartment and Charlotte slowly removed her shoes as she walked toward the balcony. Jack removed his coat and blazer, placed them on the chair then headed into the kitchen to pour a drink. As he walked out to the balcony to meet Charlotte, drink in hand, he smiled. Even broken people deserved a break. Even broken people deserved to be happy. He slid the balcony door closed, setting his drink on the ledge placing his hand in the small of Charlotte's back. The last time his hand was there he hadn't noticed that she had two dimples above each cheek.

They stood in silence; Jack sipping his drink and Charlotte smoking, just staring into the mess of lights and buildings that is New York City. Jack wished that one day he would be able to stare out into the city scape with less contempt clouded lenses because it truly was beautiful. Once Jack's drink was empty and Charlotte's cigarette finished, they both sat down in the two chairs that sat on Jack's balcony, Charlotte in the left and Jack the right. Charlotte pulled the joint that she had bought out of her purse and asked Jack if he would like to share it with her. Jack obliged and they passed the joint back in forth until

Charlotte broke the silence, "If we ever get out of this mess, I hope I can go back home, there is a boy that I left there. If I ever marry, it will be to him. I will take his name and leave my blood red ledger behind me."

Even through the dulling sensation, Jack's mind raced. Was she human Afterall? Was she telling the truth before? Was the crazy display of emotions in the bar on account of her real, confused and hurt feelings? "I have been keeping tabs on him for years, he runs his family farm now. His parents both died and every once in a while, he looks at the pictures we took together at the homecoming dance, freshman year. I don't know if he would even recognize me anymore."

Jack had the same feelings about a girl he left back home, or at least he thought she was back home. His mind may be playing tricks on him but if not, she had arrived in the big apple. He thought about sharing his own desires but then decided against it. Charlotte had been more trustworthy as of late, but he didn't quite feel safe enough to tell her his deepest desires, at least not right there in that moment.

"Times were a lot warmer back then, maybe one day I will be able to get back to a real life," Charlotte said, her eyes still fixed firmly on the scenery. Jack's thoughts fell back to his past. His freshman years were a kinder and as Charlotte had said 'warmer' time. Money was still scarce in the Hanson household, but Jack was wrapped in his mother's love. By his sophomore year that blanket that once kept him safe and warm had been stripped away leaving him naked and naïve. Jack knew he had better say something but at a loss of words all he could think of was, "Maybe."

A wave of depressing sadness washed over him. "Until then we have to be able to rely on one another. I have to be able to trust you and you must be able to trust me." Jack meant it. If they were going to beat Paul, Alexander, and the whole damn GWA they would have to stick together and would undoubtedly need to outsource some help. At one point, someone with more power than the two broken young adults sitting on a balcony in the middle of New York was going to have to be told something.

"I know you don't trust me, but I swear on my father and your mother that I want to leave just as bad as you." Swearing on his mother was something Jack didn't take lightly, if Charlotte broke his trust now she would be dead to him.

"You can trust me to do everything in my power to get us both out of this mess that I dragged you into," Charlotte said as a single tear drop rolled down her cheek.

Jack reached his hand out and Charlotte shook it. Unlike the silent bond that they had made all those weeks ago, the shake was unbreakable. It meant— at least to Jack—that he would have to die protecting her if it came down to it. Their hands broke apart and Charlotte took her last drag from the joint and handed it to Jack so that he could take one last drag. He slowly felt the smoke fill his lungs, let it sit there a moment, then let it escape, snubbed out its embers and threw it off the balcony. They both stared unblinkingly at the cityscape for a few more moments, before standing in unison and heading back into the apartment.

Instead of Charlotte's usual upbeat and slightly annoying mannerisms she moved slow and barely made a sound. Instead, of the couch she sat down on one of the bar stools that sat in front of island and asked Jack if he could pour her a small drink. He didn't object, he unscrewed the lid from the bottle, picked a clean glass from the cupboard, poured a small amount into the cup, and handed it to Charlotte. Then poured a sizeable amount in his own glass, leaned on the counter and pressed his lips against Charlotte's. He felt her weight shift as she began kissing him back. After a few fleeting moments, they broke the bridge and sipped their drinks, still staring into each other's eyes.

"I know you love the guy you left back in Ohio but while we are together do you think it might be okay if we lean on each other like two rocks in the middle of a relentless sea?"

"Yeah…I think that would be great. I could use a rock to lean up against, I've been standing alone so long I don't even know what it would feel like to drop my guard." Jack thought that she may have already dropped her guard in front of him but didn't want to ruin the moment, so he shut his mouth. "You know we have a tough patch ahead of us. Alexander and Paul won't let us go easily."

Jack knew that all too well, he had already begun preparing for it. "I will do my best to make sure you can go to the Founders gathering alone, but I can't make any promises. Paul is the cruelest person I have ever met but he is also one of the smartest and he knows how to break people. He masterfully dangles hope in front of you, and then when you finally have the courage to take a swipe at it; It morphs into a knife that cuts you as soon as your hand wraps around its glistening blade."

"I know Charlotte, but if we work together, we might have a chance. I don't think he has much in the way of foresight," Charlotte's face fell into weak smile. "He has been wrong about me twice since I've been here, and I know you will shake his very core when you take your mask off."

Jack knew that her mask might not actually be a mask, but he hoped for his own sake that it was. With their eyes glued to each other, they both finished their drinks and slowly shuffled around the counter. The tension was so thick that it could have stopped a bullet in its tracks. Jack grabbed Charlotte's waist with both hands and placed her on the counter, she gently shifted her hair to the left side of her face, leaving the right side unbarred. Leaning her head down slowly, she kissed him. Their lips pressed together, occasionally repositioning.

Each one half of a whole, sustained by the others unbroken pieces. Their souls melted together to create one mutual, unbroken whole. At least for that night, in that moment, they would be happy, they would be safe in each other's arms.

After what felt like an eternity, Charlotte broke the connection and jumped down from the counter, softly interlocking her fingers with Jack, leading him toward his bedroom. Once they had arrived, she turned her back to Jack, reached behind her and unbuttoned the lone top button holding the dress above her shoulders allowing it to fall. It fluttered to the floor with so much grace that Jack thought it may never reach the ground.

Its absence left Charlotte completely naked and all of a sudden Jack realized that he was completely clothed and quickly unbuttoned his shirt, unbuckled his belt removed his pants that fell at his feet, then removed his socks. Leaving only his underwear to cover himself. Once he was finished, he ran his hands against Charlotte's skin, it was warm and soft like a newborn babies. As the soft skin ran underneath his hands, he spun her around to face him and saw the ghastly scar running from her upper left ribs to her lower right ones. It was purple and thick, out of place on such a beautiful tapestry. He thought that he might ask her about it once the moment passed but for that momentary ripple between hells fiery rage, he just wanted to stay in the present.

Not wanting anything to break through the fragile atmosphere that surrounded them both. He placed is left hand lightly on her right shoulder while his right ran through her hair pushing it behind her ear, revealing her stunning eyes. Then tenderly, leaned down and kissed the soft skin just underneath her jaw, then let his lips once again meet with hers. The heat radiated from each figure keeping the other safe and warm. They both wished that they could stay in that moment forever. If they could, all the sin, pain and cold would retreat and their broken souls could begin to heal. Mended by the others intact pieces, creating one whole human out of two broken ones but just like anything life gives us, they both knew that the pure moment would as sure as day, pass.

Chapter 11

The air raid siren squealed loudly, effectively ripping Jack from the peace the black void of sleep offered but Jack had heard the alarm every morning, so he woke without moving a muscle. Charlotte however was not accustomed to the terrifying wake up call. She jumped out her skin ready for a fight, Jack felt her jerky movements and sat up quickly reassuring her that it was only his alarm, nothing to be worried about. Then he grabbed his shorts and a t-shirt and started heading off to the gym, as he did every day.

"Going somewhere?" Charlotte asked from the bed. She had wrapped the blankets around her body acting as a makeshift dress for the time being.

"Oh sorry, I'm just going to the gym, I will be back in like an hour. You can go back to sleep or take a shower and take some of my clothes, or you can get dressed and leave if you want," Jack said although he hoped she would decide to stay in bed and go back to sleep. He needed to talk to her about the night before and hoped his mind would be made up by the time he was back in the room. The decision was almost impossible to make but no matter which way you looked at it there had to be a choice made.

"I'm going back to sleep, wake me up when your back. I don't think I'm going to head into school today," Charlotte said slipping back under the covers, she was sound asleep before Jack made it out of the room. He grabbed his bag and headed down to the gym.

He changed into his gym clothes and shoes then headed to the bench press and loaded the bar with his usual warm up weight. Jack was amazed that the large chunk of metal that made him stronger each and every day was made from the same material as the knife he killed with. One shape created strength and safety, the other configuration of atoms made him feel small and helpless.

As he lifted the weight his mind ran over his options again and again. Accept Confucius' offer and have a chance at a better life, or maybe a life with different sins involved, but that remained to be seen. In any case, the

Dr. would be a good ally to have if he ever decided to take his stand. On the other hand, if he declined Alexanders offer, he would be punished, or killed. Jack couldn't believe Charlotte when she said they respected him. They weren't the type of men to see strength and respect it. They saw strength and put more effort into breaking the strong individual.

Paul and Alexander would undoubtedly force him kill more often, he would have to pick from the table and steal souls time and time again in the coming weeks. The sins he had already committed were on the verge of breaking his spirt and imposing imminent domain on his soul. Neither option was ideal, but one was clearly better than the other. Jack knew what he had to do but he still wasn't confident he would be able to live with the consequences.

Jack finished his workout and then headed back up to his apartment. When he stepped back into the elevator, his mind flashed back to the night before, Charlotte's gentle but commanding push into the wall and her lips grazing his and then finally landing, interlocked like two puzzle pieces. Jack let a smile spread across his face. He knew that he only had last night to be truly happy. Although the memories could bring back the same feeling, couldn't they?

As Jack's mind drifted back to reality, he was sure that Charlotte wasn't the one he would end up with, there was too much distance between them; the woman Jack had left back in his first life was the one. He was sure of that. An impenetrable mountain range erected with resentment, secrets, and a touch of fear, kept Jack rooted to that belief but Charlotte would be a good friend and ally – that was if she was telling the truth. If she wasn't, Jack would be all alone. He didn't want to be all alone again; sure his last week had been bearable, but it lacked the joy and passion Charlotte could provide.

When the doors opened to his apartment, everything was just as he had left it. Jack walked slowly, making sure his footsteps were silent and as he opened the door to his room, he saw Charlotte still laying on the left side of the bed fast asleep. Jack knelt on the bed and gently grazed her bare shoulder; the skin was soft and warm under his fingers. It was almost enough to entice him to undress and cuddle up next to her, but he thought better and softly shook her awake. Charlotte jumped up just about knocking all of Jack's front teeth out of his head but once she realized where she was, she covered herself up with a sheet and asked, "You want to shower first, or should I?"

"Whatever you want, I don't mind," Jack said, startled by her abrupt waking habits.

Charlotte looked at him and then back down at her sheet dress and said, "You go first I need to find some clothes to steal so that I can get home."

"Sounds good," Jack said walking into the closet and grabbing some jeans, underwear, socks, and long sleeve shirt. There was a chill in the air and as strong as Jack was, he hated feeling the gnawing cold against his bare skin. Even though Jack had seen Charlotte naked last night and she had seen him, he didn't want to get any more familiar with her. If she was Paul's spy, less familiarity would make it easier for him to cut her out in the long run. In his new life, he couldn't fully trust anyone, it was one of the new traits he was being forced to adopt. It wasn't a trait he welcomed; solitude was a frigid, lonely island to inhabit but he knew standing alone among the snow drifts was the closest he would be able to get to safety.

Once Jack and Charlotte had both showered and dressed, Jack cleaned up the apartment, packed his backpack and sat down. He ran the question he had through his mind a few times and went over his decision once more, making sure it was in fact what he wanted to do. After a few moments, he decided it was the right, and only feasible choice. Charlotte was busy folding her dress and recovering all her possessions that had been scattered around Jack's apartment, so she didn't hear him the first time he called her name but on the second try his voice finally broke through her concentration.

"Yes?" She answered.

"You're okay with us staying friends, right?" Charlotte looked at Jack with a completely blank expression but then as realities curtains whipped open, she said, "Yeah totally, I love the boy I left in Ohio. I just need someone to count on and someone to hold close every once in a while. Are you okay with that?"

Jack breathed a sigh of relief; he was always worried the morning after that the girl he was with would have attached onto him like a remora to a shark.

"Yeah, I am, I need someone like that too...Okay next question. Where did you get your scar?" Charlotte dropped all the items she had collected and immediately started frantically picking them up. Her face had turned bright red and her hands begun to shake. "Oh...just a childhood injury, I'm pretty sure it was piece of farm equipment. Can't really remember though."

Jack knew she was lying, not just because of the shade of her cheeks or her stunned reaction to the question. The purple coloration of the scar gave it away; a childhood scar would have been turned white by the gentle kiss of time. He

117

didn't mind though, maybe as they grew closer she would tell him its real origins.

"Oh, sorry I asked, I was just interested. You are still the most beautiful girl I have ever seen in real life, even with the scar."

"It's alright, thanks for saying that," she said with a shy smile. He had run out of meaningless questions, there was no more delaying the inevitable, it was time for the declaration of his fate. He had to tell her what his decision was and she needed time to get Paul and Alexander on board.

Jack whispered it so quietly that Charlotte had to ask him to speak up, "I would like you to take the man in red to the function, I want to take my chance with Confucius. I think it's the best option and if I make a good impression, you never know, we could finally find a way out of this shit show." Once the words left his mouth and were spoken aloud, he felt sure of his decision. He would be trading souls for an opportunity and potentially be putting himself and Charlotte in danger, but he would have to make peace with that.

Over the span of two more months Paul would make him take a lot more than three souls. Putting all his faith in Dr. Confucius meant that he may not have to endure two more months of tyranny. It meant that he may be able to lead Charlotte and himself into the promise land and maybe just maybe, he might be able to personally deliver the devil back to hell.

"Perfect, I was hoping you would take the path less traveled. I think we have a greater chance at freedom if we have Confucius backing us."

"Yeah, that's what I was thinking." It sounded like he was having silly conversation about a bio project, with his lab partner as if he had just said 'Yeah I was thinking we should include the embryo growth cycle on the poster' when in reality he had just said that he would rather kill Paul then attempt to run away. "We will have to ensure that we both play our parts perfectly though. If Paul ever smells something fishy, we would be more than fucked," Jack said.

"I know, we also have to make sure he is okay with me taking Alexander instead of you before we get ahead of ourselves. I will call him later and ask and I will give you a call after, no matter the outcome."

Jack nodded in agreement. He knew that the plan might still go awry but he had a good feeling that it would work perfectly. All he had to do was make sure he was ready for Confucius, make sure he made a lasting impression. "Thanks for letting me stay over and thank you for keeping me warm last night." Charlotte said as she walked to the elevator and got in, keeping her eyes fixed on Jack as the doors slid shut. Jack focused hard on the closing metal doors, unblinkingly trying to recreate Charlotte's face, wanting to know what was going on inside. What was her end game? Was the snakeskin she wore in front of Paul a fragile costume or was it her true identity?

Chapter 12

Jack stood in his kitchen sipping coffee, he had just finishing getting ready for the day, and had already completed his morning workout. It was Friday morning; classes had been cancelled due to some sort of student appreciation day, 'Mental Health Day' as they called it. So, Jack decided that he would go out and buy a brand-new suit especially for the event the next night with his day off. He wasn't sure what color he was going to wear just yet, although green had always been his favorite. Its lush soft nature brought back memories of his mother and their long walks through Rein Forest. It was their safe place, free from bills, jobs, and exhaustion, which at all times were always trying to rip the two of them apart. As he looked back on that time he would accept the bills, jobs, and poverty with open arms, but he knew that those walks through the Rein were the best memories he had.

They were the strongest tie he still had to happiness, maybe one day he would be able to go back. Maybe he could buy a part of the forest and build a house there, secluded from the world, wrapped in happy memories. Safe from the ball of chaos that had had been set into motion when cancer had snuck into his mother's bed while she slept. If he was carving a path into a free life, or at least a life free from the darkest evil he had encountered up to that point in his life, he wanted to begin with the color that had nourished his happiness all those years ago.

Charlotte called a few hours after she left Jack's apartment, the morning after they hatched the plan, saying that Paul wasn't happy but that the plan would work. Under the condition that he understood that he was the on-call employee for all 'jobs' for the next three weeks. Other than that 'slight road bump' as Charlotte had referred to it, they were in the clear. She made sure to remind Jack that he had promised to take her with him in the case that Confucius decided to help them. Jack assured her that he would, but he wasn't sure what he would honestly do if the Dr. did choose him. He needed Charlotte to prove herself before he even considered letting her into his inner circle.

But first and foremost, he needed to focus on the task at hand. He wouldn't even have a place within the ranks until he proved he was the best choice to succeed Fergus Confucius and the first way he could do that would be to dress perfectly. It would be the first building block that would ensure the Dr. saw him as a man who could handle the stresses that the position—which was supposedly up for grabs—brought with it. He needed a haircut, a new suit and he had to do something about the dark bags that had been growing underneath his eyes.

The bags would be the hardest but the other two would be easy enough. His hair had become unruly and shaggy, all he would have to do was get it trimmed and wrangled into a powerful, confident outward visage. The suit was the easiest, given the fact that he had unlimited funds backing him. No suit was too expensive, it would be effortless to purchase the perfectly fitting, jaw dropping suit. The bags would be the hardest, but Jack had learned that with money anything was possible. Once the day was over, he would have an solution to all three. He vowed that when he arrived at the Founder's function, he would emit confidence and status. His soul would remain the same. Underneath the mask he would still be the same boy damaged by the meat grinder of life, but his outer appearance would be one of a man who could control every room. A man who belonged at the right hand of a leader. A good man who would one day be remembered as a great man. As he grabbed his coat his skin felt like iron. Paul's evil couldn't slither and hiss through, he felt impenetrable. Although, as he stepped into the elevator, he was almost melted by the fact that he didn't know what Saturday night held in store for him.

He exited the elevator into the lobby and pulled his phone out of his pocket to search the best tailor in New York. It was paramount that everything from his shirt to his shoes be brand new, each individual inch of his outward charisma needed to emit confidence. A shop called Master Threads popped up and he pressed the direction button, it was thirty minutes from the apartment. He would have to take a taxi. Jack exited the building, hailed a taxi and told the driver that he was headed to Master Threads. The driver inputted the name into his GPS and drove away. Jack decided that he would pay the driver to drive him all day and make sure that he waited in front of every building he decided to peruse.

When the driver finally stopped at one of the oldest buildings Jack had ever seen, he looked up and saw that it was dwarfishly short compared to buildings surrounding it. The upper windows were filled with dust from the inside, the bricks were cracked, spider webs hung off the windowsills like strands of thin white hair and the entire building looked as though it was about to crumble under its own weight. Jack made sure to tell the driver that he would pay him $5000 dollars if he drove him around all day. The driver agreed without so much as a second of hesitation and Jack exited the cab.

As he walked up to the front door his peripheral vision caught a glimpse of a wooden sign with an arrow pointing toward an ancient set of cobblestone stairs that led down below the sidewalk. The sign read Master Threads, so Jack knew the GPS had taken them to the right place. The stairs didn't look stable and the ominous quality they possessed made the hairs ripple against the breath of unease they exhaled. Ignoring his intuition, he walked down the stairs, effectively immersing himself in the darkness. The wooden door that sat at the bottom was scratched and looked like it had been built by time itself. He drew a deep breath and knocked lightly on the door.

There was no answer, so after a few seconds he knocked harder, still no answer. Jack tried the handle and found the door unlocked. Cautiously, he entered the low-lit room, the walls were covered in different fabrics, there were tables strewn with ties, others covered in tie pins, collar pins and a few displays filled with cuff links. The room smelled musty, and the air was thick with the same damp air that filled the room under the left side of the office. The similarities were unsettling, but Jack urged himself forward. In the far corner, there was a desk with a bell and a brand-new debit machine sitting atop it. Jack walked quickly toward the bell but as he did a voice sliced through the silence in a slow monotone, "How may I be of service, sir?"

Jack whipped his head around, his heart raced as his fists clenched, and his eyes came in and out of focus, wild with fright. A white-haired man stood in front of him. The man couldn't have been more than 5 feet tall, his white hair was long and thin, his brilliantly blue eyes seemed to flow like they were nothing but glass balls filled with water straight from the sea and his clothes were worn. They could have been sewn by the same hands that constructed the front door. Jack wondered if the garments were older than he was. Once Jack had regained his—now shaky—composure he said, "I would like to buy a three-piece suit, collar tie pin, and cuff links. I would need it by tomorrow at ten pm at the very latest. Would you be able to do that?"

"Yes sir, it will cost more because of the time constraints but I would be able to do that for you."

"Money is not an issue, and I will pay more for your troubles," Jack said politely, "I would like the suit to be forest green. Other than that, I am not all that picky about anything. As long as I convey a look of confidence and power. Is that doable?" The man's blue eyes glistened with wisdom and intelligence like the sun brushing gently against the ocean at sunset. Even though the man was at least a foot shorter than Jack, he realized the shop attendant was twice the man he was and probably ever would be.

The old man had somehow evaded the snakes and sidestepped the mud that plagued the 21st century. He had remained pure despite the evil that lived in the shadows, even the shadows that covered his own shop door hadn't been able to swallow the man's youth.

"Yes sir," he said as he showed Jack to the far-right wall, grabbed a forest green material, ripped a square off and then ripped three more squares of different material from their wholes. Fists gripping the material, he headed down to the opposite wall and ripped off a few white squares of fabric. Then over to the tables holding the cuff links and tie pins, grabbed three of each and headed to an empty tabletop and laid all the items on the table, carefully placing them in three rows.

"Pick one row, sir. The green fabric will make up the suit, the pants, and the vest. The white will be the shirt and each tie pin and cuff link in the row will go with any one of the fabrics so those aren't stuck in their respective rows. After you choose, I will take your measurements and start creating your suit, it should be ready by 10pm tonight."

"Sounds good. Thank you, sir."

The title of sir didn't fit Jack. To his ears it sounded tainted an unearned, but it fit dwarfish man like a glove. Jack looked the fabrics up and down and finally settled on the first row, the green was perfect, it matched the trees he used to walk through with his mother. The white had tiny forest green dots spalttered across it, not too many but just enough to cut holes through the stark wasteland of white. The tie pin and the cuff links were harder. He narrowed them both down to two choices, for the pin it was between one with two black buttons on either side or one with two tiny silver roses on each side.

As for the cuff links, it was down to triangles with a green gem imbedded in the silver or links in the shape of J's. Jack wondered what had made the old man choose them, it was curious that he would choose the letter J. How the man knew the letter J was significant to his costumer, Jack thought he would never know. He hadn't told the man his name or anything about his past. It was as if the blue eyes could see past his clothes, pain and masks, straight into his soul. He stared the four options and after what felt like an eternity, chose the J's and the roses. Jack gathered all is choices and handed them to the man.

"Very good choices, sir." He said with a beaming smile that ventured all the way to his bright blue eyes. The man walked them over to the desk and grabbed a measuring tape to take Jack's measurements. "What is your name sir? I usually stitch each costumer's name on the lining of my custom suits."

"My name is Jack," Jack said extending his hand to shake the mans and asked, "what's yours?"

"My name is Gabriel, good to meet you, Jack." Standing up, he said, "I will have your suit ready by ten o'clock this evening," he said walking to the desk, grabbing Jack's choices, and disappearing past the curtains hanging ominously behind the counter.

Jack stood in the middle of the room trying to comprehend what had just happened. The small, blue-eyed man had somehow wrapped bandage around Jack's beaten soul. Just standing in his presence had made Jack feel safe. Safer than he had ever felt while intertwined with Charlotte. Almost as safe as he had felt in the presence of his mother. Once the wave of shock had passed, Jack walked to the door he had entered from and journeyed up the stairs into the light, got back in his waiting taxi and asked the driver to take him to the best leather store he knew. Without hesitation the driver pulled away.

As the taxi pulled to the side of the road; Jack tried to look out the foggy window but there was just too much condensation built up on the glass. He wiped away the liquid exhale as best he could and looked out. Two massive glass doors with gold trim stood in front of him, as if they were gate keepers to wealth. If Jack didn't carry around a card that could never be run dry, he would have never even attempted to step past the ominous gate keepers but he did and with it came the courage to act as if he owned every establishment he entered.

He stepped past the ten-foot slabs of glass and was immediately approached by a skinny man wearing some questionable pants. Jack didn't think he would ever put on a pair of skintight red leather pants but who was he to question the man's decisions. The man immediately asked what Jack was looking for in the same tone that all salesmen thought they needed to talk to him in.

"Some dress shoes to go with a forest green suit and a belt to go with the same suit," Jack said.

"I have quite a few options, we will try them all. Do you have a price range? I should tell you that we only carry the most elite products," The man said but all Jack could do was look back at his pants and wonder if they were sprayed on. If they weren't, how did the man get his legs into them? Baby oil, cream, powder? Whatever the method was, it didn't matter anyways. The man seemed to know what he was talking about and the store appeared to have every article of clothing made from leather that he could think of.

"Awesome, I have time. No, I don't have a price range, I don't need expensive shoes or a belt but if the right ones turn out to be expensive, so be it."

"That's a mindset I can work with," the man said, walking away. The pants squeaked with each step. He walked all the way to the back of the store where there were thousands of shoes, boots, and sandals lining the 30ft wall. "Men's shoes on the right and women's shoes on the left."

"What size of shoe do you wear, sir?"

Jack tried to answer the question but the word that he hated was impeding his neural pathways. The bitter aftertaste filled his mouth and made him shiver.

"Size nine, and my name is Jack by the way."

"Perfect, Jack. I will be right back with some options." The man said disappearing past smaller versions of the front doors that Jack thought must have led to the stock room. When he reappeared, he was carrying six boxes of shoes in each hand. Jack ran over to help immediately and asked if the man needed assistance, but the man said he was fine and set the boxes down on a bench beside a plush armchair.

Jack assumed he was supposed to sit in the chair as he tried shoes on, but he hated the idea of being pampered like a trust fund child. He hadn't even had a chair that nice when he was growing up. Even in his new, gaudy apartment he didn't own a chair that looked that plush.

"Take a seat si…Jack," the employee said.

Jack hesitated, he felt like he would be betraying his roots if he sat in the chair and allowed another human to put his shoes on for him. But after everything Paul had put him through in the last month, he decided that he deserved it. He knew what he deserved was either luxury or a chair that pulsated with electricity. As Jack sat down, he felt himself fall deep into the plush fabric. In reality, he had only sunk about an inch, but it felt like he had fallen right through. Even his couch back at his apartment didn't have that kind of comfort.

It put the comfort of his own bed to shame. The chair made every previous chair, couch, and bed he had sat, slept, or lounged in back in Maine feel like it had been made from hardened steel. "We have a few choices, Jack," the man said. "I will put each shoe on your foot, and you tell me when we have reached the right pair. Then you can walk around in them and if they feel good, I will grab the matching belt, you can pay for them and head out."

"Sounds good, thank you," Jack said.

The man put 20 different pairs of shoes on Jack's feet. Derby's, Brogue's, Monk strap's, Wing tips, and Loafers were put on and taken off. After an hour of trying shoes, Jack finally settled on a pair of light brown cap toe oxfords. The colored leather covered the top and darkened leather wrapped around the edges. After he had walked around in the pair he had chosen and was satisfied with their grip and comfort, the employee that had been helping him went back through the stock room doors, grabbed the matching belt and guided Jack to the register.

"You have chosen one of our nicest pairs. All heads will turn when they notice them." Jack thought that he didn't really want anyone to notice him but at the very least he would be dressed well enough to impress Confucius. "Your total is $2678.50; will that be debit or credit?" The man said without even a wrinkle of his facial features. Jack however chocked on his own saliva. He remembered a time when he hadn't even seen $2000 all in one place. Now he was paying almost $3000 dollars for some shoes and a belt. He was still mystified by how much his circumstances changed in such a short amount of time.

"Credit please and can I ask you a question?"

"Of course, Jack."

"Was this pair of shoes one of the more expensive pairs?" Jack thought that there was no possible way that $3000 dollars would be on the lower side of the scale, but he had to ask.

"It was in the middle of our price range sir. There are less expensive belt shoe pairings but there are also quite a few more expensive pairings." $3000 wasn't even the most expensive pairing, the thought made Jack's intestines churn. People all over the world were starving or living destitute lives and the ultra-rich were coming to the store and buying shoes that cost the same as a very high mortgage payment. It was a sad thought and what brought Jack down even farther was the fact that he was now one of those people. He grabbed his bag, turned to walk toward the door, saying thank you as he left.

Back in the taxi, he took a moment to settle himself and reassured himself that he was doing what he needed to do to escape mud he found himself in. The suit was rope, the shoes and belt were the strong tree limb and the haircut he was about to get would act as the physical strength in his arms that allowed him to pull himself out of the mud pit that was continually trying to pull his head under its surface. As he started to reconcile his obscene purchases, he asked the driver if he knew any good barbers. The driver said he knew the best in the city and made sure to add the fact that it was his cousin and that he had many famous clients. Jack told him that it sounded perfect, and they were off.

Once they reached the barber, the driver parked the car next to the curb in front of the building and exited the vehicle with Jack. He told Jack that his cousin didn't take new costumers very often and that if he accompanied him, his cousin would be more inclined to accept him. The doors to the barber shop were glass but looked much less impressive than the leather stores. The driver walked straight up to the front desk and asked for Angelo.

The woman sitting at the desk must have recognized the driver because she stood up quickly and walked straight to the man cutting hair in the far-right corner of the shop. She whispered something in the man's ear, he turned around as she spoke and smiled when he saw the man Jack had been driven around by all day. The man yelled at another barber sitting in the corner on his phone and he stood up and took over the haircut. As the man walked toward the front desk Jack saw that a large scar ripped his face in half, starting at the left hair line and ending just below his left eye. His left eye must have been in the knifes path because it was cloudy, and disfigured.

The taxi driver whispered in Jack ear, "Don't look at his scar or his eye, he hates that."

Jack didn't know how he was supposed avoid looking at the disfiguration. It laid in the exact spot that Jack taught to focus on. Was he supposed look at his feet while speaking to Angelo? It didn't seem very respectful so Jack decided he would try to focus on his right eye.

Angelo reached the desk and pulled the driver into a hug saying that it felt like he hadn't seen him in an eternity. Then asked who he had brought with him. The driver whispered in Angelo's ear in a language that Jack didn't understand. It was as if they were keeping a secret from him, but Jack decided that the driver could be trusted. If the driver had wanted to harm him, he would have done it already. After the two had finished their secret conversation, Angelo looked Jack up and down, said something in the foreign language to the driver which must have been funny because the driver chuckled and then motioned for Jack to follow him.

Angelo led Jack past the chair and through the pair of swinging doors at the back of the shop. On the other side, there was a single red leather barber chair, it looked like a chair pulled from an old Ferrari. Jack sat down and Angelo wrapped his neck with soft white material, placed two clean black towels on either shoulder and finished the preparations with a black barber cape; not unlike the ones that most barbers used. Finally, he said in broken English, "What would you like your hair cut to say?"

Say? Jack didn't know what he meant. He didn't want anything written in his hair.

"Pardon me, sir?"

Jack was so confused. He thought the man may be substituting the wrong word.

"What would you like your hair cut to say about you. What are you trying to look like?"

After the clarification, Jack understood, he wanted his hair cut to say he was powerful and worthy of the position that Confucius was undoubtedly vetting him for. Of course, he couldn't tell Angelo that.

"I want to look intelligent, well-groomed and strong."

"Sounds good, I will try to do this for you." Jack hoped he wouldn't massacre is head. He was putting a lot of faith in Angelo. "Haircuts cost money, $500 per cut. Are you able to pay for this?"

"Yes sir, that's fine." A month ago, a $20 dollar hair cut would have made Jack groan but now $500 for a haircut was 'fine'. The excess continued to leave Jack feeling lost in the vast sea of wealth. Angelo grabbed a razor and started shearing hair off the sides of Jack's head.

By the time he had competed the cut, the ground was littered with incredible amounts of hair and Jack's head felt much lighter than it had when he walked into the barber's shop. When Angelo told Jack he was done, Jack looked into the mirror and almost didn't recognize himself. The sides of his head were barely covered in a short layer of hair and the top of his head had lost sixty percent of the hair than had been there just minutes ago. What was left had been coerced into form by paste and a fair amount of pushing and prodding.

"You like this?" Angelo asked. Jack couldn't respond, he didn't know yet. It did convey what he had asked for, but it was different than the look he had always worn. A new hair cut for a new life. It made him feel strong, made him feel like he belonged to the world he had been thrust into. The only problem was that Jack didn't like belonging to the world of guns, death and money.

"Yes. Looks amazing," Jack said. Even though he wasn't sure, he believed his own words. "Good, you look like a...ahhh what is the word," Jack shrugged.

"Ah yes, a prince. You look like a prince," Angelo said, as he began removing the cape, towels and finally, the stretchy paper wrap.

After he had swept the hair into a pile away from Jack's feet, he walked back through the swinging doors without warning. Jack sat up fast and headed to the counter. Angelo had already imputed the cost into the card reader and handed it to Jack as he talked to the taxi driver in their own language. Jack looked down at the screen and inserted his card, the screen blinked and then asked if Jack agreed with the amount; Jack pressed OK and then it asked for a tip percentage or dollar value. Jack hovered above the 'No tip' option but thought better of it and tipped the barber $200 above the price of the cut.

After the transaction had gone through, he handed the machine back to Angelo, thanked him and walked back through the glass doors feeling very unsure about his new haircut. The cold winter air chilled the sides of his head now that they had been exposed. The driver walked up to the car and unlocked it, then turned to Jack and asked him, "Where to?"

Jack pulled his phone out of his pocket and saw that it was 3:30pm. "My apartment please," he said. They both got in the cab and the driver turned the car over and drove away.

When Jack arrived at his apartment, he glanced at the oven clock. It was 4:15pm. Jack knew he was cutting it close, but he didn't know he was cutting it that close. He scooped up his gym bag and ran full tilt toward the elevator doors, they barely opened in time for Jack to throw himself into the steel box. Jack never realized how slow elevators seem to go when you're in a hurry. As the elevator slid down the shaft, he got ready to run as soon as the doors opened. When the steel box finally reached the ground and the doors caging Jack opened, he took off like a bullet. He slammed into the front door but pushed past it.

When he finally hit the sidewalk, his feet flew out from underneath him sending his body into a freefall into the pavement. His shoulder slammed the ground, his head followed with a light thwack as his legs thudded into the cement and his ribs contracted stealing the air from his lungs. The hard cold cement felt like a large sledgehammer had just connected with every inch of the left side of his body; Jack laid outstretched on the ground trying to catch his breath and just as he thought that the air would never be allowed back into his lungs, he finally was able to draw a shallow breath. He sat up slowly shaking his head as if shaking the entire experience out of his mind, then hurried off on his way to the gym.

When Jack finally heard the gym door shut behind him, he withdrew his phone from its place in his pocket. 4:27pm, it read. 3 minutes to spare, heading straight for the changeroom Jack changed quickly, pausing only to check if his arm was bruised. He noticed his shoulder was already showing signs of bruising, but the rest of his arm seemed fine. He wondered when the pain would set in, when the slow ache would consume his shoulder. He knew he was lucky it was a Friday. Jack could fight off huge men, he could train every day of the week, could stomach the sight of death but concrete was something he couldn't beat, it was like time; unbreakable and unbeatable.

Once he was finished changing Jack headed out into the gym and immediately caught Jason's eye. There was no time for stretching, he was too late already. Jason waved, finished talking to the trainee he had just been deep in conversation with only moments earlier and walked over to Jack.

"Hey Bud, how was the run over?"

"Good, how did you know I ran here?"

"You burst into my gym like the fires of hell were hot on your tail."

Jack was about to say, they always are, but then thought better of it. The fires of hell had been hot on his tail from the first moment he had closed his eyes, turned his head, and squeezed. The speed of his entrance had nothing to do with the fires of hell nipping at his pant legs. If he had crawled through the gym doors as slow as a tortoise, they still would be hot on his trail.

"I was running late so I had to hurry, I ate shit on the way here just outside of building."

"Are you okay?"

"Yeah, fine," Jack said, even though he wasn't sure that he was. His shoulder had begun to ache, just as he knew it would.

"Perfect, well you're here now and that's all that matters. Nice haircut by the way."

Jack almost forgot about his new cut. He almost laughed and made some amusing remark about the price he paid for it but decided not to. He hated showing off the blood money, he had come to terms with the fact that he had it, but he hadn't come to terms with the way he received it. Jack much preferred hiding in the shadows like a dangerous invisible force. The tactic had always worked for him so he knew he shouldn't change it up now.

The rest of the session went by as per usual. Jason introduced a few new moves and Jack mastered a few others that Jason had showed him in the past weeks. Jack felt quite confident with his progress and was a close to positive as a person could be that he would be able to beat ninety percent of the population in a fight, but Jason always said confidence was the greatest weakness a person could possess; so, he contained it, focusing on learning. Twenty minutes before the end of the session Jason asked Jack if he wanted to box another trainee just for some 'extra exposure'.

Jack was reluctant to say yes because of his important function the next night plus the fact that he hadn't boxed in a while, but in the end he agreed. He wanted to be ready if Paul gave him a call before the function—or later that night—and he was in the mood for a fight. If for no other reason than to knock the rust off. Jason called a student over that was training by himself in the corner. His name was Frank. He was about Jack's height and built well. Not as strong as Jack but close. Frank hungrily looked Jack up and down and agreed to the fight, they put their gloves and helmets on, removed their shirts then stepped into the ring. Once the two men had tapped gloves and backed away from each other Jason said in a firm voice—unlike Paul's slow drawl that reeked of bloodlust—"Begin."

Frank was dripping confidence, circling Jack like a wolf pack circling a lone doe; He must have just recently joined the gym, because everyone at the gym had heard about Jack's reputation by now. Frank swung first; A sluggish shot meant for Jack's ribs, which Jack dodged easily. Jack looked into his opponent's eyes and was puzzled by Frank's confidence or was it naivety? Jack couldn't be sure. Either way Jack wanted to let him know who he was. After the next assault, Jack slapped his arm away and parried with a heavy hook that connected with Frank's ribs. He looked into his Franks eyes seeing if they had lost their hunger, they hadn't. If it was possible, they had gained intensity.

It was the first fight that Jack had been involved in which his opponent hadn't lost their mojo as soon as he connected his first blow. The ego he was supposed to keep locked in a safe was bruised, just like his shoulder had been earlier. Only this time the weapon was indifference rather than cement. Jack saw the intensity in Frank's eyes burn strong and he slammed his left fist into Frank's right rib cage, then drove his right fist into Frank's left temple and slammed his left fist into Frank's opposite temple. As the blow recoiled, he stepped back, waiting for the inevitable thud of skull connecting with floor but it never came. Frank's legs swayed, and his eyes went blank for a split second, then as if someone had relit the flame, Frank's eyes burnt with stronger intensity than before, almost setting Jack's own eyes on fire.

If Jack was going to snuff the flame completely, he was going to have to hit Frank even harder, quite possibly as hard as he hit the mountain of a man in the damp basement room all those days ago. Frank swung a few more times but despite the fire that burnt in his eyes, his fists carried very little heat. Jack applauded the man on his perseverance in the face of certain loss, but he couldn't have his reputation sullied by this red eyed nuisance. After Jack had swatted the last of Frank's valiant attempts to damage him away, he loaded all of his weight—which had now reached 170lbs, 10 more than when he had arrived in New York—into his right leg and then felt all the force travel from his toes to his quad, up to his hip then pivoted his upper body. Allowing the force to travel up his right ribs, into his unbruised shoulder, through his arm and into his fist., he connected flush with Frank's padded jaw. The force lifted Frank off his feet and the fires of intensity finally disappeared from his eyes. His body was sprawled on the canvas, lifeless. Jack didn't go over to check on him because he knew he would be back up; the intensity that resided in his eyes wouldn't let him sleep forever.

Jack unstrapped his helmet, took his gloves off, and said, "Is he new?"

"Yeah, he joined a few days ago but he has usually been coming in right when we open."

Jack was relieved he was new and wasn't just someone that saw through the snakeskin he wore at the gym; he had been wearing so many different disguises that he wasn't sure if he wore the right one at the proper times. The disguise he was supposed to be wearing when he was at the training gym was a confident, strong, ambitious man. Maybe Frank had seen through it to the scared, lonely, and small man he really was. Jason obviously hadn't seen through because he said, "He is probably the second-best client I have, you sure showed him that taking the Number one mantle is going to be a tough, almost impossible task. The funny thing though, is that Frank was the Highschool Boxing Champion in Maine three years ago. That uppercut is starting to get dangerous even with the gloves and padding. Barehand you are going to kill someone if you hit them that hard, you are going to have to be careful. I don't want you getting arrested. The moves I have taught you are definitely only to be used in life-or-death situations."

"I know, those moves you taught me might save my life one day though." Jack had allowed the word 'might' to slip from his lips, but he knew that one day they would save his life, *again*. There was no doubt about that. "Think Frank is going to be okay?"

"Yeah, he is tough he will recover, I don't know if he will be in the gym to train for a while or if he will ever say yes to fighting you again, but he will recover."

"I don't know about that; his eyes had an intensity that I have never seen before. Most other people would have hit the canvas after the first two head shots I landed." Jack knew that one hundred percent of the opponents he had faced would have at least fallen, after the first two head shots and would have lost their fire after the first rib shot. Frank however was different; he drove even harder.

"He is relentless, I'll give him that. Go shake his hand and then you can head home. Have a good weekend."

"Thanks Jason, you have a good weekend too," Jack said and then turned away to head in the direction of Frank who was sitting on the canvas, arms hanging over the last rung of the ropes. The fires in his eyes hadn't quite reached their earlier heights, and he had taken his helmet and gloves off. It made Jack feel like Paul, but such is war. Occasionally, by no fault of your own, you assume the shape of your enemy.

"You are the most relentless guy I have ever fought; you gained a lot of my respect tonight," Jack said and he meant it. Just the fact that Frank was able to force Jack to release his ego from its cage was a feat in itself.

"Thanks man, you hit so fucking hard. I wanted to quit after the first punch you landed," Frank said as he extended his hand to shake Jack's.

Jack shook it and as he did, realized that he may have just gained another ally. He wasn't sure that he could trust Frank quite yet, but Frank sure possessed the qualities of a good ally. Jack walked to the changeroom happy, or as happy as he could be with his armor as thick as it had to be those days.

When the elevator doors finally opened to his apartment, Jack dropped his gym bag by the door and took a quick shower. The cold water washed over him carrying the sweat and stench with it. Back in the kitchen, Jack put two medallion steaks on a pan and watched them sizzle as they cooked. Since Charlotte had told him that he may have a chance at getting out of the mud and finally be able to outrun the fires of hell he had been eating healthier. Jack knew he would have to be in peak physical condition if he was going to overcome Paul's tyranny and toaster oven pizza wasn't going to give him the upper hand.

Once the steaks were done Jack took a few tongs worth of salad out of the container of premade salad he had bought earlier that week, poured himself a glass of whiskey—he may have been eating better but the images of death couldn't be blurred by steak and salad—and sat down on the couch. He turned the TV, the New York Rangers were playing the Edmonton Oilers. He hadn't been a big fan of hockey or any sport other than boxing and sure didn't like watching any kind sports, but he was too tired to change the channel.

Jack had asked the taxi driver to be back at half past nine to go and pick up his custom suit. He hadn't paid the driver but had left his purchases in the car as collateral. So, Jack hoped the driver didn't just take the shoes and belt and return them at the store for cash. The payout would be less than what Jack had promised but it would surely be more than he would usually make in a day.

Jack's alarm rang at 9:25pm just as Jack had set it to; He grabbed his coat, slipped his shoes on, and walked into the elevator. The moment of truth had arrived, if the driver was waiting it meant he didn't steal the shoes and belt and if he wasn't, Jack would have to head back to the stores the next day. To his surprise, when the steel doors opened Jack saw the driver waiting outside in the cold to open the back door of the taxi. He could be trusted, or at least be trusted when $5000 hung in the balance.

"Good evening, sir," The driver said politely, opening the door as he spoke.

"How was your evening…?" Jack wondered what the driver's name was, he had never asked but it didn't seem necessary anymore he would only have two more rides with the man anyways. With that Jack hopped into the cab and let the driver shut the door for him when he was safely inside. As the door shut, he felt a twinge of regret, maybe Charlotte was a good person. Maybe he was wrong to be weary of her. After all, Jack wouldn't have let anyone open or shut the door for him a month ago. He would have been the one to open and shut doors for the people who saw themselves above him but as he lived the life of wealth, he saw that money can change anyone. Obscene wealth and the people that facilitated its possession were the real enemy, Jack had to focus on that. He had to set his sights on the dismantling of the hierarchy of wealth, not just saving himself from hells prison.

"Back to the tailors sir?"

"Yes, please. My name is Jack by the way, I would rather you call me by my name rather than that disgusting term. What's your name?" Jack felt like he was telling the man off for swearing, just like his mother had but it didn't make his insides squirm as they did when he was called 'Sir'.

"Yes, sorry sir, I mean Jack. My name is Lucien."

"Good to meet you, Lucien. Before we head off, I wanted to make sure you had a card reader. If you don't, I will also have to stop at a bank or an ATM."

"I have a card reader, would you like to pay now or later, Jack."

"I can pay now if you would like." Lucien handed Jack a portable card terminal. Jack looked at it, the number was already inputted, $5000 dollars. "Does all the money go in your pocket?"

"Yeah, I only have the one cab right now, but this is my own company."

"Sounds good," Jack said as he pressed the OK button and a tip option popped up, so Jack pressed the number value button, after all was the point of having unlimited funds other than to pass it on to others. Jack typed $145,000

135

dollars in the number value section. The tip brought the total amount owed to $150,000. Which was more money than Jack would have known what to do with in his old life but in his new, red painted life he had spent so much more than $150,000 and would inevitably spend even greater amounts in his tenure with the GWA.

Once he inputted his tab, Jack handed the terminal back to Lucien. In any other life he would have felt the warm fulfilled feeling one usually does when they do a good deed for someone else but in this instance, he didn't feel even the distant warmth of glowing embers. The blood dripping from every cent created an ice-cold barrier between good and evil. Paul had successfully sucked the good out of giving. No matter what you said about Paul, he was phenomenal at achieving his goals. He may have been the best employee since the creation of jobs. After a few minutes had passed, Jack realized that the taxi hadn't moved an inch, he sat forward in his seat, "Are you okay Lucien?"

There was no response, just silence. Worry grew in Jack's chest, had the card been declined? Had Lucien died? Jack stuck his head into the front seat, Lucien sat in his seat clutching the terminal in his hands, just staring at the receipt that protruded from the top.

"Is there an issue?"

"Nnnn…No. Did you accidentally tip me $145,000 dollars?"

"No, I meant to do that. I wanted to thank you for your service, just don't go around telling too many people about it. I know it's a shock and I don't mean to sound insensitive, but I really need to get to the tailors before 10."

Jack knew he did a good thing, but he still couldn't summon any emotion toward his own generosity. Lucien came to his senses quickly, tossing the terminal in the passenger seat, throwing the taxi into gear, and tearing off into the night.

"Thank you, Jack. Your generosity will not be forgotten, I promise you," Lucien said and then turned and stared out the front window for the rest of the trip.

The silence let Jack think about things, his predicament, his possible way out but most of all what he would do if he ever got out of the employ of the GWA. He knew he wasn't going to go back to Maine, he had been away too long, it wouldn't feel like home anymore. Jack had lived too many lives since then. Too many lives had come and gone since he was genuinely happy. Medora was off the list as well, but he had always been fond of the mountains and the fresh air they afforded. Maybe northern Wyoming, in a small cabin underneath the mountains was where he would settle. He didn't know if he would even be afforded a choice of where to live, surviving seemed to be the predominant issue at hand but no one can stop themselves from dreaming.

"Jack?"

"Yes?" Jack said snapping out of the haze he had been in.

"We have arrived."

"Thanks, I shouldn't be too long. Can you wait for me?"

"Of course, I will wait all night if need be." Jack smiled and thanked Lucien once more.

Jack stepped out into the night, holding the bag containing his shoes and belt, and walked toward the ominous steps for the second time that day. He walked slowly down the steps willingly accepting the shadows determination to swallow him whole before he turned the creaky doorknob and stepped into the damp room. Jack walked cautiously to the desk and rung the bell. He knew the tailor was a good man, his eyes gave it away but the shop still scared him. Maybe it was his time in New York that had changed him but the ominous stairs that leading into the damp room reminded him too much of the office's basement for him to stay calm.

Gabriel emerged from behind the curtain with a neutral expression that broke out into a beaming smile when he realized it was Jack. His blue eyes sparkled, and warmed Jack's frost covered soul as they gazed upon him.

"Jack!" He exclaimed. "Good to see you, I finished your suit only moments ago. I see you got a haircut; it suits you."

Jack forced his mouth into a fake smile, but he didn't feel like it did 'suit him'. Although he thoroughly enjoyed the responses, he was getting from everyone, at the very least it was worth the money he had spent. "Would you like to try the suit on; Just to make sure it fits before you buy it?" Jack knew that he would buy it either way, but it wouldn't hurt to try on.

"Sure," he said. Gabriel removed his coat for him and hung it on a rack that seemed to appear at his command, telling Jack he could go behind the curtain to change. Jack obliged and walked up to the curtain hesitantly pushing it aside. The curtains swung together behind him, but Jack didn't notice. He was transfixed by the suit in front of him, it was perfect. Gabriel had plucked the image right out of his head and sewn it into fruition. Keeping his eyes trained on the suit—scared that if he took his eyes away, it would disappear—he pulled his shirt off, kicked his shoes to the side and dropped his pants to his ankles. He carefully grabbed the shirt off the hanger it was neatly hung on, slid it around his shoulders and buttoned it up slowly.

Unbuttoning the pants, he slid them off the mannequin, and pulled them gently up his own legs. After he had tucked the shirt into them, he buttoned them up, strung his new belt through the loops and buckled it up. They fit perfectly. Jack gently shed the jacket from the mannequin and laid it on the table behind, unbuttoning the vest he slid it around his shoulders. After he realized he hadn't put the tie on yet, he flipped up the shirt collar, strung it around his neck and looked for a mirror. He found one hanging halfway up the wall to the right side of the curtains. After a few tries, he got it tied perfectly and went back to the table and poked the tie pin through his collar and tie. He noticed the two roses sat nicely on either side of the collar, as if Gabriel had melted the steel to fit.

Next, he buttoned the vest up, tucking the tie underneath and took both cuff links in his right hand and fixed them to the crisp cuffs. Jack knew some people would look at them and see vanity, but he didn't mind, he was the only one who needed to know their true meaning. After Jack was sure they were fixed snugly, he slid his arm through the right sleeve of the jacket followed by the left and then arched his back, as if cocking the hammer of a gun back and then unloaded by throwing his shoulders back into place and felt the jacket fall into position on top of his shoulders. Jack fixed the jacket's position until he was satisfied and then bent down and removed the shoes from their box, stepped in, tied the laces, and walked back to the curtains, pushing them out of his way as he walked through.

"It fits me like a glove, thank you, Gabriel."

"Don't thank me, You're the one that fills the fabric with its life. Come with me," he said leading Jack to the far-right corner of the room, opening a door which led to nothing but had a mirror on its flip side. Jack stood speechless; he looked like a new man. A worthy, successful, and confident man who knew who he was. It was all a big show but nevertheless; Jack reveled in his appearance. The suit even brought out the drop of green in his eyes. The suit may have been just another disguise, but it felt more like his true skin than any of the other skins he had shed or climbed into over the last few weeks.

After he stared at himself for a few minutes, he thanked Gabriel again and headed into the change room to shed the suit. When he had finished, Gabriel went into the back room and packed the suit into a beautiful leather suit bag and emerged with it and the belt and shoes that Jack had forgotten. He laid the suit on the table, handed the bag containing the shoes and belt to Jack and started typing numbers into the same terminal that Lucien had in his taxi then handed it to Jack. The number on the screen was $10,000. A small price to pay for the perfect disguise. Jack pressed OK just as he had done earlier and stuck his card inside to see the tip option pop up once again, Jack pressed the familiar dollar value. Then typed $100,000 into the machine and then entered his pin and handed the machine back to Gabriel. APPROVED, illuminated the tiny screen and he picked up both his bags, thanked Gabriel again and walked toward the door.

His left toes were barely out the door when Gabriel said, "I'll be seeing you, Jack. Your next suit will be even better."

Jack smiled, letting the blue in Gabriel's eyes warm his soul a while longer before allowing the shadows to swallow him whole.

Chapter 13

Jack fell deeper and deeper into the void. The darkness gently nudging him further into the vast space filled with pure nothingness. Then, as if an atomic bomb had exploded beneath him, he was shot back to consciousness. The familiar sound of air raid sirens rang around his room, bouncing off the walls allowing thoughts, memories, and pain to rush back through his synapses. Jack opened his eyes and immediately cringed at the sunlight beaming through the window burning his irises. He instinctively closed them again to shield them from the painful sensation.

After a few minutes in the adjusting period, Jack sat up, threw some clothes on and walked slowly out of his room. Most of the previous day's memories flooded back to him, he suddenly remembered his purchases and quickly turned around to check his closet for the suit, shoes, and belt. He found them laying on the table in the middle of the massive closet and breathed a sigh of relief but as he thought about it, he wondered how they had gotten there. He recalled getting back in the taxi and arriving back at his building, clutching his new disguise in his hands as the elevator carried him to the apartment but after the sight of the elevator opening and his apartment coming into view, he had nothing. The next memory he had was pitch-black nothingness, the peaceful falling sensation and the shot back to reality.

He was at a complete loss; the time hadn't just been blurred but instead erased without so much as a bread trail. Whatever the cause was, it hadn't even left fragments of hazy memories. Up to that point in his life he had never felt something so surreal, so unexplainable. The world-shattering fear of unexplained time—time in which he could have revealed secrets, time in which he could have written his own death sentence—washed over him like a bucket of syrup. It encased his entire body, acting like an impermeable membrane.

He checked his phone, no outgoing calls, no texts, nothing. At least, there was solace in the fact that the only way he could have breached his own walls was if there had been another person with him in his apartment. He looked around his room, in his closet, the bathroom, office, couch, kitchen, and he even looked on the balcony but there wasn't another living soul in the apartment. Of course, they could have slipped away in the hours he had been asleep but Jack decided that he wouldn't dwell on what he could no longer change. He knew the only course of action was to go on with his day as if the lost time was filled with smells, rough surfaces, images, sounds and the bitter aftertaste of life.

However, there wasn't much to do, not much to take his mind off the case of the lost time. It was Saturday, only one workout to complete but other than that he had no other obligations. At least, until 8 o'clock that was. Paul usually called around 8 and Jack had a feeling that he had something planned for that night. Jack had denied a direct offer to accompany the boss to a very important event, that type of disrespect would not go unnoticed.

When Jack returned from the gym, he stood still, surrounded by the safe walls of the elevator a few moments more than he should have. He was drenched in sweat and still very concerned about the missing hours. Even if a tunnel the size of a mouse was bore though the thick cement, the entire wall would fall, effectively revealing every lie he had ever told, every guarded secret and every dark desire. The workout had released most of the tension and anxiety from Jack's body, but he knew it would not be able to completely rid his conscious thought of the sinking, breath stealing intuition that in some way he had revealed something. The fleeting power that surged through his veins after a workout staved off the insecurities and doubts that Jack had always been burdened with, he imagined it was the sole reason he kept up the routine as long as he had but it would not be able to safeguard him against a massive breach of trust.

Drink was usually the only substance or activity that could unfurl his white knuckled fingers from the steering wheel it held so tight in times like the one he was experiencing but it was too early for a drink. So, he instead headed for the shower.

Jack stood perfectly still as he allowed the warm shower water to wash over his head, flow over his eyes, continue down his body, overtop the red sun—that seemed to have become a part of his body, no longer foreign, still out of place and contrasting but very much a piece of his being—and down to the drain. He wished he could just decline his invitation to Founders function but too much was riding on his presence. If he ran now Charlotte would be left to atone for his disloyalty, Dr. Confucius would be stood up and angry therefore less likely to be sympathetic to Jack's cause and about 100 other potential scenarios could play out. Plus, there was the added bonus that the GWA would never let him stop running once he started. Eventually it would be his head covered by a black hood, his hands and feet bound, and his own consciousness stripped from his body like the last shred of his dignity.

It would also force another poor soul to become a murderer, cause another to be burdened by a red medallion and could result in yet another prominent young writer committing suicide. Jack knew running was not an option, the only viable path was straight through the front gate. Jack understood that if he wished to be successful in his endeavor to break down the walls of the GWA and end Paul's reign, he needed to have a missile in his arsenal strong enough to obliterate the gates of hell. However, evil is masterful in the art of creating impenetrable fortresses fortified from every angle or method of attack.

Any attack against evil, no matter what shape or form it takes, is sure to be met with the same, if not a greater, level of force. Jack needed a very powerful missile that would hopefully result in a checkmate even before it needed to be fired and he knew if Confucius was the man he thought him to be, he would be a perfect candidate.

As Jack turned the shower dial to the off position, he realized that night was the night he could change his fate, or at least paint some white back over his blood-stained canvas. As he got dressed, he decided once and for all that the only course of action was to prepare for the night the best he could. He would try to think of every question or situation and attempt to ensure that his disguise was impervious to any form of attack.

He headed into the kitchen to make some breakfast and check on one last hunch. Jack opened the fridge, removed the eggs and bacon, placed them in their respective pans and turned the burners on. Once he was sure they were both cooking properly he raised his arm slowly to where he usually kept the whiskey. Before he left to pick up his suit from Gabriel, there was an unopened 1750ml bottle of Crown Royal and half a bottle of the same size. As Jack grasped the handle, preparing to open the cupboard he prayed there was at least a quarter of the half empty bottle left, or at least hoped the unopened bottle hadn't been touched.

Opening the door slowly he peered inside, the half-opened bottle was completely dry. Not an ounce of whiskey left, but the unopened bottle remained sealed, and Jack was thankful for that. At least he knew the criminal responsible for abducting time, it was about 30oz of Canadian Whiskey. All that was left to ensure was the gaurentee that the alcohol wasn't responsible for the crumbling of his walls. There really were two things he should be focusing on, but he never gave much thought to what was clearly the most underlying factor to all of his problems.

Jack tossed the real problem in the garbage section of his long-term memory and returned to the eggs and bacon. The eggs had begun to turn white instead of their natural transparent nature and the bacon had begun to pop and bubble. He placed some toast into the slots in the toaster and waited.

Before long, the bacon, eggs, and toast were ready. Jack poured himself some orange juice—it was still too early for whiskey—and headed to the couch. He flipped the TV on and started planning his day, or rather his night. He would set an alarm to go off at 6:30pm, when it rang, he would begin to get ready; shower, shave—but make sure to leave a little stubble around his mouth—fix his hair, cut his nails, put cream on his face and step into his first disguise of the evening. After he had put his usual work suit on, he would sit and wait until Paul called or until 11:00pm, which was when the second alarm he had set, was slated to go off. When the clock rang 11:00, whether Paul called or not, he would change into the green suit, buckle his new belt, tie his new laces, slide the pin through his new tie and affix the cuff links to the new shirt.

It was the only faux skin he had worn up to that point that displayed most of what was underneath in the clearest, truth filled light. It was only possession he had acquired since coming to NYC that reflected the man he was before the evil branded him as its very own cow.

As each second passed Jack checked his phone or the oven clock, expecting an hour to have passed, but it was only ever 5 or 6 minutes. That day each minute felt like an eternity, the weight of the evenings preceding's weighed heavy on his soul. Jack wished Charlotte would have never told him who the doctor was. He wished he could have arrived at the function completely oblivious but since the first time he had laid eyes on Charlotte, she had stolen things from him. It started with his breath and escalated quickly to his innocence.

Each time he saw her she took another piece of it, like she was trying to rebuild her own broken soul by repurposing pieces of his. Only Jack knew that's not how innocence works. Just like the world's natural resources, when innocence is gone it is gone forever, replaced by the calloused scar tissue of experience. When a soldier returns from war, they don't forget the images, situations or mud they had been stuck in. They just have to find a way to live with the pain and Jack was a solider in every sense of the word, the only difference was that he was fighting his war on the battlefield of New York's underworld instead of a dusty desert far across vast oceans. The images, pains and callouses he was being forced to pin to his uniform would never leave, they may fade and cause less fear with time—that was if he was able to stop creating more—but they would never drop out of his consciousness completely. While he stared at the TV, fake scenarios, death and anxiety gyrated in throngs through his mind, until the familiar sound of air raid sirens blared from his phone's speakers. Half past six.

Legs numb with fear, Jack shakily stood up and walked to the shower, the first step of the plan had begun. Icy cold water splashed over his head running down his body until he finally turned the tap off and the water stopped flowing out of the shower head. Jack dried himself off and wrapped the towel around his waist. He grabbed the nail clippers from the drawer, placed the sharp teeth around his nail and began to clip, the excess nails began to build up in the sink, forming a mountain of imperfections. Once all the nails were perfect—even his toenails—he shaved the excess hair that had grown along his jaw and down his neck.

He was careful not to cut any of the stubble around his mouth. He wanted to convey the look of perfection but still needed to keep a little piece of his old self intact because he was scared if he shaved all of his former self from existence, he would never be able to find it again. Once his face matched the picture he had in his mind, he lathered his hands in paste and forced his hair into the perfect shape just as Angelo did. Once he was sure it looked identical to how it had when Angelo styled it, he wiped the excess paste off his hands and generously administered a healthy layer of cream on his face, brushed his teeth and exited the bathroom. He walked down the hall, into his room and further into the closet.

Looking around at the generic suits Charlotte had picked out, he chose the grey pinstriped suit, matching pants, black shoes, black belt, white shirt, and a

144

black tie. He decided he didn't want to wear green when he went into the office anymore. It didn't fit and no matter what he wore Paul wouldn't be any less evil and his job wouldn't entail any less sin. Jack knew that the only course of action he could take at work would be to complete the task as fast and efficiently as possible. Ensure that he lived another day and ensure that every one of the men that Paul forced him to punish would be awarded a quick, painless death.

Jack didn't know how he would cope if he was forced to kill a man slowly. The pain he would feel from carrying out such a purely evil act would surely be greater than any pain he could ever administer or had ever received, other than his mother's death. Jack finished getting dressed, went to the mirror and wrapped the tie around his neck—compared to the first time, he had become an expert—and went to the kitchen to pour a drink. As the amber liquid filled the bottom inch of the tumbler, his phone began to ring. Jack let it ring three whole times before he flipped it over to check the caller ID. Paul. He slid the phone icon across the screen and spoke, "Yes sir?"

"Did you have a good week?"

"Yes sir, how was your week?" The words left his moth with a sour aftertaste. Jack didn't care how Paul's week was, he wouldn't care if the man dropped dead in front of his own mother. Jack didn't know if Paul ever saw his own mother but if he did, the very idea that Paul could look into his mother's eyes after all the evil he had brought into the world was unthinkable. Just the thought of it made Jack squirm as if worms were trying to eat their way through his heart.

"Good, good. Mine was fine. I have a job for you tonight. The car will take you straight to the warehouse. It will be there in 5 minutes; will you be ready?"

"Yes, sir I will be waiting in the lobby."

"Good," As the final syllable slipped into Jack's ear, he heard the line go silent. Paul had hung up, but Jack didn't mind. Jack actually preferred the white noise; Paul's voice stirred the anger that always sat deep in his heart. He had been given five minutes, time enough to finish his drink. The alcohol would be just strong enough to take the edge off. The alcohol would endow just enough haze to allow Jack to carry out the deed. He didn't sip slowly, Jack took two massive gulps and gently placed the cup on the counter, stood up and walked to the steel doors. Grabbing the leather coat on his way into the elevator he stepped in and steeled himself for the first difficult task of the night. Steadying his breathing he prepared his soul to carry the weight of another sin, another occupant of the red sun.

The black car pulled up to the curb just as Jack stepped out of the elevator, unlike Lucien, the driver did not get out of the car to open the door for Jack. There was no respect shown to him by the man. It probably meant that he placed himself higher up in the hierarchy of the GWA than Jack was, but it could also mean he didn't respect people that killed others. Not even those under the fear of being killed themselves. Jack didn't think he would ever get the chance to find out, but crazier things had happened.

Jack walked past Angela without saying a word, pushed the front doors open and felt the cold sting his cheeks. Opening the door, he climbed into the car and shut it behind him. The black car pulled away from the curb and sped off toward the warehouse. The well-lit streets faded away and all that remained were the ominous streets that lead to the warehouse. It was nestled in a neighborhood that didn't care if gun shots rang out or if screams echoed off its buildings. The neighborhood welcomed the evil like an old friend. Jack couldn't help but wonder if it had always been like that, coated in a film of tears and blood or if it had once emitted laughter and exemplified what it meant to be a community.

He wondered if at one time the only blood spilt was from a child's skinned knee or flowed from the socket of a missing tooth. Unlike the blood that was spilt each night at the warehouse, that type of blood shed could be fixed with a bandage, or an innocent dollar bill slid under a sleeping child's pillow. As the car slowed and stopped in front of the imposing, black building of death, he lost all faith in the fantasy but if the Man in Red or Paul had never heard his name, he too wouldn't be in his current predicament. Maybe the same was to be said about the neighborhood.

The gravel was uneven underneath Jack's feet as he walked toward the left side of the building. As he had on each one of other instances Jack had stood in the large buildings shadow, the two guards stood unmoving on both sides of the door. They pushed the door open as Jack walked toward them and once he was inside he heard the door close violently behind him. Paul stood only a few feet in front of the door and Jack approached slowly, not wanting to startle or anger him in any way.

"Sir?" Jack said posing the word as a question, but he really meant, 'What the fuck do you need me to do, you cock sucker?' Although if he had said it the way he meant it he would surely be hurt, maybe even killed.

"Hanson! Good to see you son, I've got a treat for you tonight."

Son. Jack felt white hot anger bubble inside of him, as the words entered his ears. The pair walked further into the room Jack realized there was no black table, no hooded man and no goliath standing behind the chair of death. In its place, there was an octagon of mats and a plexiglass cage around it with only a small chain link door allowing entry. A man sat inside; he was taller than Jack but at a glance Jack saw that he had much less muscle mass. The man was very clearly awake, eyes wide with fear, hands bound with a large zip tie and duct tape covering his mouth.

So many questions flooded Jack's mind, but he stopped them from leaving his lips, Paul would surely have an explanation followed by instructions. "We ran out of anesthesia and to be honest I want this one to suffer anyways. I'm not going to tell you what his crime was, but I promise you that the sentence is justified in this circumstance. You will have to incapacitate him before you can kill him, which shouldn't be a problem for you, but I need you to hit him at least 5 times before you rob him of his consciousness. It's imperative that they be hard hits, bone breaking hits. Once you have hit him 5 times you can knock him out and when I make sure he is out cold, I will give you a gun in which to conclude his…transaction."

Of course, they didn't run out of anything. It was his punishment. The denial of a 'kind' offer, undoubtedly had to be met with severe consequences. "Sounds good to me sir. Where should I put my clothes?"

A guard walked over with a chair and Paul waved his arm as if to say, there, put your clothes there. Jack began to undress and once his pants and underwear were the last articles of clothing left, Paul walked into the cage, cut the restraints from the man's hands, and ripped the tape off his mouth. The man jumped to his feet quickly and began to plead with Paul, "Don't. I will make it right. Don't do this," Paul didn't show an ounce of empathy. His heart had been removed long ago. A void of darkness filled with money, blood lust and power-hungry violence now sat in its place.

"Get in there Hanson, and if you go easy, I will know. Just so you know the price for sympathy is the same as if you stole from me."

147

Jack already knew that and wasn't about to allow this man to destroy the last shred of respect Paul held for him but secretly he hoped the man fought back as hard as he could, it would make him feel less guilt for what was about to happen. Jack walked shakily toward the entrance and stepped in, Paul shut the door and slid the dead bold across. Jack stood facing the man, his shirt had been stripped from his body, obviously by force. The fabric burns on his neck sat as irrefutable evidence of that altercation.

The man was more muscular than Jack had observed earlier but still looked like a skinny little girl compared to him. The man's eyes cut into Jack's soul with the same pleading look that a dog looks at his owner when he is about to leave the house for the day. The look of pure, innocent desire. The man's eyes threatened explode Jack's heart into a million pieces, but the tractor beam of guilt was broken by Paul's voice which had morphed into a slow, hungry drawl, "Begin."

Jack moved his weight onto the balls of his feet, moving purposely around the cage. The pleading looks quickly left the victims eyes, all that was left in its place was pure desperation. Jack decided that the only way he would be able to hit this man 5 times before knocking him out or worse, would be to focus on the area below his head, broken arms, ribs and collarbones would make Paul happy. Plus, Jack also had to take his later commitment in mind, if he got hit and it created a visible mark, he would have to explain to Dr. Confucius what happened. He couldn't jeopardize his escape plan just for this criminal.

The man had obviously committed some crime, he deserved it Jack said to himself. A multitude of reassurances played over and over in Jack's mind as he circled. Once a minute had passed Jack decided, there was no use delaying the inevitable, He loaded all his weight into his legs and allowed it to travel to his fist and then aimed the force at the man's ribs, the man wasn't ready for the attack and his right ribs snapped with a sickening crunch. Jack loaded again and snapped the man's left ribs. The man stumbled back and screamed in pain.

Jack spun the broken torso around; time would only cause the man more pain and would only add to the file folder of screams that would inevitably ring in Jack's ears for weeks if not the rest of his life. The 5 hits had to be delivered quickly. He lifted the man's arm, delivered a devastating uppercut into the man's armpit, dislodging the man's shoulder from its socket. The screams continued and the man feebly tried to hit Jack with his right hand, but it was no use. Jack drew away and then began to run toward the man and jumped off the ground, driving a superman punch into the man's other shoulder, hard enough to release another blood curdling scream but not hard enough to separate the man's shoulder. 4 blows had been delivered but there was still one more left.

He decided to make sure the man's head was in the right spot so that when his knockout blow connected it would surely leave the man unconscious on the mat and effectively end his suffering. Jack placed his hand on the man's back, no longer in fear of being struck and slammed his fist into the man's stomach. As the air was stolen from his lungs, he doubled over.

His one, relatively unhurt arm pushed against his knee propping him up, keeping him from toppling over but also leaving his head in the perfect place for Jack to remove him from the world of pain he had introduced him to. Jack loaded all of weight into his right leg and felt the power build as it traveled up his quad, into his hips and at that point he pivoted, warping all the force into downward punch that connected at the man's temple and sent him flying into the ground. His head bounced off the floor with a merciful thud.

The sounds of clapping entered Jack's ears and he turned to see Paul clapping and behind him the guards' faces were plastered with looks of astonishment, or fear, Jack couldn't quite tell. Paul unbolted the door and walked in the cage, resting his hand on Jack's shoulder, "That's exactly what I was looking for Hanson! It's incredible when something you have played in your head so many times comes into reality and it's even better when it's performed better than you could have ever imagined. Great fucking work, that piece of shit deserved it."

"It should have been you. You're the embodiment of the devil. Horns should be protruding from your skull any day now," Jack whispered noiselessly to himself. "Here," Paul said handing Jack the same revolver he had used to carry out the first unthinkable deed Paul had forced him to commit. Jack took the cold steel in his hand and couldn't help but fantasize about ending Paul's life right there. Right there in that moment he could've ended all the evil, but he stopped himself, telling himself that Paul's day would come soon enough. He pointed the gun at the poor unconscious man that was sprawled on the mat.

Blood was slowly seeping out of the pressure wound Jack had inflicted just above his temple creating a small stream of thick, red life. He curled his finger around the trigger, closed his eyes, turned his head and squeezed. The shot echoed around the warehouse. Opening his eyes, Jack saw the hole that had been cleared just below the pressure wound, the blood left his face and his legs felt like the wiggly pencils kids buy at a book fair. He was barely able to hold his weight, but he pushed the urge to vomit deep down, handed Paul the gun and asked if he was done for the night.

"Yeah, you earned at least a few weeks off tonight. That was a show! God, I wish I got that on camera! I could watch that repeat all day long!"

Jack forced a thank you out of his mouth and got dressed again. It was only the beginning of the night, he had to keep himself together. After he got home from the Founders function, he could wallow in self-hate. He promised himself he would drink himself to sleep with only the screams to keep him company later that night.

Once Jack was finished getting dressed, he walked swiftly to the iron door, not wanting to spend any more time than what was required in the vile place. Behind him he heard the body of the poor man he had just traded his life for being dragged along the concrete. Guilt had begun to strangle him and the air in the warehouse was becoming too thin. Jack felt himself losing consciousness. Stumbling to the door he fell through the doorway stopping his head from plunging into the unforgiving gravel with his outstretched hands.

After a few minutes, the fresh air started to circulate through his lungs and reinstated his consciousness, he stood up slowly and brushed the dirt off his hands. During the fight he was worried the man would hit him. He was scared about the fact that he would have to explain why he was bruised but instead it was his own guilt that had left deep cuts in his hands. His own guilt that was to blame for the explanation he would have to make later that evening.

It was an impossible choice. Allow the man to hit him and explain why some part of his face was bruised or avoid being hit and instead let the crippling guilt of not giving the man at least a chance to win the fight cloud his vision and block all rational thought. Impossible choices seemed to be the only choices presented to Jack in those days. No matter which way he turned there was always a fight, ultimatum, or fake personality he had to choose from. There wasn't a single choice Jack felt happy about making, but that was the nature of the life he had chosen the day Charlotte presented the first opportunity.

If he wanted to enjoy his life once again, he would have to keep pushing forward. He took a deep breath, wiped his bloodied hands on his pants and walked to the waiting car, opened the door, and told the driver he would like to be brought to his apartment. As he sat in silence watching the dark streets turn into kinder, more welcoming ones he thought that no matter how bad the evening was, one good thing had come of it. He had been given a few weeks off because of his 'memorable' performance, Jack knew he had to focus on the positives because the negatives would just result in him passing out, allowing alcohol to steal more hours of his life or something worse. Something he couldn't take back or recover from.

Chapter 14

Jack stepped off the elevator and into his apartment. His hands burned, knuckles ached, and soul was shattered. He kicked off his shoes and headed straight for the liquor cabinet, poured himself what was sure to be a quintuple shot of whiskey and walked to the couch, letting the pieces of his broken soul sink into its plush embrace. He didn't have the strength to take his suit off yet, the soul crushing physical and emotional pain still had a firm grasp on the wheel. Jack sipped the whiskey slowly, feeling every ounce of sweet amber liquid flow down his throat. Half the glass of whiskey was gone by the time he mustered up the strength to pull his phone from his pocket and check for texts. There was only one, from an unknown number.

U: Be outside your building at 11:30pm. A car will be waiting.

It was an odd message. Jack knew it couldn't be from Paul because Jack had already saved his number in his phone. It had to be from the Founders, but he didn't give Confucius his phone number and as far as he knew Confucius wasn't in touch with anyone that did have his number. None of it made sense. He decided to text Charlotte and ask her if she had gotten a text but then thought against it. She wouldn't have gotten an invite; she was just a plus one. The yin to the Man in Red's very dangerous yang. Instead, he decided to text her and ask if the plan was still a go. He needed to reassure himself that she hadn't gone back on the whole plan. He needed to reassure himself that she could at least be slightly trustworthy. He was sure that she was most likely someone he could trust but there was still a shadow of doubt hiding in the thorn filled bushes of the GWA.

J: Plan still good for tonight?

Jack waited 5 minutes, checked his phone. Nothing. Was she okay? Was the plan still on? He had only texted her to assure himself; he didn't honestly believe that something was wrong. To calm his nerves, he stood up shakily and swallowed the rest of the contents of his glass in one gulp. Then headed to the kitchen to make one more drink before he stopped, at least until after the meeting.

Or was it a function? A party? Jack wasn't sure what the gathering would entail. Was it a board room meeting? Was it a large party with dancing and drinks, or was it some sort of secret society where one member gets up in front of the entire room full of people and talks about the future in an ominous monotone? The uncertainty ate away at Jack's sanity, feeding an animal of chaos with each bite taken. It wasn't until he was halfway done the second glass of whiskey that his phone buzzed.

C: Still good on my end, U? Do you have a nice suit ready? Did u get the text from the Founders?

J: Perfect. Yeah, all good on my end! I bought a new one. I did get the text. Super weird!

C: Perfect! I've gotta get ready, see u at the party :)

Jack set his phone on the counter, his mind could finally rest or at least be free of that one stress. Charlotte was fine, the text had in fact been from the Founders and the plan was still a go. Only one question remained; What type of gathering would it be? Jack knew he would have to wait until he got there to find the answer to that question. Sipping his drink, Jack turned around and checked the time on the oven clock. 10:30pm. He had been glued to the couch for two hours. He didn't need to get ready quite yet but decided to take another shower. The cold water might be able to freeze the guilt, shame, and haunting memories until after the meeting, or whatever it was. It also might help his hands seal their wounds.

The cold water did the trick, Jack was wide awake. His wounds were clean and had begun to seal themselves and his guilt was frozen. At least, for the time being. For the second time in the last 4 hours, he willed his hair into perfect shape, lathered cream on his cheeks and waked into the closet to grab a suit. Only this time it was a suit he wanted to wear, a suit that knew who he really was. A suit that wasn't as much of a disguise but more of an extension of his skin.

Jack grabbed the bag that contained his shoes and belt and gently picked up the leather suit bag and headed back out into his room. He placed the new shoes and belt on the bed, unzipped the leather bag and gently removed the hanger that held his extensions. Jack slid the jacket off the hanger, laid it on the bed, unbuttoned the shirt and buttoned it back up on his own body. He softly slid the pants offthe hanger and carefully pulled them over his own legs as if they were made of tissue paper.

Once the shirt was tucked perfectly inside the pants, he buttoned them up and strung the belt through the forest green loops. The belt was buckled, socks were pulled up and shoes had been tied so Jack headed back into the closet to fasten the tie around his neck. Fat side of the tie on the right side of his body and the skinny side on the left he spun the fat end around the skinny end once and placed the fat end over the skinny end once again, strung the fat end between his neck and the knot that had begun to emerge.

As he strung the fat end through the knot, he tightened. Not hard enough to crease the fabric but just hard enough to create the perfect visual. Jack liked the monotony of getting ready because it drew his attention away from the fact that his entire life had been ignited by chaos's seductive smile. As he looked in the mirror at his handiwork, he felt a sense of pride. To the naked eye he looked like a man who had his life together and more than that he emitted success.

Even though it was all a massive illusion, he still took pride in his appearance, but it wasn't complete until the pin had been stuck though the knot and cuff links had been attached to their spots on the stiff cuffs of his shirt. Once all the pieces were in place, all that was left was the jacket.

He slid his right arm then left through the sleeves and threw the collar onto his shoulders. "Nothing can touch me," he said to himself. Although he knew saying it to himself in his own apartment was one thing. Believing it was a completely different mountain he would be forced to climb very soon.

Jack walked back out into the kitchen, placed his phone in his pocket and checked the time on the oven clock. 11:15pm. 15 minutes until he needed to be downstairs. Time enough for one more small drink. Jack was never good at drinking a moderate amount after he had already started. The sweet, amber liquid flooded his stomach and let him feel a fleeting moment of happiness. That night signified his first step down a new path, he felt like a bush whacker, veering off the cleared path and forging his own that would hopefully end up in a field filled with flowers, green grass, blue skies and hopefully, her.

But Jack would settle for a crack house down a dark alley in the scariest slums the world had to offer as long as Paul was nowhere near, and she was there. The fantasy faded just like the temporary happiness, all that was left was a nervous buzz thinly laid atop the crippling guilt. 11:20pm. Pushing his feelings aside, he strode to the door, it was time to go. Nothing would stand in his way of freedom, not Paul, not Alexander and especially not the guilt that seemed determined to beat him into submission. His eyes shimmered with determination as the elevator doors opened to the lobby.

Jack stepped out and looked to the reception desk. Angela was completely asleep and snoring loudly. Jack stepped quietly past her, opened the front doors, and allowed the night chill to pierce his skin. A shimmering silver limo sat in front of building. It looked like it had been made by the gods of Olympus. The door swung open as Jack stepped within a meter of it. Jack chuckled as it slowly swung open, beckoning him forward into the folds of its wealth. Paul and the GWA were beggars in the street compared to the Founders. As Jack stepped into the limo the door gracefully closed behind him. The window between the driver and the passenger section rolled down and a man spoke, "Hello, Mr. Hanson. There is whiskey, champagne, rum, wine, and deodorant on the shelf. Take anything you want. It is about a 20-minute drive so feel free to drink or freshen up along the way."

Jack was stunned, he knew the voice. He couldn't place the exact location or date in time he had heard it, but he definitely had, that much he was sure of. Jack was beginning to say thank you, when the window closed before the words could escape his lips. Moments later a cabinet rose from the floor, shelves lined with everything the driver had promised as well as many more he hadn't mentioned. Jack grabbed the bottle labeled whiskey, pulled the stopper out and took a large swig and returned it to the shelf.

The bottle had no brand name but as he swirled it around his mouth Jack realized that it was Crown Royal, a fancy version but Crown Royal all the same. The sheer volume of facts the Founders knew about him worried Jack. He had talked to the Dr. for all of 5 minutes. Were they always watching like the party in George Orwell's 1984? If they were, how much did they know? The fear held Jack's mind hostage until the divider between the two slid down once again and the driver said, "We have arrived Mr. Hanson. Text '3' to the number that you received a text from earlier and I will be here in 5 minutes to take you, and anyone else you see fit, wherever you want to go."

Jack wasn't going to miss the window again, he said thank you as fast as he could before it rolled to a close. The driver said it was not a problem. The window rolled up once again and once it was completely closed the door Jack had entered through opened as gracefully as it could allowing Jack to leave through the portal it created in its absence. Standing on the curb, dwarfed by the goliath sized building, he buttoned the top button on his suit jacket and looked up. The outer layer of the 180ft building was made from entirely pitch-black tinted glass.

A purple carpet laid across the sidewalk, guiding the way to the 10ft, solid steel doors, with purple velvet ropes standing guard on either side. As he walked up to the doors, they swung open just as the car doors had earlier. Inside the steel gates a staircase covered in more purple velvet stood in his way. It looked as though the stairs led to heaven. There must have been 100 between him and his destination and as he climbed he thought about the room he would walk into. If it was anything like the limo or the front doors, it would be breathtaking. Jack was still terrified and guilt ridden but as he climbed, he felt a glass full of excitement bubble in his stomach.

As his left foot hit the 50th stair, the beaten man's screams filled his ears, followed by his pleas offered to Paul before Paul made Jack beat him to within an inch of his life. The screams sliced Jack's brain in half. He tripped and once again caught himself with his outstretched hands. The cuts and scrapes forged through the tough flesh of his palm opened, spilling blood on the backdrop of the purple carpet. Jack felt as though his eyes were going to pop out of his head if the agonizing screams continued, and just as every blood vessel in his eyes threatened to burst, the screaming faded. All that was left was pain and images.

The blood trickling down the man's head as he laid lifeless on the mat haunted Jack as he stood up and resumed his climb. His head sitting in the perfect place, Jack's own fist driving the man into the ground and his lifeless head bouncing off the mat. The feeling of ribs snapping beneath his fingers. The screams that could have only been emitted by a person in excruciating pain echoed in Jack's head, they bounced around his skull drenching Jack's consciousness with a bucket brimming with grief. Jack pushed the images out of his mind and locked the screams away. He had reached the top of the stairs.

The next room held his escape route, like Marilyn Monroe he would be able to sneak in and out of safety as long as he could get the king to feel sympathy for him. It was all riding on his ability to get the king on his side. Even Charlotte's future hung in the balance, so he took a deep breath, reassured himself that he would have time to wallow in the ocean of guilt later and started the climb once again.

Two 10ft oak doors stood on either side of a massive archway, beyond them Jack could see a beautiful golden chandelier, and a polished wooden banister. People walked back and forth across his field of view; Piano, violin, and cello notes filled his ears. It felt good contrasted against the screams of agony that still hadn't left Jack's brain. He walked forward, lured deeper into the room by the beautiful symphony of notes floating through the blank space.

As Jack reached the shimmering banister, he looked across to the other side, two more staircases sat on the other side, separated by a large landing with a podium standing alone in the middle. The lower floor was just as impressive, round oak tables were spread out near the walls and in the middle, a vast dance floor which was flooded with people. As he scanned the room for familiar faces Jack noticed a theme, every person was wearing a black dress or tuxedo, other than the waiters who wore purple, velvet suits with black ties and shirts. He realized he stuck out like a visitor against the sea of orange on visitation day at a prison. No one had mentioned there was a dress code, but as he looked harder, he spotted three colors. Royal blue, Blood red, and Pure white. There were four colors, including his own forest green suit.

The fact that his suit made him stand out of the crowd was very problematic, the Man in Red would, without a shadow of doubt, know who he was. All the colors were on the dance floor, except for him, so he decided he had better join them and at all costs, avoid speaking to Alexander. Turning right he strode purposefully around the balcony, suddenly very aware of the heads turning as he walked by. The turning heads and whisperers he was attracting as he walked were foreign to Jack.

Usually, he was able to slip into the crowd not inconspicuous but by no means noticeable. That night he was most definitely the center of attention and the stares made Jack uncomfortable but compared to the screams that occupied his brain only moments ago they felt like feathers grazing his skin. Nothing could stop him from setting his escape plan in motion, or so he thought.

He reached the dance floor and looked around. Dr. Confucius was standing to the right near a table, speaking to another man. The man in Red, sat to the left, Charlotte sat to his right. The woman in white was sitting at the far end of the room, her back turned to Jack. Her white dress was perfect, save for the line of red piping running vertically from her waist to her toes. The strapless fabric revealed her entire back, allowing Jack to see a small tattoo sitting directly between her two shoulder blades. The distance Jack was looking from made it impossible to make out what it was in the shape of but nestled between her shoulder blades it looked perfect.

Not foreign, and not out of place, like his red sun or Charlotte's pendant and scar. It looked as though it was a part of her, like it hitched a ride out of her mother's womb along with the perfect baby she had surely been. As he ogled her with the upmost admiration a hand tapped his shoulder, "Mr. Hanson! I'm so glad you made it."

Jack whipped around and saw Dr. Confucius standing behind him in a royal blue suit with a golden tie. A blood red broach had been pinned firmly to the fabric covering his heart. The broach was so perfectly red that Jack almost expected it to be dripping blood onto the floor. "Do you like the purple? I chose it, thinking of you. I thought your first impression of the Founders should be a grand one."

The Dr. had succeeded in his attempt. The purple was in fact very impressive. It was, however, very odd that Confucius wasn't even trying to tread lightly around him. Jack assumed the Dr. knew he had been told why he was at the event and been made aware of the courtship that would endure over the coming months.

"It's great sir, it looks like a meeting of kings! And the limo was very cool. How did you know I liked Crown Royal?"

"That's what I was going for because that's what it is. The men and women in this room run this city, in essence these are the kings and queens of New York City. As for the whiskey in the limo, I guess I just got lucky," he said with a wink.

Jack's mind raced, if the Dr. knew his favorite whiskey, what else did he know? Most likely everything, but there was always a chance that he knew nothing, and it really had been a good guess. Jack clung to the improbable chance like a pole driven into the side of a cliff keeping him from dropping down into the abyss and eventually into the jaws of chaos itself. "The waiters should be around shortly with champagne, now that you have arrived, I would like to make a toast."

As if on cue, an army of purple suited men and women appeared with trays brimming with champagne glasses. Jack gently removed a glass from the nearest tray and followed the Dr. as far as the bottom of the staircase. Dr.

Confucius continued up the stairs, holding the bubbling glass of champagne. He situated himself behind the podium, his Royal blue suit jacket, pressed white shirt and golden tie were the only clothes visible. He tapped the microphone once and soon every head turned to see what the noise was. When they realized who it was, every head turned to attention.

"Good evening. As most of you know, tonight is the 400th anniversary of the Founders Society and my 50th year as your leader. I stand here looking out into all of your brave, strong and ambitious faces, and I see a truly bright future."

Pausing for second he looked around at each face in the room. Effectively making each occupant of the room feel valued and important, finally stopping on one. Jack's. "No matter what our ledgers hold, we are united by this foundation. Bound to honor and integrity by the tattoos that were etched onto the rich tapestry of each of your bodies when you pledged your fidelity to our society. I truly believe the next 100 years will be the best yet. The world is changing around us, but we must hold steadfast through the storm. The next generation has a fight ahead of them but I believe that they will rise to the occasion."

Lifting his glass he continued, "To the next 100 years, may it be as plentiful as the 400 that have already come and gone." Every glass in the room was raised to the sky and as the Dr. brought the glass to his lips, pouring the bubbling liquid into his mouth, so did the rest. Once the liquid had cleared his mouth he spoke again. "I hope everyone enjoys the party. If each person realizes one dream tonight, I will be very pleased." And with a smile Dr. stepped out from behind the podium and walked down the stairs back to Jack.

"Very nice speech, sir."

"Thank you, Jack, have fun tonight but Wednesday evening I would love to have dinner with you, just to ask a few questions. If you are free, that is." The pain coming from Jack's hands surged when the invitation left the Dr's mouth and the screams echoed in his mind. After the speech he had just heard, Jack didn't think he deserved the Dr's company or his help, but it didn't matter. It was the only way and Jack had no real choice but to go to the dinner. So, he might as well talk to the Dr. about his unique situation.

"I would be honored sir."

"Good, I will send the car around 5:00pm, does that work for you?"

"Yes, sir, I look forward to it."

"Good, good. For now, mingle, talk, learn. Each one of these men and women have something that you can use to climb the next societal step. I will come see you later, have fun." And with that he turned away, his Royal blue suit rippling in the unseen wind that seemed to pick and choose who would be touched by its flattering exhale.

Jack finished his champagne with one quick tilt of the hand, then asked a nearby waiter to bring him a glass of Crown Royal on the rocks. The waiter obliged and returned after a few minutes had passed with a stiff glass filled with the sweet amber liquid. Jack thanked him and walked away. Faces, whispers and pointed fingers flew at him from all angles. The faces looked him up and down with admiration, fear and in one special case, anger.

Alexander, who had sat down in his chair again, kept his eyes trained on Jack as if trying to burn a hole right through his chest. The seething anger building up in his eyes would have scared Jack the day before but that night he felt powerful. If the Man in Red stood and regarded Dr. Confucius as his superior, Jack had nothing to fear. If he stayed on the path he had started down, he would soon be the most powerful man in New York and fully out of the mud Paul seemed determined to hold him under. He would have the chance to be the King in a city of Kings. Jack knew he didn't crave the wealth and stature that accompanied the mantle. He only wanted to be with her but if he couldn't get that particular trophy he would have to settle for the throne. It was the only other option that would protect him from death once he carried out his plan.

Once Jack was certain Alexander had looked away, he looked over and checked to see if Charlotte was still seated beside him, she wasn't. It was good sign; he could find her and see how deep the hole he had dug for himself was. Charlotte was the perfect spy, beautiful, cunning, and broken. The plan sat on her ability to make Paul and Alexander think she was on their side, all the while feeding Jack inside information. Jack's only fear was that she would be hurt in the process.

If she turned out to be a spy for the GWA, then that was an acceptable outcome, if not, Jack couldn't bear to think of pain being inflicted on her beautiful skin just because of his disloyalty. As the images of Charlotte being tortured danced in his eyes, he felt a tap on his shoulder. He spun around and saw Charlotte standing behind him staring in the opposite direction. Jack wondered what was going on he didn't understand why she wasn't looking at him. Was she the one who had tapped his shoulder, or had it been another?

"Go to the bathroom," Charlotte whispered behind her back. Still trying to make it seem like she didn't know Jack was behind her. Jack still couldn't figure out why she was acting so odd, but then he caught a glimpse of Alexander. The man in red was, once again, trying to burn a hole through his head. It dawned on Jack that he was in some very deep water with Paul and Alexander and that Charlotte was only trying to protect herself.

Jack understood completely, the plan couldn't succeed without the two men completely trusting Charlotte. They had to believe, without a doubt of suspicion that she was on their side. Jack had already blown his respect and was in extremely hot water with the two men. Because of that, Charlotte would be the only one that would be able to get Jack close enough to them without setting off alarms. The question of whether Jack could trust her himself still hung in the air, but it would be answered that night. Jack had a plan to find the answer to the question once and for all.

Whatever her answer was would determine Jack's future and it would determine the direction the plan took. As Jack walked to the bathroom on the far end of the room, he thought about asking Charlotte the one nagging question that would reveal her true allegiances but thought better of it. The great hall of a king was not the place, and it wasn't the time. Later that night, on the balcony Charlotte seemed unbelievably comfortable on, he would ask it. He reached the bathroom and wondered what he should do next, just stand there like a jackass, or go into the bathroom. He decided to look like a fool and stand in front of the bathroom, sipping his whiskey.

Charlotte emerged from the crowd and pushed Jack past the door to the men's room and dragged him into a stall. The bathroom, in line with the theme of the entire building, was extremely fancy. Each stall was bordered by large stone walls and the door to each stall was thick oak, completely soundproof and probably one of the saftest places in the entire building.

"How's the night going?" Charlotte asked.

"Pretty good, Confucius seems to like me." Jack decided he would wait until he was sure which side Charlotte was truly on before he revealed that the Dr. invited him to dinner Wednesday night. "I also had to work tonight. I will tell you about it later," he said as the echoes threatened to consume his mind. "Alexander seems to hate me with a fiery passion."

"Yeah, Alexander does hate you with a passion for not coming to the event with him but in reality, Paul's opinion matters more." Jack wondered how that could be if Alexander really was his boss, but he didn't question it. If Paul really was more powerful than Alexander, he was in great shape. Not in great shape mentally or physically but in Paul's eyes he was a star.

"Back up, you worked tonight?" Charlotte asked.

"Yeah, Paul called at 8 and I was home by 9:00, I think. Somewhere near there."

"What did he have you do tonight?"

"I don't really want to talk about it here. Maybe we can talk about it later at my apartment?" Jack knew his proposition sounded a lot like a late-night rendezvous, but he needed her to come back to the apartment to talk. Not about the night, he never wanted to talk about that ever again, he needed her to prove her allegiances lay with him. Jack needed to ensure she wasn't in bed with him one night and Paul the next. "The limo driver said that all I needed to do is text him the number three and he would be out front in five minutes to take me wherever I want."

"Yeah, that sounds good, just text me when you're ready to go and I will make up some excuse for me to leave." The space between the two had grown smaller and smaller as the conversation continued. Their noses were practically touching. Jack's heart had started beating harder than it ever had but the fantom screams were growing louder and louder in his ears. Just as the screams threatened to split Jack's brain in two, Charlotte pressed her lips against his, turning her head until their lips had interlocked in the puzzle like fashion they had the other night. The warm, familiar touch of safety drove the haunting screams out of Jack's ears and his heart slowed back down to its normal speed.

His hands ran down Charlotte's naked back, each bump and dip moving his fingers up and down like God running his fingers over the hills and valleys of southern Mexico until they finally rested just above her hips. Charlotte's right hand unbuttoned the lone button on the green suit jacket and slithered underneath the vest to rest on the shirt covering his stomach. Jack could feel her running her fingers up and down the abs that, after years of work, were quite noticeable even underneath a shirt. Once the screams had completely left his ears, he gently pulled his lips away from Charlotte's and said, "We should probably rejoin the party."

Charlotte's eyes opened slowly, and she sheepishly said, "Yeah, we really should."

The two stood, staring into each other's eyes for what felt like hours but Charlotte broke the silence by saying—with none of the earlier sheepish tone, "I will leave first and you wait a few minutes, then head out and rejoin the party." She unlocked the stall door and walked away without another glace back. Jack stood in the stall, trying to regain his composure. He rubbed his fingers over his eyes with some pressure, trying to shake himself out of the trance.

Without Charlotte's warm lips he dove into another convulsing memory. The images etched on the back of his eyelids consumed his mind like an epileptic attack on his consciousness. The man lying lifeless, blood trickling, his sense of sound added to ambiance with a reiteration of gunshots, screams, pleas, and the thud of the man's head hitting the ground. Jack's legs faltered and finally failed, dropping him onto the seat of the toilet—which thankfully, was cleaned—while the horrifying images and sounds of death consumed Jack's brain, holding him hostage. They played on repeat like a never-ending movie, in addition to his mind being held hostage the red sun hanging around his neck gained weight.

The pendant weighed him down with more force than it ever had before. Jack didn't know how to take his mind back from the grasp the crippling memory had on it but he knew that somehow he needed to find a way past it. He needed to get back to the party. The only way was to fight through the pain. To get up, splash water on his face and walk out like nothing ever happened, but he had no idea how he was ever going to accomplish that task. Just then, as if responding to his desperate plea for strength a piece of his unbroken soul took over. It moved his legs into standing position, jerkily opened the bathroom door, stumbled chaotically into the wall of sinks, jerked the tap on and splashed water all over his face.

The cold water awoke Jack from the crippling dream he had been chained to. His eyes could still only show the images of death but the piece if him that was still pure, the piece of him that was her, had opened enough vision and gained enough control that he was able to consciously think about something else. Something other than death. He thought about the day that she had taken him to the river. They had swung from the ancient rope all day and once the sun started creeping underneath the horizon, they sat together on top of the blanket that she had insisted on bringing.

The safety and serenity Jack felt that day at the river flooded back to him. They allowed him to completely wake up and shut the crippling memory back in its box. As he wiped the water off his face the warm, kind, and loving memory receded back to wherever it had been stored, to regain strength until it was needed again.

Jack stepped back out into the room, the music and lights overwhelmed his senses, but he welcomed the distraction. It kept the memories at bay. He finished his drink, the alcohol dulled his senses and helped bury the guilt that had permanently nestled itself in his heart, letting Jack know that it wasn't going anywhere anytime soon. So, when the first waiter walked by, he asked for another and continued on his way. He knew the waiter would remember his suit if not his face. As he walked, he looked around at all the faces that occupied the room, even though Confucius had told Jack each one was worth talking to and that the wisdom he could gleam from each would move him up the hierarchal ladder, he didn't want to speak to anyone.

He also didn't care about moving up any ladder, he was just fine where he was. Well not right where he was, he desperately wanted to get out of the situation he was currently in but regarding the hierarchal level he was on, Jack was very comfortable. He had never truly wanted to move up, even all those weeks ago in Medora. Greed had forced his hand then, now he just wanted her, and to get as far away from the city as he could. Jack felt bad about giving Confucius false hope, letting him believe that he had found his replacement, but Jack was desperate.

Like a coyote knowing it only has one way out of a farmer's trap, Jack would do anything he could to get out of his own trap, even if it meant completely fucking Confucius over. After the things he had done and seen, Jack couldn't afford to honorable, he had to chew his leg off in order to preserve the rest of his body until he was far enough away from the farmers. Then and only then he could begin to be honorable again.

As he walked aimlessly through the crowd he spotted the white dress, the stark beauty shocked him. Even though he could only see her from behind, he knew she was beautiful, he knew her face would make Charlotte look like a short, fat, bald man. The loose curls of golden blonde hair, the small strings of muscle running up her back and the perfectly placed tattoo sitting in-between her shoulder blades all radiated beauty. It was beauty that Jack could barely comprehend.

There was also an air of familiarity that Jack couldn't quite place. The waiter that he had put his drink order in with appeared on Jack's side holding the tray with only one drink atop it. Jack took the glass and thanked the man. As he stared at the beauty across the room, Jack sipped his drink slowly, trying to place the woman in his bank of names. Where had he seen her before? She seemed so familiar. Jack couldn't think of a name to place with gorgeous woman. The name was buried beneath years of grief and sorrow. It sat on the tip of his tongue, so close yet so far.

As he racked his brains for the name, she began to walk away from the men she had been talking to. The dress rippled, touched by invisible wind that seemed only to grace a select group of people with its warm breath. Jack stood rooted in place, transfixed by her movements. He finished his drink and set it on the nearby table. As she walked Jack realized that she was leaving, but he hadn't spoken to her yet. He needed to know the face behind the beauty. Shaking himself out of yet another trance he walked swiftly toward her, but she kept moving further and further away.

When she reached the stairway, she flipped her hair, leaving the right side of her face open to Jack's vision. Jack saw a scar sitting just below her right eye socket, her eyes shone bright blue and Jack finally placed a name to the woman who was about to walk out the room. It was her. She had been standing across the room from him the entire night. Now the transfixion made sense to Jack, as did the inability to place where he had seen her. His brain had been in disbelief induced shock. Jack broke into a full sprint, frantically pushing anyone and everyone in his path out of the way. When he finally reached the stairs, he saw that she had already reached the top, and as Jack started up the stairs, he saw that she was gone.

She had slipped into the crowd or into some secret dimension that Jack wished he could see the entrance to. Even though he knew he probably wouldn't be able to find her again, he ran up the stairs, tripping twice in his haste. He pushed by the crowds occupying the balcony, fighting his way to the entrance of the massive room. When he reached the stairs, he saw she was already halfway down. She hadn't slipped into an alternate universe as he had thought, just been swallowed by the crowd. He shouted out but the stairs were so tall that she didn't hear, he ran past the oak doors and down the stairs, slowing only because he knew if he continued at the pace, he would fall down them and break his neck.

If that happened, he would never get to see her but when he saw that she had reached the doors he resumed his earlier speed. Wind whipping past his face he ran as fast as his legs would carry him. She continued through the doors and disappeared into the darkness. Jack finally reached the door and waited for them to open, there was no way he could push them open; the sheer weight was too great. The doors opened in the type of slow motion only elegance can incite and he finally felt the cold air sting his face. Whipping his head in every direction, he tried to determine which direction she could have gone but as he whipped his head to the right he saw a limo, just like the one that had brought him there, pulling into traffic. Jack's heart sunk; she was gone.

The adrenaline had begun to wear off and he realized his breath was terrifyingly shallow. The cold air burned his windpipe as it was pulled in with a ferocity only a chase could warrant. He put his hands on his knees, doubled over by exhaustion. The night was over, and Jack didn't care that he hadn't said goodbye to Confucius. He texted 'three' to the number he had received the text from earlier and made sure he texted Charlotte, letting her know he was leaving. No longer caring if she came or not. All he wanted, was to see her face one more time.

Once the limo arrived, Jack waited for the door to open for him and got in, making sure the driver waited for Charlotte. Even though he didn't care for her company that night, she was integral to the plan and Jack really did need to know if she was on his side. Seeing her face again would be bliss, but it couldn't help Jack out of the mud he had waded into that fateful snowy night.

Or could it? What was she doing at a party for the Founders? The questions kept piling up in Jack's brain, add the guilt and memories and Jack's mind was utterly overwhelmed. He wondered how his life become so overwhelming. Just a month ago he was a nobody, the biggest source of anxiety or pain was his mother's death. As hard as that was and continued to be, lots of people had parents and loved ones die in front of them. It wasn't an overly special case but that night he was in a very special case. He was in essence, a killer for hire, set to inherit a kingdom.

The most prominent kingdom in western society. Jack couldn't even fathom how it started; a simple opportunity had blown the reality he once held dear to smithereens. The thoughts were banging around in his head so hard that it had begun to ache. As Jack rubbed his temples, trying to alleviate the pain, he spotted the bottle of whiskey. A drink would dull the pain. It had always worked in the past, why not now? Pulling the stopper out of the fancy bottle he held it up to his lips and took a heavy swig.

The alcohol had taken effect and the nauseating ache in his skull dulled. So, he kept drinking until he reached the desired effect. By the time he reached the point of no return, the same door he had entered through, opened once again. Charlotte stood on the curb taking stock of the situation she was walking into. Jack sat perfectly still, the bottle of whiskey in his left hand, his eyes dulled by inebriation and face flushed by the chase he said, "Ready...to go?" Charlotte got in reluctantly against her better judgement.

"I know I'm not one to talk but are you okay?" She said, each word dripping with fear and concern.

"I'm fine don't worry about me. We are good to go driver. Take us to my apartment, the same one you picked me up at." The driver didn't answer but instead rolled the window between him and passengers up, pulled the limo onto the road, and drove away. Jack placed the bottle back on the shelf and tried to pull himself back to reality. If he was going to get answers from Charlotte, he needed to crawl, at the very least, a few inches closer to sobriety.

For the rest of the drive, Jack fought the alcohol, and by the time they reached his apartment he had won—partially. The memories were forgotten for the time being, but his mind was still hazy. Jack knew he had only himself to blame for the haze, but he didn't regret it. The alcohol had done its job and he was still able to act normal. Sure, it was more difficult to act normally but not impossible by any means.

Once the door to the limo door opened again and the cold air stung Jack's cheeks, even more clarity was afforded, he would easily be able to find out what he needed to. After all, he had acted sober under much more influence than he was burdened by in that moment. Charlotte exited the car first, Jack followed suit, quickly walking past her and opened the door before she reached it. If he wanted her to trust him, he needed to act trustworthy himself. The pair walked in silence past Angela who was still sound asleep at the front desk and waited for the elevator door to open. It quickly did and once the door had shut tightly Charlotte spoke, "Seriously Jack what happened tonight? You seem worse than I was when Paul made me kill that guy with a dull knife." As she finished her sentence a shudder ran down her spine.

"Yeah...I'm obviously not fine, but we can talk about it later, I have a question for you first." The elevator door opened to Jack's apartment and they both stepped in breathing a sigh of relief. They were relatively safe for the time being. "Want to go out on the balcony?" Jack asked with only a slight slur chasing each syllable, like they were tripping over his tongue as they drunkenly stumbled out of his mouth.

"Sure, do you want to smoke? I am going to if that's okay with you of course."

"Sure, it might erase the memory that has been burned onto my eyelids and if not, it sure will make me feel good for the night."

As they walked to the porch Charlotte pulled Jack back, and with her hands resting gently on his neck she leaned in and kissed him. Her soft, warm lips interlocked with Jack's, and he couldn't help but feel like they had been made for each other. There was no other reason their lips fit together like two pieces of a puzzle; they must have been created for each other. There was no other explanation. After a few minutes, Charlotte pulled away. She threw her shoes off and asked Jack if she could change into some of his clothes.

Jack said of course and continued out to the balcony. It had started to feel as though she wore his clothes more than he did, and now that he thought about it, he hadn't got a single article of clothing she had 'borrowed' back. Not that he minded, he had enough money to buy an entirely new wardrobe every single day if that's what he wanted. Jack sat down in his usual chair and waited for Charlotte to take her seat to the left.

After what felt like an hour, she emerged and took her seat in the left chair. She had chosen one of his larger hoodies and hadn't bothered to grab any pants. Jack didn't feel any need to comment on the lack of clothing. He waited for her to light the joint, take a few drags, then he took a few of his own, passed it back to Charlotte and asked his question, "What is the real story behind the scar? I need to know, Charlotte."

She coughed on the smoke that filled her lungs, but once she had gotten the coughing under control, she said, "I told you, a childhood injury."

Jack knew that she was lying so he said in the most calm and safe tone he could muster, "C'mon Charlotte, I know that's a lie, the scar is way too fresh for it to have happened that long ago. You can trust me, this is your last chance to tell me, otherwise I will never be able to fully trust you."

"Okay." Many silent moments passed before she continued, as if she was waiting for the words to come to her. When they finally materialized, she continued, "I told you that I've worked for Paul since I was 17, right?"

"Yeah."

"Well, there have been many people like you that have come and gone, either dying by their own hand, Alexander's, or Paul's dirty, grime covered fingers or simply ran away, just to die at another date. I got tired of it. You're not the first to realize the only way to slip through the cracks is to work on Paul and Alexander instead of work for them. I have always known that the only way out is to chop the head off the snake. So, two recruits before you there was a girl named Marissa. She was a master in taekwondo and smart as whip...a lot like you if I'm being honest...We became best friends quickly, but she too had a conscience, she wanted out just as bad as you do. Just as bad as I do. One night we decided that the two of us were going to cut the head off the snake, I was the spy, she the assassin. We decided she would kill Alexander on her own and then we would kill Paul together. But she never made it past Alexander, he overpowered her and killed her in the most inhumane fashion he could think of but that wasn't even the worst part. Don't get me wrong it was horrible, but before she died, she told Alexander I was in on the whole thing and that I was going to kill Paul with her after she had killed him."

"It just so happened that I was keeping Paul busy while she was supposed to be killing Alexander. So... when Alexander called Paul and told him everything, he grabbed me, and tied me to a chair. He left me there for hours. When he came back, he had a blowtorch and a massive hunting knife. He lit the blowtorch and as the flame glinted off the steel and he grinned. He seemed excited for what was about to happen. I pleaded, cried, and tried to bargain for my life, but he said in that horrifyingly slow, hungry voice he uses when he wants to see pain or death, that he wasn't going to kill me, just mark me so that I knew he owned me."

Jack sat in his chair, not quiet comprehending what he was hearing. Was it the fate that awaited him if the plan wasn't executed perfectly? It was exponentially more horrifying than the images that had been burned onto his eyelids earlier that night. The images danced around in his mind as Charlotte continued, "He ran the flame up and down the blade until it was white hot. Now I realize it was so I wouldn't bleed all over the office when he cut deep into my skin. At the time I thought it was to ensure the pain would be at the highest possible threshold. Once he was satisfied with the color of the steel he sliced my shirt in half, the blade skated through the fabric like butter. With my stomach exposed, he grabbed my face with his right hand, fingers digging into my cheek, holding the white-hot knife in his left and said in the same slow, hungry and horrifyingly distant drawl, "my sweet girl...I am going to enjoy this." Still crushing my face with his hand, he looked down at my exposed midsection and dug the searing blade into my skin, deep enough to deface it but shallow enough to keep me alive."

"Then slowly dragged it across my stomach. The pain was too much for me to handle, at first I screamed the most guttural scream that I had ever heard. I didn't know I could even make a sound so mortifying but after what was probably only a few seconds but felt like hours, I passed out. When I woke up, I was still in the chair, my stomach had been slashed open and the pain was so thick that I almost passed out again but this time I fought it and looked down in horror at the burnt skin and the ugly puss filled gash leaking blood. Paul came back in and untied me. Then told me to do some thinking about what I had done."

"I crawled to the elevator, across the lobby, into a black car and straight to the hospital. When we arrived, I realized I couldn't explain what had happened to me. So instead, I got the driver to buy me some stitching supplies and bring me home. Once we were there, he carried me up the stairs, into my apartment, stitched my wound and laid me on my bed and left."

Jack couldn't fathom what he had heard, it was appalling. He felt more than trust for Charlotte. It was empathy, maybe even love. How could she have handled so much pain, how was she still walking? No human could make it through something so awful—well except his mother but he knew he wouldn't be able to. He would have run away and taken his chances on the run. It was paramount that their plan was foolproof. They had to stick together. Paul and Alexander would have to be in the same room when it happened. That was vital. Jack sat on the chair in absolute awe of Charlotte.

She was nothing if not strong. Mentally he was one millionth as strong as her, his evening with Paul was filled with puppies and ice cream compared to what she had just told him. Charlotte waited for Jack to say something, but he couldn't find the words, so she said, "I told you my sob story, it's time for yours." Jack's mind had gone blank, and he was having trouble remembering to breathe but he was brought back to reality by Charlotte's request. He started at the beginning and told Charlotte everything. The cage, the pleas, the cries for mercy, the five-punch minimum. The feeling of bones breaking underneath his fist, the screams of agony, which in hindsight, probably sounded a lot like

Charlotte's scream as the searing knife was dragged across her perfectly pure skin. Then the man's body being blown off its moors and the sickening thud of skull connecting with rubber. Finally, reaching the end, he painted the picture of the lifeless body sprawled on the rubber mat, blood trickling down his forehead and the bang and the hole cut cleanly through the man's temple. He told her of Paul's gross comment and adoration of him for his 'performance'.

Once Jack had finished, Charlotte said, "Jesus, that's way worse than anything he has made me do. Now I understand why your so out of it. He made you torture and kill a man who pleaded for mercy."

Jack knew Charlotte was right, but he didn't care about Paul's lack of humanity. He only cared about his own actions; he had looked the defenseless man in the eyes and killed him. The memory of beating a man who didn't even fight back made Jack feel like a building had crashed down on top of him. The guilt weighing on his soul was so heavy, it had grown too heavy. The sheer volume was threating to stop his heart.

"Yeah," Jack whispered, he had revealed the worst of himself. The worst sin he had committed and was ever going to commit. He didn't think anything could get worse than what he had done earlier that evening. It was so deeply wrong that Jack didn't even fully understand what had made him do it. He should have refused, should have died to save his soul from such evils. By committing the evil, he had let the flames of hell ignite his pant legs, they no longer bit at his heels, they were a part of him and all he could do was try to extinguish the flame. Then try to reinvent himself once he had gotten as far away as he possibly could from the hellish gladiator arena. In that moment, he decided he would get his diploma, for his mother, and once that had been accomplished, he would finish it. Extinguish the evil, cut the head off the snake. Whatever you wanted to call it, he was going to kill Paul, Alexander, and anyone else who had pledged allegiance to the devil. "I don't know what to do, the memories just circulate through my thoughts like a furnace circulating warm air in the winter. I don't know how I'm going to sleep. The images are legitimately burned on the inside of my eyelids. Whenever I close my eyes, I see his pleading, scared eyes staring back at me." Jack whispered.

Charlotte turned to Jack, tears streamed down her face, but past the tears there was something else. Another quality shone underneath. Shame? No,

Agony? No, it was either guilt or love. Jack couldn't tell which, the tears were blocking his view.

"I don't know Jack; how do you push feelings like that down? I sure haven't figured it out, I've been doing this for eight years and I still haven't figured it out. How do you kill the devil?"

"I don't know, but somehow we are going to have to find a way. If we don't, our souls will be warped into the very thing we hate. Souls can only resist so much before they give in to the pressure," Jack said with tears welling up behind his eyes. He pushed them back down, a man doesn't cry, he protects. Although Jack didn't know how a man was supposed to protect another when he himself should be locked away in a dark hole that has been purged of all traces of light.

"The only way is to be as evil as Paul and that would make us worse than the devil. I don't know how I am going to do that," Charlotte said as tears cut red lines down her beautiful face. They were as foreign and out of place as the scar. Both had been caused by Paul. There was no other alternative than to snuff the fire that Alexander or whoever actually gave Paul a second chance ignited that day. The day the devil was born.

After Jack and Charlotte's tears ceased to flow, they sat in silence looking out onto the city as the sun began to rise for a few more minutes before heading back into the apartment. Jack slid the patio door open and let Charlotte walk through. As she walked past him, he noticed that his hoodie was just short enough to reveal the bottom half of both of Charlotte's cheeks. They swayed left to right, luring Jack toward them like a shiny fishhook on the end of a line.

Watching them bounce left and right made him realize he was still wearing the green suit, tie pin, cuff links and all. By the look of Charlotte's attire, he knew he needed to get out of it. It was too symbolic, and he knew he would need to wear it again someday, it couldn't be ruined. So, he headed to his room quickly to change, checking the oven clock on the way by he saw it was 5am. "Jesus," he whispered. He had almost been awake for 24hrs. Charlotte hadn't moved since he had been gone, she was still sitting on the couch wearing the same broken, hungry look. Not quite the same as Paul's but awfully close.

Jack knew she didn't want blood or death, but she did want, no, she needed something just as primal. Jack was wearing nothing but gym shorts that left little to the imagination. All his hard-earned muscle rippled beneath his skin, the red sun contrasting against his light skin, digging into his chest with its newfound weight. He stopped just before the coffee table that sat in between the couch and TV, Charlotte stood up and stepped onto the coffee table and off the other side, her body heat radiating onto Jack's bare skin.

She seductively ran her hands up from Jack's abdomen to his chest until her left thumb hit the red pendant that split his chest in half. She took it in her hands and rubbed the cold metal between her fingers, as if trying to rub a genie out of a bottle. He watched as nothing happened and then watched as she jumped up wrapping her legs around Jack's hips interlocking her fingers behind Jack's head. Jack stumbled back, surprised by the attack but then stabilized himself, locking his eyes with Charlotte's. The tears had stopped and the only quality her eyes held in their glossy spheres was desire. Pure animal desire.

Jack knew that it was only sorrow and impending doom that made her want him so bad, but he didn't mind. It would tug his thoughts away from the plague of horrors that had set up permanent residence. She closed her eyes, breaking the tractor beam holding Jack's eyes in a fixed position and pressed her soft lips onto Jack's with a firm aggression. Jack tilted his head until they locked. They remained locked for an eternity but when Charlotte finally pulled away, she jumped off Jack, grabbed his hand and led them down the hall to his bedroom.

All the pain and guilt Jack held was sucked away by Charlotte's touch. If only for one obliviously childish moment of passion, he was safe, happy, and content.

Chapter 15

When the air riad sirens blared, signaling it was time to wake up, Jack still hadn't drifted into the void of pure darkness. He turned it off and tried to slip into the void. He was safe or he thought he was—Charlotte was next to him; the sirens hadn't even stirred her awake.

Jack was woken hours later by someone jerking his arm, it was Charlotte. "I'm heading home, thanks for the great night. We are in this together, remember that."

Jack barely registered what she had said but when the mattress bounced, unburdened of her weight, he saw that she was wearing all his clothes. The same hoodie as the night before but now she had a pair of his sweats on her legs, a pair of his socks on her feet and one of the many pairs of sandals she had picked out for him during his first week in the city keeping her feet from touching the floor. He didn't mind though, they weren't really his, all the articles of clothing were purchased with blood money. Groggily he said, "Okay have a good day. I know and is it okay if we keep the things we said to each other last night to ourselves?" Jack said, not wanting Charlotte to say anything to Paul, even though he didn't think Charlotte would like him talking to anyone else about her secrets either. After all, they were horrific and probably traumatizing.

"Yeah, I wasn't going to, you better not tell anyone my secrets Jack. Otherwise, I might have to tell someone yours," she said with a playful wink that didn't quite reach its desired effect. It sounded like a joke, but the humor didn't quite reach her eyes.

They remained cold, burdened by the truth of her past, present, and future. They told him that even though they were partners in the endeavor, she wouldn't mind dragging him under the bus with him if she ever thought she was about to be thrown under.

"I promise I won't," Jack said, and with that Charlotte disappeared out of sight. Jack was too tired to walk her out, so he stayed in bed, he had no obligations. All he had to do was write a paper on the book 1984 by George Orwell, assigned by the King himself who seemed to know everything about everyone. The absolute power shown in the book reminded Jack of Paul. 'The party' was made up of Paul and Alexander; There was no doubt about that but speaking in terms of the book, Jack still didn't know all the members of the thought police.

The guards belonged for sure, but he still wasn't quite sure who else was involved. Jack sat in bed thinking about the topic of the essay until all the cool pockets of air the bed provided had been used up. Finally, he reluctantly got out of bed to make a coffee. As the coffee brewed, he kept thinking about the essay. What would it be like if George Orwell had really predicted the future? Jack thought that he might as well have. After all, how much freedom did the people of America have? How much of their life wasn't captured by a camera, video tape or prying eyes? Whether it was a CCTV camera, accidental footage from a smartphone or just a bored house dweller with nothing better to do than keep tabs on their neighbors, almost every second of life was recorded.

The government still preached the idea of freedom but how much of it was reality, and how much was just fiction. Did the people of America even make their own choices? Being in the city had shown Jack that every purchase or thought was, in one way or another, guided or influenced by some form of propaganda. Billboards, television ads and social media influenced all decisions in one direction or another. Jack guessed that the only real decision a person made in a day was which propaganda to believe and follow.

Individual thought was only held for a select few. The only decision that remained pure was who a person chose to love and even that was blemished, love could be swayed and forced. As he pondered the scary truth the coffee machine beeped. The coffee was finished, and the theme of his essay was, in essence, chosen. He would write about the fact that, in most ways, George Orwell had predicted the future. It wasn't a question of if, it was a question of how well.

He brought the coffee mug to his mouth. Jack was impressed with himself. It had taken him less time than usual to figure out the topic of his essay, the writing part was easy, but the topic was always the time-consuming step of his process. As he tilted the cup back to allow the caffeine to wake him up and clear his mind the hot coffee scaled his tongue.

The pain woke all the feelings and memories he had acquired at the warehouse the night before that had laid dormant since his lips had locked with Charlotte's. Just as they had in the bathroom of the massive ballroom the night before, they assumed control of his eyes and violently consumed his brain. The blood tricking, screaming, pleas, the fight between his own moral compass and his will to live accompanied by the bang of the gun overwhelmed his psyche. There was no way out of the prison his own mind had created for the sheer volume of guilt.

Jack hastily set his cup down on the island, stumbling to the bathroom. As he ripped his underwear off, he turned the shower on, keeping the temperature at the lowest setting, he laid on his back against the tile covered shower floor. Jack let the frigid drops of water slam into his face until the memories subsided.

When he was sure they had been vanquished for the time being, he stood up, washed himself and turned the shower off. Even though the memories had vacated his vision, he was still shell shocked. Jack walked slowly to the closet, pulled on some fresh clothes, and returned to the kitchen to pick up his coffee and continued to the office. The sight of the MacBook sitting in the center of the massive oak desk warmed his heart like a flashback to a simpler time. It made him imagine what his life would consist of if he hadn't accepted the 'perfect' opportunity. What would have been if he had seen the blood stains blurring the picture Charlotte had shown him. If only he had seen the spikes hidden in each syllable waiting to sink their barbed tips into his soft, innocent flesh.

It would have been beautifully simple. The tiny apartment that smelled like a garbage dump, seemed like the four seasons now. The bar, his table in the corner with its beat-up chairs and the snow fluttering gently through the door, unwelcome intruders at the time that would now be cherished guests. Jack thought of the university, its tiny campus and its mediocre writing department. They made Jack feel like a failure at the time but looking back at it, Medora University seemed like NYU had all those weeks ago. Maybe one day he would get back to that simplicity, maybe one day he would lead a simple, happy life.

Never in his life had he longed to be poor but now he realized that with depravity comes innocence and true happiness. Maybe he had always known it but now the fact was slapping him in the face saying, "You didn't have to be in this mess, your greed brought you here. It's your own fault you are stuck in the mud, and now that you are, you and you alone must find a way out."

Jack drifted back into reality and realized that he was in an office with a desk that undoubtedly could be sold for the same amount as his rent for the year back in Medora, sitting in an apartment five times the size of the trailer he grew up in.

He sat down at the desk in the brown leather chair and opened his MacBook that he had saved a year to buy but now would be able to buy as many as he could fit in his arms at the drop of a hat. One day he might buy 100 MacBooks and give them away to kids like him. Kids who were looking for an opportunity to change their own lives. But unlike Paul, the gesture wouldn't be a veiled attempt to crush their dreams. It would instead lift them up to the heights only a child can dream of.

Maybe one day he would even write a book about his deadly opportunity. They were all nice thoughts but there were vast, steep, and unforgiving mountain ranges to cross before he was in a position to bring them into fruition. Jack kept the beautiful images in the fore front of his mind as he began his essay. They eventually began to drown in the sounds of keys being pressed and the brilliantly worded sentences being formed in his brain. For hours, the only sounds being emitted into the apartment were the sounds of typing, occasional sip of coffee, a crack as Jack adjusted his spine or the sounds of leather squeaking beneath his ass.

They were happy, non-threating sounds; They were the sounds that once played in throngs of symphonic harmony in the home he had fashioned for himself in Medora. The apartment might have fostered his vice, but it also was the place where independence flourished. It was the place where he began to heal from the trauma of his mother death and the traumas endured in his last years of high school. His new apartment only fostered pain, regret, and soul crushing guilt. The sounds eventually stopped, and Jack stood up, pacing the room to stretch his legs, and then sat back down to complete a final check of his work.

Once he was happy with it, he handed it into the online drobox, closed the lid of his laptop and then stood up, opened the door to the office and stepped back into reality. The warm, happy environment was replaced with a cold, foreboding one. It was the reality he had come to know but not love like his last life, instead he hated it with a white-hot fury.

Jack went back to the kitchen to check the clock; he imagined it was around 4 or 5 but looking at the clock he realized it was 6:00pm. He had yet to eat anything that day, so he decided he would go to the Four Roses, have one of their disgusting burgers and then maybe check out a bookstore after. He had read every book that he currently owned and in the next three months he would have lots of time he needed to fill with something, lest he get lost in the minefield of memory.

TV and movies always missed the best parts, and a book was much more intimate anyways. They captured thoughts and feelings in a way that the screen usually couldn't. As he stepped into the elevator, he thought about the countless times books had allowed him to hide within their pages when reality became too much of a burden. The words scrawled on the pages always seemed like the true reality, good authors always found a way to create a world in which nothing was wrong, or a world in which the main character always had some special quality. Something better than the life he had been forced to endure.

The books he read in his childhood were able to keep him out of trouble, make him forget that his mom was working three jobs and when she got sick, they silenced her screams and cries. Books allowed him to turn a blind eye to the blood-stained sheets and vomit-stained carpet.

He hoped they would be able to erase the images burned on his eyelids, retract the sounds of death from his ears, and if not erase or retract maybe they would gift him a few fleeting moments of naivety. Jack exited the elevator and caught Angela's eye, she beckoned him toward the front desk, "How's it going Jack?"

"Really good, how are you?" He said trying to sound polite but really, he didn't honestly care how she was doing and obviously wasn't 'really good'.

What he should have said was, "It's going fucking awful, my bosses are having me kill people, last night I beat someone to death and then put a bullet in his head just to make sure. Now because of those horrors I am crippled by flashbacks that are like my own personal horror movies up in my head. It's so bad that I would gladly kill myself if it wasn't such a selfish thing to do." But of course, he couldn't say that. First of all he would be arrested, Angela might pull a gun out and kill him—It was the USA, the land of the free and brave after all—for being a murderer and then if she didn't call the police or kill him, she might say something to someone else and then the gossip train would eventually lead to Paul and it would result in death yet again. None of the options seemed all that appealing so Jack kept his mouth shut.

"That's great, Jack!" Angela said with a supreme excitement, she seemed almost giddy. "Thanks to you I don't have to force my kids to stay in a disgusting apartment with a man who uses and beats them. My life has changed so much since you came into it Jack and I just wanted to thank you for your generosity."

Jack grinned, at least someone was profiting from his misery, it didn't make up for the three souls trapped in the red sun hanging around his neck, but it may help keep him from losing his mind.

"No problem, Angela, if you need anything else just let me know."

"I will. You are great man Jack; I hope you know that." If only she knew the evil, he had helped keep its firm, grime covered grasp on reality.

"Thanks," Jack said as he turned away and continued out the door. He didn't need any more reminders of how 'good' he was. The only reason he was giving so much to everyone was the soul crushing guilt festering inside of him.

He reached the Four Rose's with his stomach twisted into knots due to the lack of nutrition. Anything would calm it, even the Four Rose's disgusting burgers. Jack walked into the restaurant, or was it a café? Jack wasn't sure, in a book set in the 90s it would have been called a diner but he wasn't sure what modern society would label it. He sat down at his regular booth and looked for a server but there was no one around. He waited a few more minutes but when no server materialized he walked up to the front counter and rang the bell.

It took 5 rings before a face emerged from the swinging doors behind the counter. By the third ring Jack was tempted to go into the back and demand to talk to an employee but when the face finally emerged from the door, he was thankful he didn't. It was her. Jack stared at her completely star struck. The scar just underneath her eye, the perfect loosely curled hair flowing over her shoulders like a golden brook. Charlotte was beautiful but compared to the woman standing in front of him, she was nothing. Jack's tongue had been tied into knots. He blinked twice and rubbed his eyes to make sure he wasn't hallucinating. When he opened his eyes again, he saw that it really was her and she wore the same look of disbelief that Jack knew was etched into every one of his own facial features.

"Jack?" She said.

Jack's brain registered the words, but he couldn't untangle his tongue fast enough to respond, so he just stared back in complete disbelief. He had thought he would need to go back to Maine to find her but here she was, standing right in front of him. The night before at the Founders party, he thought he had seen her but convinced himself that it was just a figment of his overactive imagination. Now he couldn't turn a blind eye, if he would have known she was working less than 5 minutes from his apartment he wouldn't have ever run after her, instead he would have memorized her face, dress, and tattoo.

As the image of the girl he had chased the night before was brought to the forefront of his mind, he remembered the tattoo, it was a J. It could be a reference to her name but just as his cufflinks symbolized something else, he thought it too, may have a dual meaning. Jack was drowning in thought, but she was still waiting for an answer, so she asked again, "Sorry sir, is your name Jack Hanson?"

"Jessica?" He asked dryly, fighting to get enough moisture in his mouth to talk.

"Holy shit, it really is you! I thought I saw you last night at the Founders thing but now I know it was you."

Jack's mouth lost all the moisture he had fought so hard to produce. Now that he knew it was really her at the Confucius's grand soiree he was even more worried about who invited her. "I can't believe you are here, I thought you would still be in Maine. You sure have changed since the last time I saw you; you look good."

Jack couldn't believe the words coming out of her mouth, how did she have no questions? How was she so happy? Maybe it was a good thing she was happy; it might mean she hadn't been corrupted by a devil masked by riches quite yet. Once he was sure she hadn't been corrupted he wouldn't sleep until he was positive she was safe.

"It's really good to see you Jess, you have no idea how much I missed you. I don't think a day has gone by that I haven't thought about you." Jack realized that what he just said might have come off as creepy or pathetic, but he didn't care, it was the truth. When he was back in Maine, she was second best thing in his entire life, the first was his mother. But even now it would be impossible to topple her off the number one spot. "You were wearing the white dress last night, right?"

"Yeah! No one told me it was a black dress event. They really should have included the dress code on the invitation! You obviously didn't get the memo either, but forest green suits you." Jack felt his face flush, he hadn't been given a compliment from a person he respected in a very long time. Sure, Paul liked to compliment him on his ability to inflict pain on others but that was vile and that form of compliment made him feel sick and dirty.

"Yeah, they really should have! But thanks!" An unfamiliar warmth was growing in Jack's belly, he thought it might be the memories coming to ruin his conversation but when the images kept their distance, he realized it was happiness. It reminded him of his mother giving him a hug. Her strong arms pushing against his back, her body shielding him from the harsh cold that is reality.

It made him believe that one day his life might turn around, it was incredible that mere hours ago he was sure his life was over. "Sorry to sound weird but I saw you had a tattoo, what does it mean?" Jessica's face turned beet red, and Jack saw that her hands had begun to sweat.

Clearly embarrassed, she said, "Remember when you were taken to the orphanage?" How could Jack forget, before he met Paul it was the saddest moment he had been forced to endure. Well, the second saddest. He remembered her face as he drove away, he never wanted to forget it so he committed every perfection and flaw that it held to memory. It was one of the only things that kept him going in those years.

"Yeah, it was one of my top ten worst days for sure," Jack said quietly.

"Well for weeks after that day I cried myself to sleep and didn't leave the house much. You were my only friend, and I didn't even get to say goodbye. I was so sad I can't even tell you how hurt I was but one day my dad came into my room and told me I needed to get on with my life. At first, I was angry with him. I slammed the door in his face and told him he could go to hell. Even though deep down I knew he was right. But I couldn't go on living without you there by my side every step of the way, so I went to the tattoo shop and told the man I wanted a J on my back. That way you would be with me every day, no matter where I went you would have my back."

Jack wasn't all that surprised; he was pretty sure when he saw it that it was his initial but as she said out loud, he felt honored. Never would he have guessed he had made that type of impact on her. "So, to answer your question it means Jack."

Jessica looked so embarrassed that Jack started to smile. It was like the two hadn't ever been apart. It was like they were 16-year-old kids making fun of each other again. Jessica saw that Jack was smiling and slapped him hard in the shoulder.

"Shut up! I didn't think I would ever see you again, it was traumatic."

Jack burst out with laughter. He knew that she must have been crushed when he left, Afterall he was devastated and so deeply depressed, he still was. But in that moment, everything was good, she was back. Jack was elated, all his energy was returned, and the memories were driven from his mind. Between breaths Jack said, "I know I'm sorry, I just can't believe your back! You have no idea how much I needed you." As the last few words left his mouth the laughter stopped.

Jack and Jessica stared at each other, both thinking the same thing. Jessica jumped into his arms and wrapped her hands so tightly around Jack's head that he thought he might pass out. Right before he lost consciousness, she let go sinking into a much softer, gentler, and more sensual hug. All the emotions that they had both obviously kept locked away for an eternity away were released.

Lonely, painful and despair filled tears streamed down both of their faces, wetting each other's shirts as they poured down their cheeks and fell through the empty space. After so many years apart, it felt like their two souls had once again, melted into one. Almost like Charlotte and Jack but instead of two separate pieces fitting together, Jack and Jessica were one. They clung to each other like a child clinging to a blanket or stuffed animal, not wanting to ever let go. The warm, fuzzy and safe feeling that passed between the two of them was ten times greater than anything Charlotte could give Jack.

Their lips may have been meant for each other, but Jack's soul was meant for Jessica's. Nothing could stop him from clinging on to her for the rest of his life or she him. When the two finally let go, their cheeks were stained red, but their eyes glowed with happiness. A new sense of strength was released in Jack's heart. Not a physical one but one that began to sew the pieces of his broken soul back together.

"Want to sit and talk? There's no one else here so I'm free," Jessica asked.

"Of course, you have to tell me everything that you have done since I left. But is there any chance I could get some food though? I'm starving I haven't eaten since sometime yesterday." Jack was the happiest he had been since he had lived in Maine. He couldn't remember a single time since he had left Cielo when he had even felt a fraction of the happiness he felt right then, right there in that dingy diner with Jessica.

"Yeah of course, what do you want?"

"I don't really know, what's good here at supper time?"

"Nothing really, the burgers aren't terrible, better than the ones served at the drive in back in Cielo," Jessica said with a chuckle, like she was laughing at an inside joke. At first, Jack didn't understand, he had forgotten many little things about his hometown, he had been away for so long and it was bound to happen, but it hurt his heart all the same. He thought hard, finally extracting a faint memory.

It was of him and his mother pulling up to the burger shack after a little league game, he couldn't have been more than 10 years old. He remembered the smell of grease and salt, ice crem and milkshakes. He also remembered the truck next to them was blowing black smoke from its tail pipe and his mother told him to roll the windows up to keep the diesel emissions from getting in the car. She told him it was bad for his lungs, so he rolled up the windows fast and let his mother roll hers down when the server came out to take their order. It was a nice memory; his mother was so full of life. He wished he had only that type of memory to look back on. He wished they weren't stained by the sad, weak ones. The ones that slunk out of the shadows when alcohol was in control.

"Yeah…That place was nasty, but if I'm being honest, I would give all the money I have to be back in that parking lot right now."

"Yeah…" Jessica's eyes gave away the fact that she was far away in thought but almost fast as she had gone, she returned to the harsh present. "I'll make you a burger quick, just take a seat in the corner and I will be right there." Jack watched her walk away until she disappeared.

When she disappeared out of sight, Jack walked to the far-right end of the diner and took a booth at the back. Being with Jessica anywhere felt like home. Still, he couldn't help but reminisce about the time they had in Cielo. It was so happy and carefree, well not carefree but it was theirs. No one owned or guided their days. Those hot summer days by the river or the cold winter days they spent sledding on the hill in the middle of town were some of the best memories he had. His mother was always his best friend, and he would trade anything to see her again but see her as her true self, not the withered, broken shell of the woman he had come to know even if it was just for a few fleeting moments.

Even so, Jessica knew him better than anyone ever had, or at least she did before he was carted off to the orphanage. Now she didn't know much about him, and he didn't know anything about her, or why she was in New York. Why would she move to New York just to work at a diner? He wanted to ask her and figure everything out but first he wanted to revel in the purely happy moment he had stumbled into.

Before long, Jessica returned with a plate holding a burger and fries and a second plate adorned only by a mountain of fries. Jack wondered how she looked so beautiful in her apron and stained, blue shirt and skirt. It was almost like a dream. A figment of his imagination created by his own grief.

"Orders up!" She said with a smile. Jack looked at her with pure joy, but just as Paul had slithered into Jack's life, the question of why she was here slid into his brain poisoning his innocent bliss. He shoved it aside, picked his burger up and took a bite, it was inedible, but he was so hungry that he scarfed it down. Once his mouth was empty and the corners cleaned, he asked, "So, what have you been up to all this time?"

Jessica cleaned her mouth and started her story. She told Jack that she finished high school at Cielo High and was offered a scholarship at The University of Iowa for winning a big writing competition in Maine. She had taken a four-year program in creative writing and lived in a one-bedroom apartment—that was 'pretty dingy'—near the university full time since her parents passed in her senior year. After she finished that part, it took her a few minutes to continue but when she finally did, she told Jack that that they had died tragically in a car crash.

She told Jack how much she liked living in Iowa city. She had made some great friends and had dated a few boys. Jack hated that part of her story, but he couldn't control it, so he let her continue. She said a writing agent had come up to her at graduation in her senior year and told her that he would sign her to a three-book deal, so she had taken him up on first offer. Which was in her words, the opportunity of a lifetime. She had worked on her book for a year and had gotten it published early last year.

She said it was published under a different name because she didn't want to become a 'big star' but it had done quite well and her agent told her that she should move to New York to be closer to his office and according to him, all successful people live in New York. She had taken his advice and had been living in New York for 2 weeks. Jessica told him that it was her agent who had invited her to the party the night before. Jack was extremely impressed by her story and was even more impressed that she had published a book already, after all she was only 24 and that was in fact very impressive. But the agent seemed too good to be true.

Why would a writing agent be a part of the Founders? It was all a little bit too perfect for Jack to accept so easily. After all, naivety had not been the cause of any good fortune for him. After congratulating and giving his condolences to her for her parent's death, he asked, "What's your agents name?"

"Fergus Confucius. Apparently, he is one of the best agents in New York, do you know him?" Jack was frozen. Was it a coincidence that Confucius had picked her? It must have been, there's no way that Confucius would know she was important to him, plus she was approached for the first time a year ago and as far as Jack knew no one in New York even knew his name before he arrived a month ago. Did they? What would the professor's motives be to bring Jess there if he did know that she and Jack were extremely close just a few lifetimes ago? "Jack are you okay?" Jessica asked in a very concerned tone.

"Oh yeah, sorry I just zoned out. I thought I might know him, but I guess not." It was a bald-faced lie, but Jack didn't know what else to do. If Confucius did know he was close with Jessica, others would too and the others would have much worse intentions than Confucius did. Maybe the best thing for Jessica was if he never saw her again. He had a terrible feeling that just by sitting in the diner with her, he was putting her in danger.

As much as Jack loved sitting there with her, he cared about her way too much to lose her. He could live with never seeing her again if it meant she was safe but if he knew he had caused her pain he would never be able to live with himself. "So, where are you living?"

"Just down the street in a one-bedroom apartment, it's much better than my last one. You'll have to come over one day soon."

"Yeah, that would be great, maybe…" Jack's sentence was cut short by the buzz coming from his pocket. He slipped the phone from his jean pocket and saw the name. Paul. "Fuck me," Jack whispered under his breath. He knew the call was coming but he had hoped it wouldn't be for a day or two.

"Sorry I have to take this," Jack said and walked out of the diner.

"Yes sir?"

185

"Hanson, I have a few friends in town, and I've been bragging about you to them. I know I said you would have three weeks off, but they are dying to see if I've been exaggerating your skills. It won't be your usual work; they just want to see a fight. Could you come by the office in half an hour?"

"Sure sir, as long as the opponent isn't too good," Jack said followed by a hollow chuckle.

He hadn't expected a call, he hadn't expected mercy. He expected to be taken from his bed in the night and killed for lying and fraternizing with the enemy, but he wasn't complaining. Although the fact that they hadn't done anything yet made him uneasy. All things aside, a quick fight was better than all the other punishments Paul could have used.

"Perfect, I will see you then. But I can't promise it will be an easy fight I've been talking you up quite a bit. Better not let me down son." Then the line went dead. Jack thought that Paul meant it as a joke, but it absolutely sounded like a threat, like a veiled warning for what lay ahead.

Chapter 16

Jack had been in such a rush to get back to his apartment that he forgot to tell Jessica that he was leaving. But as he rode the elevator, he had time to think and realized it was the best thing that could have happened. He didn't know how to have the conversation about his involvement with Confucius and he knew he couldn't lie to her again. They had known each other for too long, she knew his real self. The masks he wore in every other facet of his life wouldn't fool her; she would see right through the paper-thin lies. Or at least she would have been able two before he left Cielo.

Jack didn't know how to tell her what was really happening in his life. He didn't know how to explain the opportunity, the killing, his relationship with Charlotte, or the fact that he had a plan to wiggle out from under the of the tyrants thumb he was currently pinned under. She wouldn't possibly be able to understand the need to kill in order to escape. She would insist that he go to the police or find another way even though Jack knew there was no other way; if there was, he would be planning to escape in that way. Killing wasn't his first choice, it was his only choice.

At least the Jess that he had known so long ago would want him to find another way, he didn't know what to expect now that she was working with Confucius and why he would have told her he was a literary agent. His list of questions had been piling up since his arrival. They would have to be answered soon but Jack didn't know when or how to uncover them. The only thing he knew for sure was that he would have to find them before he made his move, because without fortified walls he was vulnerable to attack from any angle. Even angles he didn't yet know existed could be his downfall.

If he wasn't able to zoom out and see the whole picture, he would be dead, or his soul would be ripped from the weak grasp he still had on it. As of that moment all he had were blurry images of puzzle pieces, with no sequence or vague idea of how they all fit together.

The steel doors opened to his apartment, he walked in and set his coat on the back of one of the chairs that sat at the island and went to the bathroom to shower and fix his hair. Jack knew it didn't really matter what he looked like; he would have a head of unruly hair by the end of the night anyways. But the mask he put on when meeting Paul was of a confident, clean shaven, smartly dressed, punctual and impressive young man. The thin yet convincing costume he fashioned for himself on the first job he ever did for Paul was quite possibly the only reason he was still alive, so it was important to maintain the curtains opaque nature.

Before stepping into the shower, Jack stared at himself in the mirror, Jessica had allowed the color to return to his face and had driven the waxy, pale broken shell back beneath the surface, but no human would be able to take the broken, sinful pain from his eyes. Jack knew it might never leave him. He carried three lost souls around his neck, his eyes would always betray the weight he carried. The feelings rippling just beneath the surface of his retinas made Jack sad and the more grief stricken he became, the more pity he felt for himself, the looser the chains keeping the horrors locked away became.

Inevitably, they gave into the pressure and the memories flooded his vision. The screams filled his ears. The blood trickling, the pleas, the bones breaking beneath his fists and the horrifying bang of finality overwhelmed his senses. But Jack was ready, he could feel the onset of the crippling visions and steadied himself for their attack, he pushed his feet into the ground as hard as he could, trying to break through the floor. As he pushed, he fought the memories with joyous ones of his own. Memories of he and his mother sitting next to each other on their small couch were the first that popped into his head.

Jack tried as hard as he could to suck the happiness out of the memory and use it as a knife and slash holes in the memory's curtains drawing to a close in front of his vision. After three swipes, he was able to make a hole big enough to see through, turning the shower on he fought his way into the stream and let the frozen water wash the tattered curtains away. Once the curtains woven with pain and suffering were completely dissolved, he shut the water off, wiped the straggling droplets from his skin, fixed his hair and headed to the closet to grab a suit.

It was a special night; Jack had no idea what was in store for him. Of course, he didn't normally know what was in store for him but that night he knew he had messed up. He had shown a quick glimpse of his true self, and that was more dangerous than any bullet fired from any gun. Paul may have been telling the truth on the phone, but it was just as plausible that he was lying. Death, pain or more grief could be waiting for him at the office. Jack decided to make sure that he looked the part of the good employee while he still had the chance, it might make Paul rethink the punishment that he had instore for him.

It was still plausible that it may not but still, Jack had to try. He wasn't done living quite yet. Jack picked a navy-blue suit with a black tie, black shirt, black belt and black shoes. The outfit reflected him perfectly while keeping his faux skin intact. He laced his shoes and buckled the belt and then headed to the mirror to affix the tie to his neck. Jack was nervous about looking back into the mirror because he knew his eyes would trigger the memories, so he forced himself to focus on the tie, never making eye contact with himself.

Once he looked presentable, he checked his phone, he had 5 minutes until he had to leave, time enough for a drink and then run to the curb to catch the black sedan that would undoubtedly be waiting for him. He poured a stiff glass of whiskey, downed it all in one go and headed into the elevator, slipping his suit jacket on as he crossed it's steel threshold. The elevator began its plunge downward, the night had begun. Jack prayed to every god he could think of that he wouldn't be forced to allow another soul's weight to pass the semi permeable membrane of the red sun hanging heavily around his neck.

He knew it was a possibility, with Paul it always was but he also knew he might have to surrender his own soul in the coming hours. After all, he had forfeited quite a bit of the respect he had worked so hard to earn since he had arrived. Jack had made peace with the fact that he may die by the time the elevator doors opened but he still held strong against the knowledge that he may be forced to kill once again in the coming hours.

Jack walked past Angela without a word and stepped into the night, since he had entered the building the sun had taken its leave and draped a blanket of darkness over the city that didn't seem to sleep. The black sedan Jack knew would be waiting for him sat on the curb. He paused and stepped in without a word. Once he was inside the driver pulled away without so much as a curt hello.

The car drove without stopping at a single light until they reached the office. The familiar but no less ominous building sat in front of Jack as if telling him he should just leave before hell was released from its cage but despite the

189

glinting steel blade of dread threatening to slide itself through the gaps in his rib cage, Jack opened the door and stepped onto the sidewalk. Looking straight ahead at the threshold of hell he forced his legs into motion and walked up to the doors, opened the right one, and walked through. The massive hall leered at him, making him feel like an ant under a very large boot that was willing to crush him at any point. As he walked through the hall to the right elevator, he felt the desk attendant's gaze burning his shoulders.

"Watch yourself tonight, Paul says you're the best but the man he has for you tonight may best even you," she whispered. At first, Jack didn't know where the voice had come from but after a few seconds he realized it had been the voiceless, motionless woman who sat at the desk night and day. Her raspy voice made Jack's skin crawl, but she saw everything that came in and out of the building.

"Who is he, what is your name?" He asked quietly without turning around.

"New recruit, just like you at the beginning except he has a thirst to prove himself. Something you never had if I'm not mistaken and don't worry about my name, I am you 10 years from now."

Jack was silent, scared to say anything, how could he trust the gatekeeper of hell? Yet somehow, she knew his real self, maybe he hadn't hidden it well enough, and if she knew Paul must know as well. If she had stayed alive for ten full years, then she must be loyal to Paul, and loyalty was dangerous to Jack, so he continued to the elevator, turning to look at her only when he stepped inside the steel box. Before the doors closed, he saw her face plain as day. Her eyes burned with defiance and anger; they made Jack rethink his earlier assumption.

Maybe she really was trying to warn him, maybe she really wanted him to live to see the sunrise. Her eyes stayed at the forefront of his mind until the elevator doors opened once again. The multitude of questions that had been fluttering around his brain in a chaotic tornado of unknown vanished when he saw Paul sitting with his legs on the desk, arms crossed in front of him.

He looked like a man who was burdened by nothing, a man without morals who truly believed to his core that he ran the world. Jack walked in and he slid his legs off the desk and walked toward Jack, even under the suit Jack could see the toned muscles contracting and releasing with each step. Paul stood silent and motionless in front of him for a few moments and Jack feared he would pull a weapon and kill him where he stood there in that moment but instead, he

190

stuck out his hand to shake Jack's. Jack obliged and shook the gnarled hand firmly.

"Damn kid, you look like a man in charge. It's good to see you Hanson, I hope you can put on a show for my colleagues tonight. I have recruited another guy, so tonight you will have a fight on your hands. I don't think you will be able to steamroll this one, although that being said, I invite you to prove me wrong. Oh, and by the way I know you were at the Founders party the other night but don't worry, even though Alex might be mad I don't care. I'm happy you are doing so well at school." Jack didn't know what to say, how could Paul be so flippant about him disregarding such a generous offer. It was such a blatant display of disrespect.

"I will try sir. Thank you for being so understanding, I will put on a great show for your guests." Jack truly meant each word; he wouldn't have to kill anyone, and he would be able to save the kid from a life of horrific memories and guilt, so he would put on a 'show'. Maybe Paul would see it and think he shouldn't be used for killing and switch his job to 'entertainer'. Jack knew it was a pipe dream, but he still wanted to do something as a thanks for the mercy.

"No problem, Hanson you're my best man," Paul said draping his arm over Jack's shoulders. Jack was so lost in happiness that he forgot to feel enraged at the show of fatherly love. The pair walked to the elevator and headed down to the damp room. When the doors opened to the room that always seemed to be thick with moisture and mold, Jack was brought back to reality, it was the place where he had signed his soul off to the devil. He remembered the first man he had ever beaten in the room.

Henry had been beaten in 'record time'. In the moment it had felt like a terrible sin but in the months since he had carried out so many more and far deadlier transgressions. The first fight might have been the one that had kept him alive all these weeks. So maybe it was okay to take pride in what he was about to do. The unknown kid that he was about to beat senseless would eventually thank him for the inevitable violence. "Go ahead and put your stuff over on that chair," Paul said pointing to one of the rickety wooden chairs on the right side of the room.

As Jack walked over to the chair he looked over at the left side of the room and saw eight, massive, brown leather chairs. Jack knew he would have a crowd but eight people was quite a few. He wondered if they were all for Paul's friends or if they would be occupied by people Jack had already met. Jack removed all the usual clothes, belt, shoes, jacket, shirt, tie and socks. Once he was covered from ankles to hips, he stretched his arms out wide making sure the elasticity he would need was still there.

As his arms reached their limit, he knew it still was. He wiped his fingers over the lids of eyes trying to remove the layer of fatigue from them. When he opened his eyes again, he saw the first of Paul's friends walking in from the hidden door on the other side of the room. Four men walked in that Jack didn't recognize. Jack assumed they must have been the friends but once they had filed into the room, familiar faces followed. The first was the Man in Red who looked just as angry as he had at the party. The second was Charlotte, wearing her patented black dress with the red pendant resting against her beautiful skin, her personal siren of sin. As she walked to her seat, she flashed Jack a fear filled smile.

The next was a young man Jack assumed to be his opponent and when the man started to undress at his wooden chair Jack knew he was right. The man was about the same height as him but unlike Jack his eyes held the same look Paul's did. They were hungry, angry, and glistened with confidence. The next figure to enter the room shook Jack to his very core. A white dress with red stitching was all he could make out at first but once her face appeared from the darkness Jack just about passed out. The innocent eyes were perched atop a small scar. Her face almost looked fake against the backdrop of the damp, moldy room.

Jessica sat on the last chair closest to the far door and stared directly at Jack. Her unsurprised expression made Jack seethe with anger. How could she have not told him that she knew he worked for Paul and better yet what in the fuck was she doing at the fight. Jack knew he was unbelievably naïve to think that he had gotten so lucky as to meet Jessica 10ft from his apartment. It still didn't answer the question of why she was there, but it didn't matter. Jack was so filled with anger that he almost pitied the young man who was supposed to be proving his worth that night, the boy had no chance. Jack would beat him to within an inch of his life just to show Jessica he was dangerous. To show her that she may have outsmarted him, but she would be explaining herself in the near future. As his eyes attempted to burn holes in Jessica's perfect face, he saw Paul walking toward him in his peripheral vision.

"You ready, Hanson?"

"Yes sir," Jack said, words dripping with white hot fury. "You are going to see one hell of a show tonight sir, I hope your kid can fight because he is going to need to know something, lest he die right here on the mat."

Paul chuckled, with a wolfish amusement. "I think he does, are you okay Jack?" He said although his tone betrayed the fact that he already knew what he had done. He knew he had blindsided Jack and set the monster Jack kept locked away free.

"Fine…Sir," Jack said softly to avoid strangling Paul. Jack was ready to show what he could and eventually would do to the man who was the author of every morsel of pain he had been forced to swallow over the last month.

"Good," Paul said walking back to his chair and whispering something into the ear of the small Asian man sitting next to him. Once he had finished his private conversation, he sat straight up and asked loudly so both fighters could hear.

"Ready, fellas?" Jack was silent but the young man that clearly wanted Paul's respect said loudly, "Yes sir."

Jack hated the enthusiasm in the unsuspecting victim's voice. It almost made him lose his nerve but one look in Jessica's direction made the fires of anger flare up once again. He stepped into the ring and looked his victim up and down. The man was strong and quite a bit of impressive muscle rippled beneath his skin, but Jack knew he had him beat and summarized that the boy would be out cold in 20 seconds. He only gave the kid that long because he wanted to inflict pain. He wanted to show Paul that he could beat anyone if he was angry enough, he wanted the room to know he was angry. Paul needed to know what laid in his future. When the two fighters stepped onto the mat, the slow, hungry drawl was released from Paul's mouth.

"Be…gin," Jack circled his prey like a lone wolf circling a wounded pup. He was going to show every inch of his anger and pain. The only downside was that it was a boy standing in front of him instead of Paul himself. The only solace came from the evil residing in the boy's eyes. The boy swung with his right hand first; Jack swiped it aside as if it was a feather glancing his arm. His right hand connected with the boys left arm.

The boy drew back in pain, but his eyes showed the same thirst for respect as they had before. Jack waited another few second before driving his fist into the boys' ribs, the bones snapped under his fingers and the memories threatened to take over once again but the anger had control so they were driven back.

193

The boy let out a yelp of pain and a trace of fear danced in his eyes but was quickly replaced with the same wolfish thirst for power and stature. Jack mentally applauded the boy for his perseverance but a quick glance at Jessica made him flare with anger once again. The boy aimed a devastating blow at Jack's head, but he easily dodged it and thrust his shoulder into the boy's midsection.

Wrapping his arms around the boy's legs Jack heaved his weight over his shoulder and slammed his boy's body onto the mat. Jack looked down and saw that the boy was still awake, so he paced back a few steps and let him stand back up. When the boy got back to his feet Jack went in for the kill; He drove his fist into the boy's head, not hard enough to kill but hard enough that Jack knew he would be asleep for a while and when he eventually came to, his head would pound with pain. Even though the punch didn't set the boys soul free, the power still lifted him off his feet and hit the floor with a satisfying thud. Jack knew he had proven his point.

Looking at the panel of spectators he saw only amazement and approval. Jack had not let Paul down and that was the last time he would do something for the man without a gun to his head. Paul's friends looked upon him with supreme approval, all wishing they possessed Jack's poetically violent gift. Paul himself looked even prouder than he had the first time Jack had won a fight in front of him and the sight of the proud devil made the monster inside Jack slink back into its cave, coated in a film of embarrassment.

The anger stayed but Jack felt foolish. He had proved his point but at what cost. Jessica seemed thoroughly unimpressed and uninterested with Jack's performance, but Charlotte looked melancholily happy. Maybe it was because she knew he was her partner in their fight against Paul, but Jack couldn't help but wonder if it was because she really was loyal to Paul and like him, she too enjoyed the spill of blood.

Jack walked to the wooden chair to the right of the mat. Turned to the wall trying to tie his tie without having any sort of mirror to check his work, he felt a warm hand on his shoulder. It belonged to a man half the size of Jack. The small Chinese man stood staring up at him and said, "Very impressive work Mr. Hanson, I am very pleased to have you as a part of this organization."

Jack knew Paul didn't have friends; the so-called 'friends' were business associates. Men who were under his boot just as Jack was, although they had the unique perspective of thinking they were a part of the boot. When they were in fact just another ant like Jack who could be squished by Paul and his inner circle at the drop of a hat. As Jack turned around, he saw a line of the 'friends' all waiting to offer their compliments.

"Thank you, sir, it's very good to meet you," Jack said offering his hand for the tiny man to shake. He knew that although the line of men were just ants under the boot like him, they were much bigger ants who could snuff him out before the boot ever got a chance. That was the trouble with being at the bottom of the totem pole, the number of angles to fortify became overwhelming. Jack knew he had to be very careful around the men Paul considered friends.

"Pleasure's all mine son, have a good night," the small Chinese man said, moving aside so that the next man could offer his own praise.

The trend continued until the last man, a bearded, muscled Russian man who towered over Jack spoke, "Good fight, I have seen better but this is all we can expect from you small Americans." Jack knew that he might be able to knock this man out or at the very least make him feel a considerable amount of pain. But he decided to hold his tongue and put his confidence to the test another day. "One day you will come to Russia to see how to fight for real?"

"Yes, sir I would be honored," Jack said not wanting to insult the behemoth.

"Good, good, have a fine evening boy," The large Russian said. Being referred to as boy made Jack smirk, he had just been thinking about his opponent as a boy. It was amazing that the higher up on the GWA's ladder you climbed, the more you thought yourself better than the people stuck on the rung you had already climbed past. It was a false sense of superiority that Jack would have to get under control very soon. If he didn't, he would be no better than the men he despised. Jack couldn't help but marvel at the extent of vanity's poisonous tentacles.

Once the Russian man had finished his string of comments the four 'friends' walked in lock step toward the door and disappeared into the unknown space behind the door at the far end of the room. After they had all been swallowed by the darkness, Jack took inventory of the room. The only ones left were Paul, Charlotte, and the boy he had knocked senseless. Somehow in the time Jack had been barraged with compliments and veiled insults, Jessica and Alexander had slipped away.

Jack looked over at the boy, he was now sitting on the wooden chair beside Jack's looking very unsure about what to do next; Paul and Charlotte had remained seated in their chairs and were deep in conversation; they weren't talking very loudly so Jack couldn't make out what they were saying. But Jack knew it wasn't a pleasurable conversation by the way Charlotte was tensed. Every muscle in her body tightened, keeping her figure in the perfect position. Her legs crossed, fingers interlocked and resting in her lap with her head turned toward Paul and tilted slightly so that she would be able to hear perfectly.

To the untrained eye, she may have seemed calm. A woman having a regular conversation with her boss, but she and Jack had been as close to each other as two people could be so Jack knew every inch of her body as though it was the back of his own hand. There was nothing he could do except wait; he unbuttoned the lone button on his suit and sat down on the wooden chair his clothes had rested on moments ago. He turned his head and saw the boy dressing himself, his left eye had started to bruise and swell but Jack assumed that was the least of the boy's pain.

Now that the monster had retreated to its cave, he felt a twinge of guilt for beating the boy so relentlessly, he felt like a bully in the school yard. The bully was never actually mad at the kid they beat they usually were sad about their home lives or some other outside influence. The same could be said for Jack. The only difference was that the boy would eventually thank Jack for showing him what pain really felt like. But although he needn't feel guilt Jack decided that he would apologize to the boy and then interrupt the deep conversation Charlotte was having with Paul.

He didn't want to stay in the room thick with moisture all night, he wanted to leave as quick as possible. The memories were starting to come back, and he didn't want to be near anyone other than maybe Charlotte when they finally made it to the top of the hill and took control.

Jack stood up, clasped the lone bottom on his jacket and walked toward the boy. "What's your name kid?"

The boy stared at him with a confused or scared expression. It was hard to tell and took the boy a long time before answering.

"Luke, and yours is?" The boy said quietly. He looked like he was on the verge of tears but struggled to stand up and outstretched his hand to shake Jack's. As he stood, he kept his left hand on his ribs as if he was trying to keep them in place. Immediately Jack understood why it was such a struggle for him to stand, his ribs had been broken. Jack reached out and shook his hand.

"My name's Jack, sorry about the ribs by the way. I shouldn't have gone so hard on you, there were a few surprises that may have clouded my judgment. Lost control a bit."

"All good, Paul told me you were good, but I wasn't expecting that. Henry was much easier to beat."

Jack's face went paper white as the blood fled from it in search of a safer more secure part of his body. Jack's show of force had been for nothing, Luke was already a part of the GWA, there was no stopping it now. He had beaten Henry, and Paul wasn't going to let him go just for losing in a fight that didn't mean anything. The guilt gained weight in his heart but was lightened when Jessica's face reappeared in his mind. Her unsurprised expression when he had lifted the boy's lifeless body off the ground left Jack feeling utterly unnerved. The Jessica he used to know would have been appalled with the display of violence, the Jessica that lived in Cielo didn't even understand when Jack started boxing at the local gym.

She had said, "Why do you need to fight? Love will always win Jack; you don't need to fight to prove that you're a man." At the time Jack believed her and every time he went to gym, he felt like he was betraying her but in his situation there was no other choice, he had to fight to survive, and she didn't seem to mind violence anymore, in fact it didn't elicit any sort of emotion at all. The only question that remained was: What had changed?

"You are 100 times better than Henry. How long did it take you to beat him?" Luke asked.

In Jack's ears, he sounded like a star struck child asking their favorite athlete questions, eager to learn the craft. Jack hoped he hadn't done any real work yet. If he had, the boy was even more terrifying than Paul was.

"I can't really remember, 45 seconds I think," Jack said.

Luke's eyes widened in awe. "I can't believe Paul said I would have a chance to beat you. It took me 3 whole minutes and even then, I just barely won." Jack was confused, Paul had said he would have a tough time with Luke. The kid had taken more than triple the amount of time he had taken to prove himself. If three minutes was an above average time, then Charlotte must have been close to death before she beat her opponent. But as he thought about it, neither Paul nor Charlotte had spoken about her first fight—first was presumptuous, she had probably only had to fight once. Jack assumed Paul just liked to watch him inflict pain on weaker men. He craved power and an uneven fight is the greatest concentration of power a human can get near enough to spectate.

"Three minutes is a good time don't be too hard on yourself, I must have just gotten lucky. How old are you kid?" Jack asked glancing in Charlotte's direction, she and Paul were still in deep conversation.

"23. But I turn 24 next month."

Jack was speechless, Luke didn't look a day over 18. Now that Jack knew that he was only a year older than him for the next month it made even less sense that Paul would have ever thought that he would be able to put up a fight against him. It wasn't even as though he had years to grow into an adult. His figure was as big as it would ever be. Paul must have tried to ensure that Jack would use the maximum amount of force he possibly could. Paul was in the mood to rile Jack up that night, that much was clear as day.

"Oh, I see, well…have a good night, sorry about the ribs again," Jack said, turning away and walking toward Charlotte and Paul. Paul looked up as he approached them and spoke, "Hanson my boy, you promised a show and my God did you produce an award-winner! Thank you for providing some entertainment for my guests tonight, I'm sure they were very happy with what they saw."

Being referred to as 'my boy' lit the fire of rage again and Jack fantasized about knocking Paul out right then, tying him up and repeating the ordeal over and over until he never woke up. But he had yet see the whole picture and the pieces he thought he possessed were becoming increasingly blurry. New players and questions had been introduced and Jack needed time to fortify the growing number of angles.

So, he bit his tongue and said, "Of course, sir. Although I feel like you may have overestimated your new recruits' skills. I didn't expect it to be that easy."

"Well, I didn't expect you to go so hard on him Hanson, you were especially dominant tonight. Not that I'm complaining, I loved every second of the massacre," Paul said with a grin that told Jack he knew exactly what he had done.

Jack shuddered at Paul's words, the thought of making him happy was horrible. How could he have been so blinded by gratitude? He wouldn't make that mistake again. Jack was beginning to realize that every move Paul made was to hurt someone, the only trick was knowing who it was before it was too late. Jack forced a 'thank you' void of any sort of gratitude out of his mouth and then said, "Is it okay if I head out, sir?"

"Of course, have a good couple weeks Jack, I don't think you will be hearing from me for a while. You have definitely earned a few weeks off after your last two performances," Paul said with a big smile.

To anyone else it would look like he was being kind, but Jack knew he was only happy because he had won. He had cut Jack's soul so deep that it was barely holding onto its original form and furthermore he had made Jack lose control, revealing monster within.

"Thank you, sir," Jack said and turned in the direction of the elevator, beginning to walk away. Jack heard a chair shuffle behind him, but he kept walking stopping only when he heard Charlotte say, "wait."

He waited for her to catch up and then continued his pace until he reached the elevator doors. They opened as if the doors knew he was in a hurry to leave, and Charlotte entered alongside him. As the doors began to close Jack's eyes locked with Paul's and he waved a cheerful goodbye. Jack hated that the man could taunt him, and he couldn't do anything about it. He knew one day the roles would be reversed but for now he was firmly strapped to the torture chair. Just as the doors squeaked shut Charlotte spoke, "You made up for your defiance last night, so we really are in the clear for a few weeks. That kid you beat senseless is going to do all the jobs for a few weeks. He has performed pretty well so far so Paul thinks he should he fine."

Jack was taken aback; Luke had done jobs and still held his excitement. It was terrifying, he was a real threat not just an innocent kid but a murderer who enjoyed who he was or who he had become. It was a quality that made him even more dangerous than Paul. A leader is dangerous, but a martyr has the advantage because they have nothing to lose.

"Great. Were you that happy when you first started?" Jack asked, hoping she would say no and as soon as he looked at Charlotte, he knew she was truly hurt by his question.

Her eyes burned with a pain that could only be inflicted if the person knows the accusation could very well be true. "I cried myself to sleep for 3 years. Even now I can't go to sleep without being drunk or stoned."

A lone tear fell down her cheek. "I can't believe you would even ask me that."

Jack thought that if she was lying, she was the greatest actress of all time. "Sorry, it was just a question," he said looking in the opposite direction of Charlotte to hide the embarrassment on his face. Paul had successfully sowed fields of mistrust and doubt in Jack mind. He hated every part of Paul; every inch of his soul was poisoned—that was if he even possessed a soul. Charlotte reached over, straightening Jack's tie, as if to say she forgave him for what he had said.

"Want to come over?" Jack asked. He did have a few questions—It seemed like he always did these days—but he honestly had started to enjoy her company and needed it that night more than most.

"I was about to ask you the same question Mr. Hanson," Charlotte said mockingly and then giggled at her own joke. Jack's face lit up when he saw the smile stretch across her's, it made him think that he still had a chance at happiness. It allowed him to believe that maybe, just maybe the world wasn't all red, maybe it still contained a few drops of green.

The pair stepped out of the elevator and made their way to the door, both warm with happiness. Jack welcomed the feeling like an old friend. Being touched by happiness's gentle touch had become a foreign concept to him.

"How was the night sir?" The voice startled Charlotte who whipped around to see where the noise had come from, but Jack knew who it was. He turned around slowly.

"I won Ma'am," He said calmly. He wasn't sure if he could trust her, so he decided to keep his true feelings about winning to himself.

"He didn't just win ma'am; he destroyed the new kid. He was brilliant," Charlotte boasted.

Jack blushed and pushed gently on Charlotte's lower back as if to say, "Shut up, let's get out of here."

"It was nothing ma'am. Just did my job. We better be going, have a good night." Jack was lying of course; it was a huge deal no matter which way you sliced it. In Jack's brain, it meant he was a bad person and made him doubt his self-control. In Paul's eyes, Jack was a hero, an unstoppable weapon that he could point in any direction he saw fit. In the GWA representative's eyes, he was a champion, a great fighter, and an irreplaceable asset to the organization. The only perspectives that Jack couldn't quite figure out were Charlotte and Jessica's. The ironic part of it was that the two people who Jack knew the most, the two people that Jack thought he knew inside and out were the two that he was unsure about.

"Okay Jack, you have yourself a good night. Don't stay up too late you have a class tomorrow," the woman said and then turned back into the statue that Jack had grown accustomed to.

Jack couldn't make up his mind about how he felt about the woman. She was very odd, there was no doubt about that. But was she on his side or was she on Paul's? Of course, there was the chance that she didn't even know there had been a line drawn in the sand and furthermore an opportunity to pick sides but then why would she have warned Jack about Luke? It didn't make sense, either did the comment about him having school that night, or the comment about he and Charlotte staying up too late. She was either using the same tactics as Paul, or she really cared about his well-being. The only question was which side she had chosen. It was just another piece of the puzzle that Jack had to find before he was able to make his move.

When Jack and Charlotte finally exited the gates of hell, she pulled his head toward his until they were so close that Jack could feel her breath on his lips, thoughts were almost being exchanged through the air as if it were a synaptic cleft, then she pressed her soft welcoming lips to his. Jack tilted his head until his lips were perfectly interlocked with hers. Her tongue touching his and then receding back into its own mouth, Jack loved that part of the kiss.

It was like she was tempting him to come closer, inviting him to become a part of her, and instead of each of their souls residing in different bodies they would share one. Yet something always stopped him, his broken soul hanging on to its mortal form for dear life. Maybe it was because his mother only knew him in that form or maybe it was because there was so much pain and grief in his own body that he didn't want Charlotte to have to live alongside it. It was bad enough for him to live with it every day. He didn't want her to have to find a way past the pain every minute of every day. But he suspected that Charlotte was stained red just as permanently as he was, if not more so.

Jack pulled away and rested his head against Charlotte's, trying to hold on to the bliss for one more moment but when he heard tires screeching to a stop at the curb, he knew it had flown past. Charlotte cut the connection and began to walk toward to curb, Jack followed her slowly at first and then remembered that he was a man and hurried around her to open the door. Once they were both inside the car, it immediately drove off.

Charlotte and Jack sat in silence for a while, both not wanting to speak first but eventually Jack cut through the silence, "Do you know who the other woman who was at the fight was?" He asked. He hoped she wouldn't know, and it was just Paul who knew her true identity. He prayed that she was oblivious to the mental war Paul had decided to wage.

"Yeah," Charlotte said in a whisper. "I thought she was dead, Paul told me she was dead. That lying piece of shit. I thought I saw her last night at the party but told myself I was seeing things. After seeing her here tonight I see that she is most definitely not dead."

Jack was confused, why would Jessica be dead and how did Charlotte know her. Nothing she was saying made sense. Jack decided to get her to say the name she knew Jessica by. He had a terrible sinking feeling that he knew what name Charlotte knew her by. He just hoped he was wrong.

"What's her name?" He asked.

"Marissa…she was my best friend, or what I thought was my best friend. Really, she was just a little snake, tightening her coils until the final moment when she must have decided to let go and tell her master everything. God, I hate that cunt. Our plan is going to have to revised. She will be the hardest to snuff, by far. If you don't count that new psychopath Paul hired."

Jack's heart dropped even farther with every word. Jessica was Marissa and Marissa was Jessica. Marissa wasn't dead, and the worst part was that Paul had found a way to kill his best friend and replace her soul with something much different. He had been away from her too long, there must have been a terrible accident. Maybe she was telling the truth about her parents, maybe they were the origin story to the devil she had become.

Even so, how did she come to be employed by Paul and why would she say she was employed by Confucius? The picture had become so blurry that he could barely make out his own figure amongst the masses. Jack couldn't find the words to tell Charlotte that her real name was Jessica, and she was the girl that Jack loved. How to tell her that for the last ten years she was the one that he couldn't get out his mind. The one that he had longed to get back to Cielo to see. So, he didn't, at least not at that moment. He would just let her only have one life shattering truth unveiled that night. Instead, he changed the subject to the second question he had wanted to ask ever since Luke had said it had taken him three minutes to prove his worth.

"I was apologizing to Luke for breaking his ribs after the fight and he said it took him 3 minutes to beat Henry, and I was wondering how long it took you," Jack said, cheeks warming with a shy apprehension.

"Oh," Charlotte said absent mindedly, obviously chained to her own sub conscious. No doubt trying to see where her relationship with Marissa had soured. But Jack could see his question breaking her concentration and he watched as the thought grew smaller and smaller until it seemed to disappear completely. "It's kind of embarrassing but I was only eighteen so don't judge me. It took me half an hour. I was near death before I won. My ribs, jaw and arm were all broken.

My shoulder was dislocated, and I had a serious concussion, but Paul must have admired my unwillingness to give up because he carried me to the car and made the driver take me to the hospital. He might have just saw my soul was strong and the challenge of breaking it excited him. I don't know which it was but either way I survived that night and became a part of the GWA."

The story and the thought of Charlotte being in that type of crippling pain made Jack sad. Even now after all that had happened Jack was appalled by the extent of Paul's evil. The depths of his resentment, and hate were limitless; they formed a never-ending hole filled with souls that never got full or even satisfied after seeing so many souls shattered. The appetite Paul had for the souls of the already broken was amazing, Jack wondered when the craving started. It must have come out of the blue one day, after a traumatic event. It couldn't have been after his life was saved, there had to have been an instance after that in which his own soul was ripped from his chest and replaced with something darker, something tough and without weakness.

"Have you fought again since that night?" Jack asked because the frequency in which Paul was making him fight was insane. It hurt his soul to hurt innocent people—well some innocent people, Luke didn't seem all that innocent—day in and day out.

"No, he was my last fight and I hope he is the only one I have to fight for the rest of my life," Charlotte said.

Jack knew they had the fight of their lives ahead of them and that she would most likely be forced to protect herself, but he kept that sliver of truth for himself. "Then why does Paul keep making me fight? It's getting ridiculous and the stronger he sees me get the more dangerous it gets for us. The more he sees, the more he will be on guard when I am around, and the less likely it is that our plan works out," Jack said exasperated. The plan was being wrestled from his hands by the new players, the tyranny of Paul and about 100 other factors. The likelihood of it coming to fruition was growing smaller in Jack's eyes and he was becoming more and more sure that his future was going to be successfully wrestled from his grip.

"He wants to show you that no matter how strong you get he still owns you. You may be a well-paid slave, but you will always be a slave. He also likes watching you fight though, and I can see why. When you fight, you're an artist, the way you dance around your opponent's blocks and strike exactly where you mean to, your eyes shimmer with intelligence when you see the opening to send the opponent into oblivion. You know, the only time I have seen your eyes burn with anger during a fight was tonight. Why were you so angry, what made you so irate? I would have thought that the fact you didn't have to do any real work tonight would have been a relief for you."

Jack thought for a moment. He knew he would eventually have to tell Charlotte something, he knew he wouldn't be able to keep his secret forever. If not from his lips, she would hear it from another's. There was no way around it, but he had prayed for more time to uncover the perfect way to tell it. The truth was funny, it had a way of eliciting anger and sadness. It set you free and locked you away all at once. Jack had never told the truth and had it met with a happy response.

The truth had a way of telling people exactly what they didn't want to hear. It was like a juxtaposition; truth making way for anger and sadness and lies making way for happiness and oblivious contentment. It wasn't fair, but of course life for Jack never was.

"She was there," Jack said softly.

"Who Jack? Marissa? How would you know her and why would she make you so angry?" Charlotte said.

Jack just looked at her with desperate pleading eyes, as if begging her to drop it. Silently telling her that she didn't want to hear the answer. But all she did was sit perfectly still, arms crossed, looking for an answer, an answer that Jack knew wouldn't be met with a safe warmth. It would make contact like a penetrating frost.

"Her name isn't Marissa," Jack said, a lone tear leaving trail of red skin in its wake down his cheek. "Her name is Jessica; she is the girl I left back in Cielo. She is the girl I have loved since I was 14 years old. I saw her earlier today at the Four Roses, she told me she works with Confucius." His heart threatened to beat out of his chest and the memories fought their way into his vison while the blood trickled down the lifeless head. Fantom bones broke under his fist's powerful strength, but he fought through the horrors. "I have no idea what all of it means and I am dangerously close to losing my mind." When he finished speaking, the memories took hold. They consumed him with an oceanic force of horrors. As he felt himself leaving the land of the living and drifting further and further into the crippling wasteland of memories, lips pressed against his. He latched onto their strength and warmth for dear life.

Before long, the memories faded away like the ice on a windshield after a few minutes of the defrost blasting. Jack's vision became clear, and he felt safe at last, his heartbeat slowed, and his breathing resumed its normal pace. He knew that if he and Charlotte stayed together, they would be able to get through this hell they found themselves in. He could physically beat every man in New York, and she would be able to calm him if it got too much or if the memories, that were sure to rear their ugly, red stained heads, made an appearance.

The only question still blocking the floodlight of hope was, could he truly trust her with his life? Jack knew that he should be able to, he knew that she was exemplifying many trustworthy aspects, but something still gnawed at him. Something that told him she couldn't be trusted. It was like a voice in the depths of his soul saying that everyone was out to get him. The fact that Jessica had obviously betrayed him made him even more weary but if he wanted to get out, he would certainly have to put complete trust in someone, and the list had been whittled down to one name. Charlotte Jones.

She pulled away and wiped the tears that had been steadily streaming down her face. "I know Jack, I hoped you wouldn't recognize her, but I have known since I went to Cielo and found out all I could about you. The only thing I didn't know was that she was alive. I thought that I had gotten your best friend killed even before I knew who you were. But when I saw her at the party last night, I knew it was her."

Jack looked at her in disbelief, the words had not registered in his brain yet. He just sat there, his face a blank canvas. Before long, anger, pain and sadness painted themselves across the untouched canvas. The fires lit in his heart, and he had to fight against everything inside of himself not to lash out and hurt her.

"Driver, please take Mrs. Jones back to her apartment," Jack said in a dangerously sharp tone of calmness. The driver looked into the rear-view mirror, his eyes caught Jack's and Jack could tell he was very confused but just said, "Yes sir."

Jack sat straight forward seething with a white-hot fury for the rest of the drive to his apartment. Not only had Charlotte known Jessica was alive and decided not to tell him but she had known her and what she meant to Jack before she had presented Jack with his opportunity. It was so innately wrong that Jack could barely think. Streams of apologies and begs for forgiveness flowed out of Charlotte's mouth for the rest of the ride but they never got past the wall of betrayal that had been erected between the two allies.

When the car finally pulled to a stop outside of Jack's building, he thanked the driver and stepped out without so much as a formal goodbye to Charlotte. As he stepped out of the car, he noticed that it was snowing, the pure white flakes fell from the sky covering the ground in a purely white layer of deceit and lies. Jack looked up and allowed the snow to fall on his face, maybe it would make him pure again, maybe it would erase the plethora of truths that had been revealed in the last few hours. As he stood with his eyes closed, head tilted to the heavens he heard the tires of the car screech, letting him know Charlotte had left. She had really gone.

He opened his eyes again and trained them on the ground at his feet, the snow covering the ground reminded him of the white sheet that covered a body at a crime scene. It was as if God was covering the world in a white sheet, not wanting Jack to see any more of the darkness that inhabited its darkest corners as well as its most beautiful skies. Like he was ashamed of his creation. But through the gaps in the white Jack could still see the pavement just like he could see all the evil and darkness that hid in the shadows and only reared their ugly heads to wrap their tentacles around him, trying to pull him into the shadows to join them.

Their forked, serpent like tongues slipped into Jack's ears making way for the darkest evils and allowing them to streak across his consciousness. The cold was eating at Jack's ears, nose, lips, and fingers so he decided he would go inside but before he made it to the door, he remembered that he was close to running his Crown Royal reserves dry. He decided to go to the liquor store next door to buy more. He was going to need it.

Chapter 17

When Jack arrived at the door to the liquor store, he decided to turn around, maybe that night was the night he could break the pattern of liquor being his only medicine but as he tried to turn away his legs pulled him inside. The broken teenager sitting on the uncomfortable seat of the police car on his way to a new home pulled him to the shelf carrying the whiskeys. His arms raised of their own accord and pulled the largest bottle of bottle of Crown from the shelf. Once the bottle of emotion suppressing, amber colored liquid was in his hands he submitted to his body's need for its effects. He walked slowly to the counter and placed it down, the cashier said, "Hey Jack!"

All the cashiers knew his name and he knew theirs. This one's name was Faith. She was a student at NYU, and she worked at the small liquor store for something to do at night because she was on a scholarship, so she had no real need for extra money. They usually had a brief conversation when Jack came to the store, but not that night. That night, Jack wasn't in the mood for a stupid, meaningless conversation and if he didn't know the cashier as well as he did, he would have been rude but since he did, he said, "Hey Faith, I'm in a bit of a hurry if you can ring me up quick, I've got to go. Sorry."

Jack felt a little guilty for his haste and dismissive tone, but he pushed it down. That night, he just wanted to forget, he just wanted the whiskey in his blood stream, and wanted the numbness to flood over him allowing him to relax and hopefully slip into the void quickly. He would have to make sure he didn't go too far. Since he had made new memories he didn't know if they would consume him in all their vivid color or if it would be the usual vision he was shown. He hadn't gotten drunk enough the previous night to find out and he didn't want to find out that night either.

He didn't think he could live though the evils he had committed in the 4k definition they usually were presented in. He tapped his card, grabbed the bottle and ran out of the store before the receipt had even finished printing. He pushed past the front doors and walked swiftly to the elevator doors, bottle in hand. He ignored Angela's 'Hello' and stepped into the steel compartment.

Once the doors were safely shut, he unstopped the bottle and put it to his lips, the bittersweet taste filled his mouth and flowed down his throat, he only stopped when the need for air became too great. Tilting the bottle back down he took a deep breath and stoppered it, looking down he realized that he had only drank a small amount. Maybe subconsciously he didn't want to drink himself into oblivion. Just as the thought flashed through his mind so did the face of Jess or Marissa or whatever she wanted to be called at that particular moment.

The elevator doors opened once again and Jack walked slowly into his apartment, a pack of Charlotte's cigarettes sat on the counter, his jean jacket hung on the back of the chair and the whisky tumbler sat in the middle of the counter as if beckoning him forward, willing him to pour a glass. Jack obliged without faltering. Pulling the stopper from the bottle, he poured as much liquid as the glass could hold, took a lighter from the drawer under the counter, took the pack of cigarettes from the counter, grabbed a bowl from the cupboard to put the ashes in, made his way to the couch and flipped through the movies until he found one that suited him.

He hated the numb feeling his brain was filled with when he watched movies on a good day but that day was anything but a good day. Just like the effect he craved from the nicotine and the alcohol, he wanted to be numbed. If he had access to morphine, he would have filled his veins with the white liquid made for physical pain and let his body turn it into a mental numbing cream. As he sat staring at the TV he felt the alcohol taking a hold of his senses and once he got a taste he couldn't stop.

He emptied the contents of the drink into his mouth and walked to the kitchen to pour another. When he sat back down on the couch, he lit one of the cigarettes and pulled the smoke into his lungs, left it there for a few moments, allowing the nicotine to enter his bloodstream and then released the other contents back out into the air. The tendrils of smoke escaped from the tip of the cigarette and dissipated into the atmosphere living no trace behind. Jack wished he was aboard one of the tendrils. He wished he could be accepted by the oxygen and nitrogen that always existed around him, never to be seen again.

But the world wasn't done with him and in his mother's words, *He hadn't completed the work he was sent to the earth to carry out.* Deep down Jack knew he had more to offer, he knew his life held more than a dead mother, an orphanage, alcohol, and killing. He knew he had more to offer but he wished the next chapter would come sooner rather than later, he wished he could press fast forward on the abomination that his life had become. Sitting in a pool of gilt and sadness, sipping his fifth glass of whiskey he couldn't even think past the next day never mind past the next week or month.

If he had any chance at a better life, a life in which he wasn't a thorn in society's humiliating crown he had to make it past the unbeatable force that was pushing his head under the mud. It was his fault that he was drowning, after all he had been the one to willingly step in but that didn't matter now, he needed to find a way out. Someone had to throw him a rope. He would have to hold on tight and pull himself free, but some miracle needed to take place before he had any sort of hope at a fight for his life. At that moment, the man sitting beside the endless pool of mud was only pushing his head further down. Confucius was supposed to be his rope but Jack had started to get a sinking feeling that the rope he could offer would snap as soon as Jack put any weight on it.

As the sixth and final glass of whiskey flowed past his lips, he felt the alcohol take hold, the dull, peaceful feeling he had grown accustomed to, filled his consciousness just like the memories did. "Maybe there is a secret passageway into my brain," he whispered into the empty room as he snuffed the final cigarette in the bowl, flipped the TV off, stood up and started the long journey toward his room. The only difference between that lonely night and the night Charlotte had told him of the 'opportunity of a lifetime' was the fact that instead of walking all the way back to his home all he had to do was make it down the hall.

That night, more than most, he had a burning desire to be back out in the cold. Maybe it was all a terrible dream, a figment of his imagination that would conclude with him waking up on the cold, black leather of his old couch. But the hope was gone as soon as he started walking in his drunken state making it impossible to walk in a straight line, he had to steady himself against many different pieces of furniture and against many walls. The hope of the whole experience all being a fucked up, alcohol induced dream was erased as he touched each wall, piece of furniture and eventually his bed.

The reality of his situation was made clear as he touched the bed's soft, plush comforter. It was real, he could feel it, memories were woven into the fabric, the first night he spent with Charlotte, the first night he laid his head on the pillow after he had killed, and the first night he ever slept in the bed. That first night was filled with uncertainty and fear but also wonder and potential, both of which had been stripped from his hand like a baby from an unfit mother arm's.

The only difference between him and the mothers whose babies have been stolen was the fact that he didn't protest, he willingly allowed Paul to take his freedom, wonder, youth, and his last shred of dignity without so much as a whimper. He just stood at attention and unblinkingly offered his greatest virtues as collateral for his life. The thought sent a shiver down Jack's spine as he steadied himself, stood straight up, and peeled the clothing from his body.

When the only clothing left was the thin fabric covering his genitals, Jack closed his eyes and let himself fall backwards, knowing the mattress would catch him before he hit the floor. But as he continued to fall, he realized he should have stopped long ago. Opening his eyes he saw no room, no mattress, no apartment. It was just black. It was the void he usually resided in as he slept. He knew not to struggle; he learned long ago that struggling never helped anything. There was no stopping the relentless nature of a land without time. The same void that lay between reality and one of his memories. As he fell, he prayed that it would be a memory made long ago, if it was a memory he had forged recently, he may die of guilt and shame.

The void of darkness was suddenly pierced by light. Jack flipped around in mid-air and saw the hole he was headed for, there was no stopping his descent. There was only falling, until he found himself in the memory. The darkness gave way to a room lit by florescent lights and white sterilized walls. Jack breathed a sigh of relief, at least the memory wasn't from the past two days, it was a version of hell but not one he himself had walked into of his own accord. Instead, a hell he was forced to endure. His feet hit the cold white tile, he looked down and saw only boxers covering his naked body.

He was thankful that he had been afforded a night of relief from the soul crushing weight only recent memories could impose. Jack walked up to the glass window between his mother and him. He looked down, there was a boy with tear-stained cheeks staring unblinkingly at the horrors unfolding behind the glass barrier. Jack wished he could turn the boy's eyes away from the massacre, but he knew that he could not change any part of the memory, he was sentenced to watch it unfold. So, he stood there with the boy, watching his mother being cut up like a cadaver that had already passed. He had seen this memory so many times over the years that he just looked on in horror as the doctor's scalpel sliced into his mother's soft flesh; when he could not bear to watch anymore, he trained his eyes on his mother's lifeless face.

The doctors hadn't bothered to wipe the blood from her mouth and chin, it just sat there like a white cloth in a boxing ring. But beneath the bags under her eyes, blood drying on her chin and skin clinging onto her bones for life he could see the woman that had rubbed his stomach every time he was sick, nursed his broken bones back to strength and had worked three jobs just to make ends meet. He saw the selfless human underneath, the woman she used to be, he saw his mother. Once he could see past the sick, tired features he saw her, the real her not the daisy wilted by pain.

He saw his mother, and a lone tear slipped from his eye hitting the floor. Not that anyone could see it, but Jack could, and it only made his heart break more than it already was. At the time, Jack would have sold his soul just so his mother could survive but now he wished that she could have just died right there on the table. He wished the doctors would see that there was nothing they could do to save her and just let her rest. Instead, they fixed what was broken, at least temporarily, giving enough time for Jack to have a few more days with her but not long enough to end her pain indefinitely. Instead, they offered one soul a few days of soul crushing goodbyes and another a few days of torturing pain.

The doctors had begun to stitch his mother back up and the monitor had begun to pulse steadily. Jack looked down and saw the light return to the young boy's eyes. His prayers had been answered but not in the way he had hoped for, he too would come to learn that he should have been praying for the sweet release of death. The doctors began wheeling the bed out of the operating room, the young boy saw it and ran as fast as his adolescent legs would take him in the direction he assumed he needed to go. Jack walked slowly in the boys' footsteps; he had been down this hallway more times than could be counted.

Jack knew each door, each hospital cart, each word spoken by each tenant of the hospital, and each broken tile that littered the ground was a flaw he had memorized. There was no need to rush, his mother would not be awake for at least 20 minutes—23 minutes and 36 seconds to be exact. The memory of his mother ordering him to call the ambulance hadn't been played a fraction as many times as this one had. Probably because it was the most traumatic ordeal he had ever lived through. Maybe that was the reason he always saw it when he drank himself into oblivion. Maybe because it was the root trigger of his dependence on the vice.

It was only fair that drink would bring him back to the root of why he abused its prescribed amount. Whatever the reason was, Jack hated it no less, he hated the fact that he knew very inch of this hospital and that he could recite each word spoken by the doctors and his mother that night. As he walked into the room that his mother had been placed in he heard the conversation starting between the 16-year-old version of himself and the doctor. Jack knew exactly how it would unravel but he listened anyway.

"Jack, we removed a tumor the size of a football that had attached itself to the side of your mother's liver, but she is riddled with cancer."

Jack always hated the way the doctor phrased the statement. 'Riddled'. It was a comment void of sympathy, but he still listened intently. "The cancer has spread to her lymph nodes and there is no stopping it when it reaches those, I would give her two or three days maximum. I'm sorry son, she doesn't have much time left; If it were me, I would start saying my goodbyes now," the doctor said before turning away and leaving the room.

The amusing thing was that even though the doctor said it with such certainty and intelligence Jack knew his mother held onto her life for five more days. Even in the face of undeniable death she wouldn't stop fighting. Up until her dying breath she fought to protect Jack. He was always told that when a person dies, they have a moment of clarity in which they are completely cut off from pain and they act as though there is nothing wrong with them but that must be reserved for people who have accepted their deaths.

Jack's mother was never granted that moment of peace, she denied the angel who was sent to take her away and spent every waking moment trying to prepare Jack for the world that would be forced into his lap without the proper training or learning period in which a teenager is hardened into an adult. As his mother's eyes sleepily opened, he saw his younger self's face light up with relief and happiness, but before he could listen to the only part of the memory he could bear, air raid sirens blared. He grasped at the bed sheets, but the memory faded away like whisps of cigarette smoke and he was ripped from the void back into reality. Monday morning had arrived, another week in hell with no sure path out.

Chapter 18

Jack opened his eyes slowly, letting fractions of light in and shutting it back out again and again until his eyes had been sufficiently adjusted. He didn't need to throw the covers off himself as his mortal body did in fact land on the bed as he suspected it would. It was only his broken, tortured soul that fell through reality into the void and further into memory's punishing cage. When he sat up on the bed, he felt the crushing weight of the three souls and looked down to see the red sun hanging around his neck once again. He was tempted to take it off, after all no one had told him he needed to wear it every minute of every day. Paul hadn't even told him he needed to wear it at all, it was just a 'token' but in reality, it held the three souls he had stolen from the earth.

If Jack removed it and set it down, it would be unprotected, and someone would be able to steal them. The least he could for the three men he murdered was keep their lost souls safe for as long as he could. After all, he was the reason they had yet to find peace. Maybe on the day of his own death, when his soul was released from his body, they would follow him to the city of light. Jack stood up, grudgingly made his way to the closet, pulled on some sweats and a loose-fitting shirt and made his way to the gym.

When he returned sweat poured from every possible open pore, but his head was clear, ready to tackle another day. After he showered, shaved, and threw some casual clothes on, he began to think about breakfast. The Four Roses immediately came to mind followed closely by Jessica's unwavering expression. The Four Roses was no longer an option. Jack decided the next time he saw Jessica it would be at a 'work' venue. He held no sympathy for her and didn't care to listen to the lies and justifications she had for her actions.

There was no 'book of truths' that Jack could read from to decide if what she was saying was in fact truth. There was only her word and that held as little weight as a feather in Jack's opinion that day. Maybe for the rest of his life. She had broken the bond of trust they had once held so dear and that was a hard bond to mend. No one seemed to put much weight on truth those days, or at least the people that surrounded the mud pit Jack was currently drowning in didn't. It made him angry and weak but something—maybe it was his mother's sprit—pushed him forward. It urged him to keep going, pushed him to find person he could trust with his life.

The only name that came to mind was Charlotte's, and even she tended to not tell the whole truth or just leave it hidden until the date in which it was vital it be released. Even so, it was the only name that would even be worth trying to learn to trust. So, Jack picked up his phone and texted.

J: Know of any good breakfast places? The Four Roses have wilted.

Charlotte's response was almost instantaneous, as if she was waiting by the phone for a call or text from Jack to patch that which had been ripped from their fragile tapestry of trust the night before.

C: Yeah, should I meet you at ur place or at Veritas?

J: I'll meet you there. See u in 10min?

C: See u in 10.

Jack placed his phone back down on the table. He had extended the olive branch, all he could do now was hope he hadn't shown a serpent the soft flesh covering his exposed neck. He slipped his shoes on, pulled his coat over his shoulders, grabbed his school bag and waited at the elevator doors. Once he had entered, he felt a wave of anticipation was over his head and bubbling anger start to boil inside his belly. If Charlotte couldn't or wouldn't give him the truth for every uncertain question he had, he would be forced to cut the bond and take the GWA on his own. If she stumbled or if he suspected that she was lying, he would cut the tie. Just the thought of doing so sent a wave of misery over him.

She had become the only person he had but if he had to, if he was given no other choice, he would make the tough one and save himself. He had to save himself at all costs for his mother's sake. Jack would not let his mother die just so that he could let himself be manipulated by a serpent. When the steel doors opened once again, he stepped out and was prepared for the worst yet hoped for the best. He hoped he would finally see the real Charlotte, free from lies and masks.

Jack stepped out into the morning light; the warmth of the new day warmed his cheeks as he stood on the curb. He saw a taxi rounding the corner, so he stuck his hand out to tell the driver he needed a ride. The driver slowed to a stop before him and he opened the back door, the hinges squeaking and screeching at the sudden movement. He sat down and investigated the rear-view mirror as he usually did when he stepped into a cab.

Jack liked knowing the face of the man who held his life in his hands. Immediately he recognized the face staring back at him, it was the same man who had driven him around Saturday. Angelo's cousin. But Jack couldn't remember his actual name. The driver obviously recognized him as well because his eyes lit up as if the president had walked into his cab.

"Jack! Come sit up front," he said excitedly. Jack was in a hurry but there was something about this man that made him feel safe, made him feel like he wasn't the villain he saw every time he looked in the mirror. The tone and expression the man held when he looked at him made him feel like he was a good person, an important person worthy of something more. Maybe worthy of a better life. The feeling warmed Jack's heart so fully that he opened the back door and climbed into the front seat beside the man whose life he had changed.

He had changed it with blood money, but the man didn't know that, and Jack liked being seen a different light than the one he was so often sitting under lately. It was a merciful escape from the mud. "How are you doing Jack! How was your event?" The driver said.

Jack wanted to tell the man everything. Somehow the man's lips formed a smile that not only crept into his eyes but emitted enough light to make the darkest dungeons of hell indistinguishable from heaven. He wanted to tell the driver that he killed a man, that he tortured a man, that he shared rooms with what could possibly be the most evil human beings in the entire world. Jack wanted to spill his entire story of woe but he knew he couldn't. There was no scenario in which it could help so instead he just let a lie slither out of his mouth poising the angelic ears of the man sitting next to him.

"It was great, thanks to you I was able to look my best for the big night! Thank you." The words sounded harsh and guttural as they fell from his lips, but they were all he could summon.

"Very good Jack. Happy to help, but I should be thanking you. You changed my life with the money you gave me. Your contribution gave me the opportunity to make a better life for my family." 'Opportunity'. The word used to elicit hope and dreams took a different form when it touched Jack's ears. All he could think of was death, murder, chains, and blood seeping slowly, pathetically down the lifeless man's head. The word had zero positive connotations, only negatives. Jack felt the memories seeping into his brain like water into a hole dug too deep, but he fought them back, willing them to wait until he was in Charlotte's presence. Once he was there her magical lips may be able to offer some form of consolation.

"No problem…" He realized that he didn't know the man's name. "Sorry sir, I can't for the life of me remember what you name is." Jack felt terrible but the light radiating from the man's eyes didn't waver.

"No problem, Jack, my name is Lucien," The name fit the man like a glove, somehow it encompassed his soul entirely. Jack wondered if his parents were psychics. They must have been if they had come up with the perfect name to encompass a soul they had not yet met.

"Your name fits you like a glove Lucien," Jack said, and it was the truth.

"Thank you, Jack, yours fits you just as well." Jack had never been told that before and he was taken aback but he realized that it was probably something nice people say when complimented. After all, it was rude to receive a compliment and not give one in return, but something about the way Lucien said it made him believe it. It was incredible how much a simple taxi driver could make him feel.

Lost in thought, he just about forgot that he was supposed to meet Charlotte in 10 minutes but once he did, he told Lucien that he needed to be at Veritas quickly. The man didn't falter, just put the car in drive and tore away from the curb. The speed in which they were hurtling toward their destination distracted Jack enough to push the memories from his head. By the time they reached Veritas, Jack was fully awake and ready to endure the meal.

Jack paid Lucien $3000 for the ten-minute ride to Veritas and stepped out of the cab as Lucien showered him in thanks. Jack didn't mean to be rude but all he could focus on was the breakfast he was about so share with Charlotte. Was she going to be a serpent, twisting her forked tongue into his ears, feeding him lies or was she going to be more like Abe and tell him the honest truth? Jack didn't care if it hurt him, all he wanted was to know everything. All he wanted was to be given the puzzle pieces in which to build his picture. Jack didn't even need every truth, he just needed enough of it so that he could mend the trust that had been frayed.

Looking through the huge picture window placed underneath a tattered green and white striped awning, Jack could see that the café seemed nice enough. Quaint little tables were littered around the room; one waitress milled around the tables covered by the same fabric that the awning was made from. It looked like the owner had built the tables right in the store and left them where they were completed. The café emitted a faint odor that filled Jack's nose and slowly reeled him in. As Jack reached the door, he pushed it open and saw Charlotte sitting at a table nestled at the back right corner of the room.

Her eyes were glued to Jack as he walked in, as if he she had been staring at the door willing him to walk in, but the look painted on her face as she stared in Jack's direction was pure anger. He pulled the phone out of his pocket and checked the time; he was thirty minutes late. That would account for the anger. How had he spent so much time in the taxi? It felt like minutes, and the drive had only taken five minutes. Jack pushed the confusion out of his mind and made his way to the corner table.

"Sorry I'm late, somehow…I lost track of time," Jack said. As soon as the words reached Charlotte's ears her expression softened. The anger was reduced to peace in a matter of seconds.

"All good, I was trying to pretend to be mad, but I can't," Charlotte said with a shy smile. It was the type of smile that crinkles one corner of a person's mouth but never quite reaches the other.

"I ordered for you; thought you would be pretty hungry after your workout. I got orange juice, three eggs, bacon, sausage, hash browns and some toast. Is that okay?" The nonchalant nature in which Charlotte was talking startled Jack, it was like she forgot all about their conversation the previous night, but he rolled with the familiarity thinking it would be easier to get the truth if she was in a good, sharing mood.

"Yeah, that's great, thank you," he said, building himself up before confronting her to tell her how much her lies had hurt him, no matter the reasons she had for telling them.

"Charlotte, I need the truth, I need to know everything you know, I can't be learning new developments after you have already known them for a while. We can't be partners in crime if you have other partners, other debts, and other motives. I just can't Charlotte. Even you must be able to see that the plan will go to shit like this, if we continue down this road," Jack said snapping his fingers.

"We have to be united front in this and if it goes well enough maybe we can be together after the gates of hell come crashing down. But none of that can happen if you can't be honest with me," Jack said breathing a sigh of relief as the last word hurtled through the air. He had always been told the truth could set a man free. Jack didn't believe it set people free, but it certainly lessened the weight on his soul. There was no defiance in Charlotte's face. Jack could tell his words had been registered. The only thing that remined to be seen was if she would tell the truth or just tease him with half-truths as per usual. After a long pause, she spoke. "What would you like to know?" she asked in a slight whisper.

Jack thought about his answer. What would he like to know? Maybe whose side Confucius was on. Maybe whose side she was on. Maybe he wanted to know who the third partner was, or why he hadn't seen him yet. But he knew the first question he had to ask was about Jessica. More specifically who she was working for, who she was honestly working for. Not bullshit about her being dead, maybe Charlotte really didn't know but she had to know something more. After all, she had been mutilated because of Jessica's betrayal, that much was clear. The only blurry part was what Charlotte really knew.

"Who does Jess work for, is it Confucius, is it Paul or is it someone else? Is it the third partner?" Jack asked. He knew there were five questions mixed into one sentence, but he couldn't help it. He felt like a kid who was just starting to understand the world, asking his parents every question his little brain could produce.

"I don't know who she works for or reports to, but I imagine it's Paul just like before. Maybe Alexander but who knows. It's not Confucius I know that for sure, as far as I know he is one of the good guys."

As she said it, Jack watched her lips, her expression and her hands. As far as he could tell they were all truths. "As for the third partner I honestly don't know who that is, I know there is a third man, but I have never seen him or heard his name."—Little did either know that they both knew his name and both greatly underestimated his reach. Jack studied her like a book but as far as he could tell she was telling nothing but truths.

"Okay, I believe you, but you have to know something about Jessica. Why would Paul introduce her now, why not right off the bat, why let me settle in?" Jack knew the answer to his question, but he wanted to hear it from Charlotte's mouth, he wanted to hear what she thought the reason was. He wanted to know what Paul had told her and what she had been forced to infer on her own.

"Paul told me after the fight that I was supposed to keep you close, make sure that Jessica doesn't send you over the edge but not let you get comfortable. If I had to guess, he is going to uproot what's left of your life soon. I would imagine he has kept his pocket ace for so long because she was so powerful that she would be able to break you even if he failed."

The man didn't fail, he was broken. The shards of his soul littered throughout his dreams were proof that Paul had succeeded, his mission had been completed. Maybe Jack had been doing a better job at hiding his broken nature than he had expected, maybe he was succeeding in fooling everyone to the fact he was fine. Succeeding in making everyone believe that he wasn't a broken shell of the man he used to be. "The only fear I have is that she isn't going to be used in a conventional way. I think something horrific is going to happen. I would guess that it's either your life or hers that will be taken. He will break you down to small enough pieces that you have no recourse other than to give in to the evil, allow the evil to pick the pieces of your soul up and put it back to together or he will just kill you."

"To him you are the pinnacle of human achievement. In the 8 years since I have arrived here, I have never seen someone threaten him so much. In his eyes, you are strong, smart, successful, ambitious, and worthy. Worthy of what? I'm not sure but he uses the phrase 'Jack's worthy' so often that it scares me to say it. The only one that came close to the effect you have on him was Jessica and now I see how that turned out I'm terrified for what will happen to you and me. He is ruthless Jack, and you are in the same position Jessica was all those years ago. If you double cross me as she did I will have nothing left, there will be no reasons for me to live any longer."

The words were as truthful and set in stone as the ten commandments. Jack was sure of it. The passion she spoke with couldn't be faked and her fear was as real as his own, the air around them was thick with its pungent odor.

"I won't, Charlotte, I promise," Jack said. As his own words fell upon his own ears, he knew they were binding. Jack knew in that moment that there was no taking it back, no going back on his word. He had promised. There was no breaking a promise because breaking his promise would effectively shatter all the honor he had left. He would have to stay no matter what bullshit she put him through in between that moment and the moment of truth. Until the night they allotted for their murderous intentions.

"But now that I have promised not to leave you, you have to tell me whose side you're on now. Whose side you were on at the start, and I need to know that all of the stories you have told me are real, that they are not just slivers of truth woven between lies," Jack said.

The words had come out like an order but in truth they were a plea. Charlotte must have known they were just as much pleas as orders because her face fell. She looked like a person who had been set free, a prisoner of war finally freed, a wrongfully convicted prisoner, or an eagle finally being allowed to spread its wings after years in captivity. Her stiff posture and perfect face fell as her eyes lost their violent, dangerous edge. She looked like a woman at peace, finally allowed to reveal her real truth.

"Jack I…" The pain, suffering, and loneliness of his entire life faded away. His eyes widened as if to soak in the entirety of her truths. Jack's jaw hung loose below his tongue. As candor prevailed, sweat started to seep out of his pores carrying all the lies, half-truths and hidden lies away. By the time she had relieved her soul of the unfathomable weight that she had been burdened with since she stepped foot on the Medora tarmac, Jack's hair was soaked, breakfast untouched and his hands shook with a tremor of pity, empathy and anger.

He couldn't choose a single feeling, they all raged inside him like a costal storm, the winds whipped, whistled and the pounding rain soaked him through, as the massive, devastating waves of honesty slammed into the rocks. "Jack, you have to say something, I can't sit here and imagine what's happening in your head."

Nothing, Jack couldn't think of a single word.

"Jack."

If Lucifer had stepped into the small café, Jack wouldn't have been able to sell his soul in exchange for words. Her candor was wrapped around his tongue, held his vocal cords at gunpoint. It filled the space between his lips, an impassable wall of overwhelming shock. "Jack we are in this together, no one knows what you know now. My cards are in your hands and yours in mine," Charlotte said.

The gravity of the situation loosened his tongue and he was able to break a small hole in the impenetrable wall of shock. Jack felt a sentence start to form in his mind but all he could force through was, "Thank you."

Simple, yet strong. It was everything that needed to be or would be said between the two of them for now. Jack knew every deep dark secret, every misconception, every nook, crevasse and hidden passageway through Charlotte's brain. He knew her better than she knew herself, he knew every passage in out and around her psyche. Yet she didn't know every last thing about him. Jack knew there was solace in the fact that he still had secrets.

There was solace in the fact that he was not tied to one person but rather tethered tight enough for trust to be shared between the two of them. He had his partner, he had his confidant, his better half and the picture had begun to lose its fuzzy edges, he could see pieces of it clearer. Jack couldn't see the whole picture, he couldn't even see half the picture, but it was a start. The journey upwards had begun, the slow downwards descent had slowed to a standstill, and he had not been forced to lay his secrets down to have a base to stand on.

"I have to go; I need to get to class. If you want, I can come over tonight, just let me know," Charlotte said. Standing up, sliding her coat around her shoulders, she walked around to Jack's side of the table and kissed his cheek before walking out of the café. In Medora, she had stolen the breath of every occupant of the little bar but there in the city of lights she was able to flow between the crowd and mix into the grand New York experience. In Jack's eyes, he still saw her in the same dim, neon, dive bar light, every time she spun on her heels and left.

Every time she turned her back to wink goodbye his breath was taken if only for a second of peaceful, fleeting pain. A pain he enjoyed and even craved. The burning of his lungs as they fought for the air she had so cunningly stole, like a pickpocket victim searching for the wallet they know isn't there. Jack marveled at the ease in which she was able to take his breath. It had been so long. He now knew her, he had seen her in every light she hid from the world and still somehow, she was able to leave him in awe.

Once his breath returned, Jack looked down at the meal that had grown cold since it had been placed down in front of him. As the cold shower of truth washed away, the hunger returned. He dove into the meal, letting the rich flavor put his hunger at ease and as he ate, he began to think. He thought about Charlotte's truth, about the blurry edges of his picture yet to become fully clear. His mind wandered back to the first night they had spent together. He thought about how he had believed they were two bags floating in the wind, by some freak chance they had become intertwined with each other, and how Paul had reached out and grabbed them both but now he knew the story was different.

They weren't bags floating on a breeze, they were two stones released at the top of a mountain, destined to reach the same end. The only unknown was the journey and while they may have taken different paths, ran into different bushes, rolled through different streams and hopped over different logs, their paths were always destined to come to the same end. Even though they had been down different routes, they had still rolled down the same mountain.

When the food filled the void in his stomach to his satisfaction, Jack asked the waitress for the cheque and told her he needed the machine. She returned moments later with the bill and the machine, $11.50 was all he owed but when asked what he would like to tip he entered $1200. Just before he pressed enter a plate smashed from a table near the door, the waitress ran over to clean the mess and Jack completed his transaction. $1211.50 was the price for the truth. The waitress didn't know that, and he didn't want to wait around for the thanks and praise.

Jack knew he didn't deserve it; he knew he kept giving in such great excess trying to make amends for all that he had taken. He watched the waitress pick up shards of ceramic plate from the floor, slipped his coat over his shoulders and walked quickly out of the café. He would allow himself to be showered in thanks the next time he entered the café, that was if the waitress remembered him.

When he reached a safe distance from the café, he checked his phone. He had completely missed his first class. In a past life, his mother would have been mortified. In that one, in that muddy existence, he didn't think it mattered all that much. Yet a pang of guilt continued to stab at his chest, as if he had let his mother down. Even though Paul had given him a murderous opportunity, it was still an opportunity, and he couldn't squander it. There was too much riding on it, he had traded too much for it to be squandered. Jack didn't know it yet, but he would not finish his degree. He would not finish his schooling or at least he wouldn't finish it the way other people did.

As he walked to Confucius' class, he came up with a plan. The man he had once held in such a high light was now stained with questions. The unknown had a way of making you forget, making the truth foggy. It had a way of blurring the lines of even the greatest portraits. So Jack decided he would not see the man in any light he would not look at him as part of any organization, just regard him as a teacher, a vessel of knowledge. The class was being introduced to a new work of art, and even though he was burdened with questions and uncertainty he felt the same excitement he had on his first day. He wondered what book would be introduced, he wondered what light it would shed on his life. He wondered what truth it would uncover, what muse it would reveal.

Jack stepped into the well-lit classroom. Many of his classmates occupied the room. Some deep in conversation, some staring off into space and others engrossed in their phones, none of them had a care in the world. They all had problems of course; How they were going to pay rent, tuition, their girlfriends cheating, their parents fighting but none of them had Jack's problems. None of them feared the buzz in their pockets, none of them had slid glinting steel across a man's neck. None of them had heard guttural screams emitted from their preys' mouth, and none of their souls belonged to another. They didn't know the pain, the cell of oppression closing around them as they fought for air, and clawed at freedom.

They may have lost people as Jack did but they hadn't been imprisoned without committing a crime. They didn't know the desperation that silently seeped out of Jack's pores. They didn't know the stench of evil and none of them were playthings for a vile, abomination of a man. The chasm of freedom between him and his classmates drove him to sit at the back and wait for the professor to walk in and begin his lecture. It allowed him to listen and learn about the normal lives of his would be comrades but it did not allow him to speak freely.

They wouldn't understand his pain, they would laugh. They would think he was joking; think he had gone crazy or think he was a compulsive liar only looking for attention. He sat still until the Dr. walked in, books in one hand, briefcase in the other, he made his way to the front of the class and cleared his throat like a mic check before he started to impart knowledge upon the hungry minds.

Confucius' eyes locked with Jack's, and he began, "You have been the best class I have had the pleasure of teaching in my 30 years at this fine institution." His eyes flitted away from Jack's for a moment but quickly returned to their original line of sight. "I wanted to thank each one of you for your efforts and insights." He stopped for a drink of water from the water bottle that had been inside his briefcase.

Once he was properly hydrated, he started again. "The next work we are going to study is the tragedy of Julius Caesar. Has anyone read the play before?" Jack looked around the room and saw that about half the students had read the play.

Some of their arms shot up with excitement but others raised their arms sadly, obviously it wasn't beloved by all. Jack hadn't read the play, so he was excited. He always liked to read the old works of art that had been carried into this century. Although he would never truly understand why Shakespeare was a prominent author, he liked to decipher the message and loved the moment when he finally realized what made the work special. In the rare moments when he couldn't decipher the message and couldn't understand why the work had been whispered from ear to ear through so many centuries, it drove him mad.

If he couldn't find a reason other than the authors name to warrant a story being carried through time, it made him angry, it was such a waste. Why would teachers, scholars and historians carry a story that meant nothing, why would they carry a story that wouldn't prevent the past from leaking into the future? Was it just the fact that the name attached to the words held meaning, or was it because they all didn't understand why they were still learning, speaking and carrying a useless story? Jack didn't know but he hoped that in this case it wouldn't be a waste.

He hoped that with the message of the story he would be able to clear his picture just a little bit further. As he thought, a brick smashed through his window of thought, "Jack?"

He shook his head to clear the cobwebs and opened his eyes wide, "Pardon me sir?"

"I can see your thought growing smaller in your eyes and I am sorry for that, but I was just asking if you have read the play."

"No sir I'm afraid I haven't," Jack said, cheeks painted with embarrassment.

"Good, I have finally succeeded in choosing a work that you will have to read for the first time," the Dr. said as a sly smile spread across his face. It seemed like he had known Jack hadn't read the play and was relishing in the embarrassment he was causing Jack. He had promised himself that he wouldn't see the professor as anything other than a teacher, but it was growing harder as time went on. The feeling that everything Confucius said was to his benefit was inching closer to certainty. But Jack stuck close to earlier belief, he needed to if he was going to have any chance at being awarded the piece of paper he coveted so deeply.

The class went on without any other questions and comments blatantly directed at Jack and once the bell range he began to pack up just like the rest of the students, but Confucius stopped him.

"Mr. Hanson, may I have a word?"

Jack didn't raise his head and kept packing his bag, only stopping when he heard his name again.

"Mr. Hanson." The mentions of his last name made his skin crawl. It was yet another thing Paul had successfully tarnished. His own name had been stained with red just as so many other things had been in the last few weeks.

"Yes sir?" He said slinging the satchel over his shoulder, eyes locking with the Doctor's. "Are you still available for supper on Wednesday, at 5:00pm?" It was phrased as a question, but Jack knew it wasn't, it was a command. No one said no to the King, the latest in the long line of leaders. Jack knew he was a king, but he wondered if the man had truly founded anything. Was he just a son born into wealth? Had he carved his own path, or had he groomed someone else's?

"Yes sir, I am looking forward to it. Will you send a car?" Jack said.

"Yes, the same as the last time, he will be at the curb at 4:30pm. Don't be late," he said and then walked past Jack, out into the hall and disappeared down the hallway. Jack wondered if all important people just walked away when they had finished speaking. He had been forced to become accustomed to the sudden departures over the last few weeks, but he couldn't tell if it was rude or not. As he walked down the hall and out into the cold, he wondered what it would have been like if he had been given an opportunity from a different set of 'influential' men. He wondered what the differences would be. Were all powerful men devils? Would they all be involved in shady businesses? Or were there a select few that had earned their money the 'right' way?

The questions swirled around his brain until he reached his apartment and grabbed his gym bag. The best part of his day had come and all that he could think about were the moves he had already learned and the new ones he would soon learn. The excitement grew inside him until he could barely contain it anymore. When he started the working with Jason, his soul purpose was to find a way in which he wouldn't have to buy a gun. At the start, he was only motivated by desperation, but it had since become fun. It had become a passion only rivaled by the other two he had collected along his path of life. Jack knew it as a good thing that he was so motivated, it allowed him to soak information into his bones. It allowed him to become dangerous. By then, the only thing that could stop him was a silver bullet hurtled at him through the deadly, silver, strafed tube that is the barrel of a gun. Even then, he would have a chance as long as it wasn't fired by a long range weapon. Paul didn't strike him as the type of person to kill a man from a distance, he liked to kill a man face to face or at least kill a man in front of him—he had a tendency to kill men that weren't awake. By the time Jack reached the gym, he wore a smile that stretched from ear to ear.

He walked to the changeroom and once he was finished, he jammed his bag in a locker, making sure to keep his phone on him. Paul had told him he had earned a week off, but he had also said that before the Founder's party. So just for his own peace of mind he made sure the phone was within reach. As he walked to his usual stretching spot he caught Jason's eye, he was working with Frank, the student that Jack had fought the previous week. Jason immediately left Frank and made his way toward Jack.

"Jack! How are you buddy?" he said.

"Great Jason, how's Frank doing?" Jack said politely, even though he didn't really care how the pupil was.

"Doing well, he wants to fight at the end of your session if you're okay with that," Jason said, and Jack knew it was a question, unlike Paul or Confucius's propositions there was no obligation to fight the man, but he still felt compelled to do it. He had cultivated the image of an unbeatable force in New York and the beatings he had doled out at the gym and in the damp basement of the office should have been a source of shame but instead he felt pride.

When he was in-between the ropes he could foresee the outcome, he wasn't watching his shadow. He wasn't scared. Jack thought back to his last fight. Luke's eyes were filled with a boyish excitement. It was pure, naïve innocence, but Frank was different. The fire in the man's eyes intrigued him, Jack wondered if it was still there even after he had cut him down so easily. Jack understood if it was, he imagined the same fire festered in his own eyes as he danced between the ropes.

"Sounds good, I think he might be the best competition I have faced yet," Jack said. It was a lie, the mountain he had fought in the room void of innocence was much more powerful and dangerous, but he couldn't tell Jason about those fights. It wasn't because he wasn't proud, it was a matter of survival. Although, the fight he had in the warehouse—if you could even call it a fight—was an endless pit of guilt. It had very nearly broken him. Some would have said that it did, but Jack knew better. He knew that as long as he kept fighting, he would be fine. A long as hope survived, so could the last few pure pieces of his soul.

The session went by just as it normally did. Jason went over old moves, he reviewed Jack's knowledge and then introduced two new moves. One to stop a knife attack and another that would come to his aid if he ever needed to disarm a man with a gun to his head. Jason even taught him a way to disarm a man when his hands were tied behind his back. By the time the larger part of his session was over, he was soaked through with sweat, his shirt clung to him like a wet suit, yet, he still felt as though he would be able to beat Frank with ease.

So, when Jason he was done teaching for the day a smile grew at the corners of Jack's mouth. He placed his helmet on his head, tightened his boxing gloves around his wrists and stepped though the ropes of the ring. He shuffled around the ring, calming his mind and pushing all thoughts that wouldn't be able to help him out of his mind. Once his head was clear, he looked around and saw Frank making his way into the ring while Jason approached the side of the ring, arm crossed, eyes wide with wonder. Jack knew that Jason liked to watch him work. He liked to watch him surgically remove the consciousness from the man opposite him. When Frank had gotten his bearings and let Jason know he was ready, Frank turned to Jack and said, "Watch yourself tonight big man, I was not properly prepared for the last fight. Tonight, I'm ready."

Jack didn't respond, he didn't like being called big man. It was like the insignificant man in front of him didn't take him seriously. Or he didn't believe that Jack was all that. Jack was going to prove him wrong; he was going to show Frank that he took it easy on him the last time. He was going to show Frank what he could do when provoked. Jack nodded to Jason, letting him know he was ready.

"Whenever you're ready boys," Jason said, each word dripping with anticipation. Jack moved toward Frank and outstretched his right glove; Frank tapped it with his left and backed away. The two warriors circled each other and Jack saw the same hunger in Franks eyes he had seen before. The same fire that had protected his consciousness in the last fight burned brighter than they had before. It was a spotlight intent on blinding Jack's blows. Jack moved like a wolf, hungry and confident. He knew that Frank was nothing compared to him. But Jack wasn't too egoistic to know that if the smaller man landed a lucky punch, he would undoubtedly hit the canvas.

Before long, Frank unleashed a well-timed, angry attack. Jack dodged, ducked and snuck away from each punch. Once the onslaught had come to an end and Frank moved backward. Jack heard a hollow chuckle escape from Franks lips. The fire in his eyes had changed, no longer was it hunger; It had morphed into pure carnal rage. Jack knew how dangerous that was for him, but he didn't care, a little bit of fear would do him good. It would keep him humble. Jack drove a low bow into Franks ribs and heard a snap, the gloves had saved Frank from a complete rib cage failure but had not stopped one of the weak ribs from snapping. Frank reeled back and grunted before stepping back into the fold. He unleashed a haymaker meant to scramble Jack's brains, but Jack ducked underneath it and drove his left hand into Frank's opposite set of ribs.

Jack heard another snap, but Frank didn't reel back in pain, instead he unleashed a massive attack. Jack was able to avoid all the punches and connect with Franks ribs yet again. It was getting close to the end and Jack knew Frank could feel it. He fed Frank a quick jab and backed off, giving his opponent a moment to collect himself before he ended the fight. But Frank didn't want it, he stuck to Jack like gum on Jack's shoe. He unleased another onslaught, and even landed a weak punch on Jack ribs that forced a giggle out of Jack's lips and then backed away. This time Jack followed him and unleased his own onslaught. Ribs, chin, ribs and then stomach. Frank doubled over in pain and Jack pulled his right arm back like an archer's bowstring and let it go. It was by far the hardest hit he had ever unleashed.

If it wasn't for the padding, Frank would have been killed but instead, he flew onto the canvas. His head slamming the floor with a loud bang. Jack didn't look back or bend over to check if Frank was breathing. He knew he would be, the man had no quit. Jack was humble enough to concede that fact although it didn't extinguish the hate Jack harbored for him. Before the fight, he was intrigued by him but now he knew it wasn't intrigue or respect, it was anger. A need to show the man he was it. He could feel the hate bubbling inside of his belly until Jason patted him on the back and the anger died down.

"Hell of a punch, bud. I was hoping you would show Frank what's what. The stupid kid had been boasting about how he could knock you out all weekend, you're sure knocked that idea out of head," Jason said, chuckling at his pun.

"Of course, he was saying something like that at the start of the fight, so I had to set him straight," Jack said. He had endured too much to be disrespected, he had been fighting against the demons of hell for weeks. One little man couldn't be allowed to stand before him and pretend to be stronger. It was a thought that had undoubtedly floated through Paul's mind, but Jack didn't care. He had earned it; he had endured more than what a normal person would believe possible for his respect.

"Still, I hope he is okay. I think that might have been the hardest punch I have ever thrown," Jack said, with a little bit of remorse seeping into his heart but when he thought back to the fury in the boy's eyes, it all but vanished.

"He will be fine; I was hoping to see you unleash a big one tonight. I wanted to see how much power you had if you hit at 100%, and now that I've seen it, I have to tell you again, you need to be careful. A punch like that without padding could…no would, end a person's life." The look in Jason's eyes told Jack that he wasn't exaggerating, he truly believed what he was saying. Jack had always known he had the power to end a life with the swing of a fist but seeing Jason's eyes filled with a weary pride solidified his belief. At least, he knew that he had accomplished his goal, no gun would be needed if Paul was the man Jack knew him to be.

"I'm going to head out, have a good night and make sure Frank is okay for me, will you?" Jack asked, even though he didn't care about how Frank was. He knew how bad it was to feel the way Frank did, but he didn't care. There was solace in the fact that the pompous man deserved it. Something he could not say for the souls of the men he had collected from since arriving in New York. As he walked to the locker and into the change room he was at peace for the most part. The only thing that didn't sit well for him was the fact that he had never been knocked down, he hadn't felt defeat during a fight for a very long time. Jack knew it had the potential to be his downfall, but he also knew that it could be his greatest ally. After all, supreme confidence and prowess never hurt anyone. Did it?

Chapter 19

As Jack walked back to his apartment from the gym, he turned the events of the day over and over again. As he mentally filled the information away, making room for new information he processed each word Charlotte had said. She had told the truth; he was sure of it. It had to be the truth because the events she had painted with words couldn't be made up. No story was that detailed or soul crushing. It would be impossible for her to make those things up, the sheer absurdity of it all was proof. When he finally stood at the glass doors, he decided he would invite her over that night. He wanted to be in her presence, he wanted to see what he had missed and he wanted, no, needed more questions answered. Jack pulled out his phone and texted.

J: Want to come over tonight? 9:00?

C: Sure, I've got some big news. See u at 9

As Jack read the text message chills ran down his spine, what was the news? Was it good? Was it bad? Jack felt the questions swirling around in his mind and knew that if he didn't calm them, the flood gates would swing open, allowing the crippling memories to flood in. He raced to the elevator and waited for it to open. The steel doors slid open in a painfully slow fashion, as if they didn't know that he was in a rush. Jack flung himself inside and sank to the floor. It was too late. The blood trickled, ribs snapped, screams echoed off the steel. His right hand felt heavy as if the gun was once again resting in his palm. He was the warehouse; he heard the man begging for his life and he saw Paul's face as he walked out of the ring and told Jack to do it. The slow hungry drawl echoed in his ears.

Begin.

The elevator slowed to a stop, and the doors slid open to his apartment. Still blinded by guilt and pain he stood slowly and felt his way to the kitchen. He had memorized the cupboards and their contents so he had no problem feeling his way to the highest cupboard containing the bottle of whiskey. He felt around the cupboard until his left hand rested against the bottle. He grasped it tight, desperately spinning the cap off with his left hand. Jack brought the bottle to his mouth and drank until a gap had been cut through the memories.

It was just a pinprick but even so, it was better than nothing. He brought the bottle to his lips once again, repeating the motion until he could finally see again. The whiskey blurred the edges of his newfound vision but at least he didn't see the trickle of blood, the hole bored through the man's temple and the screams and pleas no longer haunted his ears. The sheer volume of alcohol he had consumed made him sway, if he was going to get more answers from Charlotte, he was going to need to sober up the best he could. Jack staggered to the shower, just barely turned the dial to ensure the water would be like ice against his skin and removed his clothes. As he stepped into the shower, he felt the daggers of ice water smack him in the face and wake him from the stupor he had plunged himself into.

The fact that he needed to crawl into a bottle just to escape pain ate away at the once overflowing reservoir of happiness that had been leaking obscene amounts of its contents since the moment his mother had closed her eyes for the very last time. Jack couldn't remember a time in which he didn't use the bottle as a hiding hole. Maybe it was because before he was reliant on his crutch, he was happy. Maybe it was because before he left Cielo nothing was wrong, and he didn't need any crutch. He couldn't remember being able to cope in any other way than the way he did. If he could, he probably wouldn't put the coping mechanism he had learned into practice as often as he did.

Once the water had washed all the soap away—it hadn't completely wiped the effects induced by the alcohol, but nothing would, he had drank too much—he stepped out of the shower and dried himself with a towel. Slipping some boxers and shorts on, he headed to the kitchen and pored himself a stiff drink. He walked with his drink to the couch grabbing the cigarettes and lighter on his way. Jack sat down on the couch and flipped the TV on. He scrolled through movies on Netflix until he found one that he liked and sat back, sinking into the cushions as he did.

His drink rested comfortably in his left hand and the cigarette sat unlit between his lips, waiting to be ignited like a stick of dynamite. Jack knew how terrible the white sticks of death were for his health. He could hear his mother's voice in his ears, *Cigarettes are like a pretty girl raised in a bad home Jack. They taste so good and will make you feel all warm and fuzzy but after a few outings they will break your heart.* When she said it, Jack was too young to understand what she meant but that night, as he lit the tip and watched the paper and tobacco burn, he knew what she meant.

The nicotine slipped into his veins, and he felt it mix with the alcohol, sending a warm fuzzy feeling though every square inch of his body. The deadly mixture dulled his senses and allowed him to feel peace, it was an artificial peace, one he knew couldn't last but he welcomed the numbing sensation while it lasted. It was like cheap sex at a college party, it felt good in the moment but he knew that with time it would wear off leaving him to cope with his issues all alone. But that night all he wanted to feel was good, so he took a long drag from the cigarette's black teat. Letting the smoke encompass him in warmth, he allowed the nicotine to blur his senses.

As he took the last drag from his first cigarette the elevator doors slid open. Jack turned his head and saw Charlotte. She was wearing a jet-black dress that hugged every perfection and imperfection equally—although she didn't have many imperfections. She was a mesmerizing, like a sheathed knife. Her chestnut brown hair fell at her shoulders and flowed over in places; her eyes were bordered by black makeup. Resting in the dead center of her chest, like a deadly target splitting her body in two, was the red pendant.

A reminder that no matter how beautiful, truth filled or pure this woman was, she was still stained red. Blood had still flowed through the crevasses in her hands. Jack couldn't help but stare as she unstrapped her stiletto shoes and threw them to the side. She reached her hand behind her back and methodically dragged the zipper down her spine. The dress fell gracefully to the floor, it seemed as through the whole world had slowed and Jack was the only one who could see clearly.

The dress' absence revealed her perfect sienna brown skin, breasts covered by a black satin bra that left little to the imagination and as his eyes worked their way down her torso they landed on the scar. The long purple reminder that she had been marked, a reminder of what would happen if the plan didn't work, a reminder of what happened if anyone crossed Paul. She moved across the room as if she was floating. She gently removed the glass of whiskey from Jack's hand and poured the remining contents down her throat.

She placed one knee on the right side of Jack's body and the other to the left, sitting on his lap facing him. Jack could feel her soft breath on his neck like the whisper of an angel. She ran her impossibly soft hand over his face.

232

The roughness of his skin snagged under her gentle fingers, but she kept going, leaning in to kiss his neck as she did. Her soft lips made their way up his neck and eventually met his own lips. She grazed them and pulled away making him crave their touch. Jack grabbed her back, pulling her warmth closer to him and kissed her. As their lips moved into lock position he ran his right thumb over the scar, it was the only part of her outward body that wasn't perfect.

Of course, on the inside they were both equally shattered. Two twin towers crumbling against the force of Paul's plane. It was almost amusing that her stomach was the only part of her that had been touched by Paul's evil knife. They sunk into the couch, both feeding off the others last few intact pieces. They both felt safe in each other's arms, but Jack pulled away when he remembered what she had texted him earlier. He laid lengthwise on the couch letting Charlotte lay on top of him, her chin resting just below the red sun that rested heavily on his chest.

"What's the news?" Jack asked softly, not wanting to uproot the moment entirely. He kept his eyes closed, swimming in the peace that Charlotte always seemed to carry with her. Charlotte closed her eyes, and Jack felt a tear land on his chest. She put both fists under her chin and opened her eyes.

"Luke is dead." She whispered so quiet that if any other noise was being produced in the apartment Jack wouldn't have heard it. Jack kept his eyes closed, he thought that it was a trick of his mind. That it was imagined noise like the screams or the trickling blood. "Jack, did you hear me," Charlotte asked after a while. She sat on his hips and asked again, "Jack?"

His eyes sleepily opened and asked, "Yeah?" He said as he ran his hands over her waist, fingers slipping under the waist band of her underwear.

"Luke, the boy you fought the other day is dead," she said in a tone so sure that Jack had no choice other than to believe it. Jack sat up, eyes wide and ears alert. His heart started beating fast, sweat started pooling in his palms and suddenly he felt very venerable lying beneath Charlotte.

"What? How? When?" He asked. The questions flew out of his mouth but inside his head there were tidal waves full of questions smashing into the shores of audible speech. He sat up, placing Charlotte on his lap, but her face was too close to his. He could feel the heat coming out of her mouth. He could feel the intoxicating pheromones dulling his mind. "Can we go to the balcony to talk?" Jack asked. He knew it was the only place he wouldn't be blinded by infatuation.

"Sure, I need some clothes though. It's cold out there tonight," she said softly. To Jack it sounded like she was reassuring him, but the edge to her words made Jack believe that she wasn't done telling bad news. He knew better than press for an answer, she would tell him what he wanted to know. After all, he trusted her, he had nothing to fear. She had told him every truth, hadn't she?

"Yeah, I need some clothes too," Jack said getting up and leading the way to his closet.

They both put on thick sweatpants, hoodies, thick socks, and Charlotte grabbed a blanket as she made her way to the patio door. Jack slid the door open slowly and allowed Charlotte to walk through before he followed but she turned back almost as fast as she had gone.

"Can you pour me a drink and grab the cigarettes?" She asked.

"Yeah sure," Jack said and turned back to fill two glasses. He grabbed his glass and pulled another out of the cupboard for Charlotte before topping his glass off and pouring a small amount in Charlotte's. He wanted her to be present as she told him the story, he didn't want any alcohol to muddle the truth. Once he finished pouring Charlotte's glass he headed back into the living room to grab the cigarettes and the lighter, slid the glass door behind him and walked to his chair. Charlotte was already sitting in the chair to left of his, wrapped up in the blanket.

Jack handed her the glass he had filled, passed her one cigarette and lit it once it was tucked between her lips then took his seat. He lit a cigarette for himself and took a sip of whiskey. As he pulled the smoke through the filter, he wondered how alcohol could have cravings. It wasn't just mortal beings that were governed by vices, even liquid had tethers. When he was sober, the thought of smoking wouldn't have even crossed his mind but when the sweet, dulling liquid passed through his lips he wanted nicotine, he needed it as if the alcohol flipped a switch in his brain. Once his reality was properly dulled, he spoke. "What happened?"

"Do you remember when you finished your fight, when me and Paul were talking?"

"Yeah, I just thought you guys were talking about the fight."

"Good, well we were talking about the fight but not in the way you think. Paul was asking me what I thought we should do about the situation. He was under the impression that Luke was a liability but really, I think he was scared that there was no chance he would be able to break him. He was saying that Luke never seemed scared, he seemed excited to be given the green light to kill."

Jack wasn't surprised, he felt the same way in the ring with the blonde-haired blue-eyed boy. The kid obviously enjoyed the job, he reveled in its secret prestige. Jack could tell that the boy was going to climb the ranks fast. He knew there wasn't anything standing in the way of the boy and leadership. Nothing would have stopped him, the kid might not have been a good fighter, wasn't very strong but he was capable of anything. It was as if the kid wasn't born with a soul. Like he wasn't given a conscience at the moment of conception.

It was as if God had forgotten the boy was being born and didn't place a compass in his chest or just forgot to mix a conscience into the formula when creating. It was a chilling thought, but it wasn't the most unsettling thought that crossed through Jack's mind. The most unsettling thought was relief, his own lack of regard for human life terrified him. No matter how innately evil the boy was, a life was still a life. But there was no changing the fact that he was relieved that he wouldn't have a martyr on his hands if his plan did end up working out.

"During our conversation he asked what I thought we should do about it, he asked if he should take an even stronger approach, force him to do something so despicable that even he would have to feel guilt doing it. I told him it was a good idea, because I thought it would save his life, but it didn't work," Charlotte said with a shudder.

"What? How didn't that work? Paul is the devil, I'm sure he would be able to find a way to break even the darkest soul."

"That's what I thought too. It was a terrible thought but at least it would save the kid from death, but it didn't work. Paul made him beat a child. Luke even flinch. Paul didn't hand Luke a gun at the end to finish the job, he didn't have a hit limit like he did with you. Paul made him beat the kid until he died. Apparently, the kid was helping a group of men steal from Paul's casinos, I know that doesn't justify Paul's actions, but I want you to know he didn't just pull a child off the street."

It could barely be likened to a cold comfort. He didn't even ask how old the boy was because he didn't want to know. He didn't want to know the depth of Paul's evil. "Right after you got out of the car Paul called me and said he needed me to come to the warehouse right away, said it was urgent. When I got there, the fight was just ending. Luke was on his knees in the ring, the kids' arms were both broken, legs too and Luke was still pounding his fists into the child's head. Paul was standing in the corner, eyes glassy as if he was on the verge of tears. He looked terrified and if the door to the cage wasn't locked, I don't think he would have even been in the warehouse."

As the words came out of Charlotte's mouth a steady stream of silent tears flowed down her cheeks. The fact that even Paul feared Luke sent chills running down Jack's spine. "Luke wouldn't stop he just kept driving his fist harder and harder into the kids face until Paul told him to stop. When he finally pulled himself away from the kids' corpse, he was covered in blood. It ran down his hands and was sprayed all over his face and chest. He looked like a mad man and when he spoke it was even more evident."

Tears rolled down Jack's cheeks. He knew that if he was put in the position to kill a child he would die before he laid a finger on the would-be victim and by the look on Charlotte's face, she would obviously do the same. "He stood tall and said 'Now wasn't that fun. Fucking bastard. No one will ever steal from you get away with it on my watch sir.' It was chilling Jack. There wasn't an ounce of remorse or guilt in his voice, and his eyes shone bright like he had just thrown the winning touchdown pass in the state championship game. Paul just looked at him and stared in shock. I've never seen him show emotion but last night he sure did, he didn't even try to hide it.

So, when he pulled a gun out of his jacket and handed it to me, I didn't feel the same fear or dull sadness I usually feel before I do the job. He whispered in my ear and said, "Go in the ring and kill him, go in there and end the madness Charlotte." I didn't even hesitate," she said as she tipped the rest of the whiskey into her mouth, grabbed another cigarette, lit it, and continued.

"I unlocked the door and stepped into the ring. I saw the boy lying dead on the ground and a tear fell from my eye, and I just about fell to my knees from the weight of grief, but I was able to hold my balance. Luke looked at me with a beaming smile, he didn't even register that I had a gun in my hand. Back in Ohio my dad taught me how to shoot so even though I haven't ever killed a man without pressing the barrel to his skull I knew what I needed to do. In one quick motion, I raised the gun and pulled the trigger."

"The bullet hit him in the chest, and he stood in shock for a while. Blood started to seep out of the entry wound and mixed with the boy's blood that already covered his chest. It slowly oozed down his chest. He touched it with his left hand and brought up to eye level. Like he was unsure about what just happened. Once his eyes registered that he had been shot he turned them to Paul, but I could still see them. They still shone with hate and happiness Jack, they didn't even shimmer with sadness or terror. His legs gave way as if an invisible hand had forced him to his knees and he had that moment of clarity most people do right before they die. He spoke with confidence, directly to Paul and said, 'See you in hell old man.' A smile streaked across his face as his head hit the black mat. It was chilling. When I turned to look at Paul, he was crying, and it wasn't as if a lone tear fell down his cheek. A fucking river of tears flowed down his face, silent but no less astonishing. I handed him the gun and he told me that if I said anything about it to anyone, it would be my head and theirs on the chopping block next."

Jack chuckled and wiped the tears from his eyes. It was hilarious that Paul had said they would be on the chopping block next because they were already damned. He knew it and he assumed Charlotte did as well. It would be a miracle if they ever got out of the mud alive. The best they could hope for is to pull as many people as possible down with them before they suffocated.

"So, you killed Luke and Paul ordered it to be done," Jack said. Then threw the rest of the contents of his drink down his throat. "Maybe I should have hit him harder, all of this could have been prevented."

Charlotte looked him and smiled but it wasn't a happy smile, it was smile forged in pain. "I guess Jack, but I am sorry for not telling you this morning. I was scared to tell you. I didn't want you thinking I wasn't on your side. I didn't want you thinking that because I am, it's me and you Jack. No one else, it's just me and you."

Jack knew she was telling the truth; he knew she was on his side, yet he was still scared. He could have prevented a child's death; he should have prevented it. As he walked back into the kitchen, he asked Charlotte if she wanted anything else. Charlotte said yes so, he went back and grabbed her glass. He didn't hold back. He filled her glass with just as much liquid as he poured in his own.

Jack made his way back to living room and saw Charlotte sitting on the couch smoking a cigarette with tears streaming down her cheeks. As he placed their glasses down on the table, he took the cigarette from her fingers and pressed his lips against hers, pulling her closer as he did. It was a wet kiss, due

237

to the tears streaming down her cheeks that were mixing in between the two like a barrier stopping their souls from finding peace. Charlotte pulled away and wiped her eyes and Jack opened his eyes slowly. He knew he didn't want to hear what was coming, Charlotte had never broken the spell for a good reason, and he didn't believe she would start now.

"Jack…" Charlotte said in the same voice as before. Just loud enough to be picked up by the human ear but soft enough that nothing else could hear. Even if he had been inches further away, he wouldn't have been able to hear it. "There's something I didn't tell you. Luke is Paul's nephew. Two devils cut from the same cloth."

Jack was speechless. It didn't make sense. Why would Paul try to break his nephew and more importantly, how did Paul summon the resolve to order him dead? The pit of evil that sat in the spot a heart usually resided continued to amaze Jack. Its seemingly boundless depth was astonishing. How could one man have been cut so deep, how evil had Paul's boss been. Jack couldn't fathom it. If Paul was innately, wholly evil and he hadn't always been that way, then the evil that had broken his soul must have been unexplainable.

Even as Paul was trying to break Jack's soul, Jack had always been able to resist the evil that was constantly knocking on his door. He was always able to stop Paul from completely uprooting his life and shattering his soul into fragments too small to collect. But with Paul it was different, not only had his soul broken but it had been completely removed without a trace.

"His nephew? How do you know that? How can, you be sure?" Jack said. His words came out fast and weak, like he was pleading with Charlotte. Begging her to tell him it was a mistake. Begging her to tell him it was a lie or that she could be wrong. He took her right hand in-between both of his and looked at her like a child begging his mother for a chocolate bar. She moved her left hand on top of his.

"I know Jack, I know because he made me go pick him up just like I picked you up. Except when he told me to pick Luke up, he told me it was his nephew. He told me Luke was the future of the GWA, except now I would imagine you are next in line." Jack's expression changed from wounded to shocked. The pieces still hadn't fell into place. They were close but not quite there yet.

"Wait a minute, when did you even go and pick him up. You have been in New York the entire time."

"No, there were a few days in which I didn't see you, don't you remember?" Jack thought about it and after a lot of searching he extracted a memory. It was right after his first sin. It was the night he started collecting souls, not by choice, obviously, but nevertheless. He had gone for lunch with Charlotte, and she was out of sorts. She had been loud and disrespectful to the waitress. It was the day after Paul made her kill a man with a dull blade and left the man awake to feel the pain.

Jack remembered it had been four days since he had seen her and a week since he had seen or heard from Paul. It was all coming back to him but there was still one thing he didn't understand. If Luke had been in New York since then how had he never seen him before and if he had somehow stayed hidden for so long. How did he do it? If Luke had stayed hidden so long there was also a chance that there were other hidden sponsor students. It was a terrifying thought, but Jack pushed it out of his mind.

"Yeah, I remember. Where was he staying and why did Paul keep him hidden so long?"

"Paul left him in the shadows because he wasn't sure if he wanted to break Luke or groom him to be the next leader. He didn't know if he wanted to let him blossom into a new kind of leader or forge him in his own likeness. I guess now he has no options but to put a new type of leader in charge. That is if you don't get out of course."

Her words cut into Jack like knives. The words alone were harmless but when delivered in the tone Charlotte chose to deliver them in, he could tell she didn't truly believe in her heart that he would be able to free them from their shackles. But that was far from the worst part. He was now in line to inherit and run not one but two of the world's largest and most powerful associations and somehow Jack couldn't shake the feeling that the two were connected by more than mutual respect or fear. He feared they were linked in a far more intimate way.

If he stayed in New York, he would be the richest, strongest, and most powerful human in the world. There would be nothing he didn't know and didn't have a hand in because if New York was the center of humanity and he was set to be the king of NYC he would in a sense be the king of the world. Jack knew that Politian's were just figureheads, the real power lay in the hands of the people who had pockets full of money. Money ran the world. It was fact that Jack had been privy to from a very young age. It dictated the paths people's lives took and no matter what anyone said, everyone wanted to be rich or at least have enough money to do anything they wanted.

Every human craved the security and stability of unlimited cash flow, even Jack himself had craved it at one point. Setting aside the path his life had taken, the horrible things he had been forced to do and the impending doom cascading down upon him, the unlimited credit card made it easy to focus; It set his mind at rest. Without the credit card he would have to get a job and he would have to worry about paying for food, shelter, and warmth on top of all the other terrible things that weighed heavy on his mind. Once he finally slowed the roller-coaster his mind had turned into, he spoke.

"Did you go to Paul's hometown, or did Luke live somewhere else? And if Luke is dead and Paul was grooming him to be the next leader of the GWA, why would the mantle fall to me? Why not you? You have been here longer and your just as, if not more capable than me."

Jack waited for Charlotte's response while she took a large swig of whiskey and a long, drawn out pull from the cigarette she was smoking. As she blew the smoke out, he saw that she didn't watch it encircle her head. She didn't watch its tendrils dissipate into thin air. Instead, she blew it out and hungrily sucked more in. It wasn't a craving or a want, it was a necessity like water. It was sustenance. Jack understood that for her it wasn't a pass time. It was an addiction just like alcohol was for him. He didn't drink for pleasure, he drank because he needed the dull haze, he needed the memories to be suppressed, it hadn't just grown into the necessity it had become in his tenure with the GWA.

It had been vital ever since his first drink way back at the orphanage. After that first hazy night filled with nothing but dulled happiness, he was hooked. The orphanage was a lot like the situation he found himself in except for the fact that he didn't have to kill anyone there. Other than that, it was just as much of a hell hole as the New York he had come to know was.

"Yeah, Luke lived in the same town that produced Paul. It's a place in California called Vide de Lumiere. It's a beautiful city, but beneath the surface it's much different," Charlotte said with a shudder. "The reason the mantle will fall to you is because Paul would rather die than let a woman run his institution. In his eyes, women can't lead because as a group, we are governed by our emotions. It's true to a degree but the funny thing is that he doesn't realize a man never strays from the values instilled in them as children. If you were brought up in a different home, a different town or different time you might be the best leader the GWA could hope for, but you weren't. I would have thought he would have seen that by now, but I suspect he is blinded by your physical prowess. Whatever the reason is, he has chosen you and there is no way to change his mind once it has been made."

Jack sat still, not moving or even breathing until he finally reached for his drink which was close to finished. He poured the rest of the whiskey down his throat and turned back to Charlotte to let her know he was still listening. "The decision has been made and there isn't any changing it so now we have to figure out how we are going to go forward, at least until we put the plan into effect. Confucius thinks you are his successor and Paul thinks you are his. The problem is clear, but I can't figure out what we are going to do about it. How are we going to appease both men, how are we...I mean how are you going to make them both believe you are on their side?"

Jack thought for a moment and then spoke. "I don't know, Charlotte. All I know is that as of now I stand to inherit both governing bodies of New York and that I don't want either. All I want is to escape this place. As a kid I was always told New York is the city of 'opportunity' but in reality, it is the breeding ground for evil. It is a place filled with spiders and the insignificant bugs who get caught in their webs. Sometimes it works out and the prey profits from its capture but most times they get pulled deeper and deeper into the nest. No one in New York is innocent, no one is special. It is a place void of heroes, the best you can hope for is to escape or be taken away by the sweet release of death and I refuse to die. I will win at any cost, and I hope you will help me. I pray you are on my side because you are the closest thing I have to a hero."

When Jack finished, he felt a weight lift off his chest, in that moment he had divulged his deepest darkest secret. He had given up the farm in hopes she would help him protect his sheep. It would have been easy for Charlotte to turn around and tell Paul, but Jack decided to trust her, he decided to place his fate in her hands because he was too tired to hold it any longer. A tear escaped from Charlotte's eye, and she kissed him. She let her emotions flow through the bond. Their lips locked into place and as they did Jack knew he had his answer.

Even if Charlotte wanted to tell Paul, even if she had been instructed to tell Paul everything, she was going to stay there. She was going to protect him at all costs. As they fed off each other's virtues he knew that he could trust her with his life. The pair sunk into to the couch and before long Charlotte was standing up, grabbing Jack's hand, and leading him to his own bedroom.

After the events unraveled, Jack felt a feathery lightness. He had been filled with hope and was sure he couldn't possibly weigh more than an atom of helium. He still didn't know what he was going to do about the split personality he was going to have to produce but for the first time in a long time he was hopeful. An air of opportunity floated in the air above Jack's bed as Charlotte sleepily laid her head down on his chest. The memories, screams and smells had disappeared; Charlotte's soft, shallow breaths were all Jack could hear as he drifted into the land of absolute nothingness. The land of perpetual peace.

Chapter 20

Jack knew he drank too much, so when he found himself floating in the abyss he didn't struggle, he knew he was supposed to be there. It was his consequence for excessive drinking. He moved his head around and saw nothing but black. The impenetrable darkness surrounding him made him feel safe, it was the feeling of falling that he hated but by some miracle he wasn't being shown any memories.

As Jack floated, he slowly closed his eyes. Allowing himself to feel nothing. No pain, no happiness, just peace. Not a single thought floated though his mind. He stayed completely still, letting his dream-self float in peace, until something pulled him to the surface. It wasn't the air raid siren like most days. It was gentler, like a feather brushing against his face. The sudden change in stimulus carefully carried his body back to the hole of light that always pierced the abyss from above. It was a constant reminder that he had to go back reality at some point, ensuring he remembered that peace only lasted so long.

Jack drifted up to light slowly, a gentle breeze pushing him back to reality. Once he had crossed the threshold between dark and light, he opened his eyes. Not fast but millimeter by millimeter until they had opened wide enough to see Charlotte's perfect face inches from his. She laid still, silently memorizing his face until he couldn't take it anymore and he kissed her lips softly. His lips gently brushed against hers but fleeted away before they formed any type of attachment.

"Morning," he said sleepily.

"Morning," she said. It was like a hidden code. Each telling the other they could get used to waking up the other's face each morning. Charlotte sat up, pulling the sheet up with her as she did. "What's on Jack Hanson's itinerary today?"

"Well, I have class…but lately going to class doesn't seem as important. So, I was thinking about getting new suit. I would like to get a new one to go to supper with 'The King of New York' on Wednesday," Jack said, "want to come with me? I found the best tailor last week; I think you would really like him."

Charlotte paused for a second, clearly weighing her own plans against the new offer. "Yeah, sounds like fun. Fuck class," she said with a nervous laugh.

Jack knew she was lying. He knew she had something other than class to do but he decided not to pry because he wanted her to meet Gabriel. The feeling he got when he was around the small old man was unexplainable and he thought that if Gabriel liked her than he would know he could truly, wholly trust her. If Gabriel was able to give his stamp of approval, then it was good enough for Jack.

"Sounds like a plan! I have to go to the gym but after I get back and take a quick shower we can head out. Does that work for you?" Jack said.

"Yeah, that sounds good, I'm going back to sleep and then you get back we can hop in the shower and then head out." But as Jack was getting up, she said, "I don't have any clothes to go out in."

Jack thought for a second and then an idea popped into his head. "I could run down the street and grab some clothes from that Hollister about a block down."

"That will do!" Charlotte said with a smile. Seeing her at peace with the prospect of wearing regular clothes dissolved the last shred of hate inside Jack's heart. Maybe the girl that had left Beatrice, Ohio all those years ago was still there. She had just been beaten down so deep that it took someone like him to bring her back out. He threw the sheets off and pulled some sweats and a stained hoodie on. Then after Charlotte told him her sizes he headed to the gym.

When he returned, he had sweat running down his face and the stench that stuck to him almost made him gag. If he didn't know better, he would have thought that he hadn't showered in days. He walked into his room and saw Charlotte sitting up, sheet pinched between both armpits. He had always wondered why women felt the need to cover themselves in the morning. If she was sitting in his bed, he had clearly seen her naked all night. It was a question he would never ask but a valid one all the same.

Jack handed her the shopping, and she began removing items. He had bought two outfits. The first was a tight, navy blue shirt with spaghetti straps, and black jeans. The second one was a black, tight long sleeve shirt with regular blue jeans and another whole bag filled with underwear because he knew nothing about women's underwear and he didn't want to ask the employee, no matter how nice she was to him.

After she was finished going through the first two bags, he handed her another that held two trench style coats and a pair of brown Chelsey boots. After Charlotte had removed every item, she said it all looked great and said that she would wear the black pants and the blue 'top' that day and leave the other outfit for another day.

"Head to the shower and I'll meet you in there," she said softly. Jack understood what she was saying. She was really saying, "Get the fuck out of here so I can find something to cover myself with, so you don't see me naked because it's weird if I'm naked when we aren't about to be intimate." So even though Jack didn't understand and frankly thought it was ridiculous he got out of his own room and made his way to the bathroom.

Jack turned the dial until he knew it would warm to the perfect temperature, then took off the sweaty clothes and hopped in. He let the water flow over his face and pull every droplet of sweat toward the drain. But as the water formed miniature waterfalls over every bump and crevasse of his torso, he felt reality cracking. His ears picked up the faint screams and his eyes flitted back and forth from the cage and back to the shower. He felt his grasp on peace slipping.

He felt the pain pulling him deeper but just as it threatened to pull him past the point of no return, he felt Charlotte's soft fingers moving their way up his back. The soft echoes faded into the silence and his vision corrected itself. Her right-hand spun him, and he saw her intricately created, beautiful face staring back at him. She pushed her weight up onto her toes and kissed him. Her lips locked with his, each set perfectly created for the other.

By the time Jack finally emerged from the shower and handed Charlotte a towel to dry herself with his fingers had shriveled up like raisins. He dried himself, brushed his teeth, headed to his closet to grab some clothes and then fixed his hair. When he got back to the bathroom, Charlotte was still drying her hair and he saw that even with messy hair, face clear from any makeup and nothing but a towel covering her torso she was beautiful.

He leaned down and kissed her, but he didn't let their lips lock, he knew he wouldn't be strong enough to unlock them. He drew away, put some gel in his hair and Charlotte headed back to the room to put some clothes on. He couldn't believe that something so beautiful could have survived in such a terrible world. It was like the small white flowers that survive at the top of the tallest mountains or the dandelions that struggle for life in between the slabs of sidewalk cement.

Jack walked out into the kitchen area and cleaned up a bit from the night before, finally sitting at one of the barstools waiting for Charlotte to be ready. Before long, she emerged from the hallway in the clothes Jack had picked and he could almost see the girl she had been before Paul had broken her soul down to its most elemental pieces.

"How do I look?" She asked in a small, timid voice.

"More beautiful than anyone else in the city, maybe even the world," Jack said, eyes wild with admiration. "If writing doesn't work out, I daresay I could have a decent career in fashion."

Charlotte broke out into a full laugh, one of those laughs that gnaws at your stomach muscles if it goes on long enough. Just seeing the joy in her laugh and the way her face contorted made Jack start laughing. It was the first time in a very long time that he had laughed, really laughed. He laughed at nothing the first time since he had gotten high at a party in Medora. It had been too many years since he had laughed because he was honestly happy, because he was filled with so much joy that it needed to escape, lest he explode.

After a long while, the laughter finally clamed. "You would make a 'great' fashion mogul," Charlotte said.

Jack beamed, and just about started laughing again but he pushed it down. "Ready for some breakfast?" He asked.

"Lead the way dumbass," Charlotte said, wiping the tears of laughter from her face. He walked up to the elevator doors, waited for them to open, and allowed Charlotte to walk through before he did, watching as the metal box sealed in front of him. Charlotte put the coat on and tied the cloth belt around her waist. The doors opened when they reached the lobby and Jack put his hand on Charlotte's back, silently telling her to head out. The pair walked by the front desk, waving to Angela as the went and continued out the front doors. Charlotte stuck her hand out and a taxi pulled up to the curb. Jack opened the door for Charlotte before he got in himself. The driver looked back and said, "Jack! How are you doing today?" Jack looked up and realized it was Lucien.

"Lucien! I'm doing well, and yourself?"

"Very good Jack!" He said, "Who is your friend?"

"This is Charlotte."

"Good to meet you, Charlotte!" Lucien said as he pulled slowly away from the curb.

"It's a pleasure to meet you as well Lucien," Charlotte said politely. She glanced over at Jack as if to say, "Who the fuck is this guy?" and Jack shot her a look to tell her that he would get her up to speed later.

"Where to sir?" Lucien asked.

"Not sure yet, any breakfast places you would recommend? And didn't I tell you my name was Jack not 'sir'?"

"Yes of course, sorry Jack. I will take you to one of my favorites," he said moving his eyes forward to focus on the road.

Lucien finally pulled the car over to the side of the road and came to a stop after bumping up against the curb.

"Here it is Jack, it's called the Rising Sun," he said.

"It looks lovely!" Jack said even though it really didn't, the red paint was peeling off the side of the building and the front window was boarded up, but he remembered what his mother said, *Don't let outward appearances fool you, what lies on the surface is very unlikely to be a reflection of what is underneath.*

"How much do I owe you?"

"$10.50," Lucien said handing the machine back to Jack. Jack looked down at the amount owed and decided he would multiply the bill by 1000 if the man waited outside for him and Charlotte and took them to the tailor.

"Can you stay here for me and Charlotte to finish and then take us to the tailor you took me to the other day?" Jack asked.

"Of course, Jack, anything you need," Lucien said turning around, a beaming smile cutting a crevasse across his face. Jack looked at the man filled with joy and then looked back at the machine and typed $10,589.50 into the tip section, then pressed okay and typed his pin into the machine, waited until APPROVED came up on the screen and handed it back to Lucien.

"Perfect, thank you Lucien. We shouldn't be longer than an hour." Then opened the door got out taking Charlotte's hand as she stepped onto the curb. Jack walked purposefully toward the door and opened the door for Charlotte walk through.

When they had been seated and ordered their food, Charlotte spoke. "Did you tip him $10,000?"

"Yeah," Jack said with mixed emotions. One part of himself felt good having just given a man $10,000 but the other part felt like a dead-beat father.

A man who thought that throwing money at his problems would scrub his ledger clean. A man who didn't really care about his children, maybe didn't even want them to begin with but then when he and his wife split, he somehow felt the need to buy them gifts to make them believe he cared. The third part of himself felt like a rich child who bought expensive things just because he could, just because it made him feel powerful.

Jack liked to focus on the first feeling but the weight of the three souls handing around his neck told him different, they made him see the other perspectives. The souls had become a part of him like a scar or a new patch of chest hair. "Why? Is that not, okay? Because if it isn't I'm in some deep shit I have probably tipped $3,000,000 dollars to different people since I have been here," Jack said knowing he really didn't care if it was okay, all he wanted was to find a way to reconcile murdering three people.

"No, it's fine… I was just wondering. After the first time, I…Did a job for Paul I walked up to a girl who had been nice to me in my psychology class and asked her how much she thought she would pay for tuition in her life. She told me it would probably be somewhere near $100,000. So, I came back the next day with a cheque for $300,000. In the moment, it felt good and the look on her face was priceless, but I don't know if anything can really fill that void you know? Like I don't think any number of good deeds will make up for a human life but it's still nice to do."

Jack thought about that for a second. It scared him so bad that he could barely push the thought out of his head. If it was true, he didn't know what he would do, if good deeds didn't eventually make up for the sins he had committed then what would? All he knew was that he couldn't live with the guilt the rest of his life, he wouldn't.

"I have never really had anyone to talk to about this stuff so it's nice to know that the first person I have to talk about this stuff with actually feels the same way. Just the fact that you're doing the same things to try and stitch the wound is really…Comforting," Charlotte's said with the same shy smile she seemed to have perfected. Like a wolf in a sheep's skin. Jack knew she could be a wolf, if she didn't have the ability to be ruthless then she wouldn't have survived as long as she had but he would take the sheep he had come to know over the wolf within any day of the week.

"Well, I just think it is good to give back. Not too long ago I was the person I am in the place to tip now. If it heals me, it heals me but if not, then at least someone else has a more positive experience in this life. I think right before we carry the plan out, we should give each a person who has helped us in any way possible, a million dollars. If we succeed, then we will be changing other people's lives as much as our own and if we don't then Paul probably won't even miss it."

"Sounds like a good idea to me," Charlotte said taking a sip of her coffee. As she finished her sentence the waitress came out of the back with their breakfast and the rest of the meal was filled with useless talk about things that shouldn't have had the opportunity to flutter through Jack or Charlotte's minds but for the fleeting moment that day in the Rising Sun all their worries faded away. They turned into regular 25-year-old people on a date, no murders, no black table, no warehouses, no screams, no fantom sensations, no plan and no questions. Just two people enjoying each other's company. But the trouble being in business with Paul was that those fleeting moments that were just that. Fleeting.

As their plates were being taken away Charlotte's phone rang. She took it out of her pocket and checked the name that appeared on the screen. PAUL. She slid the electronic phone across the screen and said, "Hello"

"Yes sir."

"Can you give me 2 hours?"

"Okay."

"Yes sir," and then hung up the phone. "Sorry Jack I have to go, pick out a nice suit. Wednesday is becoming a bigger and bigger deal as this week goes by," she said as she grabbed her purse and quickly walked out of the restaurant. Jack turned back around to his now empty table shocked. So much had happened in such a small amount of time but if he took one thing from the last minute or two, it was that Charlotte was still hiding things from him. No matter what she said about caring about him, she still was connected to Paul.

Whether it was the fact that he had come into her life and become something of a father figure or if it was loyalty or if it was fear, Jack knew when it came down to it, he couldn't fully trust her to be on his side. He knew that if she smelt even the faintest whiff of Jack losing the war, she would switch sides. It was a sad thought, but he knew it to be true. The fact that she had said that Wednesday was becoming more and more important solidified it. There must have been a new development at the GWA. A development Jack knew he wouldn't like, one that would reel him deeper in, or maybe Paul was getting ready to offer him the keys to the car.

At the very least, Jack knew he wanted no part of Wednesday but also knew he had no choice but to get it over with because as his mother always used to say, *The only way through hell is forward.* Although Jack knew that he couldn't fully trust Charlotte, it didn't change the way he felt about her. He knew nothing could.

When the waitress returned, Jack asked for the bill, tipped her $5000, grabbed his coat and left before he could see her reaction. He had never spent any real time with someone that had money, so he didn't have any sayings or words of wisdom in that department, but he knew that he wanted give as much of Paul's blood money away before the end came. When he reached the curb, he saw Lucien's taxi sitting on the edge waiting to whisk him away to wherever he wanted to go. As he opened the back door and stepped in, he felt at home. He felt safe.

"To the tailors sir?" Lucien asked.

"To the tailors sir," Jack said, closing his eyes and taking a deep breath. His picture had so many holes that he feared wouldn't be filled until his time in New York was finished. The unknown had always scared Jack, so the fact that he couldn't see the whole picture overwhelmed him. It was too early to begin drinking so he thought it best to just take a second to steel his nerves. He wouldn't be able to handle much more without breaking and if he broke, he knew the monster within would be released on the person who chose to deliver the final blow.

He kept his eyes closed the rest of the ride to the tailors and focused on the sound of the tires battling asphalt and the sound of his own breath. He couldn't risk himself slipping into a memory in front of Lucien. He wanted to keep that aspect of his life as far away from Lucien as he possibly could. The man was too good to be poisoned by the cobra venom that was constantly trying to ooze out of his other life. Before long, Lucien broke the silence by saying they had arrived.

"Wait for me, will you? I won't be long," Jack said as he left the car and walked toward the stairs that led down to Master Threads. Once he made it to the beat-up black door, he turned the handle, pushed the door open and walked inside. Immediately, the damp air and clash of smells wafting off the different fabrics slapped him in the face. He made his way to the desk and just as he brought his hand up to ring the bell, Gabriel emerged from the curtained off room. Jack wondered how the shop made any money at all, he had never seen another soul between the walls other than Gabriel.

"Jack my boy! How was the event?" Gabriel said.

Jack paused for a second, he thought of all the ways he could answer that question. After all, it was a very complicated one, so many different angles could be taken. He was going to be handed the keys to New York, he had seen the woman of his dreams and he had set himself up to be the next leader of the GWA which meant unlimited money for the rest of his life, but all those things were really snakes covered in bunnies clothing.

Not one of those things had gone down the path Jack had hoped and not one would give him freedom. Each, so called 'opportunity' would ruin his life in one way or another. So, if he was being honest, it was the worst possible event he had ever attended (including his high school graduation, which had been a complete disaster) but he decided to bend the truth; Gabriel didn't need to know his woes, "It was extremely eye opening," he said.

"Well, that's better than nothing, Jack," Gabriel said. "What can I do for you today?"

"I have an important dinner on Wednesday, and I would like a new suit. It has to make me look like I belong, but I cannot look too good." Jack knew it made no sense and he didn't know how he was going to convey what he needed or better yet what he wanted. He chuckled nervously and said, "I know that's not a lot to go on but the suit you made me last time was perfect so, if you would be up for it, I would like to give you the reins and let you do whatever you feel is right. The only stipulation is that nothing on the suit can be red, not any piping, stitching or fabric. Does that work for you?"

"Yes Jack, that will be fine. I don't think anyone has ever given me free reign on one of their suits. When would you like the suit to be ready?" Jack thought about it for a moment, the next day would probably be easiest for Gabriel but if he set the deadline to be that night, he would have a full day to prepare for the dinner. Something inside of him knew that he needed to be on his A game for the next day.

Something deep inside him said that somehow, some way, Confucius was the corner stone of the entire picture that he was trying so hard to see. Jack didn't think Confucius was on Paul's team or even agreed with the devil but Jack thought that it was entirely plausible he knew more than he let on.

"Can it be ready by 10:00 tonight?" Jack asked.

"Of course, Jack."

"Thank you, sir. I look forward to seeing the final product," he said and then turned toward the door. As he pulled the door open, he turned back around to get one more look at Gabriel—he small blue-eyed man intrigued him—but he was gone. In the 5 steps, it took Jack to get from the front desk to the door, Gabriel had disappeared behind the curtains once again.

When Jack finally returned to the apartment, he saw that it was 3:30pm. He had 20 minutes until he needed to be at the gym for his evening workout with Jason. But 20 minutes in his apartment felt like years and the only activity that crossed his mind was drinking. Not a casual drink while reading or a social drink between friends but the drinking with the sole purpose of getting blackout drunk.

But he knew he couldn't do that, there would be no advantage to being intoxicated right then, even though it was the only thing he could think of. The fact that he couldn't get the idea out of his mind left Jack with a purpose filled hole, one he knew could only be filled by something he had loved since he was a boy. By something that he knew he was good at, it had been proved in the last few months and it was the only thing that would be able to steer him back on the right path if he ever found an exit off the freeway through hell.

But it wasn't the time for writing. Not because he had nothing to write about, he had plenty to write about but before he could start, he needed to find the truth, he needed to see the whole picture or at least a bigger portion of it. So, he picked up his bag and headed to the gym early, maybe an hour and a half filled with punching, kicking, holds, takedowns and the maximum amount of physical exertion would calm his thoughts, maybe he could find solace in the fact that he could expertly dismantle every member of the GWA. He stepped into the elevator with a new sense of purpose, a new drive. The gym was going to fear him, every occupant of that sweaty confinement would fear him that day.

He knew that it would most likely sway anyone from fighting with him, but he didn't care, he needed to create a sense of confidence for his meeting on Wednesday. After all, when you are in the presence of a King you don't trust you must know without a doubt that you are a better man than he, if there is even a shadow of a doubt then all is lost.

When the elevator finally reached the ground floor, Jack stepped out and walked with a new sense of purpose toward the door, toward the future that he now felt slightly more in control of. He nodded at Angela as he walked past and just as he reached the front door, he heard his name called out.

"Jack!" He turned his head to see who had called his name. "Jack!" It was Angela.

Reluctantly he walked back to the front desk. "Yes Angela? What's wrong?" He said impatiently. The focus and determination that had filled his vision only seconds ago was fading quickly.

"Sorry to bother you, Jack, but a woman came in here earlier looking for you."

Jack's mind raced. Who could it have been, he only knew a few women in New York and most of them had his phone number, why wouldn't they have just called him? The only way the woman looking for him wouldn't have called was if they didn't have his number, no one born after the 1960s would go looking for someone in person if they had their phone number. Would they?

"What did she look like? What did they say?" Jack said. Rattling off questions like he was some sort of automatic rifle.

"She was beautiful but not in the way that the woman who usually accompanies you is."

Jack's face flushed a deep shade of red at the comment. When Angela said it, he sounded like a billionaire philanthropist with a mistress. "Don't get me wrong, she was pretty, her blonde hair seemed like it was actively flowing over her shoulders, a waterfall of gold. And her face was like a sunrise, so beautiful but a scar sat just below her right eye."

Jack almost choked up; the description was like a painting. He had heard it so many times, even done it to himself but after so many years of practice he couldn't have said it better. Angela had a gift, maybe it was because she saw hundreds of people walk past her each day and it was her job to memorize faces but whatever the reason, she really did have a gift. The only thing that ruined it was that Jack knew Jessica wasn't who she claimed to be, she was a true serpent in sheep's clothing. The only questions he had left could be answered by her.

"What did she say?" Jack asked quietly. Even though he knew he shouldn't trust her, shouldn't even give her the satisfaction of a conversation, he needed to do it. Something primal buried deep inside of him needed her. Maybe it was the years of wanting to see her face one more time, years of making up fake scenarios in his head that had warped her into the angel that she never was but whatever the reason was he knew he would undoubtedly give her a chance.

The funny thing was that Charlotte had shown more glimpses of trust, but he was more inclined to give Jessica another chance and less inclined to trust Charlotte.

"She said that you can meet her at 7:30pm for supper tonight at…Give me one second, I wrote it down. It's called Hibernacles, it's on the corner of 53rd and 4th."

Jack stood in shock, how could he possibly rationalize sitting down for dinner with her given the fact she had lied to him, betrayed Charlotte, murdered people and never even tried to reach out to him even though she had the means and probably knew where he was all along. She was the devil but even Adam and Eve fell to the serpent, it was the first flaw of humans to yearn for things that were forbidden. For centuries, people have done things that they shouldn't have, it was the reason God was forced to give his only son. It is what makes us human, it is what separates us from other species.

"Thank you, Angela, I will think about it," Jack said and turned to walk away but Angela called his name again.

"Jack, I know that we don't know each other very well but I feel like we are friends and you have been very generous to me so I feel like I have to tell you that no matter what type of relationship you have with this woman I don't think you should go to dinner with her. She looks like a great woman, maybe even the most beautiful person I have even laid eyes on but something in her tells me she is no good.

On the outside she looks like a sheep but in her eyes, she looks hungry like a wolf. I know you probably don't believe me, but I see hundreds of people every day and I have never seen the sharp quality that she holds in her eyes." Jack looked her and saw that she was telling the truth or what she believed to be the truth. Jack saw that she was honestly trying to look out for him, trying to keep him safe.

"Thank you, Angela. Can I ask you a question?" Jack asked.

"Ask away."

"When you look at me, what do you see? Do you see something else in my eyes?"

"Honestly?" Angela asked as if wanting to know if she could tell the truth.

"Yes honestly, don't worry not much hurts my feelings." Which was a lie, but Jack needed to know what he was sending out into the world. What skin he was really wearing, and if it was transparent or opaque.

"On the outside, you look confident, successful and strong. But in your eyes, they look sad, broken or beaten down. Your body says one thing, but your eyes tell a completely different story. But most of the time when you are with the girl that usually goes upstairs with you, your eyes look happy. It seems like she gives you hope, she picks you up off the ground and builds you back up to what I assume you looked like before you got here. Then there is another thing your eyes give away."

"When you're drunk, a haze covers the sadness, it glazes over the beaten, sad qualities and exhibits a look of happiness and peace, but it doesn't cover it well enough to completely fool those of us who look into people's eyes all day long. It can't lie to us, and if I'm being painfully honest, I like you better when you aren't drunk."

A smile broke out across Angela's face and Jack knew that she meant what she said. Not in a mean or degrading way. She meant it as a compliment. Although she didn't know the whole story. She didn't know what he had been through, she only knew what she saw.

"Thank you, Angela, it's nice to hear the truth once in a while," Jack said as he turned and left without another word. As he walked, he thought about what she had said, he looked powerful, successful and confident. His eyes told another story, but he could live with that flaw because he wouldn't even be able to erase the things they had seen. It would be impossible for them to be wiped clean of every tragedy they had been exposed to.

The offer for dinner bothered him more than all the rest combined, what was he supposed to do? It could be a trap, a way to draw him in and make him let his guard down before extracting his true feelings about the GWA. Or it could just be an innocent dinner between two old friends. Maybe she really did just want to reminisce about old times but how would he be able to look past the vacant expression she held the last time he had seen her. The night she had seen him on the black mat in the moist, stone room where souls went to break.

Her face was even and unsurprised as he beat Luke to within an inch of his life. It was a disgusting show of violence, one that she would have been appalled at the sight of back in Cielo. It would have made her sick to see him unleash the monster and viciously attack the boy in front of him but that night she didn't care, she almost looked impressed. Almost.

Jack didn't know how he could look past that unnerving night, but he decided that he would put it behind him for the time being and focus on learning how to defend himself. Jack opened the door to the gym, his nose immediately filled with the musty scent of sweat that had been sitting on the mats for years. Making his way to his locker and seeing all the pupils training he felt something close to happiness, or was it peace?

He couldn't tell, all he knew was that he felt at home there amid all that violence. It gave him a sliver of peace knowing that all he had to fight there was people or inanimate objects. All his enemies in that gym could be seen by the naked eye. Nothing was invisible or evasive, nothing could sneak up on him from the shadows. He sat on the mat stretching until Jason came up to him.

"Jack! How are you today buddy?" he asked.

"I'm great Jason, how have you been doing?" Jack said. Even though he wasn't great he wasn't about to ruin the atmosphere by introducing negativity.

"On top of the world man, are you ready to lose your first fight?" Jason said clapping his hands together and rubbing then back and forth like he had been waiting for that moment his entire life.

"Please, who could beat me, Jason. I don't want to have to have to ruin your dreams today. But if I have to I will," Jack said wanting to seem confident but on the inside he was terrified. Was this the day his two lives would meld together and make him slip up?

Jason pointed across the room to a guy who looked like he could rip the head off a silver back gorilla. "His name is Steve. He is the best boxer and martial artist in New York. He is a dangerous dude and I think he might be a match for you." Jack ran his tongue over his lips and his palms started sweating.

"Can I warm up first?"

"Of course, do you want to box or just get in the cage and go all out?" Jack thought about it for a second and then said, "Box." He didn't want to get beat up so bad that he couldn't walk, he needed to be able to win fights for Paul if the situation arose.

"Sounds good," Jason said, and walked over to grab his gloves to get Jack warmed up.

Once Jack was properly warmed up, he walked over to the ring and put his gloves on and slipped his mouthguard in. Jack knew that he had a chance against the city's phenom, but he also knew that that night would most likely be the first time in a long while that he would be hit. Once all of his protective gear was on—except for the headgear he normally wore at the gym—he climbed into the ring and awaited his competition. Steve wasn't much taller than Jack but unlike any of the other opponents he had faced at Jason's gym, Steve was just as shredded as Jack was and Jack could tell he was light on his feet. It would be good practice for Jack's inevitable fight against Paul, but still, he was worried.

He knew that getting hit would hurt, especially now that he didn't have any padded headgear to soften the blows. As the massive man stepped into the ring Jack looked around and saw that all the other students had gathered around to watch the fight. "Ready?" Jason said. Both men nodded and touched gloves. As the man got closer Jack could tell he knew what he was doing but in his eyes he looked amused. He didn't expect Jack to be anything special. Jack knew that his underestimate was a good thing, it meant that he could slip a shot and hammer him when he wasn't expecting it. Jack knew that no matter how strong Steve was, Steve wouldn't be able to stay awake after his clean right hook connected with his head. If Jack could get a clean shot off, he might have a chance to end the fight relatively quickly.

"FIGHT!" Jason yelled and before long the two men began to circle each other like two alpha wolves. This time it wasn't just Jack who was surveying his opponent, both men were well versed in the language of violence and to Jack it seemed like one good shot would be his only chance but before he would get a chance to land one, he would have to wait for the man to throw a few. The gladiators continued to size each other up until the man threw a punch that connected with Jack's ribs hard. Jack felt one of his ribs crack.

Obviously, so did Steve because he immediately followed the rib shot with a right cross meant for Jack's chin, but Jack was smart enough to duck and slide into safety. Jack held his ribs with his left arm as he circled Steve. The man had a large tattoo sprawled across his chest. *Survivor.* Jack wondered what he had survived, was it an abusive father? Was he homeless at one point? Or did he just pull himself out of a dark hole? Jack almost felt a bond between him and his attacker, but it was a short-lived bout of empathy because a smile had started to streak across Steve's face. The man had thought he won, the man thought he had cornered a little coyote.

Little did Steve know that deep inside of Jack's heart lay an inexhaustible vat of fury and anger. The only way Jack would lose the fight was if Steve relived him of his consciousness. Jack bounced from foot to foot, loading all his anger into his fists. He allowed it to consume his vision and block his hearing. Jack had turned into a bull and his red cape was Steve's head. As Jack moved closer Steve threw some small—but powerful—shots meant for Jack's head, chest and ribs but Jack threw his fists out of the way. He allowed the anger to bubble at the skin just beneath his fists and then waited patiently for the perfect opportunity to strike.

Steve threw two more punches and connected one of them in the same spot as he had the first time, this time around Jack knew his rib had snapped. Even though the pain was immense, Jack fought through and allowed the anger to surge toward the rib, effectively numbing the pain. After Steve connected, he backed away and waited for a surrender or a fall into the canvas but to Steve's dismay it never came. Steve started to become impatient—after all he was the best fighter in New York, a 25ish-year-old amateur fighter shouldn't be able to withstand his punches—he threw punch after punch, all of which Jack evaded.

After a few minutes, Steve was growing tired and Jack could see it, it was getting close to his time to throw a punch. Steve lunged forward with his right foot, letting Jack know he was about to strike with his right but before he could finish the punch Jack ducked and slammed his left hand into the man's ribs. Steve wasn't even slightly hurt but little did he know that Jack's rib shot was only meant to startle, and that the real thing was being loaded into the chamber and was almost to the point in which it could be released. As Steve stumbled back, he was unimpressed by Jack's force, and was even expecting more. But before he could react, he saw Jack's right hand coming across his body and before long, slamming into his cheek.

Through Jack's eyes the punch seemed to be moving in slow motion, his padded fist cutting through the air on its way to Steve's cheek and then as if waking from a dream Steve finally realized what was happening. Jack felt his fist connecting with the accomplished fighter's cheek and pushing his face out of its path. Steve stood in place shocked at the amount of force that had just slammed into his face. Jack's chest heaved, his lungs screaming for air after the 5 minutes of intense physical activity not to mention the two devastating blows Steve had landed on his rib cage. Jack stepped back and clutched his ribs as his anger started to flow back down to the pit it had come from, and he watched as his opponents' eyes went blank and his body dropped to the canvas with a bang.

All the spectators that had been watching from ringside went silent. They had all hoped to see the famous fighter work his magic but what kind of man would Jack have been if he had failed at the first whiff of talent he stumbled upon. He pulled both of his gloves off and placed them underneath the ropes on the ring and then jumped down onto the black matted floor. When he felt the sweaty rubber mat beneath his toes, he looked down at his rib. It had already started to bruise he was lucky the bone wasn't sticking out of the skin. That the anger had retreated and he could feel how much pain had been inflicted but he didn't know what he should do.

Hospital? Drink? Or would Jason know of some sort of remedy, he had to get going he had a dinner he decided he should probably attend. Just as Jack was about to go looking for Jason he appeared.

"Well, you did it buddy. You can now officially say you knocked the champ out. No one else in the entire world can say that, technically you are now the best boxer in New York now."

"Thanks Jason, but honestly right now I don't feel like it, my ribs are killing me, and I have a dinner I need to get to. Any chance you know any quick remedies?" Jack said, his eyes welling with tears of pain. He hadn't looked at his reflection since the fight, but he knew he must look like shit and the plea in his face must have been quite evident because Jason rested his hand on Jack shoulder and said, "Yeah, follow me I will get you fixed up." Jason led him to a room beside the usual change rooms which must have been his office because there was a tiny metal desk with its fake wooden surface covered in papers. The walls were lined with awards, medals and posters but one stuck out to Jack. It was hung directly in the middle of the back wall; A small gold medal with blue fabric hanging from the top. Jason dug around in his desk, pulled out a needle and a bottle of clear fluid. Jason dragged a small wooden chair from beside his desk and sat down in his own rollie chair.

"Sit down," he instructed.

Jack sat but he couldn't take his eyes off the medal. "What is that medal in the middle?" He said pointing to the small, intriguing medal that seemed to fill the entire wall.

Without turning Jason began filling the needle with the clear liquid. "It's a Medal of Honor. I received it when I was a SEAL. Now hold your arm out, I am going to inject you with a small dose of morphine. It should just numb the pain, nothing more should happen but if it does give me a call," Jason said, writing his number on Jack's arm in sharpie and then inserting the needle into the largest vein he could find. Jack felt the liquid enter his blood stream and within seconds he felt the pain in his ribs sleepily drift away.

"The morphine will work for 2 to 4 hours but after that, it's going to hurt like hell again. If you just act like a man, you will be fine," Jason said.

Jack sat in the chair for a few more moments, letting the sweet dullness of the pain medication grab hold of his brain and consume his senses allowing him to feel sleepy and energized all at the same time.

"When were you a part of the Navy SEALs?" Jack asked quietly. He was intrigued but he didn't want to offend the man who had done so much for him in the past few months.

"When I was 18, I joined the navy. I fought for 6 years overseas. Then served 4 more years at home training SEALS in Coronado, California. When ten years had come and gone I decided to hand in my resignation and start my own gym. If I can give you one piece of advice, I would tell you that killing otherhuman beings eats away at your soul no matter who you do it for. I am proud that I served my country, but I would rather be able to sleep at night without the help of my good friend Jack Daniels," Jason said, with a chuckle.

"Never join the army, it is hell on earth, killing another human that has done nothing to hurt you in any way will be the end of life as you know it. I promise you. And if you ever think you need to prove yourself to anyone just know that you don't need to. Prove anything to anyone I mean. In the last few months, I have seen better combat skills from you than I saw in my six years fighting with the SEALS and my four years training SEALS combined. Well…On that cheery note I leave you. Have a good night, Jack, I hope supper goes well," Jason said, walking out of his office toward the boxing champion of New York who was now sitting on the side of the ring, arms resting on the lowest rung of the ropes.

But the funny thing was when Jack stood up to get changed, he didn't feel like a winner. He had won the fight, but his entire life had been turned into a fight. The next assault would come in an hour when he sat down to break bread with his oldest friend. It was just one large fight, complete with rounds, blows, and bloodshed.

Chapter 21

Jack stepped out of the shower and checked the time on his phone, it read 6:45. He had 45 minutes until he was supposed to be at Hibernacles to meet Jess. He had looked up the restaurant and saw that and it was supposed to be one of the most expensive restaurants in the city so he assumed he should wear a suit. He hated the fact that he was putting effort into a dinner with Jess. It was inconceivable to him that she was able to lie with such ease, he thought they had a stronger bond than that. Before he saw her in Paul's dungeon, he had been sure that he would marry her. She was the woman of his dreams; she was the sole reason he was able to get through the orphanage.

Without her face dancing through his dreams each night he would have given up in the dark ancient halls of Verlies. Granted, he did give up a piece of himself but without her face to keep him company, he would have been completely alone in his hellish home. Jack knew his drinking was a terrible habit to foster but it was much better than the other choices he was presented with at the orphanage. Something about the large stone pillars, mahogany furniture, king size poster beds and the Callused twins that ran the institution bred a need to rebel or forget. While at the school Jack had lots of other 'inmates' to talk to, but four names stuck with him. Kyle, Ruby, Alexi and Francis.

The foursome were all brothers and sisters. They were the drug dealers, terrorists, and leaders of the home. When the oldest of the group, Alexi, was just 8, both of their parents died in a tragic car crash. From the first day they arrived at the home, they caused chaos, or so Jack was told. They arrived about 5 years before he did. Jack didn't know if it was because of their parents' death or if they had always been servants of chaos but whatever the reason, they found pleasure in making the lives of the residents and caretakers miserable.

Jack had found ways to stay on their good side, to move alongside them, staying just far enough away to make sure he wouldn't be reprimanded if and when they did something obscene. Over the two years that Jack stayed at Verlies, he saw many things happen. The 100-year-old wrought iron chandelier that lit the front foyer detached from its moorings moments before a prospective adoption couple came to visit, a 10-year-old boy become addicted to cocaine, windows broken, hundreds of spiders let loose in the little children's rooms, and countless other obscenities. But Jack was always able to slide just under their radar, the only thing he ever gave into was the alcohol they peddled.

The eldest sister, Ruby, ran a monthly poker game in her room. It started at 1am and ran until 5am—when it was time to get up for chores. Jack never won, not even once but Ruby was able to get her slippery little fingers on bottles of Irish whiskey for the games. After the second or third game, Jack was hooked, the smooth, sweet liquid made the 17-year-old boy feel strong and safe. It allowed him to lose the memories of his mother's death for a few hours. By the time he reached his 11th grade summer, he was buying it by the case from Ruby, at night he would write and write until his fingers bled. The whiskey flowed down his throat the entire time.

Then when he laid his head to rest, he would drift off into the void and watch as Jessica's face danced through the endless darkness. It gave him hope that one day, when he was reunited with her, he would be able to get rid of the whiskey and instead draw inspiration solely from her face. Maybe he would be able to let her body act as his muse, maybe, just maybe, his life would be whole once again. Jack carried the fallacy every day until he saw her face appear unchanged as she watched him beat Luke to within an inch of his life.

In that moment, he saw what he had missed all those nights alone in the house of sin, the part that he couldn't even see when he looked further into her eyes on the long summer days by the river in Cielo. The darkness that lay just beneath the surface.

Jack walked out of the bathroom feeling unbearably angry at himself, at Jessica and at anyone else that he could lay blame on for leading him into the mess he found himself in. When he walked into his closet, he picked out the most basic suit he could find. Once he had laid the white shirt, blue tie, black belt, grey pants, grey jacket and a pair of plain black oxfords on the bed he went back to bathroom, fixed his hair and sprayed some deodorant under his arms. Once he was dressed and his tie was knotted, he headed into the kitchen.

It was 7:15, just enough time for a drink before he left. The morphine was starting to wear off, so he didn't feel any guilt when he poured the first shot down his throat. Jessica was supposed to be the one who would allow him to escape the deadly vice, but she had morphed into another excuse in a long line of excuses to drink. Another name in the long list of people who were the growers, suppliers, and dealers of his pain. The first two drinks had gone down smoothly so he poured another to dull the throbbing pain coming from his ribs. At least he would be able to leave by 9:30. He had an iron clad excuse. When the glass was done, he returned the bottle to the cupboard, rinsed the glass, and made his way to the elevator, picking up his 'work coat' on the way.

Down at the lobby he said goodnight to Angela—he knew she would be sleeping behind the desk by the time he returned—and headed to the front doors. As he walked through the glass doors, he thought it was funny that whatever his reason for leaving the apartment was, it effectively changed his view of the world around him. That night, the world seemed bleak and dull with a tinge of red around the corners. The streets seemed less crowded and the people who walked by him seemed to be walking at a slower pace.

The whole world appeared to be dejected, maybe they all knew he was walking into what would be a terrible night in the already unbearable life of Jack Hanson. A night that had become a common occurrence since his arrival in the city that never slept. He stood on the curb willing the universe to pick him up, drop him back in his old life and erase his memory so that he could, once again, be the naïve boy he used to be. At the time, all he wanted was to be a new yorker but standing there on the curb all he wanted was to be as far away from New York City as possible.

The universe never picked him up. It was all he could do to not let the memories he had made in the last few weeks take control of his psyche. He stuck his hand out to let a cab driver know he was looking for a ride. In moments, a dirty yellow car pulled up to the curb and he got in. The driver was a small east Indian man with a heavy accent, nothing like Lucien's broad smile and joking demeanor.

"Where to sir?" He asked. Jack paused for a second, it would be so much easier to say any other restaurant than Hibernacles, but he knew he needed to go; he knew the picture would only become blurrier if he didn't.

"Hibernacles please, sir," he said, dejectedly.

"Right away boss," the small man said as he sped away from the curb. The drive to Hibernacles was anything but uneventful. The driver had obviously not acclimatized to New York roads. He sped and weaved through traffic nearly hitting at least 20 pedestrians and 100 other cars. His reckless driving earned him endless honks, curses and a bouquet full of fingers. But by the time they had stopped in front of the massive marble archways they were both in one piece and had made great time.

"How much do I owe you sir?" Jack asked.

"$12.50."

It was a fair price for the ride, but Jack decided he had earned more on account of the hundreds of speeding tickets he would incur as a result of his breakneck speeds so when the man handed him the machine, he paid the man $5000, then left the car before the man had time to praise him for his generosity. Jack stepped onto the curb and looked up at the masterpiece of architecture that was Hibernacles. The marble archway, barred by two towering pieces of glazed glass, dwarfed Jack.

The massive silver letters that wrapped their way around the arch were awe inspiring, not to mention the fact that they likely cost ten times the cost of his first home, if not more. He made his way to the door and when he got close, the massive slabs of glass moved out of his way. As soon as he walked into the room his breath was taken away, the floor was covered in royal blue, velvet carpet. A staircase led up to the dining area with solid silver railings leading up either side.

Each table was made of silver with flowing black tablecloths cascading over the sides. In the middle of the ceiling, a chandelier hung with white gems reflecting light to all corners of the restaurant. Every table was filled with well-dressed people laughing, drinking, and eating tiny portions of food that seemed to sustain the entire upper class. It was the picture Jack had held in his mind of what the Queens dining room might look like and smack dab in the middle of the wealth was Jess.

A waiter was showing her to the center table, a waterfall of fabric flowed over her hips and a slit had been cut in the left side granting her left leg some freedom. Her back was turned, and her hair swayed as she walked, so Jack could see the black letter J standing out against her skins perfect backdrop. Her golden hair flowed over her shoulders and as she turned to take her seat, she flipped it to the left giving her the appearance of a wild lion.

The king above very rich jungle. As her face turned towards Jack's, he caught a glimpse of her eyes, blue like Mediterranean Sea save for the black void of her pupil. In the black, he could see that no matter what she tried to cover her body with, he would always see her for what she was. Just like his own eyes betrayed him, hers acted like Judas. If Judas betrayed the King of Men, hers betrayed the Queen of the Devils. She beckoned Jack over to her once she had taken her seat and Jack obliged, he had no other option but to.

He made his way up the staircase of wealth and took his seat across from Jess without a word. He had decided he wouldn't speak unless spoken to that night, he didn't want to betray any of his true feelings. He had come for one reason and one reason only. To make his picture clearer.

"Thank God your front desk lady gave you my message. I was afraid she wouldn't, she didn't seem to like me." Jessica said nonchalantly, like it was a normal occurrence that she and Jack would sit down for supper or pass messages to each other through front desk ladies.

"Yeah...Smart lady, that Angela," Jack said, ice crystalizing around his lips as he spoke.

"Well good. We are a long way from Cielo, aren't we?" Jessica said with a curt chuckle.

"Yeah, about as far as I ever need to be," Jack said as a waiter walked up to their table.

"What can I get you to drink sir?" He asked.

"Half a glass full of whiskey neat."

"What kind sir? We have Scotch, Bourbon, Japanese, and Canadian."

"Canadian please, Crown Royal if you have it."

"Great choice sir and for you madam?"

"Martini stirred not shaken, garnished with an olive. Quickly," Jessica said. Her comment startled Jack. It shouldn't have, but it did. Whatever he had seen the other night, it was still the girl he had fallen in love with back in Cielo sitting cross from him. The comment obviously didn't startle the waiter because he gracefully moved away from the table and disappeared into the back room to make their drinks.

"When did you start drinking whisky?" Jessica asked. In retrospect it was probably said in a polite tone but to Jack's ears it sounded like a sharp jab meant to wound him.

"After my mom left, you?"

"When I turned 21, Pau…some friends took me out for a few drinks, but I never really drink. Only when I am out for dinner or when I used to party in college."

Paul. She had almost said Paul took her out for a drink when she was 21 but stopped herself. Jack had seen her at the fight, he knew she was associated with Paul. He knew she had been the puppet master pulling the strings of Charlotte's darkest hour. Why would she hide it anymore? The lies made Jack vibrate with anger, but he decided to play along with the charade, at least until the drinks came.

"That's very responsible of you, I guess when I was at the orphanage I needed something to dull the pain and I didn't have anyone, so I just found a new way of achieving that goal."

"I get it, that must have been brutal. I am so sorry Jack," she said, resting her hand over his. She looked into his eyes and tried to show that she truly sympathized with him, but all Jack could see was lies, deceit and a mask. He pulled his hand away fast.

"So how did you like the fight? Was Alexander happy with the outcome?" By that point, Jack was so mad that he was sure steam was coming off the top of his head and spherical fires were burning where his eyes should have been. Jess coughed when the words left his lips but when she regained her fake poise she spoke.

"You looked like a young Zeus. Every punch you threw looked calculated and intelligent. The other guy didn't stand a chance. You were light on your feet and your head never swayed. Plus, you didn't ever look scared, in fact you looked perfectly comfortable. It was an amazing display of power, but you know I don't like fighting."

Jack felt his eyes roll in his head, it was a perfectly rehearsed speech, one Paul or Alexander rehearsed with her. "As for Gra…Alexander, he seemed to enjoy it."

Gra? Who was Gra, could it be possible that the man in red was Jessica's grandfather? Or was it a name? Grant, Grady, or Graham? It couldn't be, she was a kid from a small town in Maine, wasn't she?

"It was the first time I met him, but he said it was beautiful display of strength. He says you have a bright future ahead of you. He even said you are in line to take over for Dr. Confucius. That's a great honor Jack, I mean it. You have achieved so much since the last time I saw you. And with all the things

266

that have happened to you it's incredible. You have come a long way from beating me in that writing competition."

Writing competition? What writing competition? And then it dawned to him, he had finished a story when he was at the orphanage, his English teacher in Cielo had urged him to enter so he had sent in a story called 'The Average'. It was called the World Writers Championship, put on by the Global Writers Association. He had never received anything back, so he had thought it was no good.

It was the first time he had ever entertained the possibility of a writing career. But as re-lived the experience he remembered the competition and how 'The Average' turned into the first building blocks of his sanctuary. It now entertained multiple vices within its walls but back then all it held was writing and drink. The two mixed to create the formula for his escape, like a sip of peace he could steal a swig from in secret every now and then.

Something that was purely his.

"I beat you in the competition? I didn't even get a letter telling me my result. How would you know I beat you? I was at the orphanage by then," Jack said quietly.

His anger had completely stopped bubbling. All he wanted from her was answers. No matter how much hell he had been introduced to since his arrival in the city, it was all second to his need to become a writer. After all, it was the reason he had run out into the middle of the frozen tundra all those weeks ago. It was the pitch he had been sold, and now that the notion that that he had been a good writer all those years ago had been pulled from his file he needed to know everything. What place did he get? Who had beat him, if anyone?

Why wasn't he told anything, why was he the only one in the dark? Before getting his grade back from Dr. Confucius he had been sure he was a mediocre writer, even his acceptance to the university in Medora had surprised him. Not even Professor Laurent's praise was good enough for him to believe he was a great writer, that he was worth something.

"I know you were at the orphanage Jack! I was there the day you left remember?"

"I didn't leave of my own accord!" Jack said, his anger making its way to the surface once again.

"Sorry, I know you didn't leave; you were forced to move. But still you should have been sent your letter after the rankings were decided. It's very odd that you didn't receive it. The letter should have been there the summer of 2012."

Once the last word had left Jessica's mouth Jack pieced together what had happened. It was a hot July day in Maine, Ruby's poker games had just started. There had only been maybe four or five games and Jack was starting to get a taste for the whiskey, starting to understand where it could take him. Or rather beginning to understand what it could shield him from. The problem was that Ruby's whiskey wasn't cheap and Jack had little to no money.

When he arrived at Verlies, all he had was the money he had saved from his old life in Cielo and the little money he had earned from the twins for doing odd jobs around the property. He had already bought two of Ruby's bottles, so he was almost out of money and what he did have left wasn't enough, but Jack already knew he couldn't live without an escape, couldn't endure without a hideout from the chaos inside and around him. So, he asked Ruby for a loan, he told her he would pay the usual rate plus half another bottle if she gave one to him without being paid up front.

Being the intelligent—or rather the brilliantly, sadistic—businesswoman she was, she obliged. There was only one catch. If he didn't pay within the month, she would start relieving him of his possessions. And due to the lack of work, he wasn't even close by the end of the month, so his shoes were the first to go. Then other things started to go missing, until the last thing he owned was the picture of his mother, and no matter how long he held off paying Ruby it never did go missing. Maybe she still had a shred of decency in her heart, maybe it was because she had lost her own parents or maybe it just wasn't valuable to her but whatever the reason was Jack was grateful that she afforded him that show of decency.

Even now he would take the picture over every dollar in the world. But as he journeyed through the memory he knew where the letter went. He had no money, no possessions, owed a debt and Ruby was in charge of walking the quarter mile to the end of the driveway every morning to collect the mail so she had access and time to check every piece of mail that the orphanage received. She must have seen his name in the letter window and destroyed it.

The waiter came over and dropped their drinks on the table without a word and left without taking their dinner orders, come to think of it, Jack hadn't even seen a menu and no matter what he thought of his companion or the restaurant he really was starving. As he lifted his glass of whiskey to his lips, he saw the irony of it all. The same vice that had suffocated him back then kept its sweet sticky hand around his throat all these years later.

"Yeah, that's very odd. I had a mailbox at the orphanage. Maybe it got lost in transit, who knows," Jack said between sips of whiskey.

"No matter, you know now. It doesn't really matter anyways; you still found your way to one of the best writing schools in the nation." Jessica said, then took a prim and proper sip of her martini. She looked like a regular posh asshole, complete with a silver spoon stuck all the way up her ass. It sure as hell wasn't where she had come from, it was something she had found along the way.

"Yeah, but still, I have so many questions. Do you know where I ranked? Where did you rank? What did the winner get?" Jack said trying to keep the excitement out of his voice.

"Well, you ended up one rank higher than me. I was third place; you were second, and Charlotte Jones was first. Do you know her? She works with Paul, and Alexander, I think. I'm not sure if you saw but she was at the fight too." Jack had to stop his jaw from literally dropping. It was all too much; he was the second-best writer in the world at the age of 16? And Charlotte had won the competition? How was that even possible? How did it fit together? What did it mean?

Why wasn't Charlotte in his classes? If she had known his name for so long, why wouldn't she have mentioned it and if she was keeping that secret she must be keeping more—potentially more dangerous—secrets. "But I don't know what the winner got; it didn't say when I received my letter. All it had was the top 50 rankings, a letter I could send to colleges as a reference and a number to call if I wanted a job in the writing industry right away. But that was only for people who had made it on the podium." Jack didn't know what to say, he had missed so many opportunities just because he needed an escape. It took every ounce of strength to push the thought from his mind.

"Wow, by missing that letter I sure missed some opportunities," Jack said with a painful chuckle.

The conversation had changed his entire view on everything he knew about Paul, Alexander and even Confucius. Jack knew the king of New York was involved somehow; he just didn't know how deeply Confucius was stuck in the mud yet. If all three of the winners were now in one way or another associated with Paul's organization, then there must be a be a correlation. It couldn't just be that they were all great writers. Paul could not have had the foresight to see each great writer in America. It would be impossible for him to know which writers would be great one day and if he really did have a vendetta against anyone who might realize his own dream then he needed a method. He must in some way be connected to whoever ran the competition. The real question was: Who ran the Global Writers Association?

"You may have missed opportunities back then, but you seem to have made your way to the same end point. Personally, I think you have made it past where you would have been all those years ago. Confucius believes that you are the best writer he has encountered, he thinks you could be the leader of the new generation of writers. A modern Shakespeare he says, which for me is hard to hear as I work with him, and my future is in his hands but one day soon it will be in yours."

Despite the kindness Jessica's words left in their wake, Jack disregarded her praise. It was fake and he knew it, he knew she was buttering him up for something, she had been doing it since they were 8 years old. He knew when she was just being nice and when she had ulterior motives. The favor or proposition was coming; the only question was when.

By the time the waiter returned with their food—which was a set dish for the night Jack had found out—and two full drinks, Jessica still hadn't said anything, she had yet to ask her favor which made Jack unbelievably nervous. The only times in their lives she had waited so long to ask something it had turned out to be a huge ask and both resulted in suspensions awarded to Jack like badges of dishonor which Jess never apologized for.

The pair ate in silence until both plates were done which took an unusual amount of time because the dish was long island roast duckling. The tiny carcass sat on top of spruce sprigs and had asparagus laid neatly on the sides. Jack had never had a problem eating meat before, no matter where it came from but be had never been forced to pull meat right off a carcass. As he pulled each strand of edible meat from the tiny bird's bones it slid around his plate— the spruce sprigs must have been for show not functionality—and he was forced to center the bird once again and start the process over again.

By what felt like the hundredth time, he decided to jam his knife into the bird so he could steady the carcass and make it easier for himself, but as his knife drove through the soft meat, he forgot about the bones that would inevitably be underneath. His knife hit the small fragile bones and crunched through but the feeling reverberating up his knife was the same feeling that ran up his arm in the cage with the screaming man. It jarred the dark hole in his mind that he had trapped the horrific memories in and threatened to let them loose, but Jack quickly reacted and swallowed the remaining contents of his glass. The burn of the whiskey drowned the memories, and he was able to continue the meal safely.

Once the plates had been cleared and their glasses once again refilled Jack spoke.

"Why am I here, Jess? What did you want to ask me, and don't say nothing I know you to well for that and you better tell it quick because I need to pick up a suit from the dry cleaner in…" Jack pulled his phone out and the time read 9:00pm. "15 minutes," he lied. The truth was Jack no longer wanted to be in Jessica's company, it hurt his soul too badly. His friend who had once been his strongest confidant now lied to him at every turn. He watched Jessica's head spinning trying to think of what to say. She had waited so long that what once was a simple sentence had been warped into words that seemed to be impossible to convert into understandable speech.

"Jack…Jack, I think you will be the king of New York someday, but I think the Dr. is going to wait for a while before he hands the reigns over and I understand his reservations, method or whatever you want to call it. But he won't give me the money I deserve for my latest book. I need that money, Jack; I have earned it and I won't let it just slip away on the opinion of one stupid old man," she said and once she got the first string of words out Jack knew she regained her confidence.

He knew she had the speech well-rehearsed. It flowed out like water, not a single stumble or hitch. Even her tones and tempo were immaculate. The only thing he couldn't figure out was if it was real or if it was a well-rehearsed trap. But he had learned how to play along with master manipulators so he decided he would string the talk out a little while, see if he could get her to trip on her own words.

"I'm not following Jess, what are you getting at here. How could I possibly fix the predicament you are in? I can't change Confucius's mind; I haven't even broken bread with him yet. You would be the one I would ask if I needed to get closer with the man or if I needed someone to plant a seed in his ear," Jack said, holding in a smirk. He knew exactly what she wanted him to do. She knew he was involved with Alexander and Paul; she knew he had killed before and she was asking him to do it again, for her.

She wanted him to kill the King of New York. If she was telling the truth, then only one question mattered, why would she want him dead? He knew it wasn't because of money, if she was in cahoots with the GWA she hadn't had a need for money since she joined. She wouldn't be stupid enough to try and kill Confucius for a book publication. So, on the odd chance that she was telling the truth, why would he need to die? Sure, the man must be involved with the GWA somehow but overall, he seemed like a stand-up guy.

A man who had worked hard to get in his position and only worked with Paul and Alexander because of their position in the community. Of course, if she was lying and trying to bait him into a trap, he would have to make sure he didn't fall in. He would have to decline her offer no matter what, so that on the off chance she was lying he would be safe. And after all the lying she had done in the last few years he didn't feel all that bad for her. Enough moments had passed since Jack had spoken to make it awkward but just as the dinner tipped off the ledge Jess leaned in and said, "Jack your powerful enough that if you took over for Confucius today most people would follow you and the ones who won't fall into line can be bent into shape."

"I don't even know where the Dr's office is, I don't know who all are a part of the Founders. There's nothing I can do Jess, I'm sorry. Have a good night," Jack said as he leaned in seductively beside Jessica's ear.

Close enough for her to feel his warm breath on her neck and smell the whiskey that lay in a thin coat over his lips. "I know that big Iowa brain will find a way through." And then grabbed his coat off the back of the chair pulling away from Jessica without waiting for her reply. She had big money too; she could take care of the bill. But as he took his first step away Jess said, "Iowa brain?" and then as if the right synapse finally fired, she said, "oh yeah I get it, because I went to The University of Iowa. You've changed Hanson, I am not sure you are the same person who left all those years ago."

The comment was supposed to hurt him, it was supposed to dig deep but it just bounced off his skin like a spear thrown off a stone wall.

"We all change, Jess," he said as he walked down the stairs. The night had been overwhelming but at least he knew one thing. She had been lying to him; No one forgot their university, it is the first time in their lives they are given real responsibility, the first time they spent large amounts of money on something they didn't receive right away, it is a young adults first investment.

Even if a person hates school, they will remember the big letters they walked by every day on the way to a class they hated. It is inevitable, there is no question, everyone remembers where they went to university, so her slip up was like her signing a confession saying she was lying. The entire conversation they had at the diner had been lies. Jack didn't know how long she had been in the city but he sure as shit knew she didn't go to The University of Iowa.

Jack stepped out onto the curb and sucked in as much fresh air as he could. Instead of clearing his picture he had just made the parameters bigger by going to the dinner he had been regretting but for the first time he didn't feel like he was drowning. He felt alive, he felt powerful. He knew Jess might know he had caught her in her slip up, but it was just as likely she didn't.

Either way, he knew beyond a doubt that he couldn't trust her. Confucius and Charlotte's real intentions were still up in the air but knocking one more chess piece off the board felt like a win in Jack's books. He buttoned up his coat, there was a chill in the air that seemed to want to cut through his skin like a very small but a very sharp blade. He stuck his hand out into the road to signal to a taxi driver that he was ready to be picked up. Within seconds, a car painted yellow slowed and pulled over to the curb right in front of his feet, Jack opened the back door, climbed in and looked into the mirror.

"Lucien, how do you always know where I am?" He exclaimed. Lucien turned around and smiled.

"I don't know, Jack, I guess we are connected somehow. How was your evening sir?"

"Eventful Lucien, it was eventful."

"Eventful evenings are what we all look for Jack. You sure are a busy man! Where am I taking you tonight?" Lucien said, as he turned his head to look Jack directly in the eyes.

"The tailors, I have to pick up the suit I had made earlier today and then home if that's okay with you," Jack said smiling. It might have been the whiskey coursing through his veins mixed with the morphine, but he felt happy. He felt like there might be hope after all.

"Sounds good to me!" Lucien said and turned around and pulled away from the curb. As they drove, Jack felt completely safe, unlike the ride he had on the way to the restaurant. When they arrived at the tailor, Jack opened the door and told Lucien to wait for him before walking down the steps, past the beat-up door and inside the damp room full of fabric. Once he was inside, he slowed his steps, something about the small room made him think he had to be quiet and methodical.

Maybe it was Gabriel or maybe it was the fumes of all the dyes mixing with the water in the air but either way the tailors basement room carried a different feeling, a feeling mixed with so many emotions. Jack ran his hand along the tables covered in fabric so when Gabriel walked through the sheet separating the two rooms he didn't notice.

"Jack! Here for your suit, are you?" Gabriel said. He didn't speak above 60 decibels but to Jack it sounded like his voice was amplified by a megaphone. He almost jumped out of his skin and had a heart attack in the same moment but luckily, he didn't. Once he regained some of his conscious thought he said in a whisper, "Yeah, sorry, is it done? It's okay if it isn't." Then rubbed his eyes trying to remove the film of fear covering them.

"I just finished, come to the back, I hung it on a dummy. After you try it on, I can put it in a travel bag and then you can pay and be on your way." Gabriel said with a cheerful smile. Then turned to walk away beckoning Jack to follow as he walked. After he had regained feeling in his legs, Jack followed the tiny man into the back room behind the dingy cream-colored curtain. As he pushed the curtain out of his eyes, he saw it. A royal blue three-piece suit, it was dazzling.

Jack was taken aback, it looked like it was meant to fit a king or movie star. It was perfect, if he was going to meet the King of New York to talk about becoming the next king one day it was the suit he should wear. When Jack gave Gabriel the reins to do as he pleased, he didn't know what to expect, he thought it would be a normal suit for a special occasion but what Gabriel came up with was much more. The suit wasn't just a suit it was a statement. It was the perfect mask.

The jacket, vest and the pants were royal blue but something else had been woven between the threads. Jack couldn't quite make it out, so he leaned in for a better look. It was gold, the man had somehow woven gold in between the threads. How he had done it Jack didn't know but it was incredible. Mesmerizing. The shirt was plain white, but it brought the focus into his chest, it would pull anyone's attention into his face instead of looking around him. It created the illusion that the wearer was important, that the wearer was to be respected. Then the dark blue, almost black tie cut the viewers' attention away and delivered their eyes directly into the wearer's eyes.

"It's to be worn with a dark brown leather belt and shoes." Gabriel shuffled around his work bench and picked up a very fancy belt along with a matching set of shoes. "You can buy these if you like. Do you like it, is it what you were expecting?"

Jack couldn't speak, his breath was taken just as it had been the first time he had laid eyes on Charlotte. But once it returned, he said, "It wasn't what I expected, I don't really know what I expected but I love it. It is exactly what I didn't know I was looking for. Every part of it is perfect. I am not even going to try it on, I will take it, the shoes and the belt. Thank you, Gabriel. You have exceeded every expectation I could have ever had; it is a masterpiece. I can't wait until tomorrow night when I get to wear it." Jack meant every word he said and even some that he couldn't quite get out. It was perfection in every sense of the word.

"Thank you, Jack, that means a lot, but without you this suit is nothing. You are the reason I could create this masterpiece. And it is a masterpiece," Gabriel said with a chuckle. "You can wait at the desk while I pack it up. It won't be cheap Jack; I hope you know that."

"Oh, I didn't think it was going to be cheap. I hope it costs more than my apartment Gabriel. I would trade my leg for your suit," Jack said and then walked back through the cream curtain out into the main room.

A few moments later Gabriel made his entrance through the curtain, suit bag and shoes in hand.

"The belt is in the bag with the suit," he said as he typed the sale amount into the card reader.

"What's the big event you needed a new suit for?" Jack thought about it for a moment. If he said it was just for one dinner, he would sound like a fool because Gabriel didn't know the gravity the dinner held. It had started out as a very important dinner; being groomed to take over as the King of New York was no small event but it had since grown into an opportunity to find out even more about the relationship between Confucius, Paul and Alexander and maybe figure out the role the Global Writing Association's writing championship played.

But Jack decided to tell Gabriel it was for a simple dinner. He didn't need the ugly red ooze of his secret life to seep into the warm, kind and soft life he had been cultivating for weeks. He didn't want the experienced side of New York to ruin his mental image of the innocent side. The side filled with kind tailors, cheerful taxi drivers and compassionate front desk ladies. In Jack's eyes, the innocent side of New York was almost the same as Cielo. But Cielo was ruined by something he didn't have any control over, so he promised himself to keep the leafy green side of New York City pure.

"Ahh it's just a dinner. It's always smart to make a good impression, right?" Jack said with a chuckle.

"That's right kid you need to make an outstanding first impression because it's much harder to change it after it has been made. So, how pretty is she?" Gabriel said as a smirk started to build in the right corner of his mouth.

"How pretty is she? What do you mean?"

"Well, no one in their right mind buys a $5000 suit for a dinner with a man. No man's opinion matters that much."

"Oh, I see. I must have misheard you," Jack said, feeling quite embarrassed. "She is drop dead gorgeous." And then stuck his card into the reader, he wanted to finish the transaction as fast as possible, he didn't like making a fool of himself. Jack could feel his cheeks getting unreasonably hot especially considering he was standing in a cold damp basement.

Ironically, if Gabriel knew who he was having dinner with he would most likely have shit his pants. The Dr. had enough money to buy Master Threads 10000x over, granted he had a fraction of Gabriel's pure soul but still Jack felt a need to protect his own pride even if it was only he who knew it was under attack. When the slow card reader finally displayed his total and asked for a tip, he paused. Granted Gabriel had made some assumptions about him and wounded his ego, but the man was kind, funny and innately good, not to mention an unbelievable tailor. Jack couldn't think of a reason more than his bruised ego not to give Gabriel a tip, so he pressed on the tip option and entered $1,000,000.

To this day he still wouldn't be able to tell you why he did it, maybe it was an overcompensation or maybe it was just to show that he could pay whatever he wanted for a suit. Then again maybe something deep inside of him felt that he wouldn't have unlimited funds for much longer. But whatever the reason was, the fact remains that he did it, he had paid $1,005,000 for a suit. It was the largest transaction he had ever made up to that point in his life, but it wouldn't be his biggest ever.

After he had typed his pin into the machine and the blinking approved message appeared on the tiny screen, he grabbed his purchases and turned away toward the door. Jack didn't want to stick around for the praise he knew he didn't deserve. But when he reached the door Gabriel cleared his throat, Jack spun his head to look at the tiny old man. And with his blue eyes shimmering he said, "Nice tip."

Then shuffled into the back room once again. Jack had spoken to the man four times since coming to New York and before that if he the two had crossed paths on the street Jack wouldn't have even looked up. But somehow there was a connection between the two men as if they had known each other their entire lives. It was like Gabriel had snuck into Jack's brain to see his deepest desires, faults and triumphs. It was like they had met before, but Jack was sure he had never seen the tiny man with brilliantly blue eyes before he walked down the concrete stairs and passed the threshold between the outside world and Master Threads. Had he?

The thought haunted Jack as he got back into Lucien's taxi. Cars passed by on the right and left and Jack sat in the middle seat watching out the front window. The night had brought so many questions. An overwhelming number of questions that Jack wasn't sure he would ever find the answers to but maybe that was a good thing. At least he knew the relative size of the picture he needed to make clear.

When Lucien finally pulled the car over to the curb and handed the machine back for Jack to pay for his ride, his brain was numb. The sheer amount of stretching, beating and infiltrating it had endured made it soft and slow. So slow that it wasn't even able to hold the buzz Jack had been riding like a wave. Without even registering what he was doing Jack typed $10,000,000 into the machine, then his pin and handed it back to Lucien without any second thoughts and dragged his unresponsive limbs from the car and into his building. The exhaustion had set in, he didn't even hear Lucien crying tears of joy from the car.

As he walked toward the elevator, he saw Angela sleeping out of the corner of his eye, and all he could think about was the fact that he hadn't felt peace or safety or whatever it was that allowed her to fall asleep in an empty lobby without a care in the world for a very long time, at least not to the degree she felt it to. He had been given all the money in the world, he was in line to inherit

277

even more, and he was, in the eyes of some very prominent men, the pinnacle of human performance.

Granted, he was forced to do unspeakable things to save his own life, but the underlying issue was that no amount of money could buy him peace. There was no dollar value on happiness, hope, success or love. The money he traded pieces of his soul for couldn't bring his mother back, it couldn't turn back time to re-establish Jessica's innocence or his own naivety. All the good, warm, and confident emotions he had been filled with over his dinner with Jessica or Marissa or whatever she now wanted to be called, along with his interaction with Gabriel had been sucked into the void no money would be able to fill.

As he stepped into his apartment, he felt empty. Jack walked to his closet, pulled the suit from its bag and hung each individual article of clothing he had bought for a million dollars on individual hangers. Once the perfect costume was hung safely in his absurdly large closet, he made his way to the kitchen to pour his woes down his throat. The void that he had been trying to fill since his mother died, the one money didn't have any hope of filling had one flaw that Jack knew how to exploit. It was the thing he learned the first day he drank with the sole intent of getting drunk.

A film of alcohol could be woven over the entrance, allowing the hope and happiness he felt during the few hours the alcohol prevailed to be enjoyed. The only trouble was that too much would send him careening through the weave, locking the lid as he fell, effectively trapping him in his deepest darkest memories.

But he didn't care what would happen that night, all he wanted was to be blind to the fact that his life and soul were lying in shattered fragments at his feet. He knew he had consumed more than enough to send him into a memory as soon as he gave in to the exhaustion, but the buzz had worn off and he needed the buzz to cope with his situation. So, he poured the whiskey to the top of his fancy glass, grabbed two cigarettes from the drawer he had stashed them in and made his way to the couch without so much as a tug at his tie.

He flipped the TV on and sat back watching some ludicrous TV show about good and evil, as if they honestly existed. He was too tired to change the channel so he just sat back and wondered what it would be like to be naïve again. What it would be like to believe that some people are good, and some are evil. It would be a simpler existence, but Jack knew that good and evil was a brainchild of the people who knew that the only thing that really exists is grey. The world isn't black and white, it is filled with people who strive to be good, sometimes failing and others who are innately evil who occasionally, by no fault of their own, do good.

Jack had consumed what probably equated to about a full bottle of whiskey that night, so as he made his way to his bedroom to fall asleep or rather to explore his memories, he could barely stand. He made his way down the hallway to his bed, bouncing off the walls like an unbelievably sad pinball. On the last bounce, he ricocheted off the right wall and fell right through his doorway.

After picking himself up off the ground, he fell again, but this time it was much farther, the space where the bed should have been, turned into a void of nothingness. Jack fell and fell, further and further so far that at one point he thought he would just continue to fall and fall until the sirens pulled him from the drunken cage. But after what felt like days of falling, his feet gently landed on a hard platform. Slowly opening his eyes, he realized he was back in the hospital room he had been dropped into the last time he drank himself into the cage of memories. It was exactly where he left off. His mother batting her eyes, about to speak. Her legs moving, trying to adjust to her new surroundings, the fear in her eyes that consumes all surgery patients.

It was the look of a person who had been prepared to die only hours ago but is now breathing, using a tube to do so but breathing, nevertheless. Jack saw the doctor who had just told him that he should say 'goodbye' disappearing around the corner and he saw his mother's brittle hand wrap itself around his younger self's forearm and begin to speak. His eyes began to tear up and his legs felt weak. As bad as his life had become since his mom had left or even the terrible truth about the memory he was sentenced to watch, wouldn't stop Jack from trading every cent he could get his fingers on just to speak to her one more time.

He would trade his life just to hug her, feel her warmth wrap itself around his shoulders, feel her warm breath softly graze his cheek. But he couldn't, so he settled for the words he knew he was about to hear. He watched them form on her lips as he had so many times before.

"Jack, Jackie?" she said.

"Yes Mom, what do you need? Water? Do you want your bed adjusted or anything Mom, anything?" The young Jack asked desperately. Hoping that in some way he could fix the situation or wake up from the awful dream he was sure he was in.

"I am fine my boy," she said in a raspy, dehydrated voice. *"Thanks to you I am alive. Are you okay? Does the breathing tube make you uncomfortable? I can take it out if you want,"* she said knowing full well that if the tube was ever to be taken from her nose she would die. This was the part of the memory that Jack still couldn't process, even 9 years later it stumped him.

How could a person be so selfless? How could a woman on the cusp of death be so selfless? So selfless that it bordered on stupidity. She was so worried about her only son that she would have given her life just to make him comfortable. It was why he hated being called sir, or never felt pride when he gave others obscene amounts of money; Compared to his mother, Jack felt like a failure. He was a glutton sitting in a house of glass, killing for money, giving just so that good people wouldn't see through his costume.

Being selfless just so that people wouldn't be able to see through his sheep's clothing and uncover the real snake underneath. As he watched his younger self's eyes opened wide at the sound of his own mother's words, he was filled with a shame 10 times more potent than polonium.

"No Mom, of course not. How are you feeling? Are you okay?"

"Oh, I will be fine Jack, your mom is a fighter. Nothing as silly as cancer is going to beat me without a fight," she said with the cutest smile Jack had ever seen. Young Jack chuckled, but as he did a tear fell down his cheek. He had been in the doctors' offices. He knew she had a week left a few weeks ago, he was just waiting for the day she really did say her last words to him.

Jack watched the tear streak down his own face, even from across the room he could see the pain in the boys' eyes. He could see how bad the sacred teenager wanted to trade his life for his mother's. He could see the primal urge to kill anything that tried to hurt his mother growing in his eyes but in his situation, he wasn't able to do anything. All he could do was savor each moment he was able to spend with her until she left him to go to a better place.

As the memory went by Jack saw her condition turn, writhe and warp into something he always hated seeing but never walked away from because it was the only time he was able to hear her voice. It was the closest thing to a physical connection he was able to have with his mother. He saw her morning vomit sessions; he watched as his younger self held her hair back as she lost all of the meager nutrition the hospital provided her over the four days she was in their 'care'.

Jack saw her scream in the night because her morphine supply had run out or had stopped working, now he knew that the only pain that screaming could have succeeded would have been excruciating. Since the night in the cage, the ribs breaking underneath his fingers and the man's hair flipping to the left side of his body as his lifeless corpse flopped to the ground, he had gained a new appreciation for the amount of pain his mother battled through just to stay with him a few more days. Jack watched as his 16-year-old self, slept in a curled ball in a hospital chair while his mother's raspy breath fought for life.

And then finally, he watched himself hold her hand tight on her final day. Tears flowed down his cheeks paralleled only by his younger selves' tears, and he watched as she held his hand tight and told him it would be alright although Jack knew it wouldn't. He knew it would end in death; it always did. No matter how many times he was shackled to the memory of his mother's death it never strayed from the facts he knew to be true, it never warped into a better or worse outcome, just the facts played on loop.

So, he knew she would cough blood once, tell him it was nothing to worry about, then cough the second time, then the third until a nurse walked by and upon hearing the horrifying cough go running for the doctor. He also knew what would come next. They would be the last words his mother ever told him. He watched as she wiped the blood from the corners of her mouth, took his innocent, terrified, naïve face that hadn't yet been withered by experience in her hands and say in a raspy broken voice, *"Jack, I love you. When I am gone, I want you to know you are a good person. Nothing you will ever do will ever change that fact. I will be with you until the day you die my little boy. I will wait by your side until we can both move on together. I will always love you."*

And as her last word slipped from her weak lips, her hands fell from the scared little boys face. Jack had seen it a million times but no matter how many times he witnessed his whole world shatter he couldn't bear its weight any easier. It was like Jesus carrying the cross and falling, but instead of someone coming along to help bear his cross, he fell to the ground and stayed there. Moments later, he saw his younger self do the same, their faces practically touched as they laid together in pain. The little boy did not know that his broken, future self was there with him. The little boy did not know then that his older self would lie on the floor with him as he screamed in pain, not because of an ailment that the naked eye could see but because of an ailment that would never heal. One that was still open and fresh. One that could only be filled with a vice like alcohol but never truly healed. A wound that was the reason he was never able to stand and watch his mother get rolled away from the room, a wound that was the root of why he was in the place to lay on the ground next to the broken teenager that had just lost the only role model, friend, family and confidant he had ever had.

Jack even reached over to touch the boy's hand as he always did at that part of the memory but was always disappointed when his own fingers fell through the memory's fingers. As he laid on the floor listening to the screams, he heard an alarm go off in the other room. It was one he had never heard before, so he got up to see what had made the abnormal noise but as he did his body was sucked from the hospital. The noise had been the air raid siren telling him it was time to go on with his life. Reminding him that no matter how close he got to his mother, she would always be an alcohol induced phantom. He opened his eyes slowly and realized that he hadn't even made it to the bed. He was laying back to the ground almost the way he crumbled to the floor that night in the hospital. He laid there for a while, waiting for the courage to seize the day to overtake him but it never did. So, he stood up by himself and loosed his tie. It had been a long night and he was in for an even longer one, only he did not know it just yet.

Chapter 22

The day dragged on like Christmas eve, the weeks leading up to a trip or the hours preceding a major surgery. Jack had worked out, read an old book that he had read more times than he could count and moved from the couch, to his bed, to the bar style island. He ate some hot pockets that he had kept in his freezer since the first time he had bought groceries. He had trained with Jason for 2 hours in the middle of the day, which was very irregular, but he didn't feel like going to school. He couldn't fathom sitting through classes that meant nothing compared to what the night potentially held.

Jack wasn't sure what the Dr. would say, he didn't know what the dinner was for. Maybe it was just a formality, a nicety, or an olive branch but it could also be a trap. The endless possibilities would have consumed Jack if he went to school and sat through mind numbing lectures about things he didn't honestly care about. He didn't even care about finishing his degree anymore, surviving was the only thought that ever ran through his mind. Survival, shame, and missed opportunities were the roots of every thought that ever popped into Jack's head for the past weeks.

But when his phone alarm rang at precisely 3:30pm Jack shut his book without marking the page and headed for the shower. He knew the only way he wouldn't be figured out—that was if Confucius didn't already know he lived multiple lives—was if his costume was perfect, flawless in every conceivable sense. The only possible way to survive the opportunity was to lie and lie well. He needed to make the King believe he was the prince he already hoped Jack was.

Jack turned the water to hot, as hot as he could possibly bear. He needed to scrub every impurity from his skin and needed to evict every scent from every pore. The hot water ran down his face scalding his skin as it did. It continued down his shoulders all the way down to his feet. It burned the soles of his feet as is slithered like snakes between his toes as it made its way to the drain. Jack grabbed the loofah he had picked up from the convivence store down the street from his building earlier that day.

Jack had never used a loofah before in his life, but he knew a prince never smelled like whiskey, blood, or sweat and if the costume wasn't perfect in every way, then the King of New York would know he was a fake. So, Jack scrubbed like his life depended on it, he scrubbed until his skin was pink, the cleanest he had ever seen it. He washed his hair twice and scrubbed his face clean, then turned the water to the coldest setting. He let the water heal the abused skin for 15 minutes and then shut the water off completely.

Jack dried himself off, making sure there wasn't a drop of water left on his skin and meticulously clipped each nail on his hands and feet until they looked perfectly manicured. After his nails met his standards, he brushed his teeth until his gums bled, then applied whitening strips to them and fixed his hair while he waited for the strips to do their job. His hair took longer than usual because, in that particular situation, each strand of hair needed to be in perfect orientation. Once he was sure they had done their job, he removed the whitening strips, brushed his teeth again—gentler this time—and applied a thin layer of cream to his face.

Just enough to hydrate the skin but not enough so that it shone in the light. After the cream was perfectly applied, he walked to the kitchen, placed two spoons in the freezer and continued to his closet where the perfect mask hung neatly on the rack. First, he put on some brand-new underwear that he hadn't won since it was bought a month earlier and then swung the crisp white shirt over his shoulders, buttoned the cuffs and the buttons splitting his figure in half but left the top button undone and slipped the red sun underneath its expensive fabric.

Jack pulled socks over his feet and up his calf. He did the same for the pants, tucked the shirt in and buttoned his pants around his waist, careful not to crease the shirt as he did. When the pants had been buttoned, he slid the dark brown belt through the loops, buckled it and adjusted its position until it was directly in the middle of his body. Once he was sure it was perfect, he slid his feet into the new shoes and tied the laces with a degree of grace that only the most anal person on the planet would appreciate.

When he was satisfied with the underlayer of his costume, he walked out into his bedroom tie, vest and jacket in hand. Laying the vest and jacket on the bed, he turned to the mirror on the wall beside the door he had fell through the night before. Just looking at his reflection startled him, he didn't quite recognize the face staring back at him. It was perfect in almost every sense, the only things that were not an example of perfection were his eyes and the bags that sat underneath.

He couldn't do anything about the eyes, but he had an idea for the bags. First he had to affix the tie perfectly. There was no room for error in this task, it was almost the most important part. After all, a real man should be able to tie his tie perfectly. It took over half an hour of pulling tying and untying to get to the desired look, but it was worth it, he had never seen a tie more perfectly tied and placed around a man's neck. He slid the vest around his shoulders and buttoned the three buttons, making sure the tie didn't stick out of the bottom as he did.

Then he slid the jacket over his shoulders making sure to only affix the top button. When he was sure he looked perfect, Jack walked out into the kitchen, removed the spoons from the freezer and placed them on the bags underneath his eyes for 10 minutes.

When the cold got to be too much even for him to bear, he threw both spoons in the sink and made his way to the bathroom for one more check. When he looked into the mirror he was proud, not just because his appearance was as close to what a prince should look like as he could get but because he looked like the man his mother had raised him to be. He had finally become a man, a proper, well-dressed, well-mannered man. All that was left to do was to act like one and the dinner was the first step on his quest to do so.

The dinner could change everything. Of course, it would change everything one way or another, he knew that for sure. He only hoped it would change everything for the better. Jack checked his phone and saw that it was 4:45pm. His ride would be waiting outside, so he headed for the elevator. And for the first time in months, he didn't even think about having a drink before he left.

When Jack reached the curb, he saw Confucius's car waiting for him. As he got closer to the back door, the door opened by itself and he let himself in.

"Good evening, sir, feel free to take any refreshments you want. The ride shouldn't be more than 15 minutes," the driver said as the partition between passenger and driver rolled up and he pulled away from the curb into the steady flow of traffic. Jack watched as the miniature bar rose from the floor carrying every whiskey brand a person could think of, and three different types of whiskey glasses. As tempted as he was to have a casual drink before he got to dinner he decided against it, he needed to be in tip top shape to meet the King. It was curious that even though Jack knew Confucius was the King of New York, the most powerful man in the city maybe even the country, he still didn't fully see the man as a king.

In Jack's mind, he would always be the balding, greasy haired old man that taught an English class at NYU. He didn't seem like a king, a figurehead maybe, but not a king. He knew that there had to be someone else pulling the strings from behind the scenes, because at his age Confucius wouldn't be able to take care of all the day-to-day tasks an organization as big as the Founders would require by himself. Jack was sure that was why Confucius had plucked a boy from his senior level English class to be a strong candidate to take over his operation, to inherit his legacy. Jack was so deep in thought he didn't realize the car had pulled over to the curb until he heard the partition begin to roll down.

"Have a good night, sir," the driver said handing him a card. "Call this number when you would like to be picked up and I will drive you where you want to go. I can also make a stop on the way back to the place you will spend the night if you would like." Then the partition rolled up and the door opened.

Jack was puzzled about the comment regarding a stop on the way home. But he pushed it out of his mind, the man was probably just being nice as per Confucius's request. After all, he had more important things to worry about, he was a gazelle walking into the lion's den covered in a lion's pelt. Anything could happen and Jack needed to be as clear minded as he could if he was going to survive the night.

Jack thought he knew the gravity of the situation when he was getting ready but as he walked out of the cab and looked up at the restaurant, he knew it was heavier than he could have ever predicted. As he looked toward the glass doors adorned by gold handles, surrounded in a gold trim, and headed by the words *AITE NAN RIGHREAN* all forged out of solid gold blocks his heart began to beat harder. Jack had searched up the restaurant earlier that day and it had been acclaimed by the citizens of New York as one of the greatest restaurants in the city, but Jack assumed they had come under much different circumstances.

They didn't know the fact that if Confucius ate at a restaurant, he probably owned it, which meant he was in complete control.

They didn't know that they were being watched, studied, and vetted at every possible turn and if they did, they didn't have to worry because none of them were lying to the King of New York. Jack took a deep breath and walked forward, there was no straying from the path he had set out on, the only way was forward. The man his mother raised him to be was courageous; he wouldn't flee. He would look his problems in the face and attempt to make the best of them. So, he walked toward the ominously transparent glass doors and pushed the right one open. As soon as he was inside, he was met by a maître d'.

"How can I help you sir? Do you have a reservation or are you looking for an available table?"

"I don't have a reservation; I was asked to meet Fergus Confucius here for dinner," Jack said and watched the man's face change instantly. What had once been a snobby, fiery gaze of a man who had been forced to deal with rich assholes for the better part of his eight-hour shift now wore the most fearful expression Jack had ever seen.

"Yes…sir, I have the Dr's table ready. I sincerely apologize…for…the mistake, I should have known," he said stuttering. Jack didn't see how the man could have possibly known who he was and couldn't see how the man had made a mistake. He wanted to give the man a pat on the back to tell him it was fine and that no disrespect was taken but he wasn't sure who was watching. Acts of kindness didn't fit into either of the alter egos he was forced to assume in those days, so he shut his mouth and tried to act like the superior man. Although he didn't know how to do so, he had never been superior to anyone in his entire life.

"Right this way sir, the Dr. isn't here yet, but I am sure he isn't far behind you, he is rarely late. For… anything," he said with a shiver. Jack noted the shiver as another strike in the con column under Confucius's name and followed the terrified man up the stairs, through two large oak doors and into the main dining room.

The dining room was unbelievably large. Paul's private plane would have sat snugly between the walls. The room was filled with aristocrats, artists, scientists, billionaires, millionaires and even a few professional athletes Jack recognized. They were all sitting at tables around the room, eating what looked to be delicious food, expensive alcohol and enjoying great company all on the backdrop of what Jack imagined a fancy restaurant looked like in the 50s.

287

The polished oak tables were covered with pristine white tablecloths and surrounded by red velvet chairs that matched the red roses set into the black velvet carpet. Hanging in the middle of the room was a golden chandelier lit by 40 red candles. At the very back of the room, there were two staircases covered in the same velvet flooring, flanked by golden rails leading up to a half moon shaped balcony, wrapped in the same golden rails, overlooking the entire restaurant.

As they got closer to the foot of the stairs Jack realized it was where he was going to be eating. The maître d' continued up the stairs and once he reached the top, he waved his hand toward the table and said, "Your table sir. Can I bring you a drink while you wait for the boss?" There it was, Jack was pretty sure Confucius owned the restaurant, but the comment solidified his belief.

"A glass of Crown Royal on the rocks please, and my name is Jack by the way, not sir."

"Sorry, Jack, I will bring your drink as quick as possible," the waiter said as he half jogged down the stairs to fetch Jack's drink. Once the man was gone Jack looked down at the people below him, he didn't feel right being placed above so many people who deserved the seat more than he did. He imagined he could throw a rock and hit at least one person who was more qualified for the job the King wanted him to take and that was only if the rock didn't ricochet and hit another diner.

But aside from the shame that as flowing through his veins Jack was in awe of the restaurant, there was no breaking away from the truth; It was breathtaking. Even the music playing behind the constant drum of conversation was impressive, a soft melody with a sharp edge just loud enough for anyone to hear but quiet enough for conversation to continue fluidly.

The waiter returned with Jack's drink in less than 5 minutes and just as he set down Jack's drink the music, laughter, conversation, even movement stopped as if Christ had come down from the heavens and was now hovering in the empty space just beneath the chandelier. But the fact was that no one Jack could see had even entered the room, the room looked the exact same as it had five seconds ago when he was admiring the beauty the restaurant offered.

But then, out of nowhere Jack saw the top of Confucius's head appear from below the front staircase. In a panic, Jack stood up and fixed the front of his suit jacket. He immediately understood what was happening; The King had entered; it was a reaction he hoped never to have to endure. Jack would have been mortified if people blindly respected him.

When he was 10 years old, a man had walked into the tiny restaurant called The Diner in Cielo, he and his mother were sitting in a corner booth that provided a perfect line of sight to the proceedings. The man wore a leather jacket with a crest of some kind embroidered on the back and his grey beard was so long that it would have flowed over his breasts if he were a woman. The men at the bar wearing the same jackets stood up and didn't sit until the man sat down with them at the bar. At the time, Jack didn't understand but his mother said, *Jack, blind respect is just fear. No man bows to a king they don't trust, they will only bow because of the fear of the repercussions that not bowing could bring upon them.*

Back in Cielo he didn't understand. Maybe it was on account of his youth or maybe the concept was just lost on him because his mother had always made him feel safe but witnessing a room filled with people who could buy the grandest building in New York and not even feel a strain stop speaking as an old greasy man walked in opened his eyes. In that moment, he understood. It was sickening and the fact that he too felt the need to show the man respect made him shudder, but he needed to do whatever it took to make Confucius believe he was who he had pretended to be. It was the only way.

The alternative was Confucius finding out he worked for Paul or if the Dr. knew that fact already—which Jack assumed he did—was the Dr. finding out how he really felt about Paul and his business. Jack wouldn't be able to survive the consequence of either path the night could venture down.

Fergus took his sweet time as he walked up to the table on the balcony. So long in fact that Jack almost sat down but he knew better, he would have to wait the man out. Every word, action, crack of a finger or chair rearrangement was a part of the costume his decisions forced him to wear like a gold star. Confucius laughed with some of the patrons, whispered into the ears of the staff and ran his hand along every tablecloth as if he was inspecting the fabric to make sure it was up to his standards before he finally took the first step up the stairs to Jack.

When he finally did, Jack breathed a sigh of relief. He had grown tired of standing in a fake show of respect to the man who was drenched in questions, a modern-day joker in the time withered body of Bruce Wayne. Jack lost sight of the man as he walked up the stairs but once he reached the top their eyes locked, the king and the would-be prince locked in a fight of wills. Confucius finally reached the balcony and caught his breath before speaking.

"Jack Hanson, that is a suit made for a king," Confucius said as a grin formed in the corner of his mouth.

"Thank you, sir, it's good to see you," Jack said as he outstretched his hand to shake Confucius's. The Dr. paused a second as if he was making his final decision regarding the extent of Jack's prowess. But finally, after what felt like years, he outstretched his hand a firmly shook Jack's and made his way to the seat opposite Jack's.

"Sorry I am late, I had some…business to attend to."

"That is more than okay sir. I hope you were able to handle the business swiftly."

"Thank you, Jack." Jack almost laughed at Confucius's comment. It was hilarious that a man with his type of power would ever apologize to a man like Jack let alone thank him for accepting his apology. "I was able to deal with the problem with…grace. You know you speak almost as well as you write Hanson."

Jack felt all the blood rush to his face as the Dr. complimented him. So, he took a slow sip of his whiskey to gather his poise and spoke, "Thank you, sir, you are too kind."

Confucius smiled, then turned to the waiter ordered the number one dinner for himself and Jack accompanied by a scotch neat. Just as he had when Jack ordered, the waiter half jogged down the stairs to fetch his masters order. "It's not kindness Jack, it's the truth. I don't deal in kindnesses. I am sure by now you have been told who I am and why these people fear me or why there were so many people at my celebration the other night and why I am able to send fancy cars to pick you up."

"Yes, sir. I have been told bits and pieces, it's all very impressive." Jack lied. In truth, he thought it was an abomination, his mother worked 3 jobs just to keep food on the table and a roof over their heads while this man was sitting on his golden balcony overlooking the world.

"Good, because when I read your first paper, I knew you were special. You have lived the opposite of a life of opportunity. You have lived with nothing and been happy, you have grit most people couldn't even dream of. Your writing reflects it each and every time, especially your commentary on *Death of a Salesman*. It is a true reflection of how a person in your situation views the world and how people in this room should introspect into their own lives."

"Thank you, sir, I read that book right after my mom died, I assume that was what influenced my bias," Jack said, he didn't need to omit things about his past, he was sure Confucius knew it all. So, everything he would be able to make up would just feed the fire of deceit that Confucius was surely stoking.

"I am sorry to hear about your mother Jack but if that needed to happen to give you your perspective, then it was a necessity. You can and will, under my watchful eye, be the greatest writer of your generation and you obviously have your mother to thank for that."

Jack just about crushed his own fingers at the mention of his mother. The fiery anger that had reared his ugly head so many times since he had arrived in the city threatened to take control, but he held it back. Jack would have given his literacy prowess and worked a 9-5 labor job to bring his mother back. He would have cut off each of his fingers just to bring his mother back. The excellence he had attained in the world of writing and his future in the field was an outlet for his grief caused by his mother's death. It was not a gift his mother had bartered her life for.

"Yes sir," Jack said, he couldn't find any other words, they were the only ones that didn't offend the Dr. and allowed him to keep his integrity. "Why am I here sir? What did you really bring me here for? Because I know it wasn't just to compliment my writing skills or my suit."

"Nothing slips by you, does it, Jack?" Confucius said with a chuckle followed by a sip of his whiskey. "I brought you here because I am the sun. I have a part in everything that happens here in the city that truly never sleeps. I am everywhere and I am nowhere, I can't be seen or heard but I am always listening and watching. I believe that if you listen to me and only me, you will become the most powerful man in New York City. So, I have brought you here to break bread with me because I want you to take over the Founders Society. I want to groom you to be the next King of New York, instead of all these people holding their breath for me as I walk in, they will stop living for you. I would like that for you Jack."

Jack knew in that moment that his disguise had worked, he had played his part to perfection. He had successfully fooled the 'all knowing', 'all seeing', King of New York.

"I am flattered sir; I do not know what to say but are you sure I am the man for the job?" Jack said and then took a slow, drawling sip of his whiskey, allowing the alcohol to smooth and polish his words. "I know nothing of business, human relations or leadership."

"That can be learned, a dunce would be able to master those things, but you have qualities that no other candidate has. You have seen death, you have felt real heart break, you have survived Verlies, and you have learned to do whatever is in your best interest. You have even survived with next to nothing for years on your own. Jack you are special, you mean something. Just think of how proud your mother would be."

Jack had heard the man's words and obviously the man knew everything about him, but he had missed a crucial part just as Charlotte suspected. He had missed the lessons his mother had taught him. The seemingly brilliant man missed his devotion to his mother. Confucius must not have been very close to his parents because he apparently didn't understand the devotion a boy has to the people that brought them into the world, especially if it is a single parent that doesn't have any other children. Not only was his mother his first friend, girlfriend or best friend she was also his provider and like a wolf he had a primal instinct to protect his family. The only catch was that Jack's mother was his only known relative and since she was gone, all he was left with were her sayings, teachings, and ideals to protect at all costs. And not even one of her ideals included richness, power or conformity. They taught the exact opposite. So, it was damn shame that Confucius had told Jack all his virtues because in doing so he had shown his hand. Jack could once again see more of the picture. He found it funny that the people who pretended to be on his side kept saying the wrong thing at the wrong time. With Confucius and Jessica's lies put together, he was very close to seeing the entire picture. He was inches away from making everything clear. "So, what do you say Jack, I won't take no for an answer. I have been looking for a replacement for too long. I am way too old for this job as it is, I can't wait any longer," Confucius said, as his demeanor changed from bright and jovial to cold and menacing.

It was funny because Paul had never acted like Jack's friend, Paul had always been straight up about his needs and wants. That is if you exclude lying to get Jack to New York but even then, it was really Charlotte who had lied and even she had told part of the truth. It hadn't been a flat out lie like the ones Confucius was so obviously spewing out of his mouth.

Jack knew that if his mother were there, she would say that Paul was a more honest and true man than Confucius had ever been. Setting aside the fact that Paul had ordered Jack to kill people, he did trust him more than he trusted Confucius. At least with Paul, you were given the cold, bloody and insane truth up front. But it didn't really matter what Jack thought of the man across from him. If the King wanted something, he got it. Or at least he needed to be led to believe he had gotten what he wanted.

"Of course, sir. If you are sure, it would be an honor. But you will have to talk to Paul from the GWA because he is paying for my education under the condition that I do odd jobs for him," Confucius chuckled, obviously there was something Jack had yet to figure out, but he didn't mind. The amusement meant Confucius knew something about Paul.

"It won't be hard to convince Paul, don't worry. He is a good man; he will understand and if he doesn't, I will make him understand."

"Okay sir, thank you for the opportunity. I truly hope I will live up to your expectations." Just as Jack finished speaking the waiter came up the stairs with two plates filled with a very small portion of some sort of meat. To Jack's eyes, it looked as though the plate was meant for a dog or a small child. "Looks great sir!" Jack said, hoping his eyes wouldn't betray his true feelings about the dish.

"I hope it tastes as good as it looks," Confucius said to Jack while having what appeared to be a staring contest with the waiter. He took his first bite, moved the food around in his mouth and looked away from the waiter. "Bring another round of drinks for me and my guest."

The response must have been what the waiter was looking for because his face lit up and he scurried away to grab two more drinks. "What do you think Jack? Does it live up to your standards?" He said just as Jack swallowed his first cold, unappetizing bite.

"Lovely sir! I've never tasted a dish quite like this." Jack knew it was better to lie than to the tell the truth and get a hard-working waiter or cook fired or worse. Jack didn't know what Confucius was capable of. But one thing he knew for sure was that Confucius wasn't the great man he made himself out to be.

"Good, good. So, what kind of odd jobs do you do for Paul. I know he runs a few casinos around the city but what does he have you do exactly?" Jack just about choked on his disgusting, lukewarm meal. Confucius was obviously playing to his own hand just as well as Jack was. If the Dr. really was the foremost authority in New York, then he would know exactly what Paul as up to. So, either Confucius was trying to get Jack to trip on his own words or he wasn't as 'all knowing' as he thought he was. But Jack was too smart to be caught by such a poorly constructed trap.

"I do this and that. I grab deposits from the casinos, I deliver his dry cleaning and occasionally I help take out the trash," Jack said, pausing to place another bite on his tongue.

"You know, the type of things a person like me would do, and in turn he takes care of all my expenses. He is a very generous man. I think he might see the potential I have, not completely unlike yourself."

"He would be a fool not to see and nurture your potential. Occasionally me and him see different perspectives on issues but your right, he is quite generous. Did you know he used to be a writer? Honestly, he was the best writer I had ever seen until I met you." Jack smiled, curtly loading another mouthful of his dinner onto his fork. It was as if the two men were Politian's on either side of the spectrum speaking about a policy or bill that was close to being passed. Like a boxing match, each word a step, each retort a blow with every counter argument or comment acting as a doge or parry.

"I did not know that sir. Why then do you disagree on certain issues? How did you come to a place in which to read his writing?" Jack said, filling his palate with more unappetizing swill.

"I read his work when he was about 16 or 17 years old. But he never responded to my letter that contained an offer to learn under my watchful eye at NYU. The life he was forced to endure in the time it took him to make his way to the big apple changed his beliefs and the perspectives he had on the world around him. It hardened him into the epitome of a callous. A strong, firm existence with no feeling for pain or sorrow."

Jack knew he had just cleared another quadrant of his picture. If the letter Paul had received was Confucius's letter, then there was a strong possibility that Jessica's letter had come from Confucius as well. It alluded to the connection that Jack suspected lay between the Global Writing Association and the Global Wagering Association. Somehow Confucius was directly in the middle of the picture Jack had been tasked with revealing since he stepped onto the large white jet all those weeks ago. The only question left was what role Confucius played within the GWA.

"If Paul didn't live in the city at the time you read his letter, then how did you come to be in possession of his work?"

"I run the world's largest writing association. Every year I pick the three contestants from the annual competition and send them a letter containing two options, three for the winner. The first is to come to New York and start their writing career with me as their agent, publisher and editor. The second is a letter of recommendation to send to any university which will guarantee their acceptance to the universities respective English departments. Then for the absolute winner, I give one more option and that is 1 million dollars up front but if they choose the third option, I will no longer help them with their writing careers."

Jack was speechless, the Dr. had just laid out his entire involvement in the scheme that he and Paul obviously had been taking part in together for years. When Jack finally gained the strength to speak again, he decided he no longer wanted to play the diplomatic game anymore.

"That is very impressive sir. Did you know that I earned second place in your competition? Did you also know that Charlotte Jones was first place in my year and Jessica Dolus was third place? How do you explain that sir, how do explain the fact that all three of us work with Paul and that all three of us are in some way a part of your New York…community?" Confucius smirked, sipped his drink and spoke.

"I did know you earned second place. I also know you were supposed to be first place but a select few on the panel of judges thought Charlotte Jones's story was clearer and more believable. They thought she was a more…projectable writer. In my eyes, you were the clear favorite. I also know that you didn't only reject my letter, but you didn't even reply or use any part of the letter to get into university; yet you were still able to impress one of the greatest writing professors in the country to the point he contacted me to tell me that he had one of the greatest writers he had ever seen in one of his classes."

Jack had lost all diplomacy at that point; all he knew was that the man was dancing around the fact that he was part of what could only be classified as a child trafficking ring. Either that or Paul and his two partners were skimming the crème of Confucius's very large crop.

"The letter got lost, but that's not the point. Either is Professor Laurent's evaluation of my skills. The issue is that you say you and Paul see the world through different lenses, yet he employs the entire podium of your competition, and I would wager a very large sum that he has employed the podium of every competition that has happened since his rise to the top of the GWA's ranks. How do you explain that sir?" Again, Confucius smirked, sipped his drink and continued.

"Yes, at first glance that may seem troubling but remember he was a writer, he knows they type of person it takes to be a strong writer. He knows that they are hard workers who can see past the monotony of simple labor jobs. He knows that they will work hard in order to gain different perspectives or new outlooks on life. An attribute that makes them incredible workers and that is why he employs my champions. Plus, he was, probably still is, a writer. He knows how hard it is to make it in the writing scene and his financial portfolio can help the writers achieve their goals faster. So, he helps them out. Personally, I don't see any issue with that. So, I allow it to happen. I think his business of preying on poor, addicted people is wrong in every conceivable sense but who am I to judge how people make money. If he didn't do it, someone else would."

"Yes, sir I guess that is true but..." Before Jack could finish his sentence and coerce Confucius into revealing how deep he was involved with Paul, his phone began to ring. Jack knew that there were only two people who could possibly calling him, and Charlotte knew he was at supper so she wouldn't be calling. There was only one name that would pop up on his phone. Paul. He slid the phone icon across the screen and spoke, "Yes sir?"

"I need you at the warehouse in 10 minutes. Do you need a ride, or will you be able to get here by yourself in 10 minutes?"

"I have a ride sir; I will see you soon," Jack said hanging up the phone. Then he turned to Confucius and said, "Sorry sir I have to go. Thank you for the meal, it was lovely. I hope we can finish our discussion another time," and then stood up.

"Of course, Jack I would love to finish our meal another time. Be careful taking out the trash," Confucius said as a terrifyingly kind smile cut across his face.

Chapter 23

Confucius's car pulled up to the warehouse and Jack was filled with a different energy than he was used to feeling at the sight of the ominous building he knew far too well. The warehouse had always been associated with pain, death and suffering but as the left standing, black door came into view it looked like opportunity. Jack was close to finishing his picture, all the blurred edges were coming into focus. He held a firm grasp on the farfetched hope that he wouldn't be stuck in the mud for too much longer.

"When I get out you need to get as far from this place as possible," Jack said to the driver as the car slowed to a stop. "Thank you for the ride, sir."

"No problem, Jack, have a good night. If you need to be picked up from another location, just give me a call, you have my number." The driver said as the door opened for Jack to leave the car. Jack walked slowly toward the door and the two guards that flanked it. Even though he had hope for his future he knew what he was there to do, the only question was who he was here to do it to. As he neared the doors he bent down and pretended to tie his shoes as he calmed his nerves and attempted to switch the mask he was wearing as quick as possible.

The intelligent writer who had been chosen from winners to be the new King was no longer acceptable, he needed to become the animal Paul had created. Jack knew he needed to leave inhibition, kindness and morals in the car and focus on strength, poise and his own dangerous qualities.

Once he was sure he had made the correct switch he stood up and walked through the door the mercenaries had already opened for him.

The warehouse hadn't changed, it was still poorly lit with the stink of death hanging in the air, but the cage had been removed and in its place was a chair and the black table adorned with every weapon known to man. It looked just as it had the first time Jack went to the warehouse. Working for Paul was torture, so any sort of solace had to be celebrated. As if from thin air Jack saw Paul emerge from the shadows.

"Hanson my boy, how was your dinner?" Paul said as he placed his gnarled hand on Jack's shoulder. "That is a fucking fancy suit, it's good to see my money going toward the right things."

Jack didn't know how to respond; he knew Confucius and Paul were associated in some sense, but he didn't understand how Paul knew he had been at dinner only moment ago.

"It was good sir. Dr. Confucius wanted to talk about my writing, apparently, he believes I am quite talented. He also said you were the best writer he had seen, before he met me of course," Jack said. He had never dug his own knife between Paul's ribs so he wanted to see how the devil would respond to a passive aggressive blade sinking into his soft flesh. Paul smiled but underneath the smile Jack saw danger, he saw the urge to kill. In that moment, Jack knew he had pulled the right string, if Paul was ever going to kill him, he had his reason. But the danger beneath the gloss of Paul's eyes sputtered out just as quick as it had come.

"Very good Jack. You know he hasn't ever told me that you surpassed me in terms of writing prowess, I will have to have a chat with him later. But that's not why we are here."

"Why are we here sir? I don't see any problem that needs fixing."

"Yes, about that…I was under the impression that the problem would be here by now so there must have been some hold up on the road. Do you mind coming back to the office with me? I will tell the courier that we will be there instead of here, we can just as easily take care of the problem there," Paul said as he walked back toward the front door. Jack knew he had no choice; he would be killed if he didn't comply, and he wasn't ready to go yet.

At the very least, he wanted his picture to be crystal clear before he joined his mother. He followed Paul to the door and walked out into the chilly New York night, but something was off. Paul's car was gone, and the only car left in the parking stalls was the car Jack had arrived in; It was Confucius's car. Paul didn't even break stride, he just walked up to the car, waited for it to open and got in. Jack just about stumbled on his own feet but held himself firm and continued his pilgrimage toward the open door. Once he was safely inside the car it started moving.

"To the office please, Leon," Paul said and then turned to Jack. "I am not sure if Charlotte told you in the first week that you were in New York, but I have two partners in my business.

The first is Alexander and the second you haven't met yet. His office is right above mine and I think tonight would be a good night for you two to formally meet." Jack's mouth went dry, why wouldn't he have met the other partner yet and how could his office possibly be above Paul's? There weren't any other buttons on the elevator, were there? Despite the plethora of questions forming in his mind, Jack knew he had to appear strong.

"Sounds good sir, I would love to meet the man who is above you. Why haven't I met him before." Paul smiled at Jack's second dagger of the night; Jack could tell that he was beginning to venture into dangerous territory, but he didn't care. He had arrived at the end of his rope; He was growing impatient and was beginning to tire of the constant flow of lies. He was ready to know the truth behind the organization he had been killing for.

"Good, good. I am excited for you two to formally meet. I haven't introduced him to you as of yet at his own request although he has been watching all of your triumphs. I believe he wanted to stay hidden so that you would be at your strongest when you finally met him," Paul said turning his head forward to pour two drinks for him and Jack to share. "Tonight, is going to be a night you won't forget. All of our collective problems will be worked out in one way or the other," he said, passing Jack one of the two drinks.

"Cheers to success and prosperity," As the two glasses clinked together Jack felt the air change around him. What was once black and white merged to form a chasm of grey smoke.

"Cheers," Jack said as he tipped the contents of his glass down his throat.

The rest of the ride was endured in silence until the monstrosity that was the office came into view. "You have an opportunity to create the life you have always wanted here Jack, if you don't fuck it all up tonight you will be the youngest ever to do it."

"Yes sir," Jack said but he had no intention of sitting idly by as his future was determined by Paul, the unknown man, and Alexander. He couldn't stand for it because his mother wouldn't have stood for it. As the car slowed Jack steeled his nerves and tensed his muscles for a fight, if the night came to blows, he would be ready. Even though his ribs had been snapped by the boxing champion of New York, he had still won the fight.

Paul or whoever else they threw at him wouldn't have a chance at beating him to his knees, he had made sure of that. But at all costs he would try not to kill anyone, because as Jason had said and he knew himself to be true, killing eats away at the soul and his soul couldn't be taken. It was the last place his mother resided, his last connection to her was etched into its fragments. Paul stepped out of the car as soon as the doors opened but Jack paused and closed his eyes. He silently asked his mother to watch out for him and then stepped out to join Paul.

"Ready to meet your future?"

"Yes sir, I can't wait."

"Good, we will make a quick stop in my office and then head up, sound good?"

"Yes, sir. That sounds fine," Jack said as they walked through the doors and into the massive lobby. The pair walked by the front desk attendant without a word but once Paul was out of her sight, she looked at Jack, her eyes seemed to penetrate his soul and they were screaming at him to run. But Jack broke the connection and powered forward, his path was going through the office that night. Whatever happened was his destiny. He was meant to be at the office, and nothing would stop him from finding the truth because he knew there was so much he had yet to learn and without the whole picture he wouldn't be able to make a rational decision.

When the elevator stopped at Paul's office, both men exited the steel box.

"Hold the door open, I won't be more than 5 seconds," Paul said, then hurried over to his desk, pulled out a medallion identical to Jack's, pulled it over his head and laid it in the middle of his chest. As Jack stared at the red sun beaming from the middle of Paul's chest, he wondered how many souls resided inside the red cage.

"Nice medallion. Why don't you wear it all the time?" Jack asked as they stepped back into the elevator.

"It's too heavy," Paul said and then went silent. The elevator still hadn't moved, and Jack was beginning to wonder what they were waiting for. "Oh shit, do you have the card I gave to you when you arrived?" Jack fumbled around in his pocket until he felt his fingers wrap around the small metal card containing unlimited funds. He pulled it out and showed it to Paul. "Press it against the metal just above the top button," Paul said still facing forward.

Feeling quite foolish, Jack pressed the metal card against the cold steel of the elevator wall. Once he tapped and removed the card, the elevator—as if by magic—began to move upwards slowly. Paul cracked his fingers and straightened his hair as if he was about to meet the Queen.

It was an odd sight to see Paul squirm, but Jack knew it for what it was. He was nervous to meet with the third partner. Jack had never seen Paul nervous before, but everyone had a boss, or a mentor and Jack assumed the man shrouded by smoke and mirrors was Paul's. The elevator creaked to a stop and Jack saw little beads of sweat appear on Paul's forehead, it was so unusual that Jack almost began to laugh but he managed to hold the chuckle in.

When the elevator doors opened, and he laid eyes on the man Paul was so scared to meet he felt his own heartbeat faster and faster until he was sure it would beat straight out of his chest. Paul pushed Jack into the room and followed closely behind. The office wasn't unlike Paul's although it had minor changes. The oak desk was the same, the floors and the chair were almost identical. The only differences came in the form of a painting hanging behind the man and the color of wall behind it. The wall had been painted a color so close to the color blood turned when it had just been set free from the shackles of mortality that Jack couldn't be sure it was actually paint at all.

The painting was even more troubling. It depicted a man dressed in all white garb, with a cup filled with some sort of thick red liquid in his left hand and a small sliver knife in the right. Blood dripped down the knife and the front of his white mid-1600s suit was drenched in blood. The man was standing over another white man in a forest green suit that had a gaping wound in his neck and his face was leaking blood from every possible crevasse. At the bottom of the picture the inscription read, "The first King at the first meeting of the Founders."

The paining made Jack feel sick to his stomach, but it wasn't the most dangerous quality the room held. The real threat sat in the brown leather chair behind the massive wooden desk in the center of the room.

"Long time no see my boy," the man said, grinning from ear to ear. "How was the warehouse, Paul?"

"It is all set up sir," Paul said meekly. Jack couldn't find any words, so he decided not to speak, it wasn't the time to be saying the wrong words. If the right words refused to make its way to his lips, then it was better just to shut his mouth. "The others should be here momentarily sir."

301

"Good. Jack, would you please grab five chairs from that closet," the man said pointing to a small door in the left corner of the room. Jack had to use every ounce of strength just to make his feet move from the spot they had rooted into, but he knew he had to. As he forced his feet to move toward the corner, he felt a silent tear slide down his cheek and he wiped it away quickly. Failure, weakness and stupid ideas no longer had any place in the room, not because they weren't part of his current mask but because they would get him killed.

Masks would no longer suffice, he had to become an exact replica of both masks he had worn over the last few weeks. He had to be intelligently animalistic. He had to become a beast with a prefrontal cortex.

As Jack carried the final leather covered oak chair and placed it in front of the man's desk, the elevator doors creaked open. He swung his head to see who had arrived. Stepping out of the elevator was the Man in Red wearing his patented blood red suit, with a blood red pendant identical to Charlotte's swaying in the middle of his body as he walked. Charlotte, wearing a black cocktail dress with the same red pendant hanging in the center of her body, and Jessica wearing a blood red dress complete with red lipstick, red pins in her hair and an identical pendant hanging in the middle of her chest.

"Welcome my friends, have a seat. Jack has so generously laid them all out for you," the man said with a smile that didn't dare to venture into his eyes. It instead crossed his face like a roughly healed scar. His words were so strong that everybody in the room scurried with as much grace as they could muster to find a chair. Alexander sat to the far left of the semi-circle that Jack had created with Jessica sitting in the chair directly to the right. Jack took his seat to the far right with Charlotte next to him and Paul directly in the middle.

The fear hung so thick in the air that Jack was sure he was going to choke if it wasn't cleared soon. Just as his throat started to constrict the man broke the silence. "Now all of the answers our friend Jack so desperately wants are within his reach, where would you like us to begin Mr. Hanson?" Jack tried to wet his throat by swallowing but there was no saliva to swallow so he croaked out his answer.

"At the beginning Sir…Actually, I would like to know why you invited me to dinner if you knew I would end up here by the end of the night." Confucius's beady deceitful eyes looked back at him with a burning fury, but he maintained his smile.

"Well Mr. Hanson, that is an easy one. I needed to know if you would speak against me or Paul while in the presence of someone who you trusted. But you showed that you are completely trustworthy, a little quizzical but that comes with the type of intelligence you possess I assume."

"Okay…then let's hear it. Who wants to start? Who was the first liar?" Jack said, looking around the room at each individual face. First at Paul whose expression didn't falter, then to Jessica who looked sad, happy and proud all at once. Then to Charlotte who looked like she wanted to lay down and die and finally to Alexander who cleared his throat to speak. Alexanders attempt to say he would start completely caught Jack off guard. How could he possibly be the first liar or the first steppingstone on the way to Jack's inevitable arrival at the office that night? Jack had not seen him before his second fight, he was sure of it.

"It was a cold January day; I had flown out to Maine to see my granddaughter," he said, looking at Jessica and smiling. "It was her sixteenth birthday, and she was becoming a better writer as the days went by, so I wanted to reward her."

Jack thought back to the day of Jessica's 16th birthday, he was at her house all day, they had skated on the pond beside the river and watched a movie until one in the morning. He remembered it so vividly because it was the first day that his mother had allowed him to sleep over at her house and the next day she had been rushed to the hospital in an ambulance. He had chosen infatuation over family. But as he thought back, he remembered a vital detail. After skating, there was a few hours in which he helped his mom shovel the driveway, make dinner for her to bring to her night shift and wrote a card to give to Jessica later that night, but when he got to Jessica's house, she was different; Not sad, not angry, just different.

He remembered seeing an unfamiliar black car driving past him as he walked to her house that night. At the time he thought nothing of it but in that moment he recognized the car, it was the same one that had delivered him to the private jet the day he had made the choice to take the impossible opportunity.

"It was you; you were in the car that drove past me that night as I walked to Jessica's house," Jack said. He felt the anger bubble underneath the skin on his hands. He gripped the arms of the chair as hard as he could to relive some of the anger but deep down, he knew the anger would only be released by hurting someone.

"Yes Jack, I really was there to see my granddaughter, but she told me something that changed everything. As she put it, her best friend was the 'best writer ever'. I knew that if she admitted someone was a better writer than her, that person must be very special because I hadn't met anyone who could write at a higher level than her. So, before I flew back to New York, I went to your teacher's house and paid him an obscene amount of money to get you to write a story and submit it to the Global Writing Associations writing competition. He took the money and told me you were working on something and that he would make sure it was done by the deadline. But there was another setback, your mother died, and the state moved you. I still don't know where you went but it was so far off the map that none of us could find you," he said waving his arm around the room. "I promise you it wasn't the result of a lack of trying. We looked high and low for you. We spent countless dollars trying to find you, but we couldn't. Just when we thought we had lost you forever a letter came in the mail with your name on it and inside was the completed manuscript. You have no idea how happy we were that we had found you and that you were the writer my granddaughter made you out to be. Of course, Charlotte was just barely better but nevertheless, you had potential that broke every chart we had."

Jack sat still, listening to the story, trying to soak every word into his brain so that he could make sense of the fact that they had turned him into a killer instead of a writer despite his uncharted potential. "All was good in the world until the months went by and we didn't hear anything from you, you hadn't contacted us for a job, and you hadn't used our recommendation at any university. So, we sent a man to Verlies which was the only orphanage you could have possibly been at but when he arrived a 16- or 17-year-old girl said you weren't home and that you had run away."

Jack chuckled; Ruby had protected him from the devils without even knowing it. "If she knew you had money, she would have let you in immediately and you would have had me right there," Jack said.

"Hmm, we should have tried that but who were we to think a teenage girl was lying to us. But when we heard that news, we stopped actively looking for you. We made sure all of the teachers and professors in our employ knew your writing style and what you would roughly look like if you ever decided to get back into the system. Then one day we got a call from your Professor Laurent. He said he had a kid in his class who was the 'next Shakespeare'. We obviously couldn't dismiss it without investigating so we sent Charlotte," Alexander said turning to Charlotte who looked like she was on the verge of tears. It took a long time for her to speak but eventually she spoke.

"I was sent to Medora one full week before I met you in the bar on the night before I came home. When I first got there, I sat in on one of Professor Laurent's classes and he showed me which student you were."

Charlotte had told Jack all of it already in the car on the way to his apartment the night Jack had savagely beaten Luke to within an inch of his life. It was the day he had stormed out because of the complete breach of privacy but compared to Alexanders section of the past it was like she had walked around blind and paid him a million dollars for 10 minutes of his time. Jack still thought back and he honestly couldn't remember that happening at all. He didn't remember a single class in which a beautiful woman had walked into his lecture hall and listened to Professor Laurent speak. Of course, he had been very inebriated during class time on more than one occasion, so he assumed it had been one of those instances.

"After I was sure you were who we were looking for, I asked around to find out where you lived or where you usually spent your time, but no one seemed to know. I had given up hope until…on the very last day of my week in Medora an unbelievably ugly girl, who seemed to know every detail about you, told me you usually hung out at the town bar at night and lived in an apartment two doors down from the same bar."

Jack chucked again; he couldn't remember the girls name, but he knew exactly who Charlotte was speaking about. "After that, I met you at the bar, attempted to show you the magnitude of the opportunity that you were being offered and then I left you to think and by no surprise you called me to tell me that you were in. Everything after that you know already," Charlotte said sighing and scooting back in her chair.

Without hesitation Jack responded. All the fear and nervous energy had been consumed by the white-hot fury bubbling just beneath his skin and the complete psychosis of the entire situation. He knew it was most likely being reflected in his eyes, but he didn't care. "Okay, I have one more question."

"What is that Mr. Hanson?" Confucius asked with the same stupid smile cut across his face.

"Why writers, why choose writers to be your killers and successors? Why not an athlete? I feel like it would have been in your best interest to employ people who could stomach the finer details of your 'opportunity'." The hate vanished from Confucius's face. The smile darted into his eyes and all that was left was pure glee.

"Great question Mr. Hanson, I don't know why either of you didn't ask this question," Confucius said as he stared in Charlotte and Jessica's direction. "I decided to choose writers because of their unique outlook on life. People who can look at the world around them and transfer it into words are remarkable people and they should be rewarded for their gifts but that is not always the case. When I was 16, I was a writer and I wanted nothing more than to be a published writer, so I wrote a novel and sent it to multiple publishers. They all turned me down and said I wasn't ready, wasn't experienced enough to be a published writer."

"I knew I was only 16 and I knew that they presented a valid point. So, I applied to be a part of the NYU writing department. In a couple months, I received a letter saying they would take me a year early if I decided that was something I was interested in and if not, they would take me the year following my graduation. I responded quickly saying that I was ready right then. I didn't want to wait another minute for my future to start. So, the next fall I moved to New York City and lived in the school dorms. It was an extremely eye-opening experience but one that bore no fruit. The year after I graduated from NYU with a doctoral degree in Creative writing a, I sent a few more publishers another story I had written but again they told me it wasn't good enough."

"They told me I would never be a published author, and that day I decided I would become the most powerful man in New York, and decided I would publish my own book. On my journey to be the best writer in the world, I ran into the Founders Society, and they took me under their wing. I rose through their ranks until I was one step from the top, one step from realizing my dream but the day I was supposed to take over the leader that came to me told me that he wasn't going to retire in fact he was going to hand it over to his son when he was done with his spot on the throne. In that moment, I decided that I would make all the people that had pulled my dreams out from under my feet pay for their sins."

Jack didn't even blink, he knew what the Dr. was saying. Jack knew that being the great writer the Dr. thought he was, made him dangerous and the Dr.

was planning to remove him from the picture. He was never going to promote him into the position he had so clearly fought for his entire life. "I started by removing the man from power by way of a small paring knife he used to cut his apple at his desk each and every day. I removed his soul from his body and then destroyed the evidence so that the next time the Founders Society met they would have no one else to look to except me. Once I had the complete control and trust of the organization, I made a plan on how I would go about punish the writing community."

"The idea I came up with was the GWA. The Global Writing Association would make me the world's foremost authority on fictional writing. Therefore, any young and upcoming author would want to compete in my annual competition, giving me the perfect insight into the new set of prominent authors from around the world. Then I would make sure that the winners would all end up in New York working for me, but never would I ever tell anyone that I was at the helm of the ship through all the pain and hardship that the writing community was going through. Instead, I would paint myself into the image of the only light house the writing community would be able to look to in the storm."

"I knew there would always be trash to take out between the Founders organization and other companies I might acquire along to way to break the pure souls of all writers I brought into my world. Does that answer your question Mr. Hanson?"

Jack swallowed slowly and wiped the cold sweat from his forehead. "Yes sir."

"Good, because I have had enough of this question answer business. I would like to get to the root of why we are here tonight. Each of you are here for a different reason. Paul you are here because you have been a faithful deputy all these years. You have done unbelievable work since I picked you from the group of great writers in your year. Alexander, you have been most understanding of the fact that I killed your father, and I am truly sorry he had to die but ask yourself, would you be better off if that imbecile was still running the show today or if you were the one in command?" Confucius asked.

The man in red sat very still and nodded toward Confucius but his eyes betrayed his true feelings. The anger that danced behind the spherical windows to his soul gave away the fact that he hated Confucius with a passion and that the only reason he had stuck around was the fact that he was scared Confucius would kill him too.

"Yes, sir it was a tough choice that needed to be made."

"Exactly. It is a true testament to your intelligence that you realize that sobering fact. As for you three children," Confucius said somehow looking into Charlotte, Jessica and Jack's eyes simultaneously.

"You three are here because you are the three greatest authors I have had the pleasure of meeting in my shuffle along this mortal coil. Compared to you three I am about as literate as a five-year-old child. Jack is the leading choice between the three of you, but Paul also has his place on the short list of successors to the throne. So, I have devised a plan to decide which one of you shall train and learn under my watchful eye so that you will raise the Founders to the next level," Confucius said standing up and pulling a silver revolver from a drawer in his desk.

Jack looked around and noticed that no one had moved an inch, maybe because they were all too scared to pull attention to themselves or maybe it was the sight of a gun that had sent everyone into shock. The only movement in the room was coming from Confucius who was loading four bullets into his gun, cocking the hammer back and lifting the gun to aiming height. Jack closed his eyes as gracefully as he could and the gun fired. Jack tensed up and braced to feel the bullet slide through his skin relieving him of his earthly pain, but it never came.

When Jack timidly opened his eyes again, he saw that no one had moved except the Man in Red who had slouched down in his chair, a bullet hole ripped into the fine Italian fabric his suit had been woven from. Silent tears fell down Jessica's face and all Jack could think about was running over to hug her. No matter what she did to Charlotte and what she had done to him, she was still the first prick of romantic love he had ever felt. The deceit and lies made him feel a little bit better about the fact that she was being given a taste of her own medicine, but it didn't completely remove the faint drop of empathy he felt for her. No matter what she had done, it was still her grandpa sitting dead just four chairs from her.

"Now that 'The Man in Red' is dead," Confucius said mockingly. "We can get on with the evening. You should all be happy; I just widened the path to success for you." No one moved from their chairs. Even Paul was rooted in place by the sight of his friend's death. "It's time to go," Confucius said without changing his tone, but instead adding a sharp quality to his eyes.

It was one that said he would kill any one of them on the spot without a second thought. All four remaining successors jumped out of their seats and followed him to the elevator. Jessica wiped her tears away as she made her way to the elevator, but a new stream followed as quick as she could wipe the last stream away. Once all five occupants were safely inside the steel box Confucius pressed the button that Jack knew would deliver them to the room made of stone. It was the farthest from safe he had ever felt in his life, but he knew if it came down to it, he would be able to overpower every occupant of the elevator. All he had to do was ensure Confucius's gun was never pointed at him.

When they reached the room where Jack had beaten people to within inches of their lives, where he had proved himself repeatedly, they all stood in silence as Confucius paced around the room.

"I have seen each one of you prove yourselves to me inside these very walls. Some of you may have thought that you were proving yourselves to Paul, but I have always been watching. Jessica, I watched as you snapped Henry's shoulder clean out of its socket wearing a strapless cocktail dress. It was the most graceful beating I have ever seen someone give. Charlotte, I watched intently while you would not quit as Henry beat you to within an inch of your life and I saw the resolve it took for you to push through broken ribs, blood streaming down your face and relieve him of his God given right to breathe."

"It was a testament to what a person can do if the only options they have is to die or win. Paul, I watched a skinny little boy learn what it meant to win at any cost, I saw you turn from a scared kid to a killer within these walls. The day you begged for a chance was the day that I knew I could trust you because you knew that you had but one chance left. And Jack," Confucius said, looking loving into Jack eyes.

"My dear Jack, when you first arrived in New York and sat in the farthest seat from me in the first English class of the new semester I thought you wouldn't be able to handle the actual reason you were here. I honestly thought that I would have to watch you, the child with immeasurable potential, put that first gun you picked up straight to your chin and pull the trigger like so many before you, but you did things I couldn't have dreamed up in my wildest fantasies. You knocked out Henry in 45 seconds, and the only reason it took that long is because you were playing with your food as if you were a cat

309

who had just corralled a mouse and was taunting it to fight back. As if you were taunting Henry to run away just so that you could catch him again."

Jack felt a wave of remorse, regret and guilt wash over him as Confucius continued to praise him. It was shameful to be held on such a high pedestal because of acts his mother would be so sad to watch him carry out. But Confucius wasn't finished, he was building to something that Jack knew would change his life all over again. He knew that whatever Confucius had planned for that night would be something he would have to try very hard to forget or somehow learn to live with.

"When you fought Amadi, a man twice your size and held your own the entire 30 seconds it took for you to watch his head fall I was amazed and even slightly scared. Then when you hit Luke, I was convinced you were dangerous. I realized in that moment that you could be the next King. Each person in this room has proven it in different ways but each of you have proven none the less that you could rule with absolute power and strength. Each of you bring a different perspective and a different style of leadership would emerge if I gave you the opportunity to lead but only one of you can leave this room tonight."

A smile ran across Jack's face, the thing he had been waiting for had happened. The truth had finally come out, Confucius was going to kill or force another to kill each one of them until the champion among champions prevailed. "So, I have devised a little tournament of sorts. Charlotte and Jessica will start. Stilettos off ladies. The first one to be knocked out will die by way of this here gun," Confucius said waving the revolver in the air.

The two women looked at each other, fear festering in both of their eyes. They both shakily removed their shoes and made their way onto the black mat. Jack and Paul moved to the sides of the mat and Confucius stood to the left of Jack laying his hand on Jack's shoulder. Everything in Jack's heart told him to move away from Confucius, the man was the definition of chaos. At the very beginning, Jack thought Paul was the worst human he had ever encountered but now he saw that Paul had been coerced into becoming the demon he now was.

Confucius' greasy hair, snake like hands and forked tongue poisoned everything around him. He couldn't even go to a restaurant and have a meal without sowing seeds of fear and chaos. Jack knew that the only one in the room that needed to die was Confucius. If his rotten soul continued to poison the city of New York there would be no good left. The New York Jack had always dreamed of would be gone forever. Gabriel, Lucien, Maria, and Angela would have no home and they would eventually fall victim to the evil that had poisoned their great city. Jack knew that the only way to allow good to prevail would be to kill Confucius, but he didn't know if he could do it.

He didn't know if he would be able to pull the trigger, his mother's soul would break. Jack looked at the two women circling each other around the ring and all he could think of was the fact that he loved them both. He couldn't lie to himself anymore. Jessica would always be his first romantic love; she was his one last connection to the home he had once held so dear. Yet she had been the author of all his recent pain, if she hadn't told her, now dead, grandfather that he was a decent writer he would have been able to live out his days as a real writer. He wouldn't have killed a man, and he wouldn't have had to witness many of the evils he had been exposed to. But he knew that no matter what she did he would still save her from death if it came down to it. Charlotte on the other hand was his best friend, he now knew that he could trust her with anything, he could trust her with his life. He knew that she would be his last love. Despite her involvement in his capture he didn't blame her for anything. A gun was pressed to her head just as firmly as it had been pressed to his. Jessica was his first love and Charlotte would be his last. Helplessly watching them circle each other like a pair of wolves ate away at his soul. One of them was fated to die and he wasn't sure how he could stop it. He could grab the gun from Confucius and pull the trigger. It would effectively end his evil grasp on New York but that would result in Paul most likely taking the mantle of King and even though Paul had a gun to his head the entire time, the look that resided in his pupils every time Jack killed a man was far too evil to push out of his mind. No matter which way he looked at the situation Jack couldn't figure a way out. There were no chinks in the armor and no escape routes, only the inevitable death of one of the two current combatants. So, he focused on the fight, not knowing who to root for, not wanting to let himself think about who he would rather have around for at least a few more minutes.

Charlotte was slipping, parrying, and returning every blow Jessica doled out but when Jessica finally landed a clean right hook into Charlotte's jaw Jack saw something change in her eyes. What had once been a survival instinct, or a defense strategy changed to anger and offensive mentality. Tiny little fires lit in Charlotte's eyes when the keen sting of knuckles against bone sent sparks into her brain and Jack saw her plan formulating in her eyes. Jessica swung again and followed it with a strong kick meant for Charlotte's head, but Charlotte ducked and swung herself up onto Jessica's shoulders.

In one swift movement, she spun back down Jessica's body effectively pinning her on the ground. Then in one fluid motion she stood up and stomped the consciousness out of Jessica's eyes. It was a perfectly choreographed dance move; she had gracefully ended the fight and all there was to show for it was Jessica's beautiful face lying unconscious on the damp black mat. Jack turned to Confucius and saw his arm lifting as if in slow motion to point the gun at Jessica's head. Some primal instinct kicked in. Jack's arm flew up and knocked the gun from Confucius's hand. Jack hadn't even told his arm to move, it just did so of its own accord, but the damage had been done so he scrambled to pick up the revolver glistening on the floor.

He dove past Confucius's feet and felt his hands grab hold of the handle and his finger instinctively moved to the trigger. But as he turned over to point the gun at whoever had chosen this as their opportunity to wrestle the leverage from his hands and take hold of the mantle of King, he heard a gunshot. The bang ricocheted around the stone walls and reverberated in Jack's ears. He looked at the tip of his gun wondering how it could have possibly fired without him pulling the trigger, but there was no smoke climbing out of the barrel.

His gun hadn't fired, it had to have been someone else. He shook his head and looked around the room to identify the shooter and he saw Paul standing still, arm still raised, gun in hand smoke trails fading into the air from the tip of his barrel. His eyes darted to Confucius, the greasy old man was perfectly still, looking directly down at his chest. A hole had been cut through the center of his body and blood had started to darken his shirt around the exit wound. Confucius turned to Paul with the saddest, wildest look etched in his eyes.

"Why...What...How?" He sputtered as his legs gave way and he fell inches from where Jack was lying. Jack scrambled to his feet; barrel of the gun pointed directly at Paul's chest just as Paul's gun had now become trained on him.

"Now we have a bit of a predicament don't we Hanson," Paul said. His confidence had now completely returned. No more big, scary Confucius to make him wither back into the shell of his former self.

"Yes, we do," Jack said, voice quivering. Jack felt his eyes start to tunnel. All he could see was Paul and the gun he had trained directly at his chest. All other colors, objects and figures fell away leaving him completely focused on

Paul. It left him blind to the fact that Jessica had come to and was now making her way around Jack's back. So, by the time she grabbed hold of Jack's gun he was completely venerable, and the gun left his hands like water though a spaghetti strainer. By the time he realized the gun wasn't in his hands, it was too late. The gun had already fired.

Jack's ears had just processed the sound of the most recent gunshot when he heard the second shot go off. His vision realigned itself, allowing him to see the entire room and the carnage that littered the ground. Paul's unmoving body laid on the stones, a hole burned through the space between his eyebrows, Charlotte's body was just hitting the ground and blood was starting to pool just above her waist. The bullet had carved a hole in her lower abdomen, and he saw that she was going to die slowly and painfully.

It wasn't a question of if but when and at the center of all the carnage was Jessica who was still holding the gun at the ready in the direction of where Charlotte must have been standing, smoke spilling out of Confucius's revolver. It took Jack a few seconds to process all the different events that had just taken place but when they finally sunk in, his body jumped into action. His brain was still numb, but his body knew exactly what needed to happen. He tackled Jessica and wrestled the smoking gun from her hands, pointing it at her head. But as he looked down the barrel of the gun at the girl he loved for the better part of his life, something cracked in his mind.

She didn't even seem scared, she laid perfectly still arms coming to a rest at the sides of her body and closed her eyes slowly, gracefully. Every memory that involved Jessica played on a reel in his mind and he saw the 12-year-old girl he had fallen in love with all the way back in Cielo. He saw her perfect features and he saw the love that always circled her like a storm. But as the memories continued to play like a movie he saw her face change, he saw her aura change from love to hate and then he saw her soul break.

He saw the bullet hole burnt through her grandpa's chest and her saw her soul finally give into the grief, allowing all the love to dissipate into thin air like cigarette smoke in the wind. He knew the person who had slept on a blanket with him by the river that ran though Cielo was gone. He knew what he had to do but he couldn't shake the feeling that his mother was watching. As he waited and waited for the courage to pull the trigger to overcome him, he felt a hand rest itself on his shoulder and he heard a voice whisper in his right ear.

She wants to go honey; you are a good man, and I am so proud of the man you have become. It's your turn to be strong and make the difficult decision to move on. Holding on to the past is what has held you back all these years. Move on, make a life for yourself away from this place. You have worth honey, I will be with you through every decision you are forced to make, every opportunity you are forced to accept or cast aside. I will always love you, Jack.

Then he felt the hand on his shoulder squeeze hard and he pulled the trigger. Blood splattered up his arms as the bullet displaced the skin and tissue that made up Jessica's face. Jack felt a weight fall from his chest, and he stood up and went over to Charlotte who was gasping for air on the ground, a steady stream of tears falling down her cheeks.

"You…are…the best of…us Jack. You…need…to get out," Charlotte said as she cupped Jack's face with her hands. Jack felt tears stream down his face as she spoke. "Do what we planned, go to the train…take it to Canada and start fresh. Write…live. I love you, Jack," she said as she drew her final breath and Jack knew her soul had found peace. She had been set free. When he thought about it, he knew that they all had found peace. He had been left alone to take on the world.

"I love you, Charlotte." He whispered as he closed her eyes and gently kissed her forehead. He stood up, slowly letting the revolver slide out of his grasp, and clang against the stone floor. He walked in a haze of shock and grief to the elevator that would take him on his final trip out of the office.

Chapter 24

When the elevator reached the lobby, Jack walked out and made his way to the door without even a glance in the direction of the desk attendant. But as he shakily stumbled, tears streaming down his cheeks—the last marks Paul, Confucius, Jessica, or Alexander would ever make on him—he heard a voice, "Is it done?"

"Yes," he said as he continued to walk away.

"How many bodies do I need to take care of?"

"5. Four in the basement and 1 in Confucius' office."

"Good luck, Jack. I hope you can find peace. I am sorry you were ever brought into this life. I am sorry you were burdened by your gifts and I'm sorry they felt the need to exploit them." The stone gargoyle of a woman said as Jack pushed the front door open and left the office for the last time. When Jack reached the curb, he saw a taxi making its way around the corner, so he stuck his hand up to let the driver know he was ready to leave. Once he was inside, he looked into the rear-view mirror and saw Lucien's face staring back at him.

"Hello Jack, where to?" He said, a massive smile splitting his face in half.

"You look very nice Jack, how was your dinner?"

"To my apartment please, Lucien. My dinner was pretty fucking awful," Jack said, sitting back in his chair and closing his eyes, letting the tears soak his already blood-stained suit.

The rest of the ride was silent. When they stopped at his apartment, Jack told Lucien to keep the meter running, he wouldn't be long. He only needed two things. As he made his way past Angela he looked away. He knew she would be able to see the guilt, shame and secrets splashed across his face. Not to mention the physical blood splashed all over his suit and face. He got into the elevator and made his way up to his apartment for very last time. The elevator doors opened at his apartment and tears rolled down his cheeks in waves. He had made so many good memories with Charlotte in the apartment.

315

Their first kiss, their first dance, the first time he had seen her naked. They all morphed together into an image he would hold with him until the day he died. He didn't want to remember her face as she laid on the cold, damp floor dying. He didn't want to hear her final words that she should have been able to say when she was alive. She had her whole life ahead of her and it was all stolen by the anger that consumed Jessica. It wasn't right but Jack knew he needed to leave fast, he didn't have time to reminisce or mourn. He had the rest of his life to do that. He quickly made his way to the office and grabbed his MacBook and its charging cord, jammed it into the carry case he had been so proud to buy when he first bought the computer and made his way to his bedroom.

He placed his phone on the charger that was plugged into the wall and grabbed the picture of his mother. It had stuck with him since the day he was taken from Cielo, shipped to Verlies, from Verlies to Medora and followed him there to New York, where he was forced to face his destiny. He checked his arms to make sure he had everything he needed and then he grabbed his satchel from its spot beside his bed, gently placed the computer, the charging cords, and his picture of his mother in the bag and hurried out of the room. But as he made his way to the elevator doors, he looked down at the state his suit was in. Jessica's blood was splashed all the way up his arms and stained his chest. He assumed it was on his face as well. Jack decided that he would take one more shower and be on his way. He made his way to the shower and made sure that the water was as hot as it could possibly be. The blood was caked on his hands and his face making it no easy task to remove. Once the temperature was up to his standards he undressed, stepped into the shower, and let the scalding liquid rip every drop of blood from his skin. As the blood-stained water ran down his chest, he realized he was still wearing the red sun pendant. He gripped it hard in his hand and was about to rip it off his neck when he remembered what was inside. He realized that it didn't matter that he had been left to endure the world all by himself. The three souls still had to be protected.

They were lost because of him, and Jack assumed that word of Confucius, Paul and Alexanders deaths would travel fast, and people would eventually come looking for him. It was a good thing that he had a credit card that didn't have a limit. When he was finally clean, he stepped out of the shower and made his way to the closet. Underneath all the suits, trendy clothes and everything else Charlotte had insisted they buy was the pair of jeans and t-shirt he had been wearing the day Charlotte changed his life forever. He slipped his head into the deteriorating fabric, pulled the jeans that had been washed far too many times over his legs, slipped on a pair of shoes and took his final walk toward the elevator.

By the time the cab reached the train station, the exhaustion had set in, and Jack was almost too tired to get out of the cab.

"What do I owe you, Lucien?" He asked.

"$25.50 Jack," Lucien said handing Jack the machine. Jack stuck the card in and then just as he had done for Gabriel, he typed $1,000,000 into the tip option, then imputed his pin and handed the machine back to Lucien.

"Thank you, Lucien. I wish you all the best."

"You too Jack, I hope you find peace," Lucien said as Jack got out of the cab. Jack made his way to the train but as he did a thought shot through his conscious thought like a shooting star and he quickly turned around. Lucien had said 'I hope you find peace Jack.' How would the taxi driver know he wasn't at peace for the last few weeks? Jack ran back toward the taxi and ripped open the passenger door.

"What do you mean you hope I find peace?" Lucien turned slowly to Jack and shifted the car into drive.

"Gabriel..." Was all Jack could make out as Lucien sped off just about closing Jack's arm in the car door as he did. Jack stood rooted in disbelief until he heard the final warning for the train he needed to board. He walked toward the ticket booth bought a ticket on the midnight train to Montreal and then climbed aboard the train that would take him to his next home. Home, that is what Jack wanted. It was what he craved above all else and he could feel that as bad as the night had been it was the steppingstone he had been promised at the very beginning. It would propel him forward toward the life he had always wanted.

Jack climbed aboard the empty train, found a seat, set his bag down and laid across the comfortable fabric. Jack was exhausted, his body hadn't been used in the last few hours, but his brain had been in the fight of its life. When he woke up, he would try to make sense of all that had happened but as of right then, he could barely think. He closed his eyes in an effort to slow his brain down to a speed in which he could sleep or at least drift off into the void of nothingness but immediately after he closed his eyes, he fell asleep. He didn't slip into a memory; he didn't pass through the barrier between the void and reality. He didn't float into the void of darkness.

Instead, he slept in full-blown state of recovery. He had finally discovered a moment of peace amongst the storm of chaos that had held him prisoner for so long.

END

Before I start, I just wanted to say thank you to my dad, mom and my two brothers. Without you guys I would not be where I am, and I would not have been able to write this book. So, I thank you from the bottom of my heart and hope that you all know exactly how much you mean to me.

When I first started to write The Opportunity, it was called The Average. That's what I wanted it to be called. The Average. Think about that for a second. The. Average. It was supposed to be a story about a kid, Jack, who couldn't get anywhere because of his crushing averageness. The kid was me, I wanted to write myself. But, as most stories do, it changed along the way. Jack morphed into this amazing character. (That's just my opinion, yours may be different and that is perfectly fine. Subjectivity is the beauty of stories.) Jack became this man who could be hurt by nothing other than himself. He evolved into this character who is untouchable because of his good heart and strong figure. And as I wrote I began to see that maybe I was still writing myself, but instead of the man I actually was, maybe he was the man I wanted to be. Maybe he was the person I strive to be day in and day out.

One of the people I shared my rough manuscript with told me that they 'hated' Jack. So, as all people who have been given criticism do, I laughed and asked why. They laughed right back and said that they hated Jack for making the wrong choice. When Jack was presented with the ultimatum between life and death, he should have died. I laughed and said that their opinion was valid and was definitely one way of thinking about it. That night I was having a conversation with another reader—who, coincidentally, was the first reader of the book. I asked them if they liked Jack, and they said no as well. They

319

said they thought Jack was a waste of space at the beginning of the book. I laughed again and headed to sleep but for the life of me I couldn't fall asleep. I was haunted by their summaries of my favorite character—other than Charlotte—in the book. It was confusing to hear that my limited audience didn't like Jack and I think it hurt more because he was me. This character was one written in the image of the man I wanted to be. It was an unbelievable, surreal moment that had me questioning every goal I ever had. But when I thought deeper, I realized that they didn't see Jack the way I did. I didn't see his killing as an impossible, murderous or greed fueled choice. I saw it as a 25-year-old kid in the first year of his first 'real' job. I saw the sacrifice we all make to earn enough money to live comfortably in this crazy world. I didn't see an alcoholic who wasn't worth anyone's time. No, I saw the raw pain, anger, grief, accomplishment, grit, and prowess that I have always coveted. I saw him for who he was meant to be. I saw him for the boy that was turning into a man as my fingers typed the next letter, the next word and the next sentence onto the page. I saw a beautiful transformation of character that continues into the next two books of the series. As the very first reader of The Opportunity, I can say I loved it. But again, that is just one reader's opinion and an extremely biased one at that. I hope that one day I can have a conversation with a reader of this book and hear what they thought of Jack. I hope that one day I can listen to the metaphor they created in their head when they read the book. If I ever get the chance to hear someone's opinion on my book, I promise you that whether it is positive or negative, I will listen to your opinion with a smile stamped on my face.

Thank you for reading this reflection and for reading the book. Before I leave, I had one more thank you to make. I would like to say a special thanks to my guardian angel, for without you I don't know where I would be. You have done so much for me, listened when I needed someone to talk to, hugged me when I needed someone to hug and kept me on the right path all these years.

www.ingramcontent.com/pod-product-compliance
Lightning Source LLC
LaVergne TN
LVHW051519280225
804810LV00001B/76